M000083830

BLOOD SYMBOLS

www.izakbotha.com

Also by Izak Botha

Angelicals Reviewed

BLOOD SYMBOLS

IZAK BOTHA

South Africa
2017

Blood Symbols

A novel by Izak Botha

This book is a work of fiction. Except in the case of historical fact, scripture, art-work, architecture and establishments, all references are used fictionally and the product of the authors imagination.

Cover Design by Fiona Jayde Media

ISBN: 978-0-620-74785-1

In memory of Bullet

Prologue

John Yilmaz stood rigid, arms dangling, hands tense. His mother had become his enemy. The nourishment of her umbilical cord had turned vile. If he did not break free she would poison him. He would die, and her womb would become his grave. He had to escape this godforsaken place.

'Euphoria is a symptom of shock,' Yilmaz thought. But he was far from happy. He had seen wickedness at its most appalling—had even collaborated. Now the responsibility for exposing it was his. People had a right to know. He could not waste time.

Light filtered through the doorway at the top of the stairs, casting shadows on the altar before him. Further out, columns rose ghostly in the gloom. On their shoulders, gargoyles leered at the trespassers in their abode. And along the disappearing edge, darkness coalesced with granite walls.

With his eyes fixed on the figure of Christ, he knelt. 'Forgive me Lord, for I have sinned. …'

He rested his forehead against the altar frontal. Why did he do that? Praying no longer made sense. Bitterly, he crossed himself. '*In nomine Patris et Filii et Spiritus Sancti, amen.*'

As his tongue pressed the prayer's final syllable against his teeth, a figure stopped behind him blocking the light.

Yilmaz stood up instinctively. Turning to leave, he said, 'I think we should go now.'

'What are you doing?' came from the darkness.

Yilmaz froze as an adumbral hand gripped his throat. A dagger sank into his ribs, and he stumbled back against the altar. Clutching his attacker's wrist, he fought to dislodge the blade from his chest, but his arms weakened as shock set in, and the attacker's strength overwhelmed him. He reached for a candleholder, but the agony of steel twisting in his lung drew him back.

'We trusted you,' the attacker yelled.

Yilmaz reached for the altar. 'You lied to me,' he moaned.

One hand tore the knife from Yilmaz's ribs, while the other struck him on the chest. Then, in a quick, sweeping motion, the blade bit into the young man's neck.

With each heartbeat, blood spurted from the wound, soaking Yilmaz's white collar. His legs buckled, and he clawed at the edge of the mensa, but the frontal slid free like a veil, sending him and the candleholders and crucifix crashing to the marble floor.

The attacker scanned the blood-soaked predella. What he was looking for was not there. 'What did you do with it?' he screamed. 'What you have done?'

Yilmaz's chin sank to his chest. 'May God forgive them, for they know not what they do,' he wheezed.

As his heart beat for the last time, the pressure in his arteries ebbed. The last vestige of life drained from him, and his face, now relaxed with that peculiar expression of peace only the hallowed dead knew, turned a chalky grey. His spirit departed and, with it, the fear of his demise.

The killer clenched Yilmaz's hair. Jerking the young man's head back so far that the knife wound seemed to sneer, he yelled, 'You are a priest for God's sake!'

But the light in Yilmaz's eyes had already fled.

Chapter 1

Shaded by four three-story buildings that rose forty meters or more, Jennifer Jaine was the essence of decorum. Her outfit, an absorbent-black, viscose jacket with matching knee-length skirt, hugged her shapely frame like a second skin and terminated in an overlapping slit halfway above her knees. Beneath, a white blouse, lucent like her alabaster complexion, peeked out from between the buttons of her tightly fastened lapel, and her patent-leather ankle boots, smart but low-heeled for comfort, etched soft lines in her calves as she walked. To be sure, the entire ensemble was as detestable to Jennifer as it was requisite for the meeting ahead.

Glancing up, Jennifer took in the Belvedere Courtyard. Designed by Donato Bramante in the early sixteenth century, it had originated as a rectangular space flanked by a palace and a villa on its short axis and two museums on its long axis. The libraries, later additions, had cut the space in half. Having spent years investigating every detail of Vatican culture, not to mention countless hours scrutinizing its one hundred and ten acres on Google Earth, Jennifer knew almost everything there was to know about the world's smallest city-state, including this particular parcel of land.

She unclenched her fingers and, taking a tissue from her breast pocket, lifted one foot then the other to wipe the dust from her shoes. Finally, she smoothed her hand over her skirt to straighten out the folds. If it were not for the Vatican's draconian dress code, she would have happily worn a t-shirt, jeans and flip-flops; dressing smartly might give the right impression, but she still felt like a student.

Behind Jennifer, the eleven-ton Campanone di San Pietro thundered like the cannon fire of Tchaikovsky's *1812 Overture*. The previous day when she had visited the celebrated Saint Peter's Basilica, she had for the first time heard its peal. She had been standing below the south tower when the first report had struck.

When two middle-aged priests pushed open the bronze doors, she checked her watch. 'At a minute past eight they're quite punctual,' she thought. One priest, elderly and hunched over, then made his way to a notice board to change the date. 'Martedì, 20 Marzo, 2012', he wrote, tracing the letters with the precision and care of a craftsman.

Jennifer smiled. This was the year the Mayan calendar predicted the present era would end. Surely, the aging clergyman was reminded of the fact every day when he looked at the date. For goodness sake, he should be. He represented God after all.

On her flight from New York, Jennifer had been riveted by Michael Bryner's, *The Mayan Oracle*, which explained how the ancient Mayans painted 2012 as a time of turmoil. From their calculations, the ancients had predicted the world would end on the twenty-first of December. That was only nine months away. Jennifer was skeptical about most things, but it was hard not to be fascinated by the idea that *something* might happen outside the sphere of humdrum experience.

Jennifer's footsteps echoed lonesomely as she approached the Leone XIII. Marching eagerly through the doorway, the sumptuousness of the Renaissance architecture stopped her in mid-stride. Stretching seventy meters and rising ten or more, the Leonine library drew her into the sixteenth century. Crowned by barrel-vaulted ceilings adorned with colorful frescoes and bisected by a series of mezzanine-wrapped columns filled with scores of bookshelves, the library comprised a cabinet-filled index room which served as a gateway for researchers, and an adjacent manuscript reading room.

Sliding her fingers gently over the spines of several books, Jennifer slipped beneath the mezzanine. The cells of her nose tingled as the musty smell of papyrus and parchment made its way to her lungs. 'If only I could inhale their knowledge,' she thought. Crossing to the manuscript room her eyes strayed, slowly scanning the wall where vast arched windows were interspersed with portrait-decorated pillars of library prefects from ages past, sighing as they held up texts as inscrutable as the scope of the library's contents itself. In the center of it all, a seemingly endless row of desks passively awaited researchers to rest their elbows on their magnificently crafted tops.

'This way, miss. You need to be at Pio XI.' A priest perched on a ladder pointed to a doorway. 'The library is up ahead in building next-door.'

Exhaling through pursed lips, she continued towards the end of the hall. Nowhere did the Vatican allow her to stand idly or enjoy its grandeur. The gendarmes prodded her along, ensuring she did not stray from her designated path. The same had happened in the Sistine Chapel the day before. Longing to absorb Michelangelo's genius, she had sat on a step, but had hardly raised her eyes to the celebrated fresco, when a gendarme had ordered her to move along. Heaven forbid she should take a photograph. He would have arrested her on the spot.

At the reception desk, a priest stood with his eyes locked on a computer screen. His slender fingers tiptoed across the keyboard like tarantulas locked in a mating dance. At two or three inches under six feet, she could look him in the eye. His upright posture, bent head and intense concentration reminded her of a friend who owned a restaurant on Staten Island and always managed to appear busy, even when no customers were around.

'Good morning, Father. I have an appointment to see His Eminence Cardinal Cardoni,' Jennifer said, her dimples deepening as she spoke.

The priest looked up, slightly cocking his left eyebrow as the light from the Cortile del Biblioteca accentuated Jennifer's innate beauty, almost glamour, making her chocolate hair glint like wet silk. The poise of her elongated neck and slim form would have made her the envy of many a Renaissance *contessa*—her pristine skin, full lips and amber-green eyes, the idol of Italy's finest painters.

'Good morning, Miss Jaine,' the priest greeted her. 'I am Father Marco Romano. Will you please sign the register for me? And don't forget to include your time of arrival.'

Romano's sable hair was in absolute contrast to his pallid complexion. It was obvious the man needed a break—and a vacation somewhere sunny, Ibiza perhaps. *Imagine. …*

Dismissing the idea, however, she drew her pen from her briefcase. With nimble, deft strokes, she formed the simple lines and elegant curves that comprised her signature.

Romano continued typing. 'I see you've changed your hair.'

She nodded, spreading her dark tresses evenly across her shoulders. 'It used to be much longer.'

The priest studied Jennifer's curriculum vitae and background report for several minutes more before letting her pass. Ostensibly, he was now party to the trivial details of her life, as was every other gatekeeper she had encountered in Rome.

He looked up. 'You have a doctorate in religious studies?'

The priest had hit a nerve. 'Not yet, Father. I'm almost there.' Behind her back, she furtively crossed her index and middle fingers.

'And you work for?'

She hated lying, but more than anything she needed this interview. '*Geographic America*, but only part-time.'

'Your section editor, she's still there?'

'Yes, Father.' Quietly she prayed for forgivingness.

'So, *she* arranged for the interview?'

He was testing her, she knew. But instead of lying again, she kept quiet. When he raised his eyes to glower at her, she conceded: '*He* did, Father.'

Satisfied that his interrogation had elicited the appropriate responses, he continued typing. 'You are here to discuss the Codex Vaticanus?'

'And see it, Father.'

Calling him 'Father', this man who was no older than she was, made her want to titter under her breath. Luckily, she checked herself before the laugh became audible, and she decided she had better restrain her reactions to this archaic formality. It was, after all, just a title.

He held out his hand. 'I'll keep your mobile and briefcase in a safe place.'

'May I keep my notes?'

'Yes, that is fine.'

Those spidery fingers again, she thought. 'And my purse? It has my ID and passport.'

'Of course ...'

She waited as Romano placed her briefcase in a locker behind the reception desk. 'How far back do the origins of the library go, Father?'

'There is evidence that the first structure was built in the fourth century after our beloved Lord,' he said, closing the locker.

He replied like clockwork, but she was equally quick: 'Your website says the oldest documents date from the end of the eighth century?'

He straightened and passed her the RFID-enabled card he had programmed for her. 'We have poetry dating as far back as the fourth and fifth centuries, but our earliest letters, by Saint Aquinas, date from the eighth century, yes.'

She clipped the card to her jacket pocket. 'I assume they're all originals?' (She simply had to ask.)

'Some are copies, some originals,' someone said behind her.

Jennifer turned to see a priest in a black cassock extending his hand towards her. His violet zucchetto and waistband and gold pectoral cross were explicit indications of his rank within the Church. Bishop Eugene Albani—she recognized him from the photos online. She had read a lot about him, too. Born in Mexico in 1951 and ordained at an early age, the Vatican had appointed him Prefect of the Secret Archives six months earlier. Prior to this latest office, he had supervised much of the library's decade-long restoration. Standing six feet tall, he had a slender, muscular frame that showed little evidence of his age. Indeed, were it not for his greying hair, she would have thought him years younger.

She held out her hand. 'It's an honour to meet you, Your Excellency.'

'The honour is mine,' he replied, and after shaking her hand repeatedly, he shifted his gaze to Romano. 'Father, can you see if His Eminence Cardinal Cardoni is on his way yet?' Then, turning back to Jennifer: 'He won't be much longer. He is normally very punctual. Is this your first time in Rome?'

Apart from a brief stint in South Africa and her two-year stay in New York, Jennifer had only visited a handful of states outside of her home state, Florida. She was not about to tell him that though. With this caliber of man, she would need to pass herself off as a woman of the world.

'It is,' she responded, her voice infused with excitement.

'Quite a culture shock, isn't it? The States have impressive cities, but Europe's history spans millennia. Have you been sightseeing?'

She had only arrived two days before and had spent much of the time since studying her notes. She had, however, managed to visit a few places. 'I've seen Saint Peter's Basilica, the Sistine Chapel and your "Lux in Arcana" exhibition.'

'Our glorious heritage!' He lifted his eyes and palms towards the ceiling in a gesture of wonder and piety as he spoke. Then, refocusing on her: 'Which part of the exhibition did you enjoy most?'

As with Father Romano, she was not sure whether the bishop was making small talk or testing her. 'It's a dead heat between Galileo's retraction and the excommunication of Martin Luther. Both had immense impacts on the world.'

Albani lit up. 'It can be cumbersome with so many tourists this time of year, don't you think? Sometimes it is better to visit in winter.'

Not having known what to expect, Jennifer found Albani's welcome heartening. In some respects, he reminded her of her father: respectful, accommodating, well-meaning. When he led her up the steps towards Sisto V, she walked beside him. As in the Pio XI reading room, the hall had a vaulted ceiling, books covering every inch of wall space and a row of desks down the center. He showed her into a meeting room overlooking the Cortile della Bibliotheca. Drawing out a chair, he apologized for not offering her a drink. Due to the nature of the relics, refreshments were off-limits. Shortly afterwards, he excused himself and returned to the reception desk.

Jennifer's pulse quickened slightly. The closer she came to her interview, the more her gut writhed. Her chat with the bishop *had* broken the ice a bit, but the thought of interviewing a cardinal still made her nervous.

Placing her notes on the table, she sat back. She stared out of the window at the deserted courtyard outside. Catholicism differed radically from her own Calvinist beliefs. The Catholic Church might as well be a different religion altogether. It was an integral part of the ritual that, upon being elevated to cardinal, former bishops intoned a ceremonial prayer invoking divine protection, the *benedictio solemnis*. It sounded so mysterious—as if they were summoning supernatural powers. Cardinals were also required to defend rigorously any papal bulls concerning the protection of Church assets, ecclesiastical nepotism, papal elections and their own dignity. It was ironically redundant, really, for at that stage in his career a cardinal would have already been in the service of the church for decades. Surely, he would have been upholding those principles all along. At the beginning of each secret consistory, the *aperitio oris*, or 'opening of the mouth', took place, and at its conclusion, there was the *clausura oris*, or 'closing of the mouth', as these ceremonies were symbolic of every cardinal's obligation to keep the secrets of his office and give wise counsel to the pope. Finally, the Vatican would bestow upon each new cardinal a sapphire ring to show he had assumed his title and responsibilities.

Jennifer frowned. These men represented Christ for goodness sake. A religious institution should be unabashedly transparent. The Vatican should have no secrets.

Chapter 2

'What is the cornerstone of our calling?'

Cardinal Giovanni Cardoni knew exactly how to capture the attention of his protégés. His question, designed to test the young men's knowledge of the foundations of their vocation, always produced the desired result. It would show aspiring priests how little they knew about their faith.

Cluttered with philosophical mumbo-jumbo, the men would struggle to realize the essence of their new life in the Holy Church. Most believed their faith in Christ's death and resurrection elevated them above other mortals. But those were only the fundamentals. Inevitably, some young men came close, but no one had ever given him the perfect answer.

Cardoni would rest his elbows on the podium. Staring across the hall of enthusiastic but gullible faces, he would say, 'We, gentlemen, are the bearers of God's *power and authority*.'

Every time he appraised the richness of their heritage, he could not help but gloat a little.

Paging to the *Gospel of Matthew*, Cardoni would read aloud how God had bestowed 'all power in Heaven and on Earth' upon His Son Jesus, and at this point, he would wait. Sometimes it would come instantly, sometimes it took a moment, but the question always came.

'Your Eminence,' an aspirant priest would call out, his hand raised, 'how did we end up getting it?'

He lived for that moment. Enlightening their keen minds to the fact that God had bestowed His glory upon the Holy Roman Church never failed to exhilarate him.

'The *Gospel of John* teaches how the "Keys of the Kingdom" were bestowed upon Christ's beloved Apostle Peter, whom He instructed to feed His sheep. In the *Gospel of Matthew*, Christ calls Saint Peter the "rock upon which I will build my Church" and says that whatever Peter bound and loosed on Earth, the same would be honored in Heaven.'

Before concluding, he would accompany the aspirants to the heart of Saint Peter's Basilica to view the first pope's grave at the foot of the *aedicula*, beneath the floor. Flanking Maderno's nave stood stuccoed marble columns bearing the weight of the coffered barrel vault above. And directly beneath Bramante's monolithic dome, Bernini's thirty-meter bronze baldachin paid tribute to the gravesite of the Church's premier saint.

He would stop in front of the confessio and wait for one of the men to open the gate in the center of the u-shaped balustrade adorned with bronze lamps. Leading the young faithful, he would then descend the marble steps to the burial site below. Above the arched entrance of the necropolis, four words were etched in the image of an unfurled ribbon, announcing Peter's tomb:

SEPULCRUM SANCTI PETRI APASTOLI

Cardoni would pass beneath the archway that led to the back of the exedra, the exact spot where Saint Peter's remains lay. Behind a gilded-bronze gate and decorated with a ninth-century mosaic, Peter's sepulcher rested within a niche known as the 'dei Palli'. Bronze statues of Saint Peter and Saint Paul graced each side. Nearby, stood a bronze urn donated by Benedict XIV.

'A shrine to our most sacred saint,' Cardoni would announce.

Huddled in the small chamber, the men would spend hours debating the importance of the treasured relic.

When Cardoni felt sure they had understood the significance of Peter's burial on that holy ground, he would then lead them to the Secret Archives. Once there, he would present them with the inspired and transmitted Word of God, *the* most precious of all the manuscripts in the world, and *the* source for biblical translations: The *Codex Vaticanus*.

'Saint Peter's remains and the Vaticanus are infallible proof that the Kingdom of Heaven is in our hands.' He would lift his chin proudly. 'And this, gentlemen, is the cornerstone of your holy calling.'

By the time he had let those words flow from his lips, the young seminarians were enthralled, their minds defenseless against his rhetoric.

Invariably one would ask, 'Does this mean no one can go to Heaven without our blessing?'

And patly Cardoni would reply, 'It does indeed.'

*****

Cardinal Cardoni no longer lectured seminarians, but as the Vatican Librarian, he was still the foremost authority on the Vaticanus. Arriving a few minutes late, he briefly spoke with Bishop Albani at the reception desk before entering the meeting room.

Jennifer watched the cardinal as he closed the door: chic, with silver-grey hair, he was at least three inches over six feet with all the swagger of a natural egotist. He certainly was not what she expected from a priest of his stature. Before leaving home, she had researched his career with great interest. Born in 1943, he had professed in his mid-twenties and taken his final vows a few years later. After his ordination to the priesthood, he had embarked on an illustrious career as a theologian. He had received his doctorate at Rome's Pontifical University of Saint Thomas Aquinas in the seventies. Pope John Paul II had appointed him Prefect of the Secret Archives Library a decade later, and noting Cardoni's flair, had subsequently elevated him to the venerable position of Cardinal Librarian.

Jennifer was already standing to greet the cardinal as he stepped towards her. When he extended his hand, she placed hers delicately into his. Meeting his forceful gaze, she curtsied, but she deliberately did not kiss his ring; her own convictions were too strong for that.

Cardoni drew his hand back indignantly but waited for her to sit before pulling up a chair at the head of the table. He then spent some time arranging his robes.

Jennifer looked on bemused. What pomp! It must be exhausting. Aside from his Tourette twitches, she found his body language rather endearing, perhaps even a touch effeminate. Despite his age and the acne scars scattered like tiny craters on his cheeks, he was quite handsome. He was possessed of near perfect symmetry. Nature seldom achieved such delicate results. His clean, creaseless, tailormade cassock fitted perfectly, and when he folded one leg over the other to rest his foot against a table leg, his black leather shoes gleamed as if polished only minutes before. (Luckily, she had cleaned her own before entering the library.) Then he laid his hands on his lap. Hell, the cardinal had nicotine stains curling up his fingers like salamanders sweltering in the desert sun. For a man of the cloth, surely that was a blemish to moral excellence.

'How can I assist you, Miss Jaine?'

'*Geographic America* is making a documentary of the manuscripts on which The New Testament is based,' she said. 'Since the library holds one of the oldest copies of the Bible, my assignment is to examine it and obtain permission to conduct experiments.'

She felt terrible for lying again, but the Vatican had left her no choice. Only doctoral academics could access the libraries; access to Cardoni was only slightly less impossible. At the very least, you had to be a reporter in the employ of an esteemed publication. She was neither. When she had applied for the interview, she was still working on her PhD. To give her thesis credibility, she had decided to do fieldwork at the Secret Archives. Having applied through the correct channels, she had received her entry pass two years ago. But just after that something extraordinary had happened: an unexpected but crucial discovery had made her question her beliefs entirely. Someone very important from Jerusalem had enlightened her mind to good sense. For him, the life of reason outweighed that which relied on faith. Reaching an impasse, she had presented her quandary to her supervisor, but his dogmatism in asserting the supremacy of faith had shocked her. Religion hinged on faith, he had insisted. She was therefore doomed; unless she chose faith, her supervisor could not confer her degree.

Finding it impossible to compromise, she had taken a break. She did not go back, for there seemed no solution to the problem. In other words, she had quit.

But she had refused to sacrifice her visit to the Vatican.

If she harbored any faith at all, it was in the hope that at some point she would find the answer. Nothing in the world would stop her from investigating further. Convinced the solution to her dilemma lay hidden within the Vatican's walls, she had started on a new quest. Because Christianity had originated in the time of the Apostles and because the Vatican claimed Apostolic succession as well as custodianship of the Apostles' writings, she had to investigate both, hence her interview with Cardoni.

Jennifer had needed help securing the interview, and it had come in the form of a friend who worked for one of the world's leading journals, *Geographic America.* He had invented her credentials in return for exclusive rights to her material. That much she owed him.

So, there she sat, a failed scholar and wannabe journalist in need of a break. It was all very stupid, really, but she had nothing else to lose.

Cardoni's eyes narrowed. 'Dear child, the Vaticanus is not *one* of the oldest transcripts but *the* oldest. We're immensely proud of our holy scriptures.'

The hair on the back of her neck rose. Not only did he call the Bible *their* holy scriptures, he had also ignored her request to conduct experiments on the Vaticanus and negated other contenders for the title of oldest and full surviving copy, such as the *Codex Sinaiticus*.

Though the Holy See dated its codex to the first half of the fourth century, it had only been with them since the fifteenth century. Nevertheless, herein lay another contradiction. Earlier, Romano had asserted that the oldest manuscripts in their care dated around the eight century. The figures were contradictory. But since she still had a number of controversial questions, she decided not to belabor the point.

'How much of the Vaticanus has changed since its transcription?' she asked instead.

'There were at least three revisions,' said Cardoni. 'The first alterations were made soon after the original arrangement. There were a few more seven hundred years later. A third hand then retraced some faded letters early in the fifteenth century.'

Feeling confident she would remember her questions, Jennifer laid her notes on the table. 'So, that means little of the original codex is untouched?'

Cardoni tilted his head. He had already sensed she was up to something. He just could not quite lay a finger on it yet. 'That's not quite the way we would put it,' he said cautiously. 'But I suppose you could say that.'

She could not believe her ears. How would the man like to put it then? She did her best to maintain her composure. 'Where did the codex originate?'

'Its origin is uncertain. Some think right here in Rome; others attribute it to Asia Minor. Another opinion is Egypt. Personally, I'd say Rome.'

For a man credited with knowledge of the Vaticanus, Cardoni knew almost nothing. What was more, he made assumptions about things impossible to validate. That was likely how he led his audiences towards his own point of view. Did he deliberately mislead the faithful?

'Did you find a complete manuscript, or were parts missing?'

'Our holy treasure was slightly mutilated when it was discovered, but it contained most of the Old and New testaments.'

'Which parts were missing?'

'Folios at the beginning and the end had to be substituted.'

'When was this, Your Eminence?'

The quick succession of questions was more of an irritation than a challenge. None of the answers he would give her was based on actual evidence. The Church based its *noesis* on age-old traditions. 'It's impossible to say exactly when, or how much. Nevertheless, since the fifteenth century all the missing pages have been replaced.'

If she did not clench her jaw, it would have dropped. Did the man understand the significance of what he said? 'How was it replaced?'

'We believe codices like the Sinaiticus, the Alexandrinus and the Latin Vulgate were used to replace the missing sections.'

He had put his finger on the pulse of her dilemma. 'What you are saying then, Your Eminence, is that the Vaticanus is not original but merely a copy of earlier texts? And texts you do not have, I might add. You do not know who wrote it, when or where it comes from, and you have no clue how much of it was replaced?'

This Jennifer Jaine's rapid responses made for formidable verbal sparring, but years of developing his own cunning had made Cardoni an expert advocate. Soon he would show her the error of her ways.

Jennifer did not allow him any respite, though, albeit he already looked ready to devour her. Anyway, she had only presented him with the truth.

'Who wrote the Gospels?' she asked, changing tack.

'Surely you should know this, Miss Jaine.'

That was exactly the point: she did not. But neither did he nor anyone else. The Vatican certainly wanted everyone to believe the Apostles had written the Gospels, but any first-year seminary student could cite a litany of proof that they had not.

'The earliest manuscripts appeared around 300 CE,' she asserted. 'We estimate their origins to be between 65 and 125. If so, how could the Apostles have managed to write them?'

He thought of lecturing her on Church history, but decided against it. As a PhD in religious studies, she already knew all the answers. This meant that she was just being difficult to get her way. 'You should be grateful that we preserved the glorious message all this time, child.'

His words were ignored. There was no rational answer to such a statement. 'When were the Epistles of Saint Paul written?'

'About 45 to 60 AD.'

How did such a man make sense out of all this? Apart from the fact that there were no original Epistles in existence, Paul could perhaps have authored six of the fourteen letters ascribed to him. The rest were so different they could not have come from the same city, let alone the same hand. Lately, she had been finding the truth, or untruth of it all, difficult to stomach. How could anyone entrust his or her spiritual destiny to a religion whose doctrines were based on the sketchiest of evidence?

Her persistence was annoying and was now testing his patience. Cardoni was not sure how long he could bear entertaining her folly.

'What is the point of all this, Miss Jaine?' he asked irritably.

'Paul's Epistles are dated prior to the Gospels and *Acts*,' she said plainly.

Now even he found it impossible to contain his curiosity. 'And your point is?'

She could not believe he would ask that. She wondered what the Vatican had been doing for two millennia. 'Your Eminence, if the Gospels postdate Paul by decades, why don't they mention him?'

Cardoni stiffened. Her odiousness was beyond the pale. She had now trapped him not once but twice. 'You forget with whom you are speaking, child. We represent God. And God would never deceive His faithful.'

Perhaps God would not, but people might.

Jennifer had not anticipated Cardoni's hostility. Every time she had asked him a legitimate question, he gave her an arbitrary brushoff, and none of it made any sense. Yes, her subject matter had been controversial, but that was her purpose. People often posed similar questions to her. Not answering them properly, clearly made her look like an idiot.

A master's in religious studies, and she could not authenticate her faith. Imagine attempting to convince sceptics of faith with little more than a series of *dei ex machina*! It simply would not fly. If Cardoni, who claimed to be an Agent of God, could not come up with one credible argument or a speck of evidence, why should she believe him, let alone *in* him? Knowing whether the Word of God had any validity had never been more crucial.

'May I see the codex now?' she asked, already knowing the answer.

Cardoni had long before decided to end the interview. The library opened its arms to those who sought the glory of God's presence, not to rebellious journalists attempting to disgrace their treasured antiquities. 'I would suggest you obtain a Vaticanus B,' he pronounced stiffly. 'They are faithfully executed copies, perfectly crafted to reproduce the Vaticanus.'

'If you don't mind, though, Your Eminence, I'm here to see the Vatican's copy.'

Ignoring her sarcasm, he continued, 'There are four hundred and fifty numbered copies in the world. It should not be too difficult for you to get hold of one.'

As if the Vatican's codex was an original. Damn it! They were all copies, even the Vaticanus. 'Where can I find one?' she asked, her voice composed.

'The Loewen Learning Resource Centre in Providence has one. Viewing can be arranged with them.'

Jennifer did not know how long she could keep this up. For the sake of not antagonizing the cardinal further, though, she decided to hear him out. 'Who did the reproduction, Your Eminence?'

Cardoni sat up, his chin thrust forward: 'The Istituto Poligrafico e Zecca dello.'

'The Vatican's official publisher—in other words, the Vatican does its own reproductions?'

His eyes narrowed so his pupils were barely visible. 'Every detail, no matter how minute, can be seen in the facsimiles. Even the pages have the same weight and texture as the original parchment.'

'Your Eminence, I realize that, but we need to run ultraviolet and X-ray fluorescence studies.' She just made that up, but she had to try. 'They are specially developed techniques that do not require samples from the examined items and therefore wouldn't damage the Vaticanus. As you must know, such methods can extract details the naked eye cannot see. As you said yourself, the tests can reveal alterations made over the centuries. The B copies cannot provide that kind of information.'

'The Vaticanus is our holiest treasure. We do not allow outsiders like you to film it. And we certainly do not grant tests. We simply do not allow scrutiny like that.'

Outsiders? Your holiest treasure? The audacity of the man! He was merely a custodian of a fourth-century reproduction. He did not own its contents. All Christians did. He might as well lay claim to the English language. In any case, the extent to which the Vaticanus differed from original manuscripts was crucial, especially considering its status as *the* Word of God.

'As guardian of God's written word,' she continued, 'is it not essential to have original manuscripts?' She had no idea how to put that politely.

'Miss Jaine, our scriptures are a true reflection of God's inspired word. The men who wrote them were guided by the Holy Spirit, without a doubt.'

The old fool. Nobody knew who wrote them. It might as well be aliens from Mars. Will the Vatican ever answer these questions honestly?

'Your Eminence,' she said finally, 'please be straightforward with me. Do you have any original manuscripts of the *Gospels, Acts* or the *Epistles*?'

It was time to end the interview. No priest in high office would tolerate this. 'Even if we did, Miss Jaine, I cannot show them to you.'

Authentic scriptures were a double-edged sword. Revealing them could expose later texts to unethical changes. Without them, it was impossible to say whether the Vaticanus described actual events. Either way, the Church's doctrine was flawed. Unless Cardoni presented original manuscripts, no one had a clue if what was written, was true or false.

'Do you have *anything* authentic?' she asked.

'God works through faith, child,' Cardoni said. 'Faith conquers all.'

'Faith that there is a God and faith that there is life after death. Faith that we will one day meet our Maker and faith that He will judge us fairly for the good we have done, or forgiven us for the times we have erred. I'm sorry, but faith that the Vaticanus represents the truth is a different question. For that, you, and therefore the Roman Catholic Church as a source for anyone's creed, must stand up to scrutiny.'

Cardoni thanked God he had taken his medication this morning. His blood pressure had just shot to a critical level. When the telephone rang in the background, he rose gratefully from his chair.

And yet, defeat did not come easily to his interlocutor. 'The Bible is common knowledge,' Jennifer said, getting up with him. 'It belongs to every believer. Secrets are only for those who have something to hide. All I'm asking for is the truth. For the sake of all God-fearing people, I need to see the original scriptures. If it does not exist, so be it. But if it does, you should be open enough to admit it.'

Cardoni's face hardened to a mask. He had completely underestimated her. 'The Holy Church prides herself on honesty and integrity. We do not deceive the faithful.'

'That's not the ...' Jennifer rested her hands on her tummy. She had to contain the viper in her gut. But she would not retreat. She had lived with this frustration for years. This was her opportunity to let it all out. She needed answers, and she was not leaving without them.

Bishop Albani arrived from the reception area on cue. He stood next to Cardoni, breathing heavily. 'Your Eminence, forgive me for interrupting. You have a call waiting for you.'

The Secret Archives' prefect could not have come at a more opportune time. Cardoni excused himself, hiding his smile as he strode towards the door.

Jennifer followed, and when Albani tried to stop her, she quickly brushed him aside. She might as well go down fighting; if her little car was headed towards a cliff without brakes she might as well punch the gas. 'Since you claim to be the bearers of God's power and authority, at least you should have proof, yes? Something that bears witness to the fact, or perhaps something that can verify your claims to truth.'

Cardoni stopped. He swung around. Facing her like a bull about to charge, he said, 'You have no idea what you are getting yourself into here, Miss Jaine. Scores have tried to do the same. Nobody, I repeat nobody, has ever succeeded. Do you for one second think you are better than those who came before you? We control the souls of men.

We ensure every man, woman and child's salvation through sacrament and faith. Now if you'll excuse me, I have far more important issues to deal with right now.' Then, turning to Albani, 'Call the gendarmerie to escort Miss Jaine to the gate.' And, denying her another word, he walked off.

Jennifer watched as Cardoni left through the 'Staff Only' exit. She tried to follow again, but this time Albani took hold of her shoulders. If it were not for her determination to get her life back on track, she would have yielded, but she could not. Another blunder like her failed PhD would break her. She tried to pull loose, but Albani held her tightly. Tears ran down her cheeks. She brushed them away, but the sobs kept coming.

At long last, she understood their strategy: if all else fails, fall back on rhetoric and deception. It had worked for centuries. She had quit her studies for exactly this reason. She would have no further part of it, not only as a journalist, but also as a person who had dedicated her life to Christ. She had the right to know the facts about the religion she had held so dear. For Christianity to work for her, she needed to have her faith authenticated. She would question until satisfied, even if it took a lifetime.

Chapter 3

Cardinal Leonardo Santori sank to his knees and hunched over Father John Yilmaz. Cradling the Father in his arms, the limp body resting in his lap, he stared at the young man's face. The priest's death could not have come at a worse time. With years of negative publicity haunting the Vatican, the Holy See could ill afford another scandal, not now, and especially not here, in the secret vault beneath his Penitentiary office.

Santori remembered the first time he had met Father Yilmaz. It was more than a year ago, in his private library upstairs. Santori had been working late, preparing for a tribunal the next day. His receptionist, Father Franco, had introduced Yilmaz as the new filing clerk. The Governatorato had transferred the previous clerk to one of the Roman congregations, and Yilmaz was embarking on his first assignment, collecting books belonging to the main libraries.

Santori watched the young priest stack books on a trolley. Statuesque and sophisticated, Yilmaz went about his task effortlessly. His burnt-umber hair, bronze complexion and prominent nose looked out-of-place in such a monastic atmosphere. That, together with his Islamic-sounding surname, made Santori wonder. When Yilmaz walked over to collect the books at the foot of the desk, Santori stopped him.

'Those are mine,' he said, his hand pressed on the nearest pile.

Still Yilmaz began to stoop. 'Your Eminence, may I file them for you?'

'No, no, I'll have Father Franco do it in the morning.'

Undeterred, Yilmaz stacked the first pile on his arm and stood. 'Where do they go?' he asked.

'The mezzanine,' Santori yielded. 'Use the stairs in the corner there.'

Yilmaz wasted no time. He glided up the spiral staircase and, studying the different sections as he moved along the wrap-around mezzanine, swiftly filed the volumes away. When he had finished, he leaned over the wrought-iron balustrade.

'May I look around?'

Santori nodded. His library contained books rarely found on Christian shelves. In addition to the law journals and religious literature used in his own work, collections of history, philosophy and science populated the walls. He looked on, bemused, as Yilmaz homed in on a controversial section. Musing over some of the titles, the young priest at last selected a book and, returning downstairs, settled into one of the desks.

'Are esotericism and occultism the same?' Yilmaz asked, skimming the first several pages.

'Pretty much,' Santori responded. 'Both are pseudo-sciences.'

'I didn't know these books even existed. …'

'The Church rejects both. Anybody involved in esoteric practices commits a grievous sin.' And laying his pen in the spine of the book, Santori eventually asked, 'Where are you from?'

'Turkey,' Yilmaz responded. Then, tilting his head sideways as he read: 'Saint Paul's neighborhood.'

Unusual indeed, Santori thought. Fascinated, he asked a question pertinent to any man of the cloth, 'Tarsus?'

Yilmaz looked over his shoulder. 'Antakya actually.'

'Ah, Antioch, where our Holy Mother Church originated.'

Yilmaz did not challenge his superior's remark because, as someone who originated from biblical Antioch, he completely understood the cardinal's statement. With all evangelical accounts of Jesus and his disciples situated in and around Jerusalem, most people mistakenly believed that Christianity had sprung from Judea.

'You must have read these, Your Eminence, no?'

'Most, not all. Some I inherited from my predecessors.'

'I wish I could. I would like to attain the wisdom of Solomon.'

When Yilmaz smiled, his lips curved towards two rows of dimples, and tiny wrinkles along his cheekbones framed his jubilant eyes. Santori liked that. 'Then you're on the right track,' the cardinal said enthusiastically. 'Wisdom is applied faith.'

'And faith is "the substance of things hoped for and the evidence of things not seen", yes.' Then, lowering his eyes again, he continued reading.

Santori leaned back in his armchair. *Hebrews 11:1*. The priest knew his Bible. He would have to take care that Holy Scripture supported his own doctrinal pronouncements. He waited for Yilmaz to look up again before asking, 'How old are you?'

'Twenty-eight.'

The young man's charm and alertness attracted Santori like a moth to a flame. Yilmaz reminded him of himself at that age. He sighed. God, if only he could have his youth back. He would give anything to do it all over again. Not that he did not have a good life; dedicating one's life to God had its rewards. And yet, years of tribulation had sapped his vigor. He could have handled so many things so differently. If only ...

*****

Rousing himself from his reverie, Santori lowered the young priest to the floor. Yilmaz no longer bore his contagious smile and his eyes had lost their light. Stroking Yilmaz's face, Santori closed the young man's eyes. Then, he lifted his pectoral cross above his head and raised his hand to administer the last rite to this talented priest, taken at the start of such a promising career. At that moment, though, the sound of fabric swishing past a wall stopped him in mid-prayer. Not daring to breathe, he listened. Then, he heard it again. He seized the dagger from the floor and sprang up. Peering through the shadows on the far side of the room, he could dimly see the shape of a man.

'Who's there?'

An ominous figure appeared as if from the grave. Tall and powerful, the intruder approached. Santori tried to catch sight of the man's face, but the light from the office above cast a shadow across it.

'Who are you?' Santori demanded.

The intruder paused briefly, staring at the cardinal, then swung around and headed for the staircase. A few strides and he had reached the centric landing a quarter of the way up. A few more and he had made it to the second landing midway and to the left.

Still clutching the dagger, Santori followed in pursuit. He cared nothing for the vigorous appearance of the man and he did not consider the possibility that he might be armed. He simply had to stop him. At the second landing, he turned and looked up, but with the light now shining in his eyes, he could only just make out the train of a cassock disappearing into his office.

'Come back! Stop!'

Santori dashed up the steps, but his chest burned and heaved. Age was his handicap and his elaborate robes hampered him. He had just made it to the top when he heard someone banging on his office door loud enough for him to feel the vibration.

Santori had to catch his breath.

'*Maggiore!*' a voice called out.

It was Father Franco, Santori's assistant. He always arrived at around eight.

Santori did not respond. With his assistant stationed at the front exit, the fugitive had to be hiding in his Penitentiary suite. He scanned the room. Where had he gone? He rushed around the hearth and into his office. At his desk, he turned to face the room. The office entrance was just to the left, the conference table on the far side, two visitors' chairs stood before him with a lounge arranged behind them. Beyond that was the hearth separating his office from his private library. Nothing seemed disturbed, but the lavishness of the furnishings made hiding easy. He examined the curtains on the wall to his right but saw nothing to suggest a human form behind them. Only his library remained.

The banging on the entrance doors started again. 'Eminence, are you all right?'

God! Father Franco was carrying on like a lunatic. On arrival, he must have knocked but found no answer. Santori had assigned him to his office eight years ago, when he had overstepped the mark at his parish in Novara. Then thirty-five, Franco had been involved with a man the Church had excommunicated for making advances towards young boys. To ensure that Franco refrained from sinning again, Santori had had him transferred to the Vatican. That way he could ensure the priest did not revert to his wicked ways. Franco's penance and good work ethic had soon persuaded Santori to assign the younger priest to his own office. Franco had led a life of celibacy ever since.

Now preparing to open the door for Franco, Santori heard hinges creak in the library behind him. It could only be the door behind the spiral staircase. He had organized its construction recently as a shortcut to the main library. Gripping the dagger even more firmly, he sprinted between the sofas, back towards the hearth.

'*Sua Eminenza!*' Franco called again from reception.

Santori did not stop. As he passed the hearth, he heard the muffled sound of a door shutting. His chest tightened. It could only mean the intruder had escaped. Moving as quickly as he could, he slipped behind the spiral staircase. He tried to open the door, but his hand slipped on the handle. Blood dripped from his fingers onto the floor. He wiped his hand on his vestments, but they were also soaked. After rubbing his hand on the wall, he again tried the handle. This time it turned. Pulling the door open, he raced down the arched passage. Reaching the small courtyard, he had to stop, his breath coming in brief gasps. He could not carry on like this.

Returning to his suite, Santori rested his forehead against the wall behind the spiral staircase. The telephone in the library rang. Good God, Father Franco would not let up! Santori could see the chubby priest's cheeks jiggling with panic as he called security.

Santori wondered what he should do. Whether he gave chase, their secret would be exposed. But pursuing the intruder would prevent him from taking control. Choosing the lesser of two evils, he closed the door, but before entering the vault, he carefully scanned the mezzanine; he had to make sure no one was lurking up there. In his frenzied pursuit of the intruder, he had failed to consider there might be more than one. Then, with a jolt, he recalled that the mysterious priest had been carrying a rucksack. Dear Lord, he could not let him get away.

As the telephone's insistent ringing ceased, Santori made his way back to the vault. He needed to know if the fugitive had the silver casket with him. With all his heart Santori prayed he did not. Scurrying down the steps again, he searched the area where the candlesticks and crucifix lay in spilt blood, but could see nothing. He circled the altar. Maybe it had fallen off the back. No, still nothing. Darting back to the front of the altar, he stepped over the broken body. Perhaps the young priest had fallen on it as he collapsed. He rolled the corpse onto its stomach.

'Oh God, it is gone!'

Santori sank to his knees. Fear flooded his being, and his breathing came in short pants.

'Your Eminence,' Franco called out. 'What's happening in there?'

Santori dropped the dagger. He could not let his secretary wait any longer. Nor could he afford to have Vatican security on his doorstep. Only high-ranking cardinals knew of the vault and its profane artefact.

'Just a minute,' he called out.

Rising from the floor, he tramped up the stairs again.

'Your Eminence, I heard you shouting.' Franco sounded calmer now that he had had a response.

Santori shoved the marble lintel above the fireplace. Slowly, the hearth floated back. As it drew level with the library shelf behind the vault entrance, it dropped into place. He withdrew a pike from a circle-cross slot beside the hearth and slipped it into its stand against the opposite wall.

'Maggiore!'

Santori took a deep breath. He had to calm himself. He walked to the entrance of his suite, unlocked the door and twisted the knob.

*****

Father Berti Franco clutched his heart.

'Oh Jesus, you are hurt,' he yelped.

He tried to come to his superior's aid, but his legs would not obey him. Commanding punishment and reform in the Holy Roman Church and prosecuting the wicked to eradicate sin had made Cardinal Santori the most feared man in the entire Holy See. Through the sacrament of penance, he had afforded sinners absolution. Those who would not atone he excommunicated. With his thinning, grey hair cut close to the scalp, his brawny stance and his feared position as Major Penitentiary, he had earned the reputation of *Vatican gladiator*. For Franco, seeing the older priest distressed and covered in blood intensified the image.

'Summon His Eminence Cardinal Cardoni,' Santori snapped. 'It's urgent.'

Franco could not focus. He clasped his hands tightly to his chest and stood staring, motionless.

'Did you hear what I said, Father? Get the cardinal and no one else. Just him!'

'Your Eminence ...'

Santori's eyes flashed. 'Tell him. He must come at once.'

Franco's commitment to God stemmed from obedience, not bravery. He had to do as he was told. He lifted the receiver from the phone on his desk. 'Should I call security? They'll know what to do.'

'Get it together, Father,' Santori growled. 'Let no one in here other than His Eminence the Cardinal, and I mean no one unless it is the Holy Father himself.'

Franco's trembling fingers fumbled repeatedly as he dialed the library offices.

Santori turned towards his own office, yelling as he closed the door, 'No one.'

Father Franco stood rooted to the ground, frozen.

Chapter 4

'God punishes instantly.'

Jennifer's mother had warned her every time her rebellious nature surfaced.

Her mother was right.

Jennifer had blundered, and now she felt foolish. In her zeal, she had forgotten the ethics of her upbringing. Her mother was probably apologizing to Saint Peter right now. Had her mother been alive, she would have been deeply shamed by her daughter's dishonesty. It seemed only yesterday Jennifer had stood beside her mother's deathbed. The doctors had summoned her urgently. Fragile and weak, drawn and pale, her mother had lain crumpled, one hand hooked to an IV, the other tethered to a heart monitor. This was her mother dying in intensive care.

Jennifer remembered holding one of her mother's hands in hers. 'Momma, don't go,' she had sobbed softly. 'I love you so much. Please don't.'

Her mother had squeezed her hand lightly. 'God sometimes takes one person before the other, that's all. …

We don't know why He does it. … My time has simply come before yours and Daddy's. … Look after your father for me. … He needs you. …' There was a long pause, and her voice became fainter. 'I'm sorry I won't be there for you when you're older. … One day you will find a beautiful husband as I did. … I so hoped to be there for your children. …' She had struggled to keep her eyes open, but at the last they fluttered shut. 'Send me photos as they grow up. … I'd like that. … I'll ask God to forward them. … I love you more than words ...'

And that was the last her mother said; although Jennifer remembered pressing her forehead to her mother's hand and praying as she had never prayed, the older woman's eyes remained closed never to open again. She had desperately needed her mother to squeeze her hand just one last time, but there had been no miracles that day.

Jennifer's father had let her have her mother's last few moments. Afterwards, he had held his daughter close for some time. When the nursing staff arrived to care for the body, they were asked to leave.

Jennifer had not been to a funeral before. She hated every minute of it. If it were anyone else, she would not have gone. Despite what her mother had raised her to believe, death seemed so damn permanent. She was impatient for the ritual to end so she could escape to the ocean. She had needed to be alone awhile but, instead, had spent time with her dad. For someone who had just lost his wife, he seemed calm, and Jennifer never saw him get emotional after that day, nor did she ever see him look at another woman. It seemed he had decided no one could take her mother's place. Her parents had had such a beautiful marriage that perhaps a memory of perfection seemed preferable in her father's eyes to any possible future with another.

Jennifer had wept for days on end. Watching her mother die had been horrible. Her passing had brought so much pain—pain that still lingered even now in Jennifer's soul. She had experienced a similar, but less intense, pain nearly a year ago when she stopped working on her doctorate. Her fear of failure had caused this feeling. Failure had felt so permanent—like death. She had not expected failure to evoke such strong emotions. It had taken months to figure out why she had felt that way. Now, however, she knew; somehow, she had not learned how to fail. Her temperament did not permit failure, so losing her mother and dropping out had the same effect.

Now, that feeling of despair had returned. Cardoni's rebuff in the middle of their interview had been yet *another* failure. The pain throbbed in her chest and inconsolable grief began choking her. At that moment, she hated life. She was stranded a continent away from home, with no career, no money, no return plane ticket to her home country—and, at this point, not even her religion. She stood facing the exit through which Cardoni had fled.

'I *can't* fail,' she whispered. She wiped her tears again, then began praying: 'God, I'm sorry. I know I lied. I was dishonest. Please forgive me.'

'You can freshen up before you go, Miss Jaine.'

The voice was Albani's. Having released her shoulders, the bishop now stood beside her. When she nodded, he pointed her towards the lobby. She followed his directions, closed the restroom door and stopped before one of the sinks, staring at herself in the mirror; her eyes were inflamed, her makeup smudged. In a word, she was a mess.

She wondered how she had managed to regress to such a pathetic state. She lifted a towel from a pile beside the sink. Dampening it with cold water, she considered her next move. As she wiped away the smudged mascara, she told herself this was no way to act. She needed to calm down—needed, really, to settle down. Already in her thirties, she had nothing to show for her life. She had not even finished her PhD. Nor did she have any means of income. She had, in desperation, spent everything on her trip to Rome, telling her more practical side that perhaps it would lead to her 'big break'. Now, what could she do? Slum around Europe? Work at Starbuck's? She certainly could not rely on her father helping her out all the time. She was not twenty. No, she had to complete this, whatever it took. That, at the very least, was clear. Her eyes flashed a clear steely hue. She would be a damned woman if need be. She would suck Cardoni's shriveled old balls if that was what it took to see the codex. She would never have another chance. That was about the sum of it. Even if she died in the process, it was preferable to a failed mission—and the answer lay only a couple of hundred feet away in the Secret Archives.

Jennifer returned to Sisto V, where Albani stood talking to one of the staff with his back turned to her. She still had to fetch her notes in the meeting room. Treading softly, she crept past Albani's desk and down the corridor. As she lifted her notes from the table, however, she spotted something: a set of keys lay on the floor near Cardoni's chair. He must have dropped them in his rage and left without noticing them. She picked them up to give to Albani, then stopped. The key ring had an RFID-enabled card dangling from it. His security card?

She looked around the doorjamb; Albani's back was still turned towards the corridor. Without a second thought she slipped the keys into her jacket pocket, and again nearing Albani, glanced around to see if anyone had noticed. The staff, however, seemed too busy—indeed, frantic—with some other task. Then something inside her, a voice not unlike her mother's, urged: 'Go. Go find the codex.'

For Heaven's sake, what *could* they do to her if she did? They could hardly burn her at the stake!

Ignoring the additional trouble which she was about to bring on herself, she slipped past Albani and headed for the staircase. She slowed her pace, hoping to avoid drawing attention to herself. The Sisto V reading rooms contained only bibliographical aids, dictionaries and encyclopedias. There was no chance of finding the Vaticanus there. The Noble Floor above housed the Holy See's diplomatic correspondences. The Leone XIII reading room was full of documentary material and indices. They would not keep something as significant as their oldest copy of the Bible there either. However, Pio XI, where she had registered with Father Romano earlier, distributed material from the double-story bunker beneath the Cortile della Pigna. Ancient manuscripts would be kept in the bunker—probably a dedicated, air-conditioned, video-monitored, climate- and humidity-controlled and with an alarm system to boot. If it existed at all, the Vaticanus would be in such a place, and she would not get through too many doors before they figured out that she had Cardoni's key card, so the Pio XI bunker was her best and probably *only* bet.

Slipping back down the stairs again, she returned to Pio XI and cut across one of the aisles to the opposite side of the room. Fortunately, the archives had now filled with several researchers, some of them female. Her presence was no longer out-of-place, and emboldened by newfound anonymity, she pressed on. At the end of Pio XI, she slid through a doorway marked, 'Staff Only', then pausing in the adjacent foyer, contemplated her next move. A doorway to her left led to the library offices. On her right, a staircase led to the floor above. Recalling the maps, which she had pored over prior to her trip, she realized the hallway ahead of her could only lead to the Pio IV museums. Then, a ping echoed down the recess to her left, followed by the sound of elevator doors opening. She hurried towards the museum entrance and, approaching the doorway, peeked around the corner.

She drew back. A priest had pushed a trolley laden with documents from the lift and seemed to head for the Pio XI reading room. When she could no longer hear the trolley wheels trundling across the marble floor, she again peeked around the corner.

Nobody.

The lift could only go to one place—the bunker. Slipping back into the foyer again, she headed for the lift. She looked for a switch, a button, anything familiar, but saw nothing. Then she spotted a black magnetic-strip scanner set flush into the wall. She plucked Cardoni's keys from her pocket and, her hand shaking, swiped its back face past the dancing, red laser light. As the elevator's doors whirred opened, she considered thanking God, but her conscience would not let her. It was only a few minutes ago that she had pledged to pull her life together and, no matter what, to stop lying. To hell with all of it: she was not leaving empty-handed; she *had* to see the Vaticanus first.

As the elevator's doors clanged to a stop a fluorescent light in its ceiling clicked on, revealing another trolley piled with manuscripts. The priest must have left it. He would be back for it once he had made his first delivery. She would have to be fast. Before closing the doors, she thought of pushing the trolley out. At least that way the priest would think someone else had needed to use the lift. Just as she began pushing the trolley forwards, the priest returned from the reading room.

'Hold up!' he called out.

She needed the doors closed, but she had already shoved the trolley too far. The doors knocked against the trolley and opened again.

The priest sprinted towards her. 'Excuse me, miss, can you hold that for me please.'

Jennifer instinctively stepped back against the elevator wall. She pulled the trolley back inside just in time to clear the doors and prevent the priest from jamming the doors with his hand. She saw him go for his ID card as the two doors were about to meet. Her heart pounded as she saw them open again.

'I have another trolley waiting downstairs,' the priest said, waiting for the doors to open. Pushing the trolley aside, he stood next to Jennifer. 'Since you're already going down, I might as well get it.'

As the lift began its descent, she pushed Cardoni's keys up her sleeve. The priest must not see the cardinal's security card. Then she saw her reflection on the polished wall opposite her. The card clipped to her breast pocket clearly read 'Visitor'. How would she explain that?

'Didn't I see you with Monsignor earlier?' he asked turning towards her.

She locked eyes, hoping to discomfort him. 'I'm helping out at the Capitoline Museum.' That was feeble, she knew, but her mind was racing and the Lux in Arcana was the only thing she could think of under the circumstances. Her assertiveness must have worked though, because he withdrew his gaze to stare at the opposite wall. But that was where she had just seen her own reflection. To recapture his attention, she continued with her trivial chitchatting. Only this time she spoke flirtatiously: 'Have you been? It's quite inspirational. You should come.'

His gaze returned. 'Priests aren't allowed,' he said, smiling. 'There are just too many of us. I think you have to work there to have the privilege.'

His height, fortunately, made her card difficult to read without looking down again. Arriving at the first basement level the priest held the door for her, but she stayed put. 'I'm going down,' she said hastily.

'I'll wait for the lift to come back up again. I don't think there'll be enough room for the both of us and the trolleys.'

'I don't mind being squashed a bit.' She nearly pinched herself. What was she saying? What if he changed his mind!

'You're very kind, Miss ...'

'Jaine. ... Jennifer. Just call me Jennifer. I'm sure we'll see more of each other from now on.'

The priest let go of the door. Not understanding quite what she had meant, he stared, almost blankly. The doors were about to meet when his gaze fell on her card. The wrinkles in his forehead deepened and he reached forward.

'Excuse me, Miss ...'

Jennifer heard his nails scratching against the stainless-steel surface and his knuckles crack as they buckled against the closed doors.

Descending again, she tried to breathe deeply, but her diaphragm's involuntary reflexes made her gasp in short bursts. She rested her head against the back wall. Closing her eyes, she listened to the sound of the electric motor lowering her down the shaft. 'I must be crazy,' she thought. The priest would alert the entire library before the elevator doors reopened, and the staff would catch her as she stepped out. And then what? If, and only if, no one was already in the bunker, would she have the smallest window of opportunity to find the codex. She prayed for that *if* as she had prayed for her mother—and, for crying out loud, there she was praying again!

Chapter 5

Gendarmerie sub-officer, Adjutant Arno Lioni, always reported for duty at seven o'clock. After relieving the night duty officer, he would deploy men at strategic points around the city. Before returning to the command center behind la Porta Sant' Anna, he would check in at the Governatorato sub-station behind Saint Peter's Basilica. There he would make sure the officers on duty were ready for the Holy Pontiff's morning walk. Each morning, at around ten o'clock, the Holy Father enjoyed half an hour's exercise and leisure in the gardens around the Radio Vaticano.

Lioni had just entered the Belvedere Courtyard from the archway on the west wing, when the command radio operator called him over his two-way.

'Adjutant Lioni, this is Command. State your location.'

Lioni unclipped the two-way from his belt and lifted it to his mouth: 'Just arrived at the Belvedere. Is there a problem? Over.'

'We have a situation at the Penitentiary. Can you investigate?'

Lioni wasted no time. He changed direction and headed for the entrance on the far-left corner of the courtyard. 'I'm on my way. Over.'

'Do you have backup?'

'Do I need any? Over.'

'We have a possible intrusion. Screams were heard.'

Lioni shifted gears. In seconds, his brisk walk accelerated to a sprint. Cutting between parked cars, he waved on the several Swiss guards by the fire station. 'On the double,' he called out. By the time he reached the entrance to the library, one Helvetian had managed to join him. 'I have the Swiss Guard with me,' he said, the two-way pressed to his lips.

His breath now shortened by his strides, Lioni leapt up the terrace steps. His navy police uniform made sprinting easier for him than it was for the Helvetians with their puffed blue, orange and red Renaissance attire, and certainly running with a holstered handgun was easier than humping a halberd and sword. At the arcade separating the library offices from the Penitentiary, a perplexed priest pointed them towards Father Franco's reception desk. His hand on his sidearm, Lioni greeted Franco as he headed towards Santori's office door.

Franco returned the telephone receiver to its cradle and slipped clumsily around his desk. 'You can't go in there,' he said, his hand up like a traffic cop.

Father Franco knew Lioni well. Their paths had crossed several years back. As a boy in his early teens, Lioni had been a member of Franco's parish. At the time, Lioni had been something of a terror. Hanging out with a pack of pubescent miscreants, he was frequently caught up in street violence, especially after football games. Despite Lioni's unfortunate circumstances, Franco liked the boy. Just before he relocated to the Vatican, he had encouraged Lioni to become a police officer. 'If you can't beat 'em …' he remembered saying to the youngster. The adjutant had not grown taller in the intervening years. He still stood two-inches shy of six feet, but he had become far more muscular. Indeed, his pugnacious stance, bulging jaw muscles and thick neck reminded Franco of a bullterrier.

Lioni pushed past Franco. 'We heard screams,' he said.

Franco resisted. 'Stop!'

'What do you mean, "Stop"? I have to investigate.'

Franco's customary gentle manner did not prevent him from executing orders. He would not let Lioni intimidate him. 'I can't let you in, Arno,' he said in a firm tenor.

As if it were yesterday, Lioni recalled Father Franco's impact on his early life. Lioni had grown up on a small farm just outside Novara. As the resident priest, Father Franco had often visited Lioni's family. Lioni's father had an abusive streak, which intensified when he was drunk. Lioni had once discovered his mother in shock and crying in the bathroom. She had had marks on her neck from his father's attempts to strangle her. He remembered joining his father on the backyard porch where the older man sat smoking a cigarette rolled in a bit of newspaper. He had challenged the old man. Standing in front of him, he had told him he would kill him if he ever disrespected his mother again. His father had just sat there, dazed like the wino he was. They never mentioned the incident afterwards, but his father never touched his mother in anger again—not while Lioni still lived in the house anyhow.

Lioni respected the Father caring for him as a child and appreciated the help he had given him and his family, but right now he had a job to do. He pushed ahead again and once more the priest resisted.

Franco had orders to locate Cardinal Cardoni. Dialing the number of the libraries and simultaneously keeping an eye on Lioni, he waited for an answer. On recognizing the curator's voice, he froze. The curator must have also heard the cries to be answering himself. 'Most Reverend Monsignor. ... It's Father Franco ..., from the Penitentiary,' he stuttered. 'Is His Eminence Cardinal Cardoni available? It's really very urgent.'

'Pull yourself together, Father,' the curator barked. 'What's happening over there? We heard shouting.'

Franco did not have time to explain. In any case, he did not know what to say. 'Most Reverend Monsignor,' he continued, 'I'm sorry to be rude, but I have orders to contact His Eminence the Cardinal. Again, I say it is urgent. In fact, I cannot emphasize enough how urgent it is.'

'He is in a meeting, Father. Can I come over?'

Franco's heart thumped against his chest with all the force of a vengeful boxer. Between needing to respect the request of the Monsignor and having to carry out His Excellency's instructions he was nearly petrified with indecision. Still, Santori's orders had been clear: 'I'm not allowed to let anyone in except His Eminence the Cardinal and perhaps His Holiness the Pope.'

'Oh, it's the Holy Father you need. I'll be sure to get your message to him right away.'

Speaking with the curator had always been a challenge—the Spanish ancestry of the Argentinean priest did have its drawbacks. 'Most Reverend, I just need His Eminence Cardinal Cardoni,' Franco said, his voice now a quivering falsetto. 'He must come right away.'

Chapter 6

The elevator's descent into the nuclear bombproof bunker seemed endless. Jennifer moved the trolley over to the other side and pressed her sweaty palms against the back wall like a runner, readying herself to dash forwards when the doors opened. In the absence of any better plan, she would simply bowl over anyone who tried to stop her.

She heard a telephone ring. Her heart raced like a caged tiger's when the elevator's doors at last slid open. What now?

Before her was a lobby with a control desk set against one of the concrete walls about twenty feet from the elevator. A priest stood in front of the desk, his arms akimbo. Although he had his back to her, she recognized him instantly; with a heightened sense of danger, she easily spotted Father Romano's spidery fingers. Another priest sat beside the counter. He answered the phone and spoke briefly, hurrying through the required protocols. The person at the other end must have been curt with him, because the priest soon passed the handset to Romano, immediately sitting back and crossing his arms as he listened.

When Romano uttered 'Monsignor', she knew it was Bishop Albani alerting them of her breach of security. She peered out of the elevator. Passages ran from left to right. Another priest with a laden trolley was approaching from the left, removing that option. There was no time to think and no alternative; she turned right, pushing the trolley from the lift. As Romano returned the receiver to its place behind the desk, she turned to retreat, but the elevator doors had already closed behind her.

'Excuse me, Miss, can I help you?'

The priest beside Romano was pointing in her direction. Feigning deafness, she started down the passage, the sound of several sets of footsteps propelling her forwards. She had no idea why she was even attempting to reach the steel door at the far end of this passage. She glanced behind her—Romano was closing in as if possessed, while the other priest was close behind him. With about fifteen feet to go, she realized she would not make the door, so just before reaching it, she let go of the trolley. Accelerating past it, she managed to squeeze between it and the closed door. Then, using the door as support, she stopped the trolley and with all the might she could muster, heaved it and its contents back towards the approaching priests.

Romano was not expecting a trolley laden with valuable manuscripts to come speeding towards him. Stopping abruptly to steel himself for impact, he slid across the floor; instinctively flinging his arms protectively across the manuscripts to prevent their crashing to the ground. A loud groan escaped his lips as the trolley's handrail hit his solar plexus. And, though the priest behind him, apparently realizing what was about to happen, tried to scuttle past, the trolley swept sideways and both were knocked backwards, trapped beneath the tumbling manuscripts.

Jennifer watched all this, somewhat amused, despite the extreme nature of her situation. Her response was short lived, for seconds later, the elevator behind the priests dinged and out stepped Cardinal Cardoni, his temples bulging with pulsating veins and his skin crimson with anger. Close on his heels was Bishop Albani.

'Stop this instant!' Cardoni screamed.

Swinging towards the steel door, Jennifer tried the cardinal's key card. A red light flashed. Oh, God no! The footsteps behind her were growing louder causing her hands to shake uncontrollably. She swiped the card again. Please God! A split-second delay felt like an eternity. It flashed green! The magnetic lock kicked back. She flung the door open and leapt through, slamming it shut just in time to keep Romano from jamming it with his foot.

Jennifer turned from the door. Before her hundreds of steel shelves stood in rows like coaches at a rail yard. If she had ever needed God's help, now was the time. She knew the archives had only two climate-controlled storerooms with acid-free cardboard casings for the Vatican's ancient parchments. And if the ducts lining the ceilings and rows of steel cabinets were any indication, she had found one of them. Glimpsing the Vaticanus was now a distinct possibility.

Outside, Cardoni's fist crashed against the door. She turned as he pressed his nose against the reinforced glass. He demanded that she open the door, but she waved him off. She would not leave until she had achieved her objective. She heard Cardoni call for Albani's card. God mostly did not listen, but He was especially deaf this morning. Still, she had to try. Again, she prayed for a miracle.

To the rear of the bunker, a row of display cabinets stood under fluorescent lights. Hoping to glimpse something—anything—she ran towards it. The door burst open behind her as she reached the first display. She did not look back but rested her hands on the Plexiglas top. Inside the cabinet lay an open papyrus scroll. At eighteen inches by at least twelve feet, it filled the cabinet. She tried to read the text and saw it was in Koine Greek. Skimming a few lines, she recognized the dialect as that of a first-century Judean, possibly a Galilean, but certainly from the early Roman Empire, sometime between the reigns of Nero and Trajan. Scholars had long suspected the original Gospels and Pauline Epistles were in Koine, hence the term New Testament Greek. The fact that the author had used such an early dialect must mean the scroll dated from that era. But, suddenly appalled at the thought of relinquishing her freedom to read a parchment that only confirmed what she already knew, Jennifer turned away and continued her search for the Vaticanus. She recognized nothing that resembled the photos she had seen. Had she utterly failed? Feeling she probably had, she began sinking into the same despondency that had affected her earlier. Just then, though, her eyes fell on a bronze plaque below the parchment. She moved her head out of the way for the lamp above her to light the inscription. The first line was in Latin, and the second was in Koine. Without thinking, she translated both into English:

The Sayings of Jesus

At that moment, Cardoni stalked towards her. 'You've gone far enough!' he cried out.

Jennifer's eyes were deceiving her, surely. The first three Gospels, *Matthew*, *Mark* and *Luke*, differed vastly from *John*. Of course, they also disagreed with each other in many respects, but as they included many of the same stories and sequences, as well as similar wording, scholars had long ruled coincidence out of the question. Their congruities could be explained as each successive Gospel simply borrowing from its earlier predecessor, but it was their incongruities that had long made for one of history's most mysterious literary enigmas. Known as the *Synoptic Problem*, the phenomenon had left academics puzzled for centuries. Jennifer had herself spent years pondering the theoretical dilemma it posed. *Matthew* and *Luke* attributed many of the same sayings to Jesus, and of these shared quotations, nearly a quarter in each was found nowhere else in the New Testament. One theory held that a fifth Gospel, named *die Quelle* (the German word for *source*), or simply '*Q*,' was where these shared sayings most likely originated; accordingly, proponents of this view also hypothesized that *Mark* and *Q* had served as the antecedents of *Matthew* and *Luke*. Theories abounded around these *Q*-based similarities, but after more than a century of exhaustive archaeological searching and critical speculation, solid evidence of *Q* had yet to emerge. Of course, one yet unexplored idea was that *Q* represented several sources, some written and some oral, but if Jennifer had just read what she thought she had …

Cardoni grabbed her. 'That's enough. I'm calling the guards.'

Despite her capture, Jennifer was elated. If the scroll was what she suspected, she had just made one of the most extraordinary finds of the past two millennia. She yanked herself free.

'This is *Q*, isn't it?'

'I'm having you removed from the library.'

'You said you don't have anything older than the Vaticanus, but this is way older!'

Cardoni grasped her arm and gripped it even more tightly. 'There is no "*Q*". Now step away from the cabinet.'

Again, she shook him off, and this time she stepped back. No reference to *Quelle* existed on the Vatican's website or in its encyclopedia, so clearly the Holy See did not acknowledge its existence. Yet here she stood, mere feet from a text the Church had omitted from the biblical canon and hidden from the faithful since before Jerome translated the Vulgate. She stared at Romano, who now looked like a cat whose milk had been stolen.

'Have you ever seen this?' she asked.

God could strike Romano at any moment. He had never been this far into the archives before, nor had he ever heard anything about this *Q* business.

'Out!' Cardoni commanded, glaring first at the control-desk priest, then to Romano. 'Father, help me get this *woman* out of here.'

Naturally, Romano would not wish to contradict a cardinal, but he needed an explanation: 'I've never heard of ...'

'Of course not,' Jennifer said, interrupting him. 'Your See would prefer you believe the Apostles wrote the Gospels, but they didn't. The existence of *Q* proves the Gospel writers weren't even contemporaries of Jesus.'

Cardoni lunged for Jennifer's arm, but she dodged his grasp. 'Who wrote this?' she demanded.

'Are you crippled, Father?' Cardoni snapped at Romano.

'Where does it originate?' Jennifer persisted.

'She has a point,' Romano thought. His right to know made him back away from the combative cardinal.

Realizing he needed Romano's assistance, Cardoni finally conceded. 'It's from Antioch,' he hissed.

Jennifer brightened at this first blood, realizing that she too owed Romano. 'When was it found, Your Eminence?' she asked.

'The twelfth century.'

'By ...?'

'"*By!*" You think I'm on a first-name basis with long-dead monks? Enough!'

Grabbing Jennifer in one swift motion, Cardoni began propelling her towards the chamber's exit, but again she jerked away. 'If you do that again, I'll call the cops myself!' Then, avoiding another altercation, she strode back towards the door. She had seen enough. She had to get the hell out of there.

Chapter 7

Santori was pacing. Where was Cardoni? He wondered if his secretary had understood the importance of calling the Cardinal Librarian. He opened his office door.

'Did you get Cardinal Cardoni?' he snapped.

With the pane obscuring his view, he could not see the gendarme and Swiss guards talking to Franco.

'Your Eminence, he is in a meeting,' Franco responded.

On hearing the cardinal's voice, one Helvetian struck his halberd against the floor in salute.

As Lioni advanced, Santori stiffened like a drawn bow. He did not need any help from a gendarme or Swiss guards, nor was there time to explain. He gazed at Franco.

'What are they doing here?' he asked, blaming his assistant for their presence.

Lioni's initial instinct to kneel and kiss Santori's ring was short-lived, for when he saw the cardinal half-dressed and covered in blood, he leapt up to help him.

Again, Franco stepped in to block the adjutant.

Santori could not waste any more time quibbling over Lioni's presence. He gestured towards the adjutant's two-way radio. 'Sound the alarm and secure the complex,' he snarled.

Lioni was not sure he understood the cardinal correctly. 'What complex, Your Eminence?'

'The entire city, idiot. There's been a breach.'

In the six years Lioni had served as a gendarme, nobody had ever called him an idiot. Neither had he heard anyone demanding the Vatican be closed. Yet there he stood, facing a high-ranking official who was demanding just that. 'Your Eminence, we cannot simply *close* the Vatican. We have thousands of dignitaries and visitors.'

Santori stepped out of his office to face Lioni. 'Close off all entrances immediately,' he roared, his eyes baleful. 'Do not let anyone out. That's an order.'

'The entire Vatican, Your Eminence?' Lioni's name might symbolize Africa's fiercest predator, but in confronting the Maggiore, he was but a cub.

'Stop parroting me, and do as I say!' Santori barked.

Lioni stood, his arms hanging limply. 'I cannot authorize that,' he muttered. 'I'll have to report to Command.'

Every second Lioni wasted gave the fugitive more time to escape. Santori could not afford that. This predicament required immediate action. To get Lioni's cooperation, he changed his strategy. 'Get a hold of Colonel Schreider,' he said. 'He must come at once. Tell him a priest is dead.'

'Dear God!' Father Franco's blood drained from his face. Having arrived fifteen minutes late for work, he did not know who had come in before him. 'Your Eminence, who ...?'

'Father Yilmaz.'

Franco gasped. Everyone at the Vatican knew Father Yilmaz. In the short time, he had been at the library, he had become one of their most admired priests. Coming from Antioch, he had been an inspiration to them all. 'How, Your Eminence?'

'Murdered!' Santori spat. 'Now get a hold of His Eminence Cardinal Cardoni and get me Colonel Schreider. I need them both here immediately.'

Lioni felt as if a signal scrambler had blurred his thoughts. He had worked at the Vatican for three years now, but had not experienced anything as dramatic before. Santori's demanding Colonel Schreider come to the Penitentiary did not make it any easier on him either. As Commander of the Swiss Guard, the colonel only provided security for the Holy See and the pope. A slain priest therefore fell under gendarmerie jurisdiction. Lioni should be calling his own Inspector General, Arnaldo Verretti. All the same, preferring to avoid more trouble, he decided to oblige the blood-covered cardinal. Once he had reported the incident to Command his Inspector would hear about it anyway. Suddenly, though, it dawned on him that he had not even seen the body yet. How could he report a murder before verifying it?

'Your Eminence, I need to see the body,' said Lioni, fearing the answer he knew he would get.

Santori reddened as his blood sweltered. 'Give me that damned radio!' Then, snatching the two-way from Lioni, he pressed the talk switch. 'Command, this is Cardinal Santori. A priest has been murdered. Send Colonel Schreider to the Penitentiary immediately.' And, passing the radio back. 'Now do as I say. Tell them to shut the city gates.'

Hoping to prevent the Maggiore from taking his two-way again, Lioni started for the exit. He needed a moment to compose himself before he called Command.

Santori's skin felt stiff from the blood drying on it. He leaned against Franco's desk, ordering his secretary to fetch a damp towel.

Franco disappeared into the adjacent bathroom. Moments later and still shaken by the death of Father Yilmaz, he reappeared with a silver bowl half-filled with water. Damping the towel, he started wiping the blood from Santori's face. He could not believe anyone would kill their library Father. He had not heard a bad word said about the man.

Meanwhile, sitting with his eyes closed, Santori used the moment's respite to prioritize his next moves. Recovering the stolen artefact came first. Keeping the contents of the stolen items secret was crucial. Nobody could see it. That meant they would have to catch the thief. He had two choices: Colonel Schreider, Commander of the Swiss Guard, and Inspector General Verretti, head of the Vatican's Gendarmerie. Colonel Schreider was surely the best man for the job; he was Swiss, and the Swiss were the most reliable people on Earth. As Commander of the Swiss Guard, the colonel had also sworn an oath to protect the Holy See with his life. They could worry about Father Yilmaz later.

Lioni turned to Santori. 'Your Eminence, we need a description of the attacker.'

Santori opened his eyes. Staring at the floor, he sighed, 'Caucasian. Six feet, maybe more. Well built. He wore the cassock of a priest. I think he had dark hair. ... It was long for a clergyman. He had a rucksack with him. That's all I remember. It was dark.'

'Be on the lookout for a suspect. A priest ...'

A deadened two-way stopped Lioni in mid-sentence. The radio operator must have heard what the cardinal had said. Impatient for the command operator to respond, Lioni pressed the talk switch again: 'His Eminence demands a lockdown of the Vatican.'

A moment's silence followed.

'Is this a joke?'

'Negative. No drill. No joke.

'Stand by. ...'

Chapter 8

Cardinal Cardoni trotted across the Sistine Hall's black- and white-checkered marble floor. Thirty years of dedicated service at the Vatican Libraries and he still had an almost overpowering urge to stop and marvel at the splendor of the frescoes adorning its walls and ceilings. Now, though, there was no time. With his mind distracted by his altercation with Miss Jaine, as well as by the urgent summons to the Penitentiary, he might as well have been walking through a barren landscape. Descending the steps near the Gallery of Inscriptions, his breath came in short bursts. He must quit smoking. He had tried many times but with little success. He felt guilty when he preached on addiction to his congregations.

His meeting with the journalist had upset him. Miss Jaine had deliberately vented her frustration on him. But what right did she have to use him as a punching bag? The Archives should have done a better job screening her. With so many crazy people in the world these days, one could not be too careful. Had he known she would be so confrontational, he would have gone to the meeting better prepared. He could have taken her to the cleaners. Originals? What bloody originals? Good God! If only she knew. She might as well defy a hurricane. She had no idea what she was up against, or whom.

People like Miss Jaine were exactly why he needed to retire. He no longer had the strength or inclination to deal with them. He was nearing seventy. Surely, he had done his share for Holy Mother Church. Someone else could assume the reins from him now, someone younger. Albani stood next in line, though he doubted the bishop's suitability. Although the Argentinean had a dedication to the faith fitting any cardinal, he did not have the tenacity the job demanded. Anyhow, seeing Santori now would be the perfect opportunity for Cardoni to discuss his successor.

Cardoni thought about Santori and remembered when Romano had told him to go to the Penitentiary his face had appeared troubled. Something serious must have happened.

Cardoni's heart began pounding with the ferocity of a kettledrum. Together with a few other cardinals, he and Santori held the highest offices at the Vatican. They had taken up their appointments at the same time and kept adjacent accommodations in the Apostolic Palace. Pope John Paul II had nominated them while they were still in their forties. The late pontiff had spent years grooming them for their positions. Their loyalty had placed them firmly at the helm of the Vatican's hierarchy. They controlled the Church's utmost secrets. Their roles superseded everyday duties; in their powerful hands lay the life and fate of the Holy Roman Catholic Church, and they ensured the faith conformed to its stated precepts.

As Cardoni approached the Penitentiary, both Lioni and the Helvetians stood at attention. Father Franco must have ordered them to stand outside. Cardoni greeted them briefly as he passed.

Franco stood cleaning his desk and had his back turned towards the entrance. On hearing footsteps, he turned. 'Your Eminence, you gave me such a fright!' he said, clutching his chest with a wet cloth.

The priest's tears only escalated the cardinal's anxiety. He had to think quickly. 'Is he inside?' Cardoni asked.

'He's waiting only for you, Your Eminence.'

Cardoni stopped. He could not barge into Santori's office without knowing what had happened. 'Why am I here, Father?'

'Father Yilmaz, Your Eminence.' Franco's head dropped. 'He was ...' He could not finish the sentence.

Cardoni lingered before Santori's office door. 'Did you call anyone?'

'The Colonel.'

Cardoni opened the door and entered. 'Don't call anyone else,' he said, closing the door behind him.

*****

Santori stood by the hearth, his back towards the entrance. On a chair lay a heap of bloodstained clothes. 'Pass me my cassock,' he said, pulling on clean red hose.

Cardoni crossed the room. Taking the clean cassock from the hanger, he held it out to his friend. Santori looked pale as a newly washed sheet. 'What happened? Franco says Father Yilmaz has been hurt.'

Santori bent his head under the garment. 'He was killed.'

'What?' Cardoni released the cassock, letting it crumple on Santori's head. Yilmaz worked for him. He had seen him earlier that morning at breakfast. When Santori grumbled from beneath the cassock, he lifted it. 'Where?'

'In the vault.'

'Inside?!' Cardoni looked at the hearth. 'How did he get in?'

Santori prodded Cardoni's arms up to lift the cassock higher. 'There were two.'

Santori's composure surprised Cardoni, though his friend had always been the stronger of the two. He had a knack for taking things in stride. His position as Major Penitentiary demanded an astuteness and composure Cardoni had never possessed. He knew he could never take Santori's place. He would not be ruthless enough to excommunicate the sheep who strayed from Mother Church's narrow path. He pulled the vestment over Santori's head.

'Do you think they saw?'

Santori shrugged on the cassock. 'It's gone,' he said, adjusting the vestment so it fell in decorous folds.

'Holy Mother of God!' Cardoni extracted his asthma pump. He took two full puffs before putting it back in his pocket. 'Where is it now?'

'I told you, damn it. It was *stolen.*'

'I thought Yilmaz had it.'

Santori stepped in front of the mirror behind the conference table. Even in the face of crisis he never lost sight of his image. 'The other priest has it,' he said, smoothing his cassock.

'A priest?' Cardoni felt the blood drain from his head. 'Who?'

‘For God’s sake, Giovanni, how should I know?’

When Santori returned to the hearth, Cardoni sat down on a chair. ‘I thought you saw him.’

‘A glimpse of a glimpse. A cassock, a satchel. That’s it. It was dark.’

Cardoni’s mind raced. ‘We must inform the others.’

‘First we must talk.’ Santori pointed to the rest of his vestments on the hearth. ‘My sash, if you don’t mind.’

Cardoni sat staring at Santori. He remembered seeing the vault for the first time. He would not forget the day. He had felt intimidated. Only the highest-ranking cardinals knew of the Vatican’s innermost secrets. ‘You know the bloody consequences,’ he said.

‘Don’t lecture me,’ Santori snapped. ‘Help me.’

Cardoni had worked with Santori for long enough to know he had something on his mind. Standing again, he unwound the red sash. Fitting it around Santori’s waist, he said, ‘We must inform Fra’ Dubois—and the pontiff.’

‘Now, now.’ Santori draped the pectoral cross over his shoulders. Finally, he put on his plush black hat and pushed the red and gold tasseled cord to one side. ‘First you and I must talk.’

Cardoni sat again. ‘We cannot let whoever it is leave these walls. We have to get him, before he escapes.’

Santori headed for his office desk. ‘I asked for a lockdown,’ he mused.

‘Lockdown? For a murder?!’ Now Cardoni was certain of the consequences. ‘Won’t that draw unnecessary attention to the artefact?’

Santori sat down in his leather armchair. He stared across the table at his colleague. ‘Who can say? This is catastrophic. What does one do at a time like this?’

Cardoni stared back, his mind blank. A priest dying in the secret vault was tragic, but the theft was a disaster of the highest order. 'How in *His* name are we going to explain this? What if he gets away?'

'Colonel Schreider will be here any minute, I suspect. I need you here when he comes.'

Cardoni stood up and walked to the window on the far side of the lounge. 'I have a problem at the library, but that can wait.' He pulled the curtain back and opened the window. He drew a cigarette from his pack, lit it and inhaled. He held the smoke in his lungs until it burned. Exhaling slowly, he let smoke filter through his nostrils: 'We can't keep this secret forever, you know that.'

'Don't be ridiculous. We'll get it back.' Santori brooded, then picking up the phone to call Franco. 'Now where is that damned colonel?'

Cardoni hit his cigarette again, slowly blowing smoke out the window. 'I don't feel good, Leonardo,' he said, staring at the dome of Saint Peter's Basilica. 'I have a feeling—call it a portent—this will not end well.'

Chapter 9

Swiss Guard Commander Oberst Ludwig Schreider swung towards the Penitentiary at a brisk march; six-foot-six, he had a bearing so upright it seemed stiff compared with his perfectly creased, maroon uniform and black beret—the latter being starkly complementary to his pale skin, snowy, cropped hair and sparse eyebrows. Constantly prepared for the unexpected, his gaze invariably extended beyond his immediate environment, a characteristic he believed gave him twice the time to react and a trait his men revered as 'psychic'. His voice was a deep, almost bear-like, growl, such that when he spoke it commanded unconditional attention.

The Helvetians at the entrance slammed the butts of their halberds against the marble floor with enough force to bust the basalt paving stones of the Belvedere. Saluting midstride, Schreider ordered his soldiers to stand at ease.

Schreider had graduated top of his class from the Swiss Military Academy in '99. He had excelled first in training then as a field commander. Despite Switzerland's limited partnership with NATO, he had managed to have himself deployed as one of only two Swiss officers to serve with the Germans in Afghanistan after the American invasion. His reputation for honesty and integrity, strong Catholic convictions and impeccable military record had then seen him first accepted into the Swiss Guard, then elevated to the rank of security commander to the Holy See. His primary duty—looking after dignitaries during a period of religious intolerance and turmoil—had made his job arduous. He had long lived with the knowledge that he might, one day, sacrifice his life for the Supreme Pontiff. At such times as the thought of that ever-imminent sacrifice occurred to him, he would remind himself wryly, but with no less sincerity, of the old cliché 'for God and country'. And yet, he took solace in the fact that if it ever came to that, he would be shedding his blood for a good cause. He did, after all, protect God's elite.

Lioni saluted Schreider. 'Colonel, we ...'

Schreider did not allow the gendarmerie adjutant to finish his sentence. Command had already briefed him on his way across the city. Nearly an hour had lapsed since the incident and an immediate response was necessary.

'Secure the entrance,' Schreider ordered. 'I want no interruptions while I'm in here.' He continued to the reception area where Father Franco sat like a soul in anguish. He halted before the priest's desk and doffed his beret. 'Father, may I?'

Franco walked to Santori's door. He knocked lightly, waiting for an answer before standing aside for Schreider to enter.

Schreider walked to Santori's desk. On the way, he scanned the area for clues to the murder. To his surprise, everything looked undisturbed. Nor did he see a body. Confident that he had summed up the situation sufficiently, his attention shifted to the two cardinals. Santori was hunched over with his elbows pressed onto the desk, demonstrating the grievous weight he now carried. Cardoni pulled hard and fast on his cigarette, hinting at the condition of his frayed nerves. Schreider positioned himself to the side of the desk where he could maintain a view of the office suite. When Cardoni offered him a seat he declined.

'If you don't mind, Eminentia, I prefer to stand.'

'Very well then,' Cardoni said. He stubbed his cigarette out in the silver ashtray on the windowsill. Closing the window, he emptied three butts in the waste bin and sat down opposite Santori.

'What is our highest security level, Colonel?' Santori asked.

Schreider attempted to hide his confusion. Apart from searching for the escaping suspect, he needed to confirm Father Yilmaz's death. He also needed forensics on the scene. Still, with Santori's gaze locked on his he yielded: 'Alarmbereitschaft Eins; it's roughly equivalent to the Americans' "DEFCON one" of Hollywood fame.'

The whites of Santori's clenched knuckles showed through his skin. 'Yes, Colonel, I need you to go to Alarmbeits—whatever.'

Schreider had already adjusted their security level from Alarmbereitschaft V to Alarmbereitschaft IV. A murder-robbery, though heinous enough, certainly did not warrant the kind of security level appropriate for a nuclear war. Alarmbereitschaft I applied only to severe, imminent global threats. It would not only put the Vatican's entire civil defense force on maximum alert, but it would trigger equivalent alerts in Italy and therefore the EU—and after that, well, you could bet those Americans would implement their fabled DEFCON 1 as well, if only for good measure.

'I cannot invoke Alarmbereitschaft Eins,' the colonel said defiantly. 'A simple murder-theft does not constitute an existential threat to the Vatican, let alone the entire western world.'

Santori slammed his fist on the table. 'In this case, it does!'

'It's not so much the murder, Colonel, as the theft,' Cardoni explained more peaceably.

Schreider glared at him. They obviously did not understand what the Vatican's security levels meant. Lockdown occurred only in cases of imminent attack: if Muslim extremists snuck a dirty bomb into Saint Peter's, fine; if the Russians launched a forty-year-old nuke, sure; heck, if the Ayatollah decided to send a simple Super Soaker-mounted drone to take the piss on the pope's birthday, then it would probably be warranted. But war-crazed as they had been the past two decades, the U.S. would not go to DEFCON 1 without ICBMs crisscrossing the atmosphere.

'Listen, your eminencies, Alarmbereitschaft Eins requires I not only coordinate with the heads of the gendarmerie and fire department, as well as with the Prefect of the Apostolic Palace, but that I also alert every government between here and Japan. I'll have to inform the American Joint Chiefs, Interpol, Europol and the Italian military. Then, together we form one unified command. That's protocol. So, what you're talking about is an international incident of epic proportions, and for what, a theft?'

'This is unacceptable,' Santori groaned.

Schreider was sweating now. The cardinal's call for the highest alert level made the colonel feel trapped. The more Schreider thought about it, the more he suspected something sinister was afoot. Alarmbereitschaft V, or standard readiness protocol, meant there was an imminent threat to the Vatican from within. If someone made a bomb threat or if there were demonstrations at the city's gates they would declare Alarmbereitschaft IV to increase intelligence and strengthen their security measures. Due to an alleged murder, which Schreider had yet to verify, they were now at Alarmbereitschaft IV, albeit that was something of an overreaction. Alarmbereitschaft III would increase force and readiness even more and was meant for times when the pope or the entire Holy See were in imminent, life-threatening danger, and this was obviously not the case now. The only time they had implemented Alarmbereitschaft III was in 2006, during the Osama bin Laden crisis. Pope Benedict XVI had spoken out against Islam, calling it evil and inhuman. Bin Laden had then accused the Vatican of leading a crusade against Islam, which had led to several threats against the See. The 9/11 attacks had resulted in the Vatican's one and only Alarmbereitschaft II, which it had maintained for a short while thereafter, and Schreider would never forget the chaos that had ensued. Maximum force readiness could only be triggered during an impending or ongoing attack by a foreign power or terrorist group. It demanded *the* most severe threat the Vatican had ever seen. It simply was not the case here, and considering the Vatican's place in geopolitics, it probably never would be.

'Close down the Vatican,' Santori spat. 'That's an order!'

Schreider's ears burnt. Was he hearing the cardinal right? 'Is Your Eminence saying there is a severe threat to the See?' He looked around at the tidy, serene office to prove his point. 'I have yet to verify a murder that supposedly happened here, a single murder and, according to you, a robbery, and you're saying the entire city state is practically about to explode because of these two little unverified crimes that are, and let me be clear on this, not national but police concern?'

'We don't have time to explain, Colonel,' said Santori with a penetrating look.

Cardoni stepped forward. 'Our problem is extraordinary. The extremity of the situation demands a lockdown.'

'Excuse my boldness, Your Eminence,' Schreider said, 'but the safety of the Holy See is my responsibility. Right now, I'm not seeing a safety risk here, but I'm willing to listen. So, before I create a multinational panic, I need to know everything.'

'It is in our best interest that the matter be resolved quietly and expeditiously,' Cardoni said. 'You must personally take care of this.'

Schreider hated nothing more than someone questioning his integrity. The Swiss Guard had served the Holy See for five-hundred years; each guard, to a man, was a devout Catholic, and they had all, like their predecessors, sworn an oath to serve and protect the Vatican and Holy See. The cardinals would not find a more loyal force, which was exactly why he was standing there.

Cardoni drew another cigarette from his gold case and dragged nervously on the first puff. Exhaling before sitting back, he continued, 'The murder happened in a secret vault. It contains—forgive me, it *contained* something the world isn't ready to see.'

Schreider did not move. He felt as if someone had driven a stake through his heart. He wondered if he had heard right, not about the murder or the secret vault, but about something the world could not see. If he understood Cardoni correctly, the cardinal had just referred to incriminating evidence against the Faith. He could not conceive of his religion having secrets.

Finally, at length the colonel asked, 'Who knows about this?'

'Not many,' Cardoni answered.

'Who is 'not many'? The Holy See, the faithful, who?'

Santori stood up. The urgency to retrieve the stolen artefact compelled him. 'What I am about to show you has been the most safely guarded secret in all Christendom,' he said. 'Its' theft threatens our entire existence.'

'Whose existence, the Vatican's or Church's?'

'Both!' Santori snapped. 'Even Christianity's!'

Schreider felt his collar tighten. Anything *that* incriminating surely meant a fundamental, doctrinal flaw.

Santori walked to the hearth. 'You must capture the intruder and return the stolen artefact before it is revealed publicly.'

'Capture! Eminentia, you mean arrest. This is not a war.'

'It *is* a war—against none other than the Almighty Himself!' Santori howled. 'A malicious assault on Holy Mother Church!'

Yielding to the cardinals violated everything Schreider stood for. Apprehending perpetrators to recover a stolen artefact was one thing; swearing not to divulge secret information was another altogether.

'You have my word, Eminentia,' he said, marching to the hearth.

It felt as if he were now perpetuating darkness. He might as well tango with the devil. How could he agree? How had he agreed? Perhaps it was simply not in his nature to challenge a cardinal. He was accustomed to believing cardinals were as holy as they purported to be. He had to get the hell out of there.

'Now show me the body …'

Chapter 10

Dust swirled as Santori's cassock trailed across the steps behind him. Schreider remained some distance behind to avoid stepping on the sweeping garment. The colonel had thought he had scoured every inch of the Vatican City, yet this place was new to him. Rumors of hiding places rarely proved true. It amazed him that the vault had kept its secret for so long. As the Belvedere's east and west wings were five hundred years old, one would think information on the vault's existence might have leaked centuries ago. His eyes scanned the area for clues of the murder.

Descending to the underground chamber felt like a journey into hell. Supported by a series of columns, the stairway zigzagged down to a centric landing. To the front and back, abyss-like corridors replicated the layouts of Santori's office and the library above. Schreider stopped halfway down on the landing directly beneath the hearth area linking Santori's office with the library and leaned over the balustrade. Stacked crates interspersed with statues filled the room beneath the office. The Vatican had collected hundreds of pagan sculptures over the centuries, but why? Had generations of priests preached against idolatry, Bible in hand, while at the same time, restoring the very idols they decried? It made no sense. Detecting no evidence of the supposed murder victim from his vantage point, he turned and bounded down the remaining steps, two at a time, to the basement below.

The area beneath the library opened into a chapel. In its center lay a square nave. Around it, columns rose like vigilant knights. A vaulted ceiling extended over them, its ribs uniting at the columns' capitals like synchronized waves. Candelabras with battered limbs hung aslant at intervals, the soot of centuries old burnt wax creeping like ghosts up the granite walls. On the far side of the nave rose an apse and altar, and draped across the altar steps lay Father Yilmaz.

Schreider proceeded to the apse. The sight of Yilmaz caked in coagulated blood turned his stomach. It reminded him of Afghanistan. Years of collecting the body parts of comrades hit by IEDs had nearly shattered his sanity. He still had nightmares more than a decade later. He stopped in front of Yilmaz, his gaze falling on the spattered altar. Brocaded onto the frontal cloth, a converted Saint Paul presided over the reverse crucifixion of Saint Peter. He wondered why their two greatest founders were secreted in a hidden vault. The Church seldom portrayed Peter and Paul together. Yet, he had seen this imagery before. But where?

Six silver candlesticks encircled Yilmaz, and a gold crucifix protruded from under his shirt. By his head lay a bloodstained dagger; it had a golden handle with red cross insert and a double-edged blade. Schreider squatted and examined the weapon. 'Templar or Hospitallers,' he thought, but there was so much blood on the handle it was hard to tell which—in any case, it was a collector's piece, no doubt. Taking out his pocket knife, he slipped its blade under the dagger's and flipped the larger knife over. The blade's shape and size matched the incision on Yilmaz's chest. It had to be the weapon used to kill the priest.

Cardoni stopped by Schreider's side, holding his sleeve over his mouth and nose. The stench of blood was nauseating. The cardinal had been down there just the other day and had not anticipated coming down there again this soon. After this, he decided, he would never return. Few knew of the vault, and those who did preferred not to talk about it. It was not so much the vault itself that had become taboo as what it housed. He studied Yilmaz's wax-white face sadly. Having made a good impression, the young man had become one of his favorite priests. Indeed, with his dedication to his work, common sense and passion for ethics, Yilmaz could have made a great librarian. Cardoni had even mentioned this to the younger priest once. It was such a pity Yilmaz had never considered taking a degree. Every prospective cardinal had to be well groomed and academically qualified in addition to being well-versed in Church doctrine. Cardoni knew Santori had also liked the boy. His colleague had often mentioned how Yilmaz reminded him of himself. Santori had confided his hope that the young priest would follow him in studying law. His ambition for Yilmaz to become the future Major of the Penitentiary had irked Cardoni.

At any rate, Yilmaz had declined both their offers. He had had no interest in degrees, said he had nothing to prove, and now his youthful lack of drive was no longer an obstacle to his once-promising career. With the young priest lying lifeless before him, Cardoni reflected that everything he and Santori had hoped for was now no more than a futile daydream.

Schreider rose, his head throbbing with innumerable questions: how had Yilmaz and his killer known about the vault, and how had they gained access to it? More to the point, *why* had they, and how was all this connected? Yilmaz had routinely collected books from the Penitentiary; that much Schreider knew. Maybe Yilmaz had disturbed the suspect. He could have tried to intervene. Schreider lifted the frontal from the floor and draped it over the altar. Then, one by one, he returned the candlesticks to their places, setting them on the dustless prints in the frontal where they had stood for eons. Finally, he picked up the crucifix and placed it respectfully in the center of the desecrated altar, and in so doing, he saw *it*.

Tapping on the square print in front of the crucifix, he said, 'Something's missing.'

'That's why you're here, Colonel,' Santori said, approaching from the other side of Yilmaz.

'What was it?'

'A letter.'

'You don't care about the priest. It's the letter you're after.'

Santori pulled out his handkerchief and bent down to pick up the dagger. 'You have your proof, Colonel. Now get it back.'

Schreider reached for the cardinal's hand: 'We need prints first.'

Santori shielded the dagger from him. 'You don't understand, do you, Colonel?'

'We're dealing with this internally,' Cardoni interjected.

Schreider's focus remained on Santori. 'With all due respect, Your Eminence, I cannot let you take that.'

A knocking sound from Santori's office above echoing down the chamber broke the impasse. Hurriedly, the cardinal placed the wrapped dagger in his sash. 'We have to go,' he said, heading for the stairway.

Schreider was aghast that the two cardinals would not permit a proper investigation. Their behavior bordered on suspicious. Reluctantly, and with more questions than answers, he followed them back up the stairs to the office. On the way, he considered his next move. Any mistakes now and he would face execution. Then, he recalled an earlier thought. The letter obviously contained something sinister—something illicit that implicated the Church—but without information it was impossible to connect the dots. Dear Lord, it had never crossed his mind that his faith could be based on duplicity!

Chapter 11

Not far from the Penitentiary a priest hastened along an open colonnade. A breeze was lightly blowing the train of his cassock, creating drag he could ill afford. Tightening the shoulder straps of his rucksack, he briskly approached the atrium.

Three IT specialists on loan from the United Kingdom were huddled next to the Cortile della Bibliotheca staircase. They had arrived a week earlier to help install a new filing system on the archives' computer system. On hearing screams coming from the Penitentiary, they had run outside to investigate. Others had joined them. Someone said the sound had come from Santori, which instigated a fierce debate about the Vatican's most feared cardinal. Anyone facing the Maggiore in a tribunal would undoubtedly find himself transported to the Spanish Inquisition. Other than ending up in Hell with Satan, the most daunting experience would be whatever *auto-da-fé* His Eminence handed down.

From the corner of his eye, the fleeing priest saw one of the IT techs beckon, but the priest dismissed the

Englishman with a cursory wave. Only at the atrium's entrance did he stop. His shoulder pressed against the wall, he peered around the corner, scanning the area for security cameras. In the center of the atrium, an S-shaped staircase snaked towards the floor above. To the left and right, passages led to other wings of the museum.

The priest heard footsteps approaching from behind him. One glance over his shoulder was all he needed to find that two gendarmes were speeding in his direction. Slipping into the atrium, he headed for the museum's north wing. Just before reaching the passage though, he heard voices of people approaching. Trapped, he ducked behind the staircase. He just managed to hide behind the marble balustrade when the gendarmes ran into the atrium. He pressed his body against the staircase and listened.

The two gendarmes, one a lieutenant, the other a sergeant, stood before the stairway, discussing where the fugitive had gone. Then the lieutenant ordered the sergeant to check upstairs. At the top of the steps, the sergeant's footfalls stopped at the landing as he studied the upper corridor for any sign of movement. Once satisfied that there was none, he returned, skipping steps as he accelerated to the floor below.

'Let's try Pigna,' the lieutenant said, as the sergeant neared him. 'No, wait. First check the stairs.'

The sergeant settled his semi-automatic rifle on his shoulder and approached the opening behind the balustrade.

A door slammed in the passage to the right. Footsteps followed.

The lieutenant pulled back. Worried it might be the fugitive, he sprinted towards the noise, the sergeant close on his heels.

Behind the staircase, the priest waited for their footsteps to fade before exhaling at last. He rested his head against the wall behind him, sweat trickling from his brow. He glanced around the corner and, seeing no one, sneaked from behind the staircase and headed left, away from the gendarmes. Hugging the walls, he passed through an archway leading to the Cortile della Bibliotheca. At the sound of more footsteps, he slipped behind a column enwrapped with an ivory-petalled evergreen rose. As he waited in silence, he heard shouting blare through a window overhead. It seemed to be library staff discussing the slain priest. As he listened, he learned that Vatican security was now on high alert and that the security personnel were searching every building surrounding the Belvedere courtyard. An older voice, possibly a cardinal, was demanding lockdown of the entire city. Even more disturbing though, was the mention of sending more gendarmes to the secret archives, as someone had broken into the bunker.

The priest waited, listened, calculated. Patience, as he had often heard said, was a virtue.

Chapter 12

Schreider stood in the middle of the Via Sant' Anna, halfway between the Belvedere Courtyard and the Sant' Anna gate. Dark, roiling clouds were gathering overhead, causing the morning chill to linger. A complex scent of wet soil and budding grapes was wafting in from the vineyards near Marcellina to the east, and lightning in the distance portended the rumble that would soon sweep in from the Apennines.

Turning, the colonel studied conditions on the ground. An hour and a half had passed since the murder, meaning there was no guarantee the perpetrator had not escaped. At the nearby Sant' Anna entrance, additional security was scrutinizing everyone who approached the gate. The Swiss Guard had closed the portcullis and extra gendarmes were even searching the handbags of elderly nuns. To the south, at the towering Apostolic Palace, yet unapprised of events, the Holy Pontiff was eating his breakfast. To the west, officials were rushing to a meeting to determine the Vatican's official news release to the international community. To the north, workers were gathering in front of the post office and print shop, no doubt having heard that *something* was going on at the Penitentiary.

Schreider used his two-way to call command. Captain Weber from the Swiss Guard answered, his voice noticeably shaken by the reports he had already received. Deciding not to divulge too much over an open system, Schreider said he would explain the situation further when he returned to headquarters. Then, with Weber's flood of questions stemmed, he pursued a more practical topic, asking his subordinate how many men were currently on duty.

'We're fully reinforced, Oberst,' the captain replied.

A full complement meant Schreider had about one hundred and thirty guards and sixty-five gendarmes at his command at any given moment. Both forces had rehearsed Alarmbereitschaft I protocols at least once a month for years, but many of the practices in which his men had been drilled were impractical when the official alert level was elevated to such an extent. And yet, if what Santori and Cardoni had said was true—if one artefact could topple the entire Church—the present situation was no less an existential threat than if ISIS militants had dumped ricin in the Bracciano aqueduct. …

'Summon my antiterrorism squad immediately,' Schreider radioed. 'Order those already on duty to close off the Vatican. All entrances. Now. Nobody in. Nobody out.'

Still, he stopped short of requesting Alarmbereitschaft I. He knew he could not implement a full security protocol without involving Inspector General Arnaldo Verretti from the Gendarmerie, as well as the Prefect of the Apostolic Palace and the Roman police. Even then, without additional international assistance, enforcing a high alert would be in vain.

Schreider marched into a command center already buzzing with activity. He said nothing but continued towards the surveillance offices. On his way, he passed Inspector Verretti, who was giving instructions to four gendarmerie officers. Brushing back his bangs, Verretti beckoned Schreider to join the briefing, but the colonel silently declined and pointed towards the video-camera desk.

Schreider resented Verretti's attitude. The police officer had acted as though he thought a mere Inspector outranked the commander of the His Holiness's own personal guard, and indeed he often did make Schreider come to him. He probably did not do it on purpose, but in a way, that made it worse. Thus far, Schreider had ignored this behavior. Maintaining a viable working relationship far outweighed initiating a penis parade. Notwithstanding his tolerance for the inspector, there were times when Schreider would stand his ground, and this was one of them. He had promised the two cardinals he would recover the stolen letter; undoubtedly his job was on the line if he failed, but for many other reasons failure was out of the question.

The Swiss Guard and gendarmerie operated differently. Schreider served to protect his employer, the Vicar of Christ, and those under his protection, which included the College of Cardinals. Verretti, on the other hand, managed the city's general policing. In theory, their work environments overlapped, but their duties could not have been more different. That said, though each force had its own barracks, they were obliged to share the command center.

Verretti had overseen the gendarmerie for the same time Schreider had been commander of the Swiss Guard. The inspector's abrasive attitude had irritated Schreider from the start. He recalled how Verretti had initially tried to befriend him. The inspector had repeatedly invited the colonel to the amateur rugby matches he played in at weekends, and Schreider had repeatedly declined, using his duties as an excuse. Of course, the one time the colonel did go, the inspector had done quite well. He had played flank, but had incessantly picked fights with his opponents. After tackling his opponent around the neck, the referee had sin-binned him for ten minutes. Afterwards, in the pub, the inspector had accused the referee of bias and not knowing the rules of the game. Rather than behaving like one of Italy's *Azzurri*, Schreider thought Verretti had acted like a French *Les Tricolore*—comparing the Italian to a fighting cock was a more appropriate metaphor.

Schreider preferred football, a game, he felt, that had true finesse. The electric atmosphere and continuous singing at football matches exhilarated him. And, though his job did not allow him much time to follow sports, he still *made* time to watch the biggest matches, like the 2006 FIFA World Cup. Schreider had felt personally defeated for weeks after the Swiss, despite winning all their previous matches, ultimately succumbed to Ukraine in a penalty shootout. That five-minute lapse at the end of a single match had made them the first team in history to be eliminated without conceding a goal during regulation time over the course of an entire tournament.

But Schreider had no time to muse about football. When Verretti joined him at a brisk pace and asked what had happened at the Penitentiary, he replied, 'I'll fill you in as we go.' He first had to check the surveillance tapes.

A Swiss Guard corporal sat in the monitor-filled surveillance room, his fingers rotating the joystick with extraordinary skill. Within seconds, he had called up recorded scenes from around the Penitentiary on two large-screen LEDs in the center of one wall.

Flipping his curser from screen to screen, he described the different scenes: 'At 07:50 this morning, His Eminence Santori arrived at the Penitentiary. Soon after, security personnel from the Belvedere Courtyard reacted to his calls. Entering here, they immediately made their way inside. Next, a priest exited through a rear door, here.'

Verretti had something else on his mind. He did not appreciate the way the two cardinals had left him out of the loop. Now Schreider had done the same. Turning to face his counterpart, he asked, 'So you're closing the gates?'

Schreider kept his eyes fixed on the monitors. 'This thing's got them spooked. They demanded a complete lockdown.'

'Are they mad? It's only a priest for God's sake.'

Schreider pointed to the exit at the back of the Penitentiary. 'Where does this go, Corporal?'

'The library offices, Oberst.'

'Who's this?'

'Our suspect.'

'Do we know who he is?'

'No, Oberst.'

'What do you mean 'no'?'

'We're unable to ID him, sir.'

'Did you check our database?'

'Absolutely, and there's been no match so far.'

'Where is he now?'

'Gone.'

'Gone?!'

'He hasn't shown up on our library cams, Oberst.'

A Helvetian hastened in and stood to attention, his hand lifted, tense in salute.

'At ease, Halberdier. *Was ist los?*'

'We have a situation in the library, Oberst. A female journalist has breached archive security. The staff have triggered the alarm.'

'What happened?'

'She entered the bunker, Oberst.'

Schreider stepped closer to the library monitors. It depicted a female at the archives' reception room. 'Is that her?'

'Have her arrested, Colonel,' Verretti said. 'Whoever she is, she could be an accomplice to the murderer.'

Schreider studied her image on the screen. 'Give me close-ups on both.'

'We know who she is,' the corporal said. 'It's the priest we can't ID.'

Schreider hardly thought the two incidents were linked, but he could not take any chances. His job required he investigate every security breach, however small. He turned to his guard. 'Bring her in, Halberdier.' Then, turning to the corporal: 'Run them through Interpol.'

'It will take a while, Oberst.'

'Send it to my office when you've finished.'

On his way to the surveillance desk, Schreider called his officers over for a briefing. 'All off-duty personnel are to report on the parade grounds immediately. Double our guard at the gates, and make sure they're armed. Also, be extra careful when people leave and send out more patrols. Extend the perimeter. They must search all the buildings around the Belvedere Courtyard. Concentrate on the library, the museums and all the exits. Look for a priest with a rucksack. We'll have pictures in a moment.'

Verretti joined Schreider. 'I'll send my men to bring her in.'

Schreider's second-in-command clicked in from radio control. Captain Franz Weber had been his deputy for four years. Like Schreider, the captain weighed in at 90-plus kilograms, stood over six feet tall and kept himself in prime athletic condition. He was unmarried, a dedicated Catholic and of good moral character. The main distinction between them was color. Schreider was pale in every sense; Weber had inherited some of the dark skin of his North African mother, which together with his rust-brown eyes had earned him the moniker 'the panther'.

'What's the problem, Captain?' Schreider asked.

'Bomb threat at the Pietà, Oberst!'

Schreider spun around. His captain's propensity for stoicism was greater than most peoples', and little fazed him. Such a terse message meant the threat was truly serious. 'What's going on this morning?' he asked, his voice strained.

Verretti was equally perplexed. 'Why didn't my men arrest him?'

'It's impossible, Inspector,' Weber replied. 'He has a bomb strapped to his waist.'

'Fanculo!' Verretti snapped. 'A Muslim radical?'

Weber shook his head. 'Caucasian. He speaks English with a New Zealand or Australian accent—I can't tell the difference.'

Schreider was pensive. Three incidents had occurred in succession. How very strange. Though the cardinals had insisted he apprehend the escaping priest first, their demands no longer seemed to command precedence. The new threat to the Holy Pontiff's safety at the Apostolic Palace itself, left him no choice. He turned to Verretti. 'I'll take the bomber. You get the priest and journalist.'

'I'll need some of your men,' Verretti said.

Schreider pointed to one of his officers. 'Lieutenant, you help. The others should be on the parade grounds already.' The colonel did not have time to quibble with Verretti and called Weber to join him. He began disrobing and reached his office wearing only his boxers and socks. The rest of his uniform lay sprawled across the floor. 'What type of bomb is it, Captain?'

'Plastic explosives, Oberst. ... Three, maybe four kilos.'

Schreider's neck muscles stiffened. He would have to deal with the bomb threat himself. He would let his captain take over at the command center. The man's cool head would be suitable under such circumstances. Should anything happen to Schreider, Weber would be just the man to take over.

The colonel's vertebrae clicked as he stretched his neck from side to side. 'What's he doing?'

'He's ordered everyone to move away from the sculpture,' said Weber.

'What a strange request for a man threatening destruction,' Schreider thought. With no time to waste, though, he leaned over his desk and pressed down on the Command intercom's talk switch: '*Alarmbereitschaft Drei, jetzt*. And get me three snipers ASAP!'

Chapter 13

When cameras tracked Jennifer from the bunker back to the Sisto V reading room, she knew she had gone too far. She may have managed to see one of Christianity's most priceless relics but, in so doing, had landed herself in far more trouble than she had anticipated. Still, she could not understand why looking at an old parchment would spark such hostility.

Back at the Sisto V reading room, she asked if she could pick up her notes, but as she started towards the meeting room, Cardoni stopped her, ordering two clergymen to guard her. Determined to have her removed from the premises, he had Romano call security. He waited until the priest had finished speaking with Command before walking down the passage to Santori's office.

No sooner had Cardoni disappeared than a disturbance sounding like a Pamplona bull stampede resounded from the Belvedere Courtyard below. Eager to discover the cause for the hubbub some of the library officials moved to the windows. Ten gendarmes and six Swiss guards were storming through the archway by the fire station. At the fountain, they paired off, some headed for the library entrance, others were running towards the archway leading to the gardens on the western edge of the city. Meanwhile, four gendarmes hurried up the ramp leading to the Leonine index room. The officers' arrival up the steps, saw the priests at the windows scurrying back to their stations.

Jennifer saw only two of the gendarmes as they reached the Sisto V lobby. To her surprise, Romano seemed unperturbed. Unlike the rest of the clergy who had gathered at the windows, he had remained at the reception desk. From his demeanor, one would swear nothing was happening.

'That's not good,' she thought. 'He obviously knows something the rest didn't.'

The gendarmes approaching Romano distracted the priests guarding Jennifer briefly, and she began searching for a way out. Battalions of simultaneously firing neurons were grid-locking the synapses in her brain. And yet, only two thoughts registered: two aggressive gendarmes looking for someone, and the security cameras focusing on her.

It was time to get the hell out of there.

Jennifer's self-defense training from living in an American city came back in an instant. With recent terrorist attacks imprinted on her memory, she thought it prudent not to wait and see if the gendarmes were after her. She studied the hall for an escape route. The only exit near her was the lobby she had just come from. Off limits or not, she had no choice. She retreated slowly, hoping the hounds surrounding her would not notice. Their preoccupation with the gendarmes had drawn their attention to the reception. She managed to slip from view and took off like a spooked mouse scurrying from the pounce of a tomcat. Using the rows of filing cabinets as cover, she again headed for the *Staff Only* exit. Just as she thought she had made it, though, she saw Cardoni approaching from the other end of the passage. Appearing deep in thought, he was speeding straight towards her. She ducked to the right, concealing herself behind a cabinet. She leaned up against the shelves and prayed he would not see her.

At last God listened because the cardinal galloped past her on his way to the reception hall. She exhaled, but her relief was short-lived, as another security camera zoomed in on her. How the hell would she escape with those ever-present eyes tracking her every move?

'Where is she?' barked a gendarme at the reception desk. 'We have to take her in for questioning.'

Jennifer glanced at the nearest exit; did she have a clear path?

The gendarme had his two-way pressed to his lips. 'Did you say five-foot-nine, brown hair, black outfit?'

No time to think. Two belligerent gendarmes with machine guns were searching for someone of her description. The party was over. Jennifer ran.

'I see her on the monitor,' echoed the voice over the two-way. 'She's heading for an exit twenty meters up ahead.'

Jennifer refused to grow eyes in the back of her head. She was out of *gone*.

Chapter 14

Weber removed Schreider's ear-mounted headset from its charger and unwrapped the wiring for the com set. 'You'll need this for the snipers,' he said.

Schreider pressed the talk switch on his intercom. 'Evacuate Saint Peter's. Nobody is to approach this guy. He absolutely *must* not feel threatened.'

'I've already evacuated the Basilica,' Weber said.

Schreider could not have wished for a better second-in-command. His captain always stayed two steps ahead of the rest. He turned towards his steel locker and plucked a charcoal, pinstriped suit from its hanger.

'I'm going as a civilian,' he said, diving back in to pull out a pair of shoes. 'Did he say why he's doing this?'

'He says the statue is a lie.'

'A lie?' Schreider hesitated. Something must have triggered the bomber. He needed to figure out what it was. 'Why would our Holy Mother holding Christ's dying body be a lie?'

Schreider could not think of a single reason that statue might constitute a lie, except, perhaps, for its proportions—Mary would tower over twelve feet if she stood up and she resembled a woman in her twenties, rather than her fifties. But Schreider's intuition told him the nut making suicide-bomb threats was not the world's most passionate art critic. As the colonel lifted his arms for his captain to tape the com set to his chest and clip the mic to his shirt collar, his mind drifted. He had often stood in front of the Pietà. Commissioned as Cardinal Jean de Billheres' funeral monument, the late-fifteenth-century marble statue now stood in Saint Peter's Basilica. Michelangelo had carved the masterpiece while still in his early twenties. Apart from being the famed sculptor's most polished work, it was also the only piece Buonarroti ever signed.

When Weber had finished, Schreider hugged him, then stood back. 'Do we have a negotiator?'

'Not on duty.'

'Pray for me.'

Not waiting for a response, Schreider sprinted for the exit.

Weber saluted. The colonel's relentless obsession with drills and inspections had made him unpopular with the troops. They had long felt their commander was unnecessarily strict. But not a single soldier in the entire guard would hesitate to give his life for the Oberst. The man led from the front.

Weber shouted after his commander: 'God bless you,' Oberst.'

Chapter 15

Jennifer bolted for the *Staff Only* exit. The instant that she had seen Father Romano standing around as if nothing was happening, she had known they were after her.

Shouting from the reception desk, Cardoni threw his hands up in exasperation: 'You can't go in there!'

The image of her dangling from a dungeon contraption while torturers extracted false confessions from her mangled body, propelled Jennifer onwards through the exit and into the passage outside. She needed to get to the Porta Sant' Anna fast. From there she could make a break for her hotel. She searched for a way to the ground floor. When a priest passed in front of her, disappearing down a stairway, she ran after him. Then, with only a few yards before reaching the stairway herself, a gendarme stepped onto the landing in front of her.

Planting both feet to slow her momentum, she prepared to turn back, but her leather soles slipped on the polished marble, sending her skidding towards the approaching officer. Slowing a little, she reached for the stuccoed wall to her right. She managed to hook her fingers on the corner of a decoration and, using it as support, pulled herself back. Her instinct told her to head back to the library, but she had just fled from there. She barely changed direction when the two gendarmes from reception stormed through the exit in front of her. With nowhere else to go, she scrambled for the only doorway to her left. She had no idea where it led, but with a gendarme now on her tail and another two approaching from the front, who cared. She thought she had made it when an arm from behind curled around her waist, lifting her off her feet. She tensed her muscles in resistance, but the gendarme tightened his grip. Then, in one continuous motion, he swung her around and led her towards the stairway he had come from.

'What are you doing?!' she demanded.

'Just move!'

The gendarme pulled her down the first flight of steps. She caught the rail, but his strength broke her hold. The man must be a triathlete! Each time she tried to break free he overpowered her.

'Let go of me!'

'Stop attracting attention.'

She kicked at him, but he pulled her into his body. She thrust an elbow backwards and, missing his jaw by half an inch, found herself immobilized in his arms.

'I have an appointment with Cardinal Cardoni,' she cried.

'He's the last person you want to see right now.'

The gendarme hustled her to the floor below. Implacable, and as a ruckus of footsteps closed in behind them, he hefted her down a passage.

'I won't go there—you have no right!'

'If you value your life, you'll do as I say.'

Jennifer knew from her research that they were now below the Tower of the Wind. Her best bet for an escape was still the Porta Sant' Anna, but it meant she would have to pass through the Pio XI reading room and cut across the Belvedere Courtyard. Her other option was through the Pigna Courtyard or up the Pio IV wing. Both routes ended at the Viale Vaticano, near the city's north wall. She was still considering her options, when the gendarme dragged her into an alley. Ducking into a dark corner, he drew her up against his body and clapped his hand over her mouth. She tried to scream, but he squeezed her lips together.

'Quiet. Not a word.'

As the other gendarmes raced past, she stopped fighting. She had no idea why. Then, she sensed the man holding her might also be running from the police. The two gendarmes chasing them must have realized they had lost their quarry because they had stopped only a few feet from where she and this man—whoever he was—had taken cover. She held her breath. One of the gendarmes lifted his two-way to his mouth and reported the suspects' escape. Command replied that the pair had not exited the building and must be nearby. The gendarmes split. She heard their footsteps fade as they dashed off in opposite directions. One went towards the Pio XI reading room, while the other returned up the steps they had just descended. When Jennifer's captor removed his hand from her mouth she nearly screamed, but thought better of it.

'Who are you?' she whispered.

The stranger shushed her but said no more. Looking around the corner to make sure they were alone, he took off again, pulling her through the Pio XI reading room. The reading room was now filled with visitors and staff. Some froze when they saw a gendarme escorting a fugitive. Others just stared. Jennifer could not remember ever having been more embarrassed. She felt like pulling free, but that would attract even more attention, jeopardizing any chance of their escape. Besides, the stranger was too damn strong. She would have to come up with a better plan.

Escorting her now through the Leone index room, down the steps and out through the main exit, the stranger kept close to the Belvedere Courtyard's west wall. He briskly pulled her into an archway leading to the Vatican Gardens. At the Stradone del Giardini T-junction he stopped and peered around corner. With one hand clamped around her waist and the other still holding her wrist, he pulled her between a pair of parked cars.

'Stop hurting me,' she pleaded.

'Then stop resisting me,' he said. 'I'm helping you.'

Without offering more, he continued up the Stradone del Giardini towards the back of Saint Peter's Basilica.

The stranger's behavior made no sense. Every time Jennifer expected him to do one thing, he did the opposite. In addition to hiding from the two gendarmes at the library, several other actions told her he was not a police officer. For one thing, he did not have backup, and any trained officer would have already called for help under the present circumstances. Also, instead of continuing to the command center behind Porta Sant' Anna, he had brought her to the gardens. This was the least of it. After exiting the library, his other behaviors had been just as *strange*. Even accepting he was no gendarme, rather than cutting across the Belvedere Courtyard towards the Via Sant' Anna, he had chosen Stradone del Giardini, which ran directly behind the museums. But he did not make his strangest move until, in Stradone del Giardini, he turned left, pulling her away from Viale Vaticano on the north wall. Having avoided the Porta Sant' Anna, the Via Vaticano gate was their next nearest escape route. And having ignored both exits, his prospects as a fugitive—and hers, by extension—was looking undeniably bleak.

Clearly, he was also running from the city's police and was lost. Either that, or he knew of an exit not shown on any map of the Vatican. She was uncomfortably aware that their flight could result in severe consequences if they were captured. From what she knew, her own country's FBI used extraordinary methods to extract information. And given the Vatican's history, the Roman Church was no stranger to that. The stranger could be taking her to the Governatorato behind Saint Peter's; there was, she knew, a small police station somewhere behind the basilica.

They were approaching a three-story building with an archway leading towards the rear of Saint Peter's Basilica. Encircling the back were two roads, the vias del Governatorato and della Fondamento. Both exited at the Vatican's main gate, which stood near the south tower where she had heard the campani's peal the previous day. She did not imagine they were going there though; the route was twice the distance of the Viale Vaticano gate, which option they had already abandoned.

She was thinking his behavior could not get any more bizarre when he hustled her into a building across the Via del Governatorato and up a stairway. The exit opened onto a parking lot. Beyond that, the vivid green of the gardens bounded gently over a succession of hillocks. Tears filled her eyes. If only she had thought to enjoy the gardens' splendor instead of offending the most powerful city state on the planet! She had been hoping to see the gardens since receiving permission to visit the Vatican. As she gazed at the acres of trees, lawns and flowers, her mind ticked over feverishly.

'I'm not going. Not until I know who you are.'

The stranger paused momentarily. Then, as if flicking a flea, he said, 'I'm Simon.'

Without offering more, he continued forwards, this time keeping to the left of the Fontana del Sacramento.

At six or seven years, her senior, this stranger, this '*Simon*', seemed older than the average non-commissioned officer. Nor did he wear a cap so that his longish hair fluttered in the breeze like that of a boy half his age. It was time, she decided, to press this Simon for answers.

'Why are you arresting me?' she asked. 'I haven't done anything but glance at some musty, old parchment.'

'I'm not arresting you.'

'What?'

'I said I'm not arresting you. I'm rescuing you.'

'I want to go to my hotel.'

'It's the first place they'll look for you.'

Jennifer clucked her tongue sarcastically. 'How in the world would they know where I'm staying?'

The stranger stopped by an electric cart at the side of the road, shoved her into the passenger seat and slid behind the wheel. 'Who do you think you're dealing with here?' he asked switching on the battery-powered motor. 'These people are connected. They will find you wherever you are.'

The driver had been lazing on a bench beneath a nearby tree. On seeing them pulling out, he leapt up and began waving his arms like a man possessed.

'Nonono, signore, you cannot take my cart—it's not allowed!'

Jennifer screamed in panic for behind the driver, gendarmes were swarming from the building's exit. She turned and stared at the road ahead. What had she just done? By warning the stranger about the approaching gendarmes, she was now complicit in whatever he had done. He had abducted her for goodness's sake! How could she trust him—especially considering he was not a gendarme?

The stranger sped along the narrow road cutting through the center of the gardens. The blood drained from Jennifer's knuckles as she clutched the dashboard handlebar. She prayed repeatedly they would not crash. A hundred feet further at the Fontana dell' Aquilone the stranger cut left. The road circuited Saint Peter's statue. He sped over a crest, swerving several times to avoid pedestrians. On the downward slope, three gardeners were loading containers with branches. It was too late to swerve. To avoid rolling the cart, the stranger steered directly towards them. He slammed his hand on the horn, and Jennifer closed her eyes. She opened them in time to see the one gardener shove his colleague aside before diving for cover himself.

Simon sped into the next bend. Farther down, he turned into the Via Dell' Osservatorio. 'Your interview must have touched a nerve,' he said. 'What did you do?'

Jennifer knew he was trying to extract information from her. Why else would he ask such a thing? She remained silent. She was not sure if the Vatican had anything like the Fifth Amendment, but she would not say one word more without a lawyer. She was in enough trouble as it was.

'Oh, so maybe you did something worse. How about it then? You denounced the pope, didn't you?'

Damn! The man did not stop! He must be security. Why else would he ask all these questions? Suppose, despite all outward appearances, the stranger was a gendarme. Suppose this whole flight of theirs was merely some elaborate means of gaslighting her.

'No,' she huffed. 'Of course, I didn't—what good would that do anyhow?'

'Well then, what did you do?'

'Okay, okay. I broke into an underground bunker. I found a key card and used it to access the secret archives. But all I got was a two-second glance at some old scroll before *they* caught me. And when the gendarmes arrived, I was trying to get from them. But then *you* caught me.'

The moment the flurry of words left her mouth, she was aghast she had said them. She had admitted to everything and had no idea why. Perhaps telling the truth for a change would help get her out of trouble. True, she felt guilty for lying to Cardoni earlier, and every other time she had been untruthful before, it had resulted in more trouble. This was a legal issue, though, which meant she had to be careful not to incriminate herself more with stupid confessions. If the stranger, this so-called Simon, was a crack Vatican interrogator, the truth was her *worst* option. Then again, if he were a fugitive like herself, he might very well lose faith in her and leave her behind. Whatever he had done, after all, might be less criminal than her own infractions.

Jennifer did not know what to think until, finally, she found herself so befuddled that she broke down. Rivulets of tears streamed down her cheeks. The stranger had dismantled her defenses. He had forced her to accept something she had avoided admitting for so long. Her visit to the library, her meeting with Cardoni and now her escape—she had done all of it for one reason alone.

She brushed the tears away. 'I did it to confirm my faith. ...'

Chapter 16

Verretti was enraged. By the way Schreider had acted you would have sworn the Vatican had promoted him to Général d'Armée. Not only had Schreider left without briefing Verretti on the Penitentiary incident, but the colonel had barked orders at every man in the control center without even consulting the inspector. The Swiss were just there for show; even the tourists knew it. And really, on a day-to-day basis, their only purpose was to pose for photographs. You might as well have Mickey Mouse protecting the Pentagon! It was Verretti and the gendarmes, not Schreider and his costumed clowns, who took care of the city's real business.

What was more, Cardinal Santori's lapse in judgment in placing Schreider in charge had humiliated Verretti. His Eminence's oversight now reinforced Verretti's view that the Vatican needed a single police force. As a thoroughbred Italian, the inspector thought himself just the man for such a task. Surely, he and his men should oversee neutralizing the bomb threat at the Basilica. His anti-sabotage and rapid-intervention units were on twenty-four-hour standby. In situations like this, his force was ten times more prepared than the Swiss. To be sure, the colonel did have more men than Verretti, but the inspector had the entire Corpo dei Carabinieri at his disposal if necessary.

Descended from a proud line of carabineers, the inspector had followed his father and his grandfather into Rome's elite force. His two brothers currently served in the carabinieri in Florence, but they were hardly as accomplished. As inspector of the Vatican's gendarmerie, Verretti had reached the highest rank of anyone in his family. He was the pride of his entire clan. At thirty-eight, he had come a long way. And, with his pedigree and experience, he could easily direct both the gendarmerie and Swiss. In fact, without the Swiss, there would be no overlap, no fuss and no damn conflict.

The corporal at the surveillance desk reclined in his chair, but he was still intently focused on the sixty-inch LED screen in front of him, and suddenly he cried out, 'Inspector! You need to see this.'

Verretti studied the monitor and smiled. The gendarme entering the gardens had the journalist with him on the cart and was heading for the Governatorato. He must be taking her to the station at the government building for interrogation.

Verretti set off for his office. 'Have you found the priest yet?'

'No, Inspector.'

'Well, find him. He must be in the Vatican somewhere. He didn't just sublimate.'

'That's why I called you, Inspector. It's the same guy.'

Verretti returned to the surveillance room as quickly as he had left. 'Are you sure?' he demanded.

The corporal moved the mouse rapidly, feverishly clicking and rolling its wheel with his index finger. Within seconds, he had loaded clips onto several screens. Selecting two portraits, one of the Penitentiary priest and the other of the gendarme holding Miss Jaine, the corporal superimposed their faces on the central LED. They matched perfectly.

'No!' Verretti howled, throwing up his hands. 'Where are they going? There's no exit that way. They're in the gardens for goodness sake. They're surrounded by fucking walls!'

'They could be lost, Inspector.'

Verretti was still studying the image when Adjutant Lioni entered the room. He had just returned from the Penitentiary and was breathing heavily. He also carried a priest's cassock.

'Where did you get that?' Verretti called from across the room.

'I found one of our men near the Cortile della Bibliotheca, Inspector. He was unconscious and naked—this lying on top of him.'

'*Che cazzo!*' Verretti spat. 'Where is he now?'

'I called an ambulance for him. He needed stitches.'

'Fuckfuckfuck!'

Standing in the doorway, Verretti scanned the operations room looking for Weber. When he saw the Swiss officer at the operations desk, he called out, 'Captain! Where is your Colonel now?'

'He just arrived at the Basilica, Inspector.'

Verretti swore under his breath. The cardinals were right: the two incidents *were* somehow connected. Now even the bombing incident seemed to be part of it.

The inspector turned to Lioni. 'Get six men to the garden,' he commanded. 'Make sure they're armed. We're going after them.'

Verretti slid into his office and pulled his pistol from a desk drawer. Drawing the slide back halfway, he made sure there was a round in the chamber. Satisfied with his inspection, he flipped the safety on before holstering the weapon. Finally, he scanned his desk for anything he might have forgotten and returned to the operations desk.

'Who do you have in the area, Captain?'

Weber checked his roster. 'Two men are at the helicopter pad; two are at the Governatorato. And there's a patrol at Radio Vaticano.'

'Are any of them armed?'

Weber studied Verretti's face, unsure if the inspector was serious. In his eagerness to take an active role the inspector had obviously become confused. The Swiss were perfectly capable of handling the situation, no weapons necessary.

'Inspector, these people are unarmed.'

'Just answer me, Captain!'

'Only the corporal at the helipad is.'

'Get him down there ASAP.'

Weber was now glaring at the police officer. The man had lost his mind. 'I think you should reconsider that, Sir,' he said.

Verretti started for the door. 'You take charge,' he barked at Weber. 'I'm going after them.'

Weber's eyes followed Verretti as he approached the exit. 'You cannot send armed men after them,' he called out after the inspector. 'They have nowhere to go.'

Verretti pushed on, pretending he did not hear the captain.

Weber watched incredulously as the inspector left Command. ‘That’s murder, for God’s sake!’

Chapter 17

When Schreider marched through the main entrance to Saint Peter's Basilica, his three snipers were waiting in the atrium. He gave last-minute orders before sending them to their positions around the bomber.

Armed with an SG-550 NATO assault rifle, the first sniper climbed into one of the reliquary balconies. Lying on his stomach, he drew his weapon into his shoulder and adjusted its telescopic sight. The second sniper aimed around the corner of one of the basilica's monolithic piers. The third sniper kneeled beside a column in the portico of Maderno's nave.

Schreider entered the north aisle through the Holy Door. Twenty meters away, a man stood facing Michelangelo's La Pietà. As if deep in worship, he had his arms lifted in a vee.

Schreider needed to get closer, but any dumb moves and he, his men and the basilica—not to mention those he served in the adjoining Apostolic Palace—were dog meat. As he stepped forward his leather soles crunched on grains of sand, and the sound reverberated off the sheer marble surfaces around him. He might as well have bulldozed his way in.

The bomber swung around as expected, but preparedness could not prevent the blood from draining from Schreider's face. The bomber was a boy, no more than nineteen years old. Schreider quickly assessed the young man's condition. His bony build indicated extreme stress; his greasy hair and stubble evinced days of neglect; and his sunken eyes, encircled with dark rings, betrayed a lack of sleep. Neurotic and lethal, that was the colonel's interpretation of the suspect's appearance. It brought back memories of suicide bombers he had once had to shoot half a world away. Wrapped around the youngster's torso were eight bars of plastique, each with a detonator and cable, which linked to a receiver on the boy's chest. In the young man's right hand was a Bible and, in his left, a cell phone. Forget about the Plexiglas protecting La Pietà; the entire basilica did not stand a chance.

'It's a lie! A lie!' the bomber cried out. 'You all lied to me.'

Schreider stood in full view of the young man. When he spoke, he kept his voice low: 'Hey, there. I see you need help.'

'What? Who are you?'

'Ludwig Engel. And you?' Schreider did not wait for the young man to respond. Instead, he continued to move forward. 'I hear what you say. I feel the same.'

The bomber's eyes shifted from side to side nervously. 'Don't come any closer or I'll do it. I'll blow it all up.'

A flashback from Afghanistan shot through Schreider's mind. His platoon had just readied itself for night watch at their compound, and the sergeant had set off to station troops at various high points, but had scarcely placed four men, when the sergeant had shouted the words for 'halt' and 'lie down' in Arab. The approaching antagonist had either not listened or had not understood, for he had continued advancing. Then the sergeant had instructed one of the men to move in on the stranger. At that instant, Schreider had realized something was wrong. The Arab was approaching with too much confidence. Schreider had not seen the explosives around his waist until the sergeant and two troops were already within blast range. Rather than negotiate, the two soldiers began backing away, but the bomber followed. Schreider saw the Arab's grin, and his heart turned to lead. Any closer, and the bomb would take out the entire platoon. Schreider had no option but to shoot the bomber, yet therein lay the colonel's conundrum: he would have to choose between sacrificing the three soldiers nearest the bomber now or the rest of his men being killed soon enough. One way or another the sergeant and the two troops were already—they were lost before Schreider had time to squeeze the trigger.

A week later, NATO had returned three black body bags to Switzerland. And yet, in some sense, the rest of Schreider's men had been the unlucky ones. They would wear their unseen scars until their deaths. Some would eventually lose limbs; others ended up in wheelchairs. Schreider had been one of only a handful of those in the Swiss platoon whom God had protected from the physical butchery of those early years in Afghanistan. And God did not save any of the men from the deeper scars inflicted by the war; the three-inch, pink slash that snaked over Schreider's left eye was the least of the burdens he still carried. And yet, if there could be anything positive about that awful day, it was that it taught the colonel that death by bombing was instant and therefore painless.

'Thank God,' Schreider thought, he had no wish to suffer.

The sniper in the balcony above Schreider had placed his laser sight on the suspect's forehead. 'I have a shot, Oberst,' he whispered into his microphone.

The sniper in the north aisle now had his own laser point on the suspect's neck. 'Guillotine's drawn, Oberst.'

The third sniper's dot was now steadied on the young man's heart. 'All clear, Oberst.'

Schreider could not falter. He flipped his open palm behind his back, signaling the snipers hold their fire. Then, retrieving his hands again, he asked, 'What is a lie?'

The bomber gaped: 'Don't fucking patronize me!'

'I've not heard anyone say that before. What do you mean?'

When the suspect pointed towards the figure of Jesus draped over the Virgin's lap, Schreider caught sight of the phone clamped in his fist. It was an old-fashioned flip phone, probably a burner. The suspect's thumb was buried into the *one* key, indicating it was a release mechanism. The device would trigger if the phone fell from the kid's grasp. Schreider's heart sank. If only he could push the proverbial reset button on bringing the snipers. Fire now and they could all kiss Mother Mary *goodbye*.

'Look at His face!' the bomber cried.

Schreider genuinely did not understand what the young man was trying to say. 'This is the most heavenly expression known to art, our Holy Mother cradling her beloved Son after the crucifixion.'

'That's not true!'

'I agree, but what's your reason?'

The bomber dropped his arms to his sides. 'Jesus was marred, disfigured beyond recognition.' He lifted his trigger fist towards the Pietà. 'Does that look marred to you?'

A dedicated Catholic all his life, Schreider had, of course, never viewed the Pietà as any more than a beautiful depiction—an artist's rendering—of a moment in the Savior's Passion. He had certainly never associated it with lies, and if he had had his own personal doubts at times, they had nothing to do with a statue's facial expression. This was absurd! One plus one was equaling elephant for this kid, who was assuredly, absolutely crazy.

The bomber threw the Bible at Schreider's feet. 'God's Word ...,' he shouted sardonically, his now empty hand pointing to the mangled book.

Schreider felt stupid. Was this boy giving him a scripture lesson now? Who in the Vatican had not read the New Testament numerous times? At least, for his part Schreider certainly had, and he had not come across a single passage suggesting the Pietà was untruthful. If Michelangelo had deviated slightly from biblical events, he had simply taken artistic license; it could not possibly warrant bombing a sculpture considered a major world treasure. Then, Schreider reminded himself of Laszlo Toth, the thirty-three-year-old, Hungarian-born Australian who, back in the seventies, had leapt to his death from one of the basilica's guardrails, crying. 'I'm Jesus Christ!' *That* lunatic's hammer attack had destroyed parts of Mary's left arm, her nose, left eye and veil, and since then, the Vatican had kept the statue behind bulletproof Plexiglas. The number of explosives the young man had strapped to his torso now rendered that protection useless, and if he released his grip on the phone it would blow the entire nave to Hell. But what was it with this statue and nuts like Toth—and now this kid?

'How come you don't know?' the bomber cried out. 'How come nobody knows? Don't fuck with me!'

With that, Schreider realized he could not stall any longer. He had to act. 'I can't remember seeing anything like that in the Gospels,' he said.

'Prophesy,' the bomber said. '*Isaiah 52, verse 14*. Jesus came off the cross beaten and bloodied; disfigured beyond human recognition. What else is a fucking lie?'

Schreider shifted his weight and took a small step forward, hoping the young man would not notice.

'These are all idols,' the bomber said, sweeping his empty hand across the entire basilica. 'Look. Idols everywhere.' He stared back at Schreider with tortured, lightless eyes. 'La Pietà. What does it say, man? Worship Jesus, or worship his mother? No, it says worship an idol. What about Jesus on the cross? That's another idol. So are all these statues, hundreds of them, this whole damned basilica. So, all these people aren't here to worship God. They're tourists! They're here to worship Michelangelo, Raphael and Bramante—to worship buildings, art, architects and artists. It's idol worship, all of it. And what about all the people buried in this place? What about Saint Peter? The man to whom this place is dedicated. His grave and remains are yet more idols. And what about his statue outside, all five and a half meters of it? That's an idol too, man. What about the obelisk? It's a motherfucking obelisk for God's sake—a pagan Egyptian symbol! And everyone thinks I'm nuts. How crazy is it to fill a city dedicated to a religion that bans idolatry with idols at every turn?'

Again, Schreider edged forwards. He always knew the day might come when he would have to sacrifice himself for his faith. He focused his mind. He had to find a way to keep the suspect from taking his finger off that phone key.

'What about the pope—holy and all?' the bomber almost pleaded. 'What about all the popes buried here. Idol worship, that's what it is. Come on man, open your fucking eyes!'

Schreider could have understood even a little if this kid had stumbled on some proof that all of Christianity had been a brazen lie, but the ridiculousness of what he was saying was like something out of a Franz Kafka story. So, idolatry was bad. Great. Go become a Protestant or Muslim or Jew. And so, you don't like the unrealistic realism of Renaissance sculpture. Go visit the Abstract Expressionism collection at MoMA. Then Schreider remembered what Weber had said about the bomber's requesting the area be cleared. At least that was one point in the kid's favor: he did not want to harm anyone. Obviously, he was seeking something else though, but if the statue itself was not hurting him, how could its mere existence do so? Just because the faithful visited the Vatican did not mean they *worshipped* its statuary. It was certainly possible to appreciate this sculpture or any other as an expression of the artist's faith or as an example of a mastery of craft without believing, like some medieval peasant, that God lived inside it. The biblical ban on idolatry was also no great secret; hell, it was right there, repeatedly, in every copy of the Bible, in every language. The Church was not hiding anything.

Of course, whatever the reason for the bomber's confusion, no amount of empathy or reasoning was going to make disarming him any easier. At what point, exactly, would this tormented mind snap? Schreider saw the frustration in the kid's eyes. Nineteen years of obedience had made him believe things even the Church did not ascribe to, and Schreider could relate to that to some extent. He had had his own crisis of faith on the battlefields of Afghanistan, but he had later found his way back to belief. All this kid saw now was chaos. To him, the Pietà's misrepresentation was a betrayal. He was equating cheating God to treason, and he was demanding the *truth*. The problem was knowing what *truth* the kid wanted to hear—indeed, knowing what was *truth* beyond any doubt—was something perhaps only one man in human history had been capable of, and that man had died on a cross two thousand years before.

Chapter 18

Verretti got into his specially built Lamborghini patrol car. Lioni had followed him outside, and the inspector now ordered the adjutant into a second cruiser nearby. Verretti turned the ignition of his vehicle and cursed Lioni's slowness. The last thing he wanted was to be dragged down by some juvenile who could not keep up. The gendarmerie, he felt, should consist exclusively of officers with years of experience behind them. As he waited impatiently while four more gendarmes crammed themselves into Lioni's vehicle, another officer slid into the passenger seat beside Verretti. The man hardly had time to shut his door before Verretti sped away.

From their location behind the Porta Sant' Anna, the shortest route to the gardens cut beneath the Apostolic Palace. One hand on the steering wheel, the other clutching his two-way, Verretti raced for the tunnel ahead.

'I need an update on the escapees.'

'Suspects approaching the back of the Governatorato. Heading south towards the station.'

Verretti dropped the handset, pulled the handbrake and spun the steering wheel, performing an on-a-dime one-hundred-and-eighty-degree turn, a maneuver which forced Lioni to a screeching halt behind him.

'Porta Sant' Anna!' Verretti called out through his window. 'We're going around the front!'

The gardens on the western side of the Vatican comprised half the city. The most prominent building was the Governatorato Palace, a majestic five-story structure situated just behind Saint Peter's Basilica. Several roads linked it to other important buildings, including the Roman metro's Vatican Station. Dating from the early nineteen-thirties, the white marble structure lay just south of the Governatorato. Passing between it and the Governatorato, the suspects were travelling towards the city's southern gate, so circling Saint Peter's Square would allow Verretti to cut them off.

Vatican personnel in front of the Porta Sant' Anna's closed portcullis were surrounded with a crowd of tourists thirty deep. Verretti hollered for the two Swiss guards to let him through. He waited as they pushed back the crowd, then, turning up the Via di Porta Angelica, he sped off.

Accelerating towards the Via del Saint Uffizio, the inspector radioed the command center: 'I'm going around Saint Peter's Square.'

Realizing the need to keep ahead of the fugitives, Weber had already ordered the surveillance tech to pull feeds of the streets surrounding Saint Peter's Basilica up on his central screen: 'Careful, Inspector. There's a large crowd of pedestrians in the square.'

The Via del Saint Uffizio encircled the oval Largo del Colonnato. The double-banded colonnade encircled Saint

Peter's Square like two arms holding a bowl and, with the Basilica, formed the shape of a key—symbolically that of the gates of Heaven—which was only apparent from overhead. At the intersection separating Pio XII Square from Saint Peter's, Verretti honked at the slow-moving pedestrians. The beginning of Lent had seen an increase in the number of the city's visitors, and with the gates currently locked, many of those visitors were congregated in and around the Pio XII square, making the inspector's speeding even more dangerous.

Verretti accelerated into the second colonnade bend. The road ended at the Main Gate, next-door to the Palace of the Holy Office. But, halfway there, a tour bus slowed the inspector's progress.

'For goodness sake!' he howled, leaning half his body out the window to see if he could pass.

Lioni, meanwhile, had a clearer view of oncoming traffic. He waited for a break in the traffic before radioing an all-clear to Verretti. No sooner had Verretti crossed into the oncoming lane than the adjutant slipped in behind the inspector. Verretti's Lamborghini spat flames as he sped away. The powerful sports motor passed with ease, but left the adjutant facing oncoming traffic. Lioni was damned if he did not keep up, so he rammed the accelerator to the floor. The adjutant's vehicle shot forward, passing the bus with inches to spare before hitting a taxi head-on.

Verretti's Lamborghini screeched across the Piazza del Saint Uffizio and stopped at the Main Gate.

'Open!' he called to the Helvetians.

He waited as the two guards, perhaps out of habit, ceremoniously drew the gate open. At the same time, four gendarmes shoved onlookers back behind a barricade allowing the two vehicles to pass.

When he took off again, his two-way was pressed to his lips. 'Where are they?'

'Between the Governatorato and ...' The surveillance tech paused. 'They're heading for the railway tracks in front of the metro station.'

'*Merda!*'

Verretti pictured the area around the station. The Vatican's section of the railway line covered only a mile. It entered from the east wall as a subway, passed the station building, then exited the south wall above ground. Both entrances had steel gates, making it impossible for anyone to pass without permission from command.

He pressed the talk switch: 'Who do we have in the area?'

'No staff today. No trains in or out for two days.'

'What the hell?!'

'Maintenance, inspector. The council requested maintenance. They're skimming the tracks.'

'*Porca miseria!*' Verretti suddenly felt dizzy as a pang shot down his left arm. 'Did you check it out?'

'That's your department, Inspector.'

'*Culo!*' That was their escape route, Verretti was now sure of that. 'Get all the guards in the area there immediately. Do we have a sniper on the dome?'

'In place, Inspector,' a voice cut into the channel. 'Target moving south behind the Governatorato now. Have partial sight.'

Verretti recognized the burly voice as that of his own sniper. 'Thank God!' he spat. 'Do you have a shot?'

'Negative, Inspector. No clear shot. Target moving fast. Too many trees; civilians.'

'*Puttana merda!*' Verretti checked his rear-view, then spoke into the two-way again. 'Adjutant Lioni, cover my sides. If I miss them, you'd better do your damn job.'

Chapter 19

Schreider took another step towards the young man.

'What are you doing? Stay away, or I'll blow you up as well.'

'I'm here to help.'

'You? You can't do anything.'

Schreider edged forwards. 'Tell me what you've found out.'

'I've already told you. Now get the fuck back!'

Schreider recognized the quiver in the kid's voice. 'You haven't told me everything. First, tell me what else is bothering you.'

'It'll take too long. There's so much. It's too fucking late anyhow.'

'We have time.'

The bomber's emotions suddenly got the better of him. Months of pent-up frustration burst forth. He shook uncontrollably.

Schreider inched within feet of the kid. 'Don't let go now. You're not ready to let this happen. I can see that.'

The bomber could not believe someone was prepared to die with him. 'Do you *want* to die?' he sobbed.

Just then the look in the kid's eyes told Schreider he was ready to go; that bleak stare said he was willing to blow them both to the other side of Purgatory at any moment. Death had never been this close for the bomber, that was obvious. But Schreider had not felt so alive in nearly a decade.

'Put the safety on. I'm not ready to die today,' the colonel said.

'It doesn't have a safety.'

'It's right there, the *two*-key next to your thumb.'

Schreider lifted his hand and closed it around the young man's fist. He pressed down on the bomber's thumb. He was taking a chance as the safety switch programmed into the phone could be any of the keys. Still, the most popular program, the one any paranoid loon could find online, made the default safety the *two* key. As their hands met, Schreider pressed the second key on the dial pad and, taking a deep breath, ripped the phone from the kid's grasp. It shattered as it smashed against the Plexiglas glass protecting the Pietà.

'Now, let's have a talk about what's bothering you.'

Chapter 20

Verretti could smell success. He was racing up the Via Tunica, which lay just south of Saint Peter's Basilica. In mere seconds, he himself—practically single-handedly—would make an arrest. He could already see Schreider's face as the colonel realized the commander of the gendarmerie, not the Swiss, had returned to Command victorious.

He passed beneath the skywalk linking the Sacristy and the Basilica and raced across the Piazza Santa Marta. With the, Palazzo di Giustizia, up ahead, he glimpsed the helipad corporal scrambling down the grass embankment on the opposite side of the railway line.

'Move, Corporal! Move!'

'What should I do, Inspector?' the corporal replied between panting breaths.

'Is the gate closed?'

The sniper on the dome replied first: 'Affirmative, gate's closed. Suspects in sight. Heading for the station now. Can I take the shot?'

The fugitives had to be out of their minds. What were they thinking? Verretti was tempted to give the sniper the okay. They had killed a priest after all. The male suspect had also knocked one of his men unconscious and left him for dead. Finally, though, after a moment's reflection, Verretti barked, 'Don't shoot! They have nowhere to go.'

At the rate Verretti was going, the gendarmes would reach the fugitives before him. The thought of his men getting there first caused a reflex action, making Verretti flatten the accelerator to the floor. His Lamborghini shot forwards like a shark lunging after its prey.

'Problem, Inspector,' the two-way squawked. 'Suspects' headed for the rail grinder.'

Suddenly Verretti panicked. The realization that the suspects could get away caused his chest muscles to spasm. 'Can you take a shot, sniper?'

'Negative, Inspector. No current visuals.'

'Where's the rail grinder?'

'On the track in front of the ...'

The sniper's voice fell silent.

Verretti checked his radio to see if it had accidentally switched off. No, no, no, no! He pulled the mic back to his lips: 'And, sniper, and?'

'Smoke, Inspector. They've started the engine.'

The blood vessels in Verretti's neck bulged: 'You're not fucking serious!'

The corporal at the track held his aim. 'What should we do, Inspector?'

Verretti refused to give up. He raced up the Via del Mosaic, catching a glimpse of the station from the terrace separating it from the plaza above. Then, skidding sideways into the last bend, he saw the yellow rail grinder. His heart sank as the locomotive began to gain speed. Enraged, the inspector sped past the front of the Vatican Station. Halting on the platform, he jumped out, just in time to see the thirty-ton rail grinder power towards the Vatican perimeter wall.

‘Are they crazy? The gate’s closed.’

Refusing to concede defeat, the inspector ducked back into his Lamborghini. He collected the two-way handset and glanced up at the lantern atop Saint Peter’s dome.

‘Shoot them! Shoot them now! Damn it, just take the shot!’

‘I’d reconsider that, sniper,’ Weber’s voice chirped over the two-ways.

‘Come on!’ Verretti waived towards the corporal on the other side of the tracks. ‘Take the shot!’

The corporal lowered his rifle. ‘I have no visual, Inspector.’

‘Fuck that!’

Verretti plucked his pistol from its holster. Turning sideways, he locked the pistol firmly into both hands. Stretching his right arm across his chest, his chin pressed onto his raised shoulder, he fired a volley of rounds. He lifted his head to see if he had hit the target, only to witness the locomotive ramming the gate, ripping the steel apart. Debris flew and sparks exploded through the air, clattering against the perimeter wall and cement quay.

Shock flagged Verretti’s face.

‘Shoot, dammit!’ he shouted at the corporal on the opposite side of the track. ‘Take the fucking shot!’

*****

‘Don’t shoot, Corporal! I repeat! Do not take that shot!’

The words emanating from the radios were Schreider's. Accompanied by three Helvetians, the colonel passed Verretti in his 2.8 liter Mercedes Steyr Puch.

Behind Schreider a determined-looking lieutenant approached in a second SUV, the Helvetians with him clinging to their seats.

Schreider sped down the off-ramp. At the intersection with the track, he braked hard, swinging the steering first left, then right. Like a dirt truck on an off-road challenge, the vehicle bounced onto the tracks.

'The audacity of the colonel!' Verretti thought. How dare the man interfere with this pursuit?'

Diving into the Lamborghini, the inspector motioned for his officer to get back in. He slammed the door and sped down the off-ramp like a man possessed. At the bottom, he copied Schreider's maneuver, tail-spinning his Lamborghini sideways onto the tracks, but his vehicle did not have the clearance of Schreider's Puch, and he lost traction. Leaping from the Lamborghini, his ego severely bruised, he bellowed a vast assortment of profanities after the speeding train.

*****

Minutes later, Schreider tossed his two-way onto the console and pulled his cellphone from his jacket pocket. The last thing he needed now was broken teeth. With one eye on the tracks in front of him, he dialed Weber.

'I'm in direct pursuit, headed south,' he stuttered as the SUV's wheels bounced over the railroad ties.

'You're driving on the track, Oberst?'

'I have to get to them before the carabineers do.'

Schreider had no chance of stopping a thirty-ton, speeding behemoth with a one-and-a-half-ton Steyr Puch. They must be heading for the cover of the subway tunnel; he was now sure of that. The entrance was at the Passaggio Antonio Cesari and it came out at Trastevere. At best, he could order the men in the back seat to start shooting, but with the subway up ahead, that option was quickly vanishing too.

'See if you can get someone to cut them off at Trastevere,' he called out over the rattling noise of the Puch.

There was a moment's silence.

'With respect, Oberst,' Weber replied, 'you're asking me to cause a train wreck.'

Schreider weighed his options. Injuring or killing bystanders was out of the question. 'Okay. Make sure nobody shoots unless I give the order. We're outside the city, out of our national jurisdiction. We can only use minimal force.' Then, realizing he was nearing the subway tunnel, he added, 'If we lose each other, I'll call you at Trastevere.'

Chapter 21

When Simon saw the two SUVs mount the tracks behind them, he knew it was the Swiss Guard. Approaching the Stazione di San Pietro, he leaned out one of the rail grinder's windows to take another look. Surely, his pursuers would not attack the locomotive now that they were outside the walls of the Vatican.

Their crash through the gate had made Jennifer's pulse roar in her ears. Charged with adrenalin, she also leaned out of the window. To her horror, the SUVs were closing in on her side. She drew back, hardly able to breathe.

Simon leaned across her and peered out. Behind them a Swiss guard was balanced on the bonnet of a Mercedes 4x4, attempting to climb onto the back of the rail grinder. He pulled back and opened the throttle. The sign for the Roma San Pietro station and entrance to the subway tunnel were only two hundred meters ahead. Once they had reached that, their chances of escape would improve significantly. The subway also prevented vehicles from coming alongside the rail grinder. The Swiss would be forced to approach from the tracks—and, as the rail ties would make gaining speed in SUVs nearly impossible, he and Jennifer would, at that point, be all but out of reach.

Now almost paralyzed with shock, Jennifer stared at the tracks ahead of them. Just before crashing through the gates, she had witnessed a gendarme fire at them. Moments later, three rounds had smashed through the window, barely missing her and Simon. She concentrated on clearing her head, but just as she thought she had, entering the subway at full speed hit her like a brick wall. She lifted her feet to the seat, folding herself into a fetal position and cupped her hands over her ears to alleviate the immense pressure of the compressed air. Sitting like this awhile, she calmed herself enough to think. She wondered if Simon had planned their escape route. The gendarme uniform, their flight through the gardens—in preference to a gate—and the rail grinder parked at Vatican Station all seemed to indicate he had. But, that would mean he had accomplices. How else could the rail grinder have ended up at the Vatican?

Lowering her feet, she tried to deal with her situation. She had never been in trouble as deep as she was now. Aside from sabotaging her interview, she had—let's see—become a fugitive, who having committed no more than breaking and entering, found herself at the mercy of and accomplice to a stranger who, by the looks of it, had done something far worse than she could even imagine. She would have to escape from him as well; there was no doubt about that. He looked Middle Eastern. Was he a terrorist!? Her heart rate rose again. Such people had no respect for life; on missions like this, they operated in cells, meaning he might be part of a larger network. She simply had to get away from him. She would seize the first chance she got; she had to.

Then something else struck her: his going out of his way to rescue her made no sense. He had no reason to endanger himself for her. Of course, it was not that she minded. If it had not been for him, she would, at present, be sitting in an interrogation room, trying to explain to a pack of old sadists that sneaking into their secret clubhouse was not grounds for placing her on the rack. Yes, he had rescued her from the library's upper story. Either he had been lost too, or it had been his intention to help her.

'Why did you come for me?' she asked.

'I got you into this; it's only fair I get you out.'

'How did you get me into this?'

'Your break-in coincided with mine.'

'I hardly did anything.'

'That's not why they're after you.'

'What? Why then?'

'Right now, they're after anybody trespassing.'

She stared at him quizzically, but did not speak.

'A priest was murdered, okay.'

Jennifer gasped. 'What does it have to do with me?'

'They think I killed him …'

Despite the shocking news, Simon sounded annoyed—almost as if he were hiding something. Surely, he must have had something to do with the killing. Why else would the gendarmes be shooting at them? The evidence was right there above his head.

'Don't look at me like that. I didn't do it.'

'How can I believe you? You already said you stole something.'

'I *took* something.'

'Take …, steal …, what's the damn difference.' She remained still for a moment. Suddenly curious, she asked, 'What did you take?'

'A letter …'

When Simon pulled the throttle back to slow the rail grinder, Jennifer felt as if she was about to have a heart attack. 'Why are you stopping?!'

'We're getting off.'

'You're crazy. There's nowhere to go!'

The steel wheels screeched as the railgrinder rolled to a halt. Simon flung his rucksack over his shoulder. He picked up a crowbar that was lying by his feet and leapt to the gravel below.

'Come on, now,' he said, his arms stretched towards Jennifer.

She shook off his help and leapt down on her own. Hardly, had she landed when the roar of the two SUVs speeding down the tunnel towards the back of the rail grinder caught her attention.

Simon ran up the dark subway.

She did not.

She could not go with him—not after what he had just told her. She glanced back towards the approaching trucks. Gravel shot up against the back of the railgrinder, causing her diaphragm to contract. Murderer or not, she feared going back more than she feared going on, and she could escape from Simon later—he *probably* was not the type to torture his victims.

Then, she ran after him.

Chapter 22

Why had the rail grinder ground to a halt? Schreider was painfully aware the two fugitives could have an escape route for it was insane to stop with him and his men tailing them. Closing in on the front of the locomotive, he found the cabin door standing open. He raised his sidearm and, approaching cautiously, shouted for the fugitives to come out with their hands over their heads. Three Helvetians dashed up behind him. He need not check. They would all have their semi-automatic rifles pressed into their shoulders. Then he heard the lieutenant and his three Helvetians closing in from the opposite side.

'Anything on your side, Lieutenant?'

'Nothing, Oberst.'

When Schreider saw the empty cockpit, his heart skipped several beats. Then he heard footsteps echo further up the tunnel. In the distance, he saw the suspects' silhouettes growing smaller as they neared a shaft of light. The airshaft. That was where they were headed. Calling his men to follow, he lunged forwards. His lieutenant made it to the bottom of the ladder first. Schreider arrived as the fugitives reached the catwalk, just below the exit above.

'I can get the male, Oberst,' the lieutenant said, taking aim.

'No, go after them. Go!'

The lieutenant slung his rifle over his shoulder. With the agility of a trapeze acrobat, he scaled the ladder.

Schreider followed close behind. He might be older, but he was still fit enough to keep up with the youngest of recruits.

'Go,' he ordered. 'We can't let them escape!'

Chapter 23

Simon closed the hatch behind them and jammed the crowbar into the latch. He checked his watch hoping they were not too late. It was nineteen past ten o'clock.

Standing on the subway roof, he scanned the surrounding apartments to make sure nobody had seen them exit the airshaft. He was wary of old ladies with nothing else to do, but call on the carabinieri informing them about trespassers in their area. The air had warmed by at least ten degrees, and that, on top of the exertions of their escape, had drenched him with sweat.

He headed to the stairs leading to the street, which due to the slope, the property was one level below them.

Jennifer was shading the morning sun with her hand. Their sudden emergence into daylight hurt her eyes. She had no clue where they were, but needed an escape route away from Simon. Surrounded by apartment blocks, she saw none, so she followed him. On the street, she weighed up her options again. She was thankful he had helped her, but did not trust him. She had no idea whether he was telling the truth.

Simon peeled off the uniform jacket and pitched the jacket into an open dumpster on the side of the road. He swung the rucksack over his shoulder with an easy air, then, as if reading Jennifer's thoughts, he pulled her towards the Viale del Quattro Venti and the Piazza Francesco Cucchi.

Jennifer must escape from him as soon as the opportunity arose. He had already conceded to stealing a letter from the Vatican, sure, but now he admitted to being an accomplice to a murder. Why would he do that? Only true nut jobs admit to crime. How was she to know if he was speaking the truth anyway. For all she knew he was chased for being the killer. Even if he was not the killer, he must be connected with the crime. How else could he know about it?

Suddenly it dawned on her: 'Oh my God, I left my briefcase in the library!'

'What was in it?'

'My keys, phone, my notes. Part of my thesis was in it.'

'What about your passport?'

'I have it on me, I think.'

She pulled her purse from her inside pocket and let out a relieved sigh. Before she had a chance to replace it, though, Simon snatched it from her hand. She reached for it, but he was too quick and tucked it in the back pocket of his pants.

'What are you doing?'

'Don't worry. You'll get it back.'

The viper returned, stirring in her belly. He had this maddening way of making her feel helpless. For a moment, she considered screaming, but the street was deserted.

'I need to get back to New York,' she moaned helplessly.

'You won't make it. They'll stop you.'

It irked her that he was probably right, but she had to do something. She was not planning on staying with him, but how else could she get back to the States again? The scent of cocoa floated across the street. '*Di Angele Marco Cioccolateria*', read the sign on the nearest building. If she made it inside, would anyone help her? She studied the surrounding area for escape routes. On the far side of the piazza ahead, a woman with a buggy was crossing the street, a young girl at her side. A friend waved from a nearby porch. At the corner café below, four elderly men were playing cards, drinking espresso and smoking cigars. The shop to the right had a delivery truck parked in front of it and the driver was offloading boxes and stacking them on a trolley. Beneath the median's trees, a silver taxi idled. It was a Maserati sedan. How could she not recognize it? She found it laughable that someone had the gall to turn such a fine machine into a taxi. The driver had the engine idling, no doubt with the air conditioner running as well.

Simon headed for the taxi, but Jennifer resisted. She was not entering another vehicle with a killer and terrorist—even if it *was* a Maserati. She had managed to escape the Vatican with him, but her determination to escape him led her to resist getting in the car. With bystanders, close by, she was confident she could escape. She would figure her way out of Rome later; hell, all she had to do was find the American consulate.

'Forgive us our trespasses,' she whispered, not a little ironically as she considered the possibility that they might extradite her.

The cabdriver, possibly in his late thirties to early forties with solid stature and of Jennifer's height must have noticed her resisting Simon, because he got out of his vehicle and was approaching them. When he was only a few paces away, he lunged forward and grabbed Simon around the waist. Heaving the harasser like a grizzly, the cabby swung Simon around in a circle, but instead of wrestling him to the ground, the man peaceably set Simon back on his feet.

'Simon, you made it!' the cabdriver cried. 'I was starting to worry.' Then, clasping Jennifer's shoulders, he kissed her on both cheeks and standing back, gazed at her. 'And who's your beautiful companion?'

'Jennifer Jaine, Giorgio. We met at the library.'

'What a glorious place to meet. Well, I hope it was good for you too, Jennifer.'

His dark complexion, stubble-covered jaw and lumpy cheeks gave Giorgio the appearance of a South American freedom fighter. But, the similarity ended there. His black leather jacket, charcoal beret, greying mane and Latin accent lent him an unmistakably Italian flair. If only his spirited friendliness *could* raise her spirit.

'I'm not so sure it was the best place to meet,' she replied.

Giorgio looked her over admiringly. 'Yes, I think I shall go to the library myself. Perhaps they'll also let me check out a girl like you,' he teased.

Jennifer dismissed the compliment though. It had just crossed her mind to demand that Giorgio drive her to her embassy when movement behind him caught her eye. A couple of blocks away, on Via Francesco Daverio, two blue Lamborghinis turned off a side street and were roaring straight for them.

'Get in,' Giorgio urged.

This time she did not hesitate. But when Simon held the front passenger door for her, she slipped in the back. She had to escape the Vatican's hyenas first, but with Simon and Giorgio in the front, she would have a chance to escape from them as well. She just needed the right opportunity.

Simon leapt into the passenger seat as Giorgio released the clutch. With wheels spinning and tires burning, the vehicle skid sideways around the median. Simon managed to close the door, but their momentum forced him to brace himself until Giorgio had straightened the vehicle.

The Maserati shot ahead, startling a flock of pigeons. By the time they reached Viale del Quattro Venti, Giorgio had put some distance between themselves and the Lamborghinis.

'Airport?' he called out.

Simon put on his seatbelt. 'No, first you have to lose these guys behind us.'

'I think you've unleashed a demon. Perhaps it's Satan himself you've angered.'

Powering down the Viale del Quattro Venti, Giorgio thought of an escape route. The Via di Donna Olimpia intersection at the Piazzale Enrico Dunant lay a kilometer ahead. Beyond that, the Ponte Guglialmo Marconi was their fastest route to the Ciampino Airport. He peered at his rear-view. Having gained distance, the Lamborghinis were on his bumper like hungry hounds. The first Lamborghini raced towards Giorgio's side, slamming against the Maserati's left-rear door. Clearly trained in pursuit, the second Lamborghini closed in on the sedan's tail, boxing Giorgio in and preventing him from decelerating. Rather than letting the gendarmes tail-flip him, Giorgio sped up.

He checked his side-view mirror for their attack while also glancing at the road ahead. Then he saw a gap: a pack of vehicles before him was approaching di Donna Olimpia intersection a few hundred meters ahead just slowly enough that it might let him lose the gendarmes.

'Hold on—tight!' he ordered.

As his tongue struck the final t against his teeth, he cut a hard left into oncoming traffic. He sped up just enough to ensure the two Lamborghinis followed him, and as they moved in, he punched the gas once more. On passing the first car, he swung back into the flow of traffic, deftly sliding the Maserati between the back and front ends of two cars in the driving lane. This maneuver stranded the two Lamborghinis on the wrong side of the road, causing both their drivers to brake hard, and while the rear Lamborghini could swing back into the flow of traffic, the front vehicle ended up facing oncoming traffic. To avoid a head-on collision, the driver swerved out even more, scraping against several parked cars.

This bit of ingenuity from Giorgio had helped put some distance between the Maserati and the Lamborghinis, but he had not managed to lose them entirely. Then, as they entered the bend before crossing the intersection of the vias del Quattro Venti and di Donna Olimpia, a delivery truck was pulling away from a loading bay, veering straight in front of the Maserati and blocking its path. With nowhere to go, Giorgio swung the sedan back into the oncoming lane. The move allowed the Lamborghinis to catch up, but in a way, that was preferable, for it now created the opportunity Giorgio was hoping for earlier. Once he had pulled next to the truck, the Lamborghini's closely following on his tail, Giorgio matched the speed of the truck. He waited for the exact moment when oncoming traffic was right up ahead before accelerating again, swerving in front of the truck. As expected, the Lamborghinis tried to copy his move, but just as Giorgio had cut in front of the truck, instead of accelerating, he slammed on the brakes, making it impossible for the Lamborghinis to get back into the driving lane.

As before, the first Lamborghini swung left to avoid oncoming traffic. The second tried to follow suit, but it was too late. Swerving to avoid a bus the driver swung in towards the truck. Squeezed between the bus and the truck the driver had nowhere else to go, but head straight for the intersection. The Lamborghini hit the Piazzale Enrico Dunant median at eighty miles an hour sending it airborne. Its tires burst and wheels bent at ninety degree angles from its axles the Lamborghini took off like a pipped fighter jet, sliding first sideways across the second-story stone façade of a bistro, before bouncing back and hitting a traffic light. The vehicle spun seven hundred and twenty degrees before striking the next section of pavement diagonally, flipping backwards and, with glass and sparks shooting through the air, rolling three more times before wrapping its back end around a streetlamp.

Jennifer had turned back just in time to see a small coupe collide with the totaled Lamborghini. She felt for the unassuming Italian couple inside, who had suddenly found themselves in an unwarranted accident, but faced forwards again as the second Lamborghini nipped the Maserati's rear bumper.

Then Giorgio hit the brakes as they found themselves behind three lanes of traffic stacked four cars deep.

'We can't stop!' Jennifer yelled. 'Why aren't they moving?'

Giorgio leaned out of the window. 'There's a train up ahead. The metro must be passing.'

Glancing over her shoulder, Jennifer screamed instinctively as a cold hand seemed to grip her heart. Not far behind them the Lamborghini had stopped and the gendarmes were approaching on foot.

Giorgio glanced at the rear-view mirror. The two gendarmes had disembarked and were running towards the rear of the Maserati, firearm raised and ready to fire. In desperation, he slapped the hazard-light button, pressed his hand into the horn and accelerated onto the nearby sidewalk. Swerving around pedestrians, he sped past stationary cars, a set of café patio chairs and the bookshop entrance. At the Circonvallazione Gianicolense intersection ahead, three lanes of traffic were crossing their path. Between the street's east- and west-bound lanes ran two shuttle tracks, and Giorgio tapped the brakes as he considered whether he could cross it safely. The passing traffic was moving slowly, and he could slip between the oncoming cars, punch the gas and maneuver the Maserati between the speeding shuttle and a truck.

Jennifer could have touched either vehicle, so close were they to the Maserati's flanks. Turning back again, she saw the Lamborghini was about twenty yards behind them having copied their every move, but luckily, with the lack of space between the truck, the Maserati and the shuttle, it was now impossible for the gendarmes to get out and approach on foot as they had minutes before.

Giorgio waited for a second truck to pass before turning right and speeding down the Via Quirino Majorana.

Meanwhile, Simon's composure puzzled Jennifer. Since they had left the piazza, he had not said a word. She also could not help wondering why the Vatican would go to such lengths to capture them, when it meant endangering the citizens of another sovereign state so recklessly that it was bound to make the evening news. Obviously, the gendarmes were after the stolen letter. So why not just give them what they wanted? She thought of grabbing the rucksack from Simon and tossing it out, but her curiosity got the better of her. Whatever the letter contained had to be important enough for the Vatican to risk international censure to recapture it, and now she wanted to know what it said too.

'Give me the rucksack,' she demanded, stretching an open hand towards Simon. 'Just the bag. You can keep the letter.'

Recognizing her ingenuity, Simon removed the silver casket from the rucksack and handed it to her.

The Via Portuense crossing lay not far ahead. Shrugging off her jacket, Jennifer stuffed it into the rucksack. Turning in her seat, she lifted the rucksack to the rear window to ensure the gendarmes saw it. Then, leaning out the rear window, and with all the strength she could muster, she heaved it into the air. Pulling back in, she watched as it hit the bridge's balustrade, bounce back into the air again and, seconds later, hitting the Via Portuense several stories below.

'Please let them go for it!' she pleaded.

Jennifer saw the gendarme in the passenger seat shout at the driver and point to the over bridge behind them. Then, the Lamborghini swerved to the side of the road, stopping in a cloud of smoke. When she swiveled forwards again, her eyes met Simon's. He was beaming. She noted his appreciation, but something even more exciting gripped her—whatever was in the silver casket beneath his hand was so important that the possibility of its recovery had caused the gendarmes to abandon their pursuit. Naturally, her curiosity knew no bounds.

Chapter 24

Schreider had hardly returned from the subway chase when Father Franco called him from the Penitentiary for a report. His decision to deal with the bomber personally while Verretti pursued the two fugitives had made him the object of criticism. Then again, he had to accept that was just part of the job. He just did what they hired him to do.

Marching into Santori's office as the basilica's bells struck eleven, he prepared himself for the dressing down he was sure the cardinal would deliver. Still dressed as a civilian, he closed the door behind him and briskly crossed the office to the lounge. Santori sat facing him, while Cardoni was perched on a couch beside the window.

Santori's blood pressure felt as if it had risen above critical level, and a torrent of sweat was trickling down his upper lip. If Schreider only knew. …

Allowing the suspects to escape had created their greatest nightmare; the Holy See had been through trying times before, but never had it faced extinction. No one had ever successfully challenged their authenticity as the spiritual leaders of Christianity. Not even the non-conformist movement starting with the breakaway of Henry VIII in the sixteenth century managed, and the *Ninety-Five Theses* had been anything but a sneeze. Once that letter got out, two thousand years of ecclesiastical service would be down the drain.

'Halfwit!' Santori snarled. 'Rest assured you'll be court-martialed for this.'

Schreider bowed. 'Eminentissimi.'

Santori stared across the coffee table irritably. The audacity of the man; the fugitives would blend in with the millions of tourists visiting Rome. It was nearing the height of summer!

'Why didn't you go after them?' Santori exclaimed.

Schreider maintained his militaristic stance. 'Your Eminence, the bomb threat at the Basilica took precedence. It threatened His Holiness's life.'

'His Holiness's life?' Santori snapped. 'Don't you get it? The Pope means absolutely nothing without His flock. There have been two hundred and sixty-six popes since Saint Peter drew breath, and two hundred and sixty-four of them now lie in the ground. A pope's life is arbitrary. What left this city today—what you let leave—was the seed of our complete destruction!'

Schreider refused to be enmeshed in the cardinal's argument. He had asserted his allegiance to the Holy Pontiff and his commitment to defend the Papal Court with his life; he had not sworn to protect their immorality, just their lives.

'The wellbeing of Our Holy Father takes precedence according to my oath. I didn't swear to protect His lies or yours.'

Santori slammed his fist against his armrest. 'His Holiness won't exist, if ...' then stopping mid-sentence, he composed himself with rhythmic breaths. 'Why didn't you just have them shot when you had the chance?'

'I couldn't endanger civilians, Your Eminence. In any case, the woman's role in all this has yet to be established.'

'You've disregarded my authority!'

Schreider had had enough of Santori's dictatorial contempt. He was still a God-fearing man, but he was fast losing respect for God's elite. 'My order has served His Holiness for five hundred years,' he said courteously but sternly. 'Our record is impeccable. Apart from the papal throne itself, we have served the courts of France, Spain and Italy. We have fought on the frontlines of countless wars. I do not deserve your scorn.'

'Psht! You're little more than a bunch of mercenaries,' Santori shot back. 'If it weren't for Swiss law, you'd render your services to the highest damned bidder.'

Schreider's back stiffened. 'Our men have served in many armies. Many have lost their lives in wars made by people like you, who are happy to start conflicts but nowhere to be found when the shooting starts.'

'Oh, get over yourself. Men like you fight on the frontlines of both sides. You might as well be pitbulls in a dog fight.'

'Not a man amongst us has been unpatriotic!'

Cardoni shot up. Their behavior had become intolerable.

'Stop this!' he barked. They had far more pressing things to contend with than this pissing contest between the two.

The spasm in Schreider's neck eased. He had always found the Cardinal Librarian easier to stomach.

'What happened at the Basilica, Colonel?' Cardoni asked, resuming his seat.

'A bomber tried to blow up the Pietà.'

'Do you think he had any part in all this?'

'In what, Your Eminence?'

As Santori leant forward to berate the colonel again, Cardoni lifted a restraining hand.

'Your Eminence, it's hard to say. We haven't had time to investigate yet.'

Santori glanced up at Schreider. 'Because *you*, Colonel, not your predecessors, the gendarmerie or anyone else, botched the whole damn thing.' The phone on the desk beside him rang and he picked up the receiver. 'Is he here? No, it's okay. Let him in.'

The door opened to reveal a strutting Verretti, his chest puffed out like a mating cock. He approached and, as if to stamp his authority, halted inches beside Schreider.

'Inspector Verretti will handle the investigation from here, Colonel,' said Santori.

Schreider's color deepened, but he did not move. He wondered if he had heard the cardinal correctly.

Santori pushed himself from his seat and walked towards the exit. Holding the office door ajar, he announced, 'You may go now, Colonel.'

Schreider turned slowly. 'I need to examine the body first.' He could not now find it in himself to honour the cardinal with the customary title of 'Eminence'.

'Inspector Verretti can take care of that.'

'With respect, sir …'

Santori reddened as he roared through a tight larynx: 'You can see the body at the morgue, Colonel!'

Schreider marched towards the open door. Passing Verretti, he felt like head-butting the inspector right in his smug, little face. He composed himself just in time though. Losing his cool would spell defeat, and he would not be able to forgive himself for that. On his way out, he saluted Santori. To be sure, however, this was only out of habit. A salute expressed respect, and *respect* was far from his feelings for the cardinal.

Santori closed the door. Returning to his seat, he rearranged his vestments before leaning back. 'Just to let you know, Inspector, you're equally to blame for this calamity, but at least you didn't disobey my orders.'

'The colonel left me without a proper briefing, Your Eminence. Had I known what we were dealing with, none of this would have happened.'

Santori lifted his hand. He could not care less about any squabble between the two commanders of the Vatican's security forces; his only objective was to retrieve the letter. 'I cannot allow any further mistakes, Inspector. You do realize that, right? So now, tell me what happened out there.'

Verretti, though somewhat taken aback, maintained an assertive tone: 'The male suspect had his escape meticulously planned. Because the journalist fled with him, we believe they were working together. We know where the female suspect stayed last night. I've already sent men there to investigate.'

'Surely, they would think twice before going back, Inspector,' Cardoni interjected. 'They know it would be too easy for your men to find them.'

Santori frowned. 'What about escape routes out of Rome?'

'Your Eminence, it would be impossible to cover all escape routes. At best, and even with the Italians' permission, we could focus on public transport. Naturally, the airports should be our priority, as both suspects are foreigners. My guess is they're heading for one of the airports, probably Ciampino.' Seeing Santori's skeptical gaze, the inspector quickly added: 'They fled in a south-easterly direction. If they'd been headed for the da Vinci, they would have fled west. Also, there's less security at Ciampino.'

Cardoni stood up and walked to the window, a cigarette between his fingers. 'There are also private planes, and what about trains?'

'They've just abandoned that option, Your Eminence.'

'So, you're ignoring it?'

'I've sent men to the stations, but it's impossible to cover every route out of Rome. As the saying goes, all roads lead into the city, and they all lead out of it too. Right now, our best bet is to get them as they try to return to wherever they came from. If we're lucky they're already heading back in that direction.'

Cardoni lit his cigarette and inhaled. Exhaling smoke, he spoke with all the deliberation he once used when answering the question of a novitiate many years earlier: 'America. …'

'But, Your Eminence, we are quite sure the male suspect is Middle Eastern.'

Cardoni's eyes shot to Verretti. 'A Muslim?'

'God help us,' Santori said softly. This could spark the next crusade.

'It's very simple, Your Eminences,' Verretti said, his voice confidant. 'We can simply arrest them at customs.'

Santori shot up. 'No, not customs. We cannot involve the Italians in this. We must think of something else. Find out where they're going, but don't let customs touch them.' Then, though he hated going through the whole vault exercise again, he walked to the hearth. 'What I'm about to show you, Inspector, is the most guarded secret in Christendom. You must swear this secret will never pass from your lips. Is this clear?'

Chapter 25

'I didn't swear to protect your lies!'

The thought, evoked in anger and frustration, reeled in Schreider's mind. Needing time to compose himself, the colonel seated himself on a lobby bench outside the Penitentiary and loosened the top button of his collar. Resting his head against the wall, he closed his eyes and recited the oath he had taken more than ten years before:

'I vow to faithfully, honestly and honorably serve the reigning Pope John Paul II and his legitimate successors, and to dedicate myself to them with all my strength, ready to sacrifice, should it become necessary, even my own life for them. I likewise assume this promise toward the members of the Sacred College of Cardinals during the period of the Sede Vacante of the Apostolic See.'

Disregarding this oath was practically treason. Failure to protect those chosen by God meant dishonoring his oath. The incident at the Basilica had posed a direct threat to the wellbeing of the Holy Pontiff and the College of Cardinals. Handing the bomber to the gendarmerie to chase after a murderer who was fleeing away from the His Holiness, meant he would have violated his oath. It did not matter how important the Maggiore felt the letter was, Schreider had not vowed to protect the Church's dogma. He had vowed to keep the Apostolic Palace's occupants safe. If the Holy See had come to harm because of his disregard, he would have broken an oath before God.

As for the cardinals' conduct, demoting him in front of that meatball Verretti was the most degrading, demeaning thing that had ever happened to Schreider. It was a blemish on his otherwise sterling career. They might as well have court-martialed him and blown up Saint Peter's themselves. Verretti was a reckless fool whose precipitous climb up the police force's ranks had turned him into a prima donna. Schreider dreaded what the inspector would do if he captured the fugitives. The Maggiore's scorn had infuriated Schreider, but it hardly compared with the curiosity it had inspired regarding the stolen artefact. It was evident that Santori would sacrifice anyone to recover it. Even as he had stared the bomber in the eye, Schreider had wondered about its contents. If only the kid had known, as Schreider did, the extent of the Church's dishonesty. Concealing information from the faithful was immoral and contrary to the Church's own teachings.

Schreider stood up, refastened his collar and straightened his tie. Then, marching resolutely to the Belvedere Courtyard, his thoughts returned to the Pietà. The only wounds carved on Jesus were tiny nail holes in His hands and feet and a minuscule spear wound in His side. The bomber had a point. In no way was Michelangelo's portrayal of Christ scripturally correct. He could not recall reading anything or seeing any painting, sculpture or crucifix which depicted Christ marred beyond recognition. All the symbolism depicted the Savior bloodied, but unbroken, and while this imagery of the resurrection might be interpreted as symbolic, the consistency was odd.

'We have skeletons in our closet,' he thought. 'That is what, deranged as he was, that kid is trying to say.'

Nor would Schreider take Santori's drubbing lying down. The Maggiore might have taken him off the case, but the colonel still needed to learn what that letter said, if only to satisfy his curiosity and salve his conscience. He could not prove it yet, but the murder, theft, trespass at the bunker and attempted bombing, were all unrelated incidents in one particularly ill-starred day.

The gendarmerie must be questioning the bomber by now. Realizing the consequence, Schreider set off for the Governatorato. On his way, he had another realization. Strange as it seemed even to him, he felt for the bomber. The youngster had threatened the lives of bystanders and members of the Holy See, but his pleas had been sincere.

Slipping between parked cars, Schreider called Weber on his mobile. His captain was returning from the station, where he had placed several guards at the gate.

'Pick me up in the gardens,' the colonel commanded. 'I have to check on the bomb suspect. I don't trust the gendarmes on this one.'

Schreider was striding through the passage linking the Belvedere Courtyard with the Stradone del Giardini when Weber pulled up in front of him. The colonel slid into the passenger seat and ordered the captain to gun it. While Weber performed a U-turn, Schreider drew a miniature New Testament from his inside jacket pocket which he left there for when he went to Bible study.

'What are you looking for?' Weber asked.

'Matthew's account of Christ's trial.' Flipping to the *Gospel of Matthew*, Schreider began reading extracts of the passage aloud: 'The soldiers who held Jesus captive spat in His face. ... Then, they buffeted Him and smote Him with the palms of their hands. ... They stripped Him and put on Him a scarlet robe. ... They plaited a crown of thorns and put it upon His head. ... They smote Him on the head with a reed whilst He had the crown of thorns pushing into His flesh. …'

Schreider stopped. Staring out of the window, he imagined the scene. 'All that took hours,' he said. 'That means the blood must have dried.'

Then, he continued reading: 'His captors stripped the robe off Jesus and put his raiment back on. ...'

Schreider paused again. He had not thought like this before: 'Every time they removed His clothes and replaced it with something else, the dried blood would have taken skin and bits of flesh with it.'

With Schreider too deep in thought to concentrate on their location, Weber assumed control: 'We're almost there.'

Schreider turned to the *Gospel of Mark* and skimmed through the pages as Weber stopped in front of the Governatorato. 'His incarceration and torture carried on for days,' he said, reading a last passage.

Schreider hopped out and sprinted across the terrace to the entrance. Saluting the two Helvetians at the door and calling for his captain to keep up, he slipped into the north wing corridor. Just before the gendarmerie offices, he ducked into a short passage to the left and turned right into the darkroom.

The colonel needed only seconds to assess the situation. Looking through a one-way mirror he saw the bomb suspect in the adjacent interrogation room. The youngster was sitting on a chair, his face badly bruised. One eye had been reduced to a slit between two swollen eyelids, while blood from a half-inch cut in the kid's lower lip oozed onto his shirt. Probing the bomber for answers, Adjutant Lioni hovered like a hawk.

Schreider's gaze shifted to the AV technician in the darkroom with him. The gendarme sat on a swivel chair with his feet propped on his desk, his lunchbox balanced on his groin. With one hand, he was stuffing his face with a pastrami-and-cheese sandwich, while with the other he held a can of soda; he was so preoccupied with his lunch and the show in the interrogation room that he had not even noticed who was standing beside him. Glancing at the blank monitors on the desk, Schreider wanted to slap the man off his chair.

'Aren't you filming this?' the colonel snapped.

The gendarme shot up, his lunch box flying across the recording console as he saluted. Wiping his mouth and hoping his hibernating brain would boot up, he searched for an answer that would not land him in further trouble.

'I was told not to record, Colonel.'

Schreider pointed to the camcorders: 'Put that damn thing on right this instant!'

The gendarme tripped over himself as he fumbled to press the *power* button.

Once the screens lit up, Schreider turned his attention to the interrogation. The would-be bomber was slumped in his chair. Gore dripped from him; he looked broken. He had played a dangerous game, but had ultimately backed down.

He could not have picked a worse day to vent his frustrations though. His attempted suicide coincided with the murder and theft at the Penitentiary as well as the breach at the Archives, making him the only captured suspect in what was being treated as an orchestrated terrorist attack.

Schreider shifted his gaze to the gendarme. His voice shaking with agitation, he asked, 'What do they have so far?'

'He's an Australian from Perth, who stayed in Venice for a year where he tried his luck as a gondolier, but when that failed, he tried construction in Florence, Colonel. I think the man's nuts. He doesn't even speak Italian. He came to Rome a month ago to see our Holy Father, but he couldn't get past your guards. That's why he forced his way into Saint Peter's today.'

Schreider watched as Lioni smacked the bomber's head. When the adjutant grabbed the young man's hair to yank his head back and spit in the kid's face, Schreider had seen enough. He turned towards the exit to go to the interrogation room but halted as the door opened and in walked Verretti.

Ignoring the Swiss officers, the inspector marched straight to the operator's desk.

'The audacity of this gabagool!' the colonel thought. One would think Schreider's name was '*Schweinhart*' the way he had to deal with pigs like Verretti all day. In fact, this pig had done nothing but obstruct their operations all morning. Pushing Weber aside, the colonel approached Verretti. 'What are you doing, Inspector? Are you trying to kill the man? It's obvious the boy had nothing to do with the murder or the theft.'

Verretti straightened. 'We don't know that, now do we?'

Schreider's carotid arteries swelled as rich, oxygenated blood rushed to his head. 'Look at the circumstances. He's already made a statement.'

Verretti did not budge. 'And what might that be?'

'We ... the Church has skeletons in its closet, and the kid flipped his shirt over it. It's not complicated.'

'I see. So, that's *your* analysis. And I assume, then, you expect me to stop interrogating him? You make me sick, Colonel.'

'The man's no terrorist! Neither are the fleeing suspects.'

The chance to prove his worth felt like one in a million; Verretti would not let the opportunity pass or allow anyone get in his way—especially not Schreider. 'They could've worked together,' the inspector growled.

'For God's sake, Inspector, the journalist fled from *us*. You going after her scared her shitless. The real suspect here is the priest who'd escaped from the Penitentiary. You know yourself he stole an important artefact.'

'He also killed Father Yilmaz.'

'You don't know that, Arnaldo!'

Verretti detested the use of his first name, especially at work where it undermined his authority. From Schreider's lips he found it even more despicable. 'This is now my investigation, Colonel. So why don't you and your captain get the hell out and let me do *my* job.'

Schreider's muscles contracted. Fist clenched, he swung upwards. His knuckles struck Verretti's chin, sending the inspector into the wall.

Weber had not seen his commander lose his cool before; he had not therefore seen the punch coming. But before

Schreider could throw another, he had lunged forwards, grabbing his commander's shoulders.

Schreider broke free and advanced on the inspector, but before he could throw another punch, the Italian had plucked his sidearm from his holster and raised it towards the colonel's face.

'Best you pull that trigger!' Schreider snarled.

Struggling to keep his footing, Weber managed to restrain his commander. 'Not now, Oberst!'

Schreider pushed his forehead against the pistol barrel. 'Go ahead. Shoot! Shoot while you have the chance!' He waited for Verretti to show his mettle, but when nothing happened, he stepped back. Using his superior height to his advantage, he stared the man down. 'You coward!'

Schreider relaxed, and his captain released him.

'I'm not letting you off the hook on this,' the colonel said, finally. He turned and headed for the exit. Stopping at the door, he flung a parting glance over his shoulder at Verretti. 'You let anything happen to this man, and I swear to God I'll hunt you down like the swine you are.'

Eyes as wide as a spooked rat's, the surveillance officer gulped down the last of the soggy mush stuck in his cheeks.

Chapter 26

The Maserati glided swiftly through traffic, its engine growling like a tigress as exhaust filled its muffler. Since Jennifer had jettisoned the backpack from the window, the occupants of the Maserati had been silent; the significance of the stolen artefact had sunk in. Whether Simon had murdered someone did not seem to bother the gendarmes. They were after the letter. Why else would they have abandoned their pursuit?

Jennifer could not believe she had escaped the Vatican police only to find herself trapped by a suspected murderer and confirmed thief. Fear gripped her as her quandary became clear. Even if she got away, she would have no way of proving her innocence. When she had woken up that morning she had thought the day might be challenging, but not that her life would be shattered with, perhaps, worse to come. If she survived, how would she explain all this? It was bound to be a funny story to tell the grandkids, but first she had to stay alive—and avoid life imprisonment.

She wondered if she should be thanking Simon for helping her or ruing his apparent chivalry. Were it not for him, she would still be in the Vatican facing a pack of ravening wolves. Heaven knew what would have happened if he had not saved her. As they neared the city's outskirts, she studied him from the back seat. His most notable features were the tiny wrinkles that framed his penetrating eyes. He exuded confidence, and his wavy hair, greying slightly at the temples, rippled in the wind like a lion's mane. He reminded her of an oil painting she had once seen in a New York art gallery. The artist had depicted a Stone Age warrior with painted cheeks rescuing a defenseless woman and child from a burning village. The painting symbolized how an individual can shape human destiny. Simon had a similar martial presence to the warrior. But Jennifer quelled her budding fascination as soon as it entered her mind.

She tilted her head slightly. 'How did you know my name?'

Simon turned. 'I overheard it at the library. You created quite a stir.'

'Where are you going?'

'You mean *we*.'

'No, I mean *you*.'

He flipped his arm over the backrest. 'Well then, I mean we. You can't stay here—not after what has just happened.'

Jennifer remained unconvinced. She did need to know where he was heading though: 'Just tell me then. Where are *we* going?'

'Turkey.'

'Let me out!'

'I can't leave you here. If they catch you, they'll do who-knows-what—and at the very least, getting yourself a lawyer will cost more than you can afford. I know that. Giorgio knows that. Really, if you think about it, you know that too. With us on the other hand, you'll have a chance to get out of here and eventually clear your name.'

Jennifer had missed numerous opportunities to escape from Simon. She could have called for help when they crossed the Pio XI reading room. There had been another chance when he had pushed her into the cart in the gardens as well. If she had put up any fight at all, the driver had been close enough to help her. Nor did she have to get on the rail grinder with him or climb up the airshaft in the subway tunnel. Her best opportunity had come in the piazza where they had met Giorgio. They would not have managed to force her into the Maserati before the gendarmes arrived. So, if the pair were a couple of sadistic serial killers, she had only herself to blame.

'Where in Turkey?' she asked at length.

'Antakya.'

Now she knew they were crazy, and catching the first US bound flight from Leonardo da Vinci airport became her priority. Or, if that did not pan out, she would go to France or England—anywhere would suffice.

'You can't expect me to come with you,' she said, but her words had hardly crossed her lips when she remembered something Cardinal Cardoni had said—the Q manuscript had been found in Antioch, or 'Antakya,' as the Turks called it. Now she was faced with a real dilemma: as a journalist, her urge was to investigate the artefact currently in Simon's hands, and the whole murder situation at the Vatican was an absolute scoop; then again, was she not risking her life following a potential killer. This was not like interviewing a couple of mullahs who wanted to spew hatred on American television; this was sharing a car with someone who might slice her open and fry her left breast for breakfast. She sat staring blankly at the road ahead. She must be out of her mind. Going with Simon was the last thing she should be doing. The artefact would have to wait.

Simon's eyes were still locked on her. 'You have a doctorate in religion, yes?'

Now he was scaring her. What was this? How could he know so much about her? 'Are you guessing?' she asked warily.

'Not really. The archives only accept high-profile researchers, those with or pursuing their doctorates.'

He was right. Maybe she should trust him. Something about him made that difficult though. 'No,' she said under her breath. 'I haven't finished yet.'

There. She had finally said it. She had admitted her failure. That, at least, was honest. She still felt horrible for lying at the libraries, but really, she had no choice. This was different though. Simon's gaze was piercing her soul. She felt as if he knew everything about her. Not many people saw through her defenses. For some reason, he did. He must be intuitive.

'I'm an investigative journalist,' she said at last. 'Or trying to be. ...'

Tears pricked her eyes, and she blinked hard, refusing to give way to them. Her mind was playing tricks on her. She had had so many opportunities to escape yet had not.

Simon's gaze grew more intense.

Looking back up at him, she said, 'I don't know if I can come with you.'

'You have to decide now. It's one thing for me to drag you from the Vatican. It's another to take you to Turkey. That would be kidnapping. With murder and theft charges already assured, I'd prefer you made your own decision.'

'What if I don't?' When he did not answer, she edged forwards. She studied the silver casket beneath his hand. 'Is that locked?'

'You know it is.'

'Can I look?'

He waved her off, and she felt silly. She did not trust him; so why should he trust her? She sat back again. She simply had to know what lay in the casket. If it was a letter, she needed to know what it said.

'Do you have the key?' she asked.

His silence was frustrating. 'He knows exactly what he's doing,' she thought. But her curiosity left her no choice. Sitting with her hands folded in her lap and staring at the tails of the planes rising upwards in the distance, she reminded herself that going with him offered the chance of a lifetime, any journalist's dream come true. Stories like these jumpstarted careers. She would not forgive herself if she let it slip by. She consoled herself that she still had time to decide.

When Simon turned again she looked him in the eye and said, 'I've never been to Turkey.'

The corners of his mouth turned upwards ever so slightly. 'Have you been to Rome before?'

She had to give him points for tenacity. 'There is one problem. I don't have a visa for Turkey.'

He handed her passport back. 'Americans can get multi-entry, 90-day visas on arrival. It only costs thirty dollars. Giorgio, on the other hand—well, let's just say Italy and the

Vatican, and San Marino, for that matter, weren't on speaking terms with Ataturk when the Republic was founded.'

'They definitely won't be on speaking terms now either,' Giorgio quipped nervously as they approached Ciampino's customs gate.

Realizing this was her last chance, Jennifer quietly grasped the door handle and, summoning all her courage, looked for a place to jump out. That damned artefact. She had to be crazy. God help her! She turned her gaze to Simon. 'What if the customs officers are expecting us?'

He kept his hand firmly on the casket. 'I don't think the Vatican can afford that kind of setback.'

He was right. If the letter contained proof of anything substantial, the cardinals would not want customs finding it. All-important contraband in Italy would first have to pass through Interpol, at which point, even the press could get hold of it. She reflected on her escape again. Simon did not have to take her with him, and he was not insisting on it either. He had had many opportunities to abandon her. And imagine the trouble they would be in if she betrayed him at customs.

Just then, she made up her mind: 'I'll come. But my life is on your head.'

Giorgio smiled, relieved. They were only meters away from customs.

*****

Giorgio's apparent rapport with the customs officials smoothed them straight through the checkpoint. He explained in Italian why 'the woman' had no luggage. Jennifer did not understand everything he said, though her background in Latin did enable her to pick up the gist of it. She decided she would smack him for wryly telling the officers she had left her suitcase at a certain apartment at the Palazzo Grazioli. Then, she decided she would beat him senseless for saying she had lost it while attending an especially wild 'bunga-bunga party'—a phrase he was careful to enunciate slowly while using air quotes and giving a meaningful wink—and which she had been too ashamed to retrieve once she had sobered up. Nor did she appreciate how the official chuckled and attempted to look down her blouse as he stamped her passport, but in any case, they were through.

Giorgio drove down an alleyway and turned between two hangars at the end. Standing near the boom were three guards, and he rolled down his window. 'Is my plane ready?' he asked.

'It's all warmed up, Mr. Castignani,' the guard said. 'I see you have another guest today. Will she be flying with you?'

'Yes, it seems Miss Jennifer will be gracing us with her company.' Giorgio slipped the guard a tip. 'Can you keep an eye out? The paparazzi have been tailing us all morning.'

The guard slid the notes under his clipboard. 'Don't worry, Mr. Castignani. We'll take care of it. Have a good flight.'

The boom dropped behind them and Jennifer realized she had now embarked on the greatest challenge of her life. Her archives inquiry had become a journalistic investigation. Giorgio parked the car to one side of the hangar and she leapt out. A reckless feeling gripped her, propelling her forwards. She needed to read that letter and find out why her new companions were headed to Antioch. The adventure of it all was exhilarating.

Flanked by Simon on her right and Giorgio on her left, they hurried towards the Bombardier Challenger 605.

The pilot was waiting. After a brief introduction, Giorgio hung his jacket in a locker by the entrance. He waited while Simon placed the casket in an overhead compartment, before calling up the smartly dressed Martina from the back, suggesting they order some drinks.

Jennifer sat in the first seat: a plush, reclining swivel chair that looked like it had been taken from Air Force One. Her heart raced as the pilot raised the stairs and closed the hatch. There was no turning back now.

Simon turned her seat to face the console behind her and sat opposite her. She looked up nervously as Martina checked the buckle on her seatbelt. Minutes later, the jet's twin engines hummed as they powered towards the airstrip. As they took off, blood rushed to her face. Of course, she had not taken off facing backwards before. She had never flown first-class, let alone on a private plane.

*****

Now in the co-pilot's seat, Giorgio set a south-easterly course. When they reached twenty-three-thousand feet, he stepped from the cockpit with a phone in his hand. He handed the receiver to Simon and showed him to the couch at the rear of the fuselage before asking the pilot to transfer the call.

While Simon was preoccupied, Giorgio poured himself a Mai Tai. Convinced his guest might be hungry, he had Martina stack Ritz crackers in a tin marked, '*Almas*'. He also had her pile on salmon, olives and an assortment of cheeses. He waited for her to place the snacks on the console, before seating himself opposite Jennifer.

Noticing her drinking water, he said, 'How about a glass of bubbly. I have champagne if you want.'

Jennifer took another sip of her water. 'I'm fine, thank you.'

He pushed the snacks to her side. 'Here, have something to eat. It will get your sugar levels up, and I'm guessing you haven't eaten in quite a while.'

Giorgio had a pleasant demeanor. He told her how nervous he had been waiting in the Maserati for them. He had checked his watch, then his phone, then his watch again. At one point, not having heard from Simon, he had known something had gone wrong. He had even thought of leaving. It was nearly nine o'clock before he had had a call from Simon saying he would be late, if he made it at all.

As she listened, Simon caught her eye, but as if to shield himself from her, he turned his head abruptly. She could swear she had seen tears gleaming in the corners of his eyes. She shifted her gaze back to Giorgio. 'Something's wrong with Simon,' she said.

Giorgio took a cracker from the tray, bit into it and gestured for her to do the same. 'Don't worry about him right now. He'll be all right.'

The way Giorgio was diverting her attention from Simon confirmed her suspicions that he was hiding something. 'But he's emotional,' she insisted.

Giorgio held the tray towards her. 'Don't worry, Jennifer. He just needs some time to himself.'

Chapter 27

Simon reclined on the sofa. It was half past twelve and he had already been awake more than eight hours. Feeling drained, he covered his face with his hands. He pressed his fingertips down onto his eyes. Soon, kaleidoscopes of color and light flashed in his brain. When the pain became unbearable, he released the pressure. He dropped his arms to his sides. Keeping his eyes closed, he inhaled and exhaled deeply and rhythmically. It did not take long for him to slip into a meditative state, and his thoughts became pictures. He saw himself walking down the winding streets of Antakya's Uzun Carsi two months earlier. It had rained the previous night, causing the slick paving stones to glisten with subtle tones of grey. On the surrounding mountains lay a thin layer of snow like a silk mantle. The chill in the air had forced him quickly towards the undercover arcade of the bazaar. He remembered pulling his laboratory overcoat closed over his grey V-neck sweater. Having come straight from the archaeology site above the Cave Church of Saint Peter, he was still dressed in his laboratory jacket.

Father John Yilmaz was by Simon's side, matching his strides. John had flown to Antakya specially to see him. He wore a black suit jacket over a black cassock with a white clerical collar. He was also clutching a black leather-bound Bible. At the time, Simon had wondered if he would ever get used to seeing John dressed that way. He had not seen the priest since his ordination.

John loved Uzun Carsi. In continuous operation since ancient times, the colorful semi-enclosed bazaar was still a major landmark in the region. Everywhere, shoppers and merchants he had known as a boy greeted him. He had spent most of his teen years working part-time jobs for several of the shop owners. With hundreds of stores and kiosks lining its serpentine length, he had easily earned enough pocket money to buy a motorcycle. John brought a smile to the faces of many he passed. Everyone had something to say about his priestly garb. As if nobody took it seriously, many asked when he would open his own store.

Simon lingered for an hour while John worked his way past the shop fronts. Towards the end of the bazaar, they glided down a stone-paved alleyway with a vaulted gothic roof. Here, humble restaurateurs sautéed chickpeas and spinach side-by-side, jostling each other as they and their staff prepared ingredients. Between the brightly painted but crumbling walls, milk crates and vegetable boxes served as décor and furniture.

John stopped at his favorite café. It had a single display counter separating the kitchen from five tables. He chose the table farthest back, beside the display counter, then waited until Simon took his seat, before sitting down himself.

The owner, a former Turkish shot put champion, ambled over to take their orders. He had his white apron stretched tightly around his bulging waistline. Towering at nearly seven feet, the man had to dip his head as he passed beneath the brass chandelier in the center of the dining area. Then, with his chin pressed to his chest, his elbows hoisted slightly behind him and his hands flat on his belly, he stared warmly at John. In guttural tones, he joked how his wife had once threatened to become Catholic. Sensing his quip had not met its mark, he apologized for causing any displeasure and rattled off the day's specials.

Simon and John had both frequented the café in the past and therefore knew exactly what they felt like eating. Simon ordered an Adana kebab, while John chose the assorted meze with a carafe of house red.

John had not expected such a kindly reception. After his ordination, he had broken all ties with the city of his birth, thinking perhaps he would be an outcast amongst Antakya's predominantly Muslim residents. He thought his absence was due to the desire to avoid a general ridicule of his faith and vocation, but the criticism that cut most deeply was Simon's. As John's fiercest critic, Simon had bitterly disapproved of John's rejection of his ancestral religion, and for his part, John had not appreciated it. Harsh words had passed between them. John had stormed off, his final words fiercely cursing Simon's condemnation.

Simon now watched as John placed his Bible on the table before him. Eight years had passed since they had spoken. During that time, Simon had called John umpteen times, but their conflict remained unresolved. Wanting to avoid the role of antagonist, Simon waited for John to start the conversation.

'I did it for salvation, Simon,' John said. 'You know that, don't you? I've had a fascination with death for as long as I can remember. Life just seems so damn futile. What happens when we die? I can't begin to tell you how many times I've asked God that question. Nobody seems to know. You're a scientist, and even you don't have the answers. I couldn't accept that. I needed to know. I attended sermons up the road from here and I believed them. I believed they could help cleanse me, save my soul. That's why I gave it all up. It was my dream.' He sat motionless for a moment, before he concluded: 'Maybe I made a mistake.'

Simon frowned. 'What happened over there, John?'

John did not answer immediately, but sat with lips pressed tightly together. As Simon started to speak again, John lifted his hand towards him: 'Bear with me, please. I must get this off my chest.

'I collected books at the Penitentiary the other day. Our Maggiore wasn't there, so I slipped into his personal library. He has an amazing collection of rare books you can't find anywhere else—not even in the Vatican's main library. Anyway, I was up on the mezzanine when his office door opened. I heard voices. It was the Maggiore and His Eminence Cardinal Cardoni. They spoke softly. I could hardly make out what they were saying. When I heard them approaching the library, I lay on the floor. I didn't know what to do. I didn't have permission to be there. I hardly breathed. Fortunately, it was late and therefore dark. Then I heard something else: two clicks, the sound of metal tapping on metal—and then other, louder noises like something had fallen. Finally, I heard a rolling like metal wheels scraping against tracks, and the two cardinals were gone. I lifted my head and searched for them from my vantage point on the gallery above, but they had disappeared. I had no idea where they'd gone. I thought they might be right beneath me—under the mezzanine—so I didn't move. I must have waited ten minutes when, suddenly, they reappeared as if from nowhere. That's when I heard Eminence Cardoni say something that worries me; something about *a letter* that could get them into trouble and that they should destroy it. It wasn't clear what he meant by *us* and *we*, the two of them or the entire Church, but the Maggiore disagreed. As far as he was concerned, their secret was safe, and nobody would ever find out. And that's when he said something that shocked me even more. He said it was a "travesty" that he had striven his whole life to become pontiff, only to discover it had no meaning.'

The owner of the café returned with the wine. Filling their glasses, he stood back while they sampled it. Once they nodded their approval, he placed the carafe on the table.

John waited until the owner had returned to the kitchen before beginning again: 'Only one thing legitimizes His Holiness, Simon, and that is the Apostolic succession.' Agitated now, he combed his fingers through his cropped hair. 'That begs the question then of what legitimizes the Apostolic succession?'

Simon did not answer. He assumed an explanation was imminent.

'Actually, it's three things,' John stated emphatically. 'Three things are absolute requisites for our Holy Father to claim the Apostolic succession: the Jews rejecting Christ as their Messiah, Saint Peter founding Christianity in Antioch and his ministry's base in Rome. Those are *the* essentials of our faith, and if *any* of these is missing the pope has no bishopric power; in fact, there is no Church. It's that simple.'

John slumped.

'That's the problem, Simon,' he said, swiveling his glass with his index and middle fingers. 'Jesus appointed *only* Jews as His disciples, and they, in turn, reserved fellowship for other followers of the Levitical laws. The Catholic *sacred tradition* says Saint Peter received full authority and power under Heaven from Jesus and that, on appointing the second pope, Linus, he passed that authority to the gentile Church of Rome. But it turns out this isn't true!'

John pulled his Bible closer.

'Our scriptures offer enough circumstantial evidence that Peter did not convert gentiles in Antioch and that he was never in Rome. Meanwhile, Saint Paul's account states that "God shall judge the secrets of men by Jesus Christ according to *his* gospel."' He opened the Bible to *Galatians* 2 and rested his index finger beneath verses seven and eight. 'Here Paul insists the "gospel of circumcision" was Peter's responsibility, while the "gospel of the uncircumcised gentiles" was committed to himself.' Then, he quickly flipped to *Timothy*. 'And here Paul declares that *he* was the preacher, apostle and teacher of the gentiles. So, based on his own testimony, Paul alone preached to the Roman gentiles, and he also convinced the Romans that he was the only chosen apostle. His letter to them reveals how he "longed to see them so he could impart the gift of the spirit to them and establish a church there."' Turning to *Romans* fifteen, John now read verse twenty: '"I have strived not to preach the Gospel where Christ was named before, lest I should build upon another man's foundation."' Finally, frantically turning the pages again, this time to the *Book of*

Acts, John recited parts of the twenty-eighth chapter from memory: 'Acts denounces Peter's presence in Rome. Paul had to stand trial before Caesar. When he arrived, the *entire* Christian community went to meet him. The brethren of Rome heard of Paul and his entourage and came to meet them, yet Paul failed to mention Peter. These verses strongly suggest that our portrayal of history is incorrect, Simon. Not even the claim that Peter is buried beneath our basilica would suffice. Unless *physical* evidence exists to corroborate our claim—and I don't mean a few bone fragments which could belong to anyone—we must assume Peter was never *in* Rome.'

The owner arrived with their food and again awaited their approval before returning to the kitchen.

John bit into his meze and sat thoughtfully chewing for some time before reiterating his point: 'The implications if Saint Peter never went to Rome are huge. Not only is the Church's claim to the Apostolic succession false, placing all of Christendom under scrutiny, but even more crucial, it begs the question of Peter's actual location. If he wasn't in Rome, then where was he? I've been mulling over these specific Bible verses for years, but they are continuously dismissed through sophistry. This letter of the cardinals', on the other hand, I believe it holds the answer. In fact, I'm sure it does.'

Simon watched John eat. The lines framing his teal eyes harbored a great deal of pain. 'Just leave it, John,' he said. 'If you don't trust them, just walk away.'

John shook his head. 'I can't. This is just too important. I've got to know what they're hiding down there. I *need* to know. I won't forgive myself if I don't at least try to find out.'

'It's not worth getting into trouble over. Just come back here. Hell, you're already here, so you might as well stay.'

'It's not that difficult to get in, Simon. I know how their system works. Even the Penitentiary isn't a problem. It's where they disappeared to that's got me stumped.'

Simon pushed his plate aside. John's idea of breaking into the Vatican Penitentiary had upset him so much he had lost his appetite. 'I think you should reconsider. Why can't you just walk away?'

'I can't get it out of my head. I need to see it for myself. We all need to find our own truth, Simon. This is mine.'

'We all need to find our truth, John, sure, but this isn't exactly going on Hajj or walking the Via Dolorosa.'

'So what? Why is this any different?'

'Because, John, most people seek their truths meditating while burning incense, whacking wind chimes or, heck, paying thousands to attend special enlightenment retreats where they scorch their feet walking over hot coals. But most—I'd say ninety-nine-point-nine percent of human beings—don't seek God through theft and espionage. Not when it's just a matter of religion, anyhow.'

'What are you talking about?'

'Exactly what it sounds like. Grow up, John. There are no fucking answers. Religion is faith-based, meaning exactly that—you take it on faith or you don't. There are no facts, no tell-all interviews with God. You're searching for answers that don't exist.'

John sprang up. 'You don't give a shit, do you? Why can't you just stand by me for once?'

'John, sit down.'

'No, Simon. You're being ridiculous now. I'm a priest for God's sake! It's my duty to have faith—my *job*.

Millions of people have faith in the priesthood itself, and that might be wrong. But how can I walk away from that?'

'Come on, John. Let's talk this through.' When John drew money from his pocket to pay for his lunch, Simon pushed his hand away. 'Don't be silly, I'll pay. You're my guest.'

Simon would have loved to praise John that day; he had taken a stand for what he believed in, and that was admirable. But he could not be allowed to go through with his plan to break into this Penitentiary place.

Just as he had years earlier, John was storming off and, in his haste, had forgotten his Bible. Simon tossed several bills on the table and went after him, but when he reached the bazaar's main thoroughfare, John was gone.

As when John first left for Rome, Simon tried his phone repeatedly for days, but his calls went unanswered. Simon refused to let another eight years pass without speaking to John. He tried to contact him at the Vatican, tried to leave messages, and when that wound up fruitless, Simon also flew to Rome. That was a week ago. He had finally tracked John down one day as the priest exited the Porta Sant' Anna. To Simon's surprise, John had greeted him as if nothing had happened. With their failed meeting still etched in his memory, Simon had expected another hostile response. But just the opposite occurred. John had called a taxi, and they had driven to the Trevi district and had coffee at a café not far from the famed Fountain. This time, Simon gave John time to explain how he felt. It was then that Simon decided to help.

Over the next two days they had worked out a strategy to get into the Penitentiary. Simon would access the Vatican as a tourist, then once inside, he would change into one of

John's cassocks. John would then slip Simon into the Penitentiary before Father Franco arrived. Locating the cardinals' hiding place would take nearly half an hour, they estimated, and getting inside, another twenty minutes. In the end, Simon had accidentally leaned against the hearth and discovered it moved slightly under pressure. It took a while to figure out the mechanism. Then they had descended into the darkened vault. ...

*****

Simon sat up. He could not go there again. Every time he thought of John's death adrenalin flooded his body, nauseating him. His eyes rested on Jennifer to see if she was still all right. She was speaking with Giorgio and seemed relaxed. Her expression appeared more composed now. She returned his gaze with a smile, and he smiled back. Taking the Vatican on like that was audacious. But clearly, she had been acting impulsively, and had not had a clue what to do after she had broken into a restricted area. He had needed to get her to safety. Her crime was trivial compared to his; simple coincidence—and, therefore, association—had landed her in far worse trouble than she could guess.

Chapter 28

Inspector Verretti knew he should not be too cocky. He reminded himself that the Swiss Guard had been around for five hundred years and that getting rid of Schreider and his men would not be easy by anyone's measure. But Schreider's arrogance in racing past him on the station platform even now sent stomach acid surging up his throat. He shook two antacid tablets from the bottle he kept in his desk drawer and flicked them into his mouth. He chewed them a few times before washing the powdery mush down with gulps of water. He despised the colonel more than anyone.

Resting his palms on the desk, he stared down at the enlarged photographs. The sight of his quarry escaping turned his stomach again. How had they gotten away so easily? He shuffled the photographs in with his notes and, before leaving, scanned the desk one last time; he could not afford to forget anything. Turning to the door, he switched off the lights and marched to the conference room.

Lioni shot up first. Standing to attention, he ordered the taskforce to their feet.

'At ease, gentlemen,' Verretti ordered. Dropping the file on a nearby lectern, he waved the men to their seats. 'The Vatican's had a serious breach. At zero-seven-fifty-five a priest was killed at the Penitentiary—lights.'

The IT technician dimmed the fluorescent bulbs and called up an image on his iPad so it appeared on the screen behind Verretti.

'Father John Yilmaz,' Verretti said, turning towards the screen. 'The deceased worked as a filing clerk in the library.'

The men fell silent. They were hardened beat cops, but they were also avowed Catholics. A naked and mutilated priest on a mortuary table seemed too gruesome to contemplate, let alone look at.

Verretti paused until the next image appeared on the screen. It showed another priest, this one fleeing from the Penitentiary. 'Our suspect, gentlemen,' he said. 'His name is Simon. He circumvented our security checkpoints, broke into the Penitentiary and forced his way into a highly restricted vault. Once inside, he killed Father Yilmaz. He then stole an artefact of great age and value to the Church, overpowered one of our officers and, after causing a great deal of property damage during our ensuing pursuit of him, escaped using a Roman Metro rail grinder stolen twelve hours earlier—next.'

A close-up of their suspect's face appeared on the screen.

'Memorize this face, gentleman. It is the face of a suspected terrorist and murderer. A former special-forces, the man served in the Palestinian wars in the early two-thousands before studying genetics at the Hebrew University of Jerusalem and subsequently returning to his native Turkey. He currently works for the Turkish government on a top-secret project related to biblical era Antioch. The Vatican has been aware of his work for some time now.'

Verretti scanned the faces before him.

'His resume speaks for itself, gentlemen. Do not underestimate him. He is to be considered highly dangerous, so the next time you see him you have standing orders to engage.'

The next image appeared on the screen, this time a surveillance-camera of the same man now wearing a gendarme uniform.

'This is our suspect after he overpowered one of our men,' Verretti said.

'We heard he had an accomplice,' said one of the officers.

'Yes, American journalist, Miss Jennifer Jaine.' Verretti waited until the next slide appeared. 'Her appointment with His Eminence Cardoni this morning allowed us to trace her identity and origin; what we're unsure of is *how* she's involved in the aforementioned crimes. Her entry into the archival bunker occurred immediately after the murder and theft, so we believe she served as a decoy. Despite all we know, no information available on Miss Jaine as yet indicates any previous contact, direct or indirect, with our primary suspect.'

'*Che fiage*,' one of the men said.

Verretti's eyes locked on him. 'What was that, Officer?'

'I said she's sexy, Inspector.'

Verretti let the jest pass without remark and waited for the men's howling to subside before he continued: 'Born in Miami, she is the only child of an architect from Tampa and a psychologist from Santa Monica. Her father specialized in the renovation of historic buildings, while her mother cared for the mental wellbeing of the rich and famous of Hollywood. Soon after her sixteenth birthday, the mother was diagnosed with cancer. Despite surgery and chemotherapy, she succumbed. Struggling to accept the loss of his wife, Miss Jaine's father relocated to Key West.

'In the years that followed, Miss Jaine travelled and worked intermittently to support a carefree lifestyle before settling in Cape Town, South Africa. Living in Tamboerskloof below Table Mountain, she had visited nearby townships and gangland hotspots, becoming involved in social work. Witnessing the addictions, murder and rape which permeates South Africa's worst slums gave her insight into her true purpose in life.'

Verretti hesitated.

'Imagine that,' he said, scanning the ardent faces before him. 'Doing nothing makes you realize your calling.'

'Perhaps she was looking for a husband, Inspector,' one of the men called out.

He waited for the men to stop laughing, before he said, 'Jokes aside, gentlemen. She is no slouch. She had returned to the States to study religion at Miami University. From the outset, she had distinguished herself amongst her peers, winning scholarships and graduating *cum laude*. And, having completed her master's degree two years earlier, she had started working on her PhD.'

Verretti closed the file and looked up.

'I've given you what we know,' he said, scanning the faces before him. 'It's what we don't know that makes these two dangerous. Take our male suspect. As a current employee of one of our allies, he has no history of violent extremism nor any past associations with radical Muslim groups. While it is true that Antioch is near enough to Turkey's Syrian border to make it a major gateway for ISIS and Al Qaeda operatives seeking access to the West, nothing about the man would indicate he has anything but personal hatred for these groups. We therefore have no clue about his motives and are equally baffled as to how he knew about and gained access to the area where the stolen artefact was stored. Furthermore, we don't know how he and Miss Jaine coordinated before executing their plan or how the tools required for their successful escape were made available to them. Amongst the College of Cardinals, some have speculated that this level of planning and secrecy indicates their activities were an act of international espionage perpetrated by the American and Turkish governments, but again, no evidence of this has yet become available. What we do know is that he arrived in Rome on a flight from Antakya, Turkey, a week ago. That's biblical Antioch for those of you who haven't yet made the connection. Both suspects are currently returning to Turkey on the same plane, which brings me to my next point—the jet they're traveling on belongs to one Giorgio Castignani.'

One of the men raised his hand. 'Isn't that one of the Sicilian Mafiosi we arrested a while back?'

'Almost,' Verretti said. 'We arrested Giorgio Castignani Sr. along with almost four hundred others. This is that man's son.'

The officers suddenly became restless. The Mafioso's connections complicated things, as they were a handful even on good days. Not that any of the gendarmes were scared, per se, but they did prefer not to take on the Mafia.

Verretti returned his notes to their folder. 'So, this is the situation, gentlemen,' he said, making eye contact with each officer in turn. 'We're about to go undercover in a Muslim country and national ally without prior clearance from that nation's government. In other words, we're going to be pursuing two foreign nationals in a place we shouldn't be setting foot in. Our entry could spark a major international incident if uncovered. Moreover, we will be surrounded by people who hate, not only our guts, but our faith as well. It's also a time when the Turkish population has been infiltrated by extremists who would give anything to see our bloodied heads roll down a dusty road. Under no circumstances will we draw attention to ourselves, *capite*?'

'Is this why we're going and not the Swiss?' one officer asked.

'Enough! Our mission is top priority. There'll be no goofing around. Is that clear?'

Another man put up his hand. 'Dead or alive, Inspector?'

Verretti reflected beneath knitted brows. 'Our mission is to retrieve the artefact,' he said at last. 'Secondary to that, we are to bring back the perpetrators alive, but frankly, gentlemen, I don't care if you bring them in as *lola* in an ice chest. They killed a priest. They also embarrassed the hell out of me and they beat the crap out of one of your officers. One way or other, we'll make sure they pay—dismissed.'

The lights came on again, and Lioni stood up first to call the men to attention. Then the officers filed out of the meeting room, evincing a sense of purpose but no less boyish and slovenly in their behavior despite that.

When the last had left Lioni followed, and Verretti met him at the door. 'Weapons will be supplied on the other side,' the inspector said. 'And one last thing—make sure they all bring their passports.'

*****

Verretti removed his shirt and lifted his arm. The pungent smell of hormone-charged sweat wafted into his nose. Dealing with this much peril had made him discharge vast quantities of adrenaline and testosterone. He loathed the smell. It reminded him of kelp drying in the sun.

He stepped under the shower, standing still awhile to let the water cool his body. Ambition was a crucial part of who he was. He had gotten that from his father. 'Before leaving,' he thought, 'I should give the old man a call.' He would tell his father about his important mission; get his input. His dad's opinion meant a lot to them both. For his father, it was a way of connecting with his son. For himself, it was a way of gaining perspective on his work.

Moreover, victory would bring yet another laurel—and respect—for the Verretti clan. And it would also help him move one step closer to creating and leading a unified police force. A successful mission would give him the power to approach the Italian and Vatican authorities. He could not wait to see Schreider's face when he returned with both suspects shackled and the artefact recovered and intact.

He closed the tap and stepped out of the shower. Wiping himself with a clean towel he walked to his dressing room, where posing naked before a full-length mirror, he patted aftershave on his face. This done, he ran his fingers over the shoulders of his jackets. He had at least twenty, all tailored just for him, hanging equally spaced and aligned like a row of cadets at attention. 'Quality maketh the man,' he thought proudly. Color combinations, balanced designs and expensive shoes were all as essential as the impeccable presence they helped to create. But the shoes were especially important. More so than his clothes, they expressed who he was. Cheap shoes spoiled an entire outfit. They also drove women away. He had overheard countless conversations between women nit-picking men for their tacky shoes. He would rather buy less and focus on quality. He was fond of Etro when it came to shirts, jackets and coats, and he liked Armani for his suits; the elegance of their designs was, after all, unrivalled.

That afternoon, though, he based his decision on practicality. They would certainly be operating in the mountains and at night, making a turtleneck essential. And they would need to blend in as civilians, so he chose a leather-shearling jacket. Methodically and deliberately, he donned the clothes, inhaling the fresh scents of dry-cleaning fluid and saddle soap. Then still without trousers or pants, he stepped back and examined himself in the mirror. Both were a perfect fit.

*****

Verretti had Lioni pick him up outside the barracks. On their way to the helipad, he kept the Lamborghini's window down. Rays of sunlight intermittently burst through the trees. On hearing the helicopter's engines warming up, Verretti recognized the Puma. Like sports cars, helicopters had distinctive sounds. He could identify any sports car driving past the barracks at night from the sound of its engine. The Puma, though, was one helicopter he did not like. In wars, they typically served as frontline-troop carriers and ambulances. If you were in a Puma, then, you were either headed into the meat grinder or headed out mangled. Not that he was superstitious or anything, but he hoped it was not an omen of things to come.

From a distance and in gaps between passing trees, Verretti noticed the logo on the side of the Puma. Surprisingly it was that of the Order of Saint John. Earlier he had wondered who had volunteered to fly them to the airport. He had already ordered a Vito minibus, when a call had informed him of a helicopter, which was on its way to pick them up. With no time to ponder the Order of Malta's involvement, he pointed Lioni to the edge of the helipad.

The team arrived just as Verretti was passing beneath the Puma's rotating blades. Lioni waited for the men to collect their backpacks from their BMW X5s. As the last two locked up, he ordered them to fall in before him. Now dressed in civilian garb, the men stepped into two perfect lines of four.

The adjutant gave last-minute instructions before concluding that the final briefing would take place on route. Any questions from there on out had better relate to the mission ahead.

'Now stop acting like a military unit,' he shouted over the hissing engines and swooping rotor blades. 'From now on you are civilians.'

Two of the men sprang in the back of the Puma. After stacking the backpacks in the tail, the men all hopped in and took up positions in the fuselage.

Verretti waited for Lioni to give a 'thumbs up' before instructing the pilot to take off.

'Use the helmet, Inspector,' the pilot called out.

Verretti flipped the helmet on his head and secured the chinstrap, before positioning the mic in front of his mouth. He glanced over to the pilot. 'How long to Ciampino?'

The pilot synchronized the controls for lift-off. 'I have orders to get you there ASAP, Inspector. So, give or take a minute, we'll be there in ten.'

Chapter 29

Giorgio watched Jennifer gulp down her water. When she had finished the first bottle, he had Martina fetch her another. After refilling her glass, he pushed the snacks towards her, insisting she should help herself.

Jennifer knew she should eat something. In her haste to reach the Vatican Library that morning she had skipped breakfast. She spread butter on a cracker and stacked two slices of cheese on top. Seconds after her first bite, she realized just how ravenous she was. She layered her next cracker with slices of salmon and *chevre*.

Giorgio watched her gobble down one snack after another. 'You are safe now,' he said in a gentle tone.

Jennifer wanted to agree with him—she truly did—but the fact was she was trusting him merely out of necessity.

'You drive well,' she said, before licking caviar from the tips of her fingers.

Like a child remembering his favorite theme-park ride, Giorgio lit up: 'I'm an expert driver. I've done the Dakar Rally, twice.'

'You're not really a cab driver then,' Jennifer said wryly, indicating the luxurious interior around them.

Giorgio plucked an olive from the crystal bowl, flicked it into his mouth and chewed a few times. 'Ah,' he said, extricating the pit and placing it neatly to one side of the plate. 'So, you're wondering how a humble cabby can afford a Maserati, I see.'

'And a Lear.'

'And a Lear, yes.'

He snatched up two more olives as if they were captured chess pieces and flicked them one at a time into his mouth. Then, he picked up a third and held it between his fingertips. 'These olives are my own little cherubs,' he said. 'Many people think olives come from Greece, but we Italians, we have the best olives in the world. There are over two-hundred-and-forty-thousand olive farms and about fifty million trees just in Puglia alone. These are my Sicilian olives. They are for eating rather than for oil. In Italian, we call it "*da tavola*". We pick them when they are young and green and cure them until they are nice and dark violet or black, like these. After that, we preserve them in brine. That's how they survive the long voyage to America and appear on your pizzas.'

Jennifer could imagine people underestimating Giorgio. He was not tall. Neither did he cut much of a figure with his informal attire. Yet everything he owned was the best money could buy; even the tacky, creased Hawaiian shirt he had put on since they had boarded the plane was a Saint Laurent. Beneath his simplicity, informality and apparent boorishness, then, Giorgio was a very smart, and very rich, man.

'That still doesn't answer my question though,' she said, deciding she would test his acumen.

'Oh, you mean my toys? Ha! You *are* very persistent, Miss Jaine. Well, let's just say I was born with the proverbial "silver spoon". But I do work hard, too. My car is transport between the airport and my house in Rome. The Lear I bought a few years ago to fly American produce buyers to my farms in Sicily and to fly family around occasionally. All my family members are technically shareholders—so that takes care of the taxman—but they also love visiting the farms, so I take them there every holiday. Of course, my family's pretty big, and we don't have to tell the taxman my cousins Simon and Jennifer were adopted, now do we?'

Giorgio's levity relaxed the fear-induced spasm in Jennifer's neck, making her sink into the chair. Her lungs inhaled easily and she noticed that her diaphragm was relaxed. She listened as Giorgio related how, in the early 1980s, magistrates Falcone and Borsellino had tried four-hundred-and-seventy-four Mafiosi, and how his father had been one of the three hundred and forty-two convicted. He had adored his father, irrespective of the bad things he had done, and although his dad had been a criminal, he had only overseen the syndicate's betting schemes; otherwise, he had been a goodhearted man.

After his father passed, Giorgio's mother had driven him to the bank, opened an account in his name and transferred funds. Before returning home, she had led him inside the bank's vault, where she showed him a safety box containing bonds and precious stones worth millions. The Vatican Bank had received them with open arms.

Giorgio was the youngest of four children. His eldest brother had lived and died by the gun. His second brother, who lived in Sicily, had, sadly, fallen prey to alcohol and drugs, and now lived on one of Giorgio's farms. His twin sister had married a Sicilian and had two children a little older than his own.

'And your mother?'

Giorgio smiled. 'Ah, *la mia mamma.* She lives with me and my wife and helps with the kids and the cooking.'

'How many children do you have?'

'Four: two boys, two girls. A fifth is on his way. We already know it's another boy. We Sicilians—well, *amiamo le famiglie numerose.*'

It must have been difficult for Giorgio to be the son of a convicted Mafioso, especially during his childhood. She could only imagine the ridicule he must have endured.

'So now for my last question …'

'Oh, shush, Miss Jaine. You ask more questions than my attorney. Why don't you tell me about *you* instead?'

Jennifer's face turned quizzical, almost impertinent. 'Well, I would, but there's not much to tell.'

He scrutinized her through narrowed eyes. Her insistence in diverting attention from herself meant she still did not trust him. Eventually, he leaned forward conspiratorially and said, 'You're wondering why a Catholic like me is helping a man like Simon, yes?'

She blushed a deep rose-pink. 'Yes—I mean; it is unusual to say the least.'

Giorgio's mood changed suddenly to absolute seriousness. 'I owe him, Jennifer,' he said. 'He saved my life once.'

He looked over his shoulder to see if Simon was listening, but his friend had his eyes closed. Still, he continued in a whisper: 'I was skiing in the Alps, and like a complete newbie, I was there alone. But where I went wrong is when I miscalculated a ten-meter drop and clipped a rock on my way down. My leg was broken in three places, with the bone pushing through my leg right here. You have no idea of the pain, the blood! Worst of all, though, was that in all that snow my body temperature dropped just as shock was setting in. I thought I was going to die right there, and I probably would've if Simon hadn't seen me from a nearby slope. The guy's absolutely nuts. He used branches and strips of his own shirt to brace my leg. Then, he carried me down the mountain to a place flat enough for a helicopter to drop a basket. I was barely conscious when the rescuers arrived, so I didn't realize it at the time, but Simon was only wearing long-sleeved vest and trousers. It took the rescuers longer to save him from near hypothermia than it did to reset my leg. Believe me, Jennifer, that guy will never let you down.'

Jennifer's eyes grew cold. 'He killed a priest.'

Giorgio sat with intertwined fingers, his elbows pressed into the armrests. He pushed his palms together until knots of tension shone through his knuckles. Before he answered, he reflected on her accusation. He decided she was being straightforward, not malicious, and said softly, 'You couldn't be more wrong, Miss Jaine. John came to see Simon a while back. He wanted his help breaking into the Penitentiary. He'd heard about a hidden artefact that casts a shadow on Catholicism. His obsession with it became so overwhelming that he couldn't refrain from going after it. I don't know if it was guilt or stupidity that made Simon go, but in the end, he joined him. That's why he was there today, to help John. He couldn't bear to see his little brother go it alone.'

A shocking numbness coursed through Jennifer's body. She could not believe what she had just heard. She shifted her gaze to Simon who was still sitting on the sofa with his head reclined against the backrest. He seemed to have lost track of the world around him.

'I'm so sorry.'

'Don't tell me. He's the one accused of his brother's murder.'

'I didn't know.'

'How could you?' Giorgio sat up. 'Their parents died when they were both young. Simon was tiny; John had just been born. Their grandmother raised them until they left school.'

With so much to digest, Jennifer's mind drifted. When Simon told her that a priest had been killed, she had immediately assumed he had had a hand in it. What else could she have thought? Even if he had denied it, she would not have believed him.

She snapped out of her reverie, when Giorgio mentioned a name. 'Professor Rabin from Jerusalem?'

'He's waiting at the airport. Are you familiar with his work?'

Professor Uri Rabin? Perhaps the better question would be: who in her field had not heard of him? Rabin had assumed the Israel Antiquity Authority's directorship in 1967, soon after the Six Days War, and now managed all five of the IAA's departments. His knowledge of Judaism and Christianity was unrivalled, and the decades he had spent overseeing digs on some of the world's richest archaeological treasure troves had placed him at the apex of his profession. Moreover, he was one of the elite few both fluent and literate in ancient Hebrew, Aramaic and Greek.

'Yes,' Jennifer replied at last. 'I'm familiar. In fact, we've met—in New York.'

When the pilot announced their passing Tarsus on their left, Giorgio excused himself. 'I have to go now,' he said, hoisting himself from the chair. 'It's time for our descent.'

Martina started clearing the table, but Jennifer stopped her. 'I'll do that. I've often thought of becoming a flight attendant. Besides, I have to stretch my legs a bit.'

Giorgio's exit had left Jennifer with a sense of loss. Maybe it was a result of the stress of their escape and the chase, but in the short time they have spoken she felt she had become closer to him than she was to her own friends back home. Moments like these were rare; in fact, they were non-existent. Never had she found herself becoming best friends with someone in a matter of hours. It was as if they had known each other all their lives.

With so much to digest, she became manic. As she helped stack the glasses and plates in the basins, her hands trembled slightly. She lowered her head and closed her eyes. How could she have landed in so much trouble? She was mulling over this question when she felt a presence behind her. Her body stiffened when a hand touched hers. She had felt that touch before, but this time it was different. This time it was gentle.

Simon drew her round. 'We're about to land. Come.'

She looked up at him. 'I'm sorry. I didn't know.' She hoped he understood.

'You have to take your seat.'

As Simon sat down opposite her, she looked out of the window. She could not now meet his gaze. She felt terrible. For the first time since they had met, her thoughts were focusing on him. She had been so wrong about him. Until a few minutes ago, she had thought he was a killer. But he was the slain priest's brother—and her savior. She forced herself to look at him, her eyes softening into a subtle smile. She yearned to apologize, but she found it impossible to speak. She looked down at his hand, which rested on the side of the table between them. She thought of slipping her hand under his curled-up fingers. She wanted to comfort him and for him to reciprocate, to squeeze her hand lightly and forgive her for her presumptions. Inwardly, though, she ridiculed herself. The stress of this horrendous day was obviously playing on her hormones. She looked up and noticed that something troubling had darkened his eyes.

'What are you thinking?' she asked.

'I have to go back tomorrow.'

'What? Why?'

'I have to bring John back.'

'But you can't, Simon. It's suicide.'

'I'll make them a deal.'

'The letter?'

He nodded. 'First I have to make sure you're safe though.'

His concern was thrilling, but she knew she would be okay. 'I can look after myself from here.'

He shook his head slowly. 'No, they'll come after you.'

'Simon, don't say that! Not in Turkey. They'd have to go get an okay from the Turkish government to extradite me, and that would mean revealing their secret.'

She said this with absolute conviction, but then reminded herself of the crusades: how Pope Clement had convinced the faithful to wrest Palestine's Christian sanctums from the hands of the Mohammedans; how thousands had affixed the cross to their garments and taken up arms; and the eight crusades in which the faithful had wantonly murdered and even cannibalized Muslims. Things had not changed much in a millennium, she realized. People still killed to defend their faith, even when that faith ironically, preached peace and nonviolence.

'Giorgio said Professor Rabin is meeting us in Turkey. He knows me. He'll get me back to the States. I can catch a flight from Antakya.' She waited for a response. When none was forthcoming her eyes grew wide. 'I can, can't I?'

Chapter 30

Simon's watch said it was nearly three o'clock. To account for the Rome-Antakya time difference, he set it an hour ahead. As he fastened his seatbelt for landing, he decided they would have to divert their flight to Ben Gurion International in Tel Aviv instead. Not only did Israeli airports provide tighter security, they also offered direct flights to the United States. Still, they would have to refuel. Their quick stopover at Havaalani Airport would give him a chance to meet with Professor Rabin. Knowing his old undergraduate tutor, Uri would already be waiting in the arrivals hall, bookishly studying photocopies of something no one could read in two thousand years.

The approach from the Latakia Basin at the northeast corner of the Mediterranean gave Jennifer a perfect view of Antakya to their right. Between scattered clouds, mountains surrounded the city like cupped hands. Further north, shadows crept lazily across the landing strip. A momentary glance and she knew exactly why there were no direct flights between the airport and the States. Despite apparent renovations, a humble terminal ostensibly last upgraded in the seventies could certainly not offer the kind of security needed for transatlantic flights, though Jennifer suspected this lack of security would be advantageous to concealing their movements.

As the Lear rolled towards the terminal, Jennifer's nausea returned. Simon's asking her to wait on the plane while he met with Rabin did not help matters either. When he got up to leave, she decided she was not staying. Despite Giorgio's reassurances, she was not going to just sit there while they refueled the jet. As far as she knew, that was the most vulnerable time to be on board. She saw her chance when Giorgio's pilot opened the cabin door to lower the steps. Simon had barely retrieved the silver casket from the overhead compartment when she skirted past him. She hit the tarmac at a pace and powerwalked towards the terminal, counting on Simon's reluctance to cause a scene. She did not stop until she was inside customs, and Simon only caught up with her as she stood showing an official her passport. She prayed Simon's assurance that she could get a temporary visa was true. Please let her not be arrested for illegal entry.

Surprisingly, though, entry into Turkey was the smoothest check-in she had ever experienced. Not that she had travelled much, but the Turks were polite and helpful. Twenty minutes later, and with Simon beside her, she entered the arrival terminus. The knots in her neck softened, for there, just several feet away and staring around blankly was Professor Rabin. He was just as she remembered him: his greying nest of curls as rampant as Einstein's on a bad-hair day and his salient forehead and lynx-like gaze still hinting at the genius that had made him one of the world's foremost authorities on biblical history. He must have come straight from an archaeology site, as his short-sleeved cotton t-shirt, baggy khakis and brown penny loafers were all worn and caked with mud, making him look as if he were wearing a sundried buffalo carcass; indeed, his appearance was the complete antithesis of the dapper figure he had cut wearing the tweed jacket and tie for the seminar he had given two years earlier. He spotted her coming towards him, bemusement written all over his face.

After embracing Simon with compassionate warmth and whispering condolences, Rabin stepped back. Discussing John's death was not appropriate here. He turned to Jennifer, extending his hand.

'Miss Jaine,' he said smiling. 'I take it you've resolved the matter you were struggling with?'

'Please, call me Jennifer, Professor,' she said, shaking his hand. 'And no, I haven't. In fact, you've made my life hell—but only indirectly.'

'You read the book then?'

'And others,' she said, her eyes absorbing his. 'But I'm not sure I know what to make of it yet.'

'Faith cannot stand on bias alone—you of all people should know that. Anyone studying religion must also consider opposing views. In any case, the stuff in the book was nothing new, unless by *new* you mean *centuries-old*.'

Simon looked on perplexed. What his old mentor had done to Jennifer was not clear, but then, she was one of the most dogged people he had ever met.

Jennifer, meanwhile, did not expect Rabin to recognize her. He taught scores of students every year, and she had only taken one of the seminars he gave as a visiting fellow. Her meeting with him had lasted only an hour, and she assumed it impacted on her life far more than it did his. The seminar had been at the Waldorf Astoria in New York. She had approached him in the hotel lounge afterwards, as he sat sipping a gin and tonic and speaking with an older couple. She had waited until he had finished before introducing herself. Then, she had asked him about his comments on faith, and he had cut her short. His back was killing him, and his stomach was starting to dissolve itself he was so hungry.

Jennifer recalled Rabin inviting her to join him for dinner, adding that he considered the prime angus steaks there amongst the best in the world. She and Rabin hardly placed their orders when Jennifer began voicing her frustration: 'How can one not believe, Professor? Life without faith is impossible.'

'Oh, *faith*—dear, dear *faith*,' he said sardonically. 'Faith is the measure of one's ignorance. That's all. And it certainly is no substitute for reason.'

'But I and many others might find that offensive. Faith comes from the heart. It is the essence of being. It is our way of connecting with God. Without it, souls are lost. It takes faith to receive Christ and let His blood cleanse our sins. It takes faith to know we will one day stand before God and be judged for the lives we have lived. It takes faith to know we'll go to Heaven.'

Rabin ignored this as if Jennifer had not spoken at all and proceeded to talk about fishing. Fishing allowed him escape from life. His least memorable trip had taken place in Key West, where he had gone to fly fish for Atlantic tarpon, a protected species. The prehistoric fish could grow to be more than six feet and weigh in at around two-hundred-and-eighty pounds. Its strength, stamina and leaping ability made it one of Florida's premier game fish. Not knowing which tour operator to hire from the slew of brochures he had picked up at the hotel, he had booked his trip with the most highly recommended company and was looking forward to setting out the next morning.

Up at dawn, Rabin had met the skipper at a nearby jetty. The guy was a youngster, no more than twenty-five, sporting a bronze tan, with hair that curled down to the small of his back and arms lavishly decorated with tattoos. The boat, an eighteen-foot Beavertail with a one-hundred-and-twenty-five horsepower Yamaha engine, had propelled them across the Gulf's silver-blue waters beneath a red and amber sky. The skipper had chased the horizon for quite a while before stopping, and the coastline had completely disappeared. That was when Rabin had become suspicious. Tarpon did not live in deeper water; they roamed the shallows of brackish estuaries and coastline reefs. Adding insult to injury, the skipper had pulled out a drop-shot rod with a spinning reel. Rabin had protested that he specifically requested a tarpon trip with fly tackle, but the kid only responded that it was now too late to change, for, by the time they reached land again, the time Rabin had paid for would be over. In the end, Rabin had spent a frustrating three hours casting with a rod he had not planned to touch that day.

Later that evening, hoping to put the day's disappointment behind him, Rabin had taken his wife to the hotel pier for sundowners. They had watched the last of the sun's golden rays transmute into pastel, lavender and rose, before vanishing into the seemingly endless Gulf. Before retiring to their room, they had strolled along the jetty. Standing on the edge, he had read the name of a moored yacht. It was then that he had seen something he wished he had not: in the glow of the jetty's floodlights he could make out the swishing bodies and tails of a school of tarpon gliding lazily through the ultramarine waters. Instead of wasting time and money on the incompetent character who had taken him out that day, he could have simply cast his line right beside the hotel.

When Jennifer eventually attempted to steer the conversation back to faith, Rabin called it a night. She was stunned. She saw it as a lost opportunity to gain insight into the question which nagged at her. He paid the bill, walked her to the street and called her a cab. Closing the door, he told her to read Thomas Paine's *The Age of Reason*. She knew the book formed part of her curriculum, but through some lapse of her own, she had not read it yet.

Realizing Rabin would not recommend a two-hundred-year-old book he did not think significant, she decided to get a copy. When she unsuccessfully tried to buy it from her local bookstore, she thought of getting it from the library or ordering a copy online. Something must have come up, because she never got around to it. To her surprise though, a second-hand copy arrived via UPS. It was admittedly slightly creepy that a professor was interested enough to find out where she lived, but his note in the jacket allayed any fears she might have that he was stalking her. He sent her his personal copy; all he asked was that she read and took good care of it.

Paine's work impacted Jennifer's life greatly—perhaps even more so than the Bible itself. And despite her syllabus over the course of her studies including opposing views to Christianity, nothing hit home as much as Paine's words. Her years of trying to establish the authenticity of the Bible as a truthful record of the past, had been in vain. Apart from demonstrating the impossibility of her quest, Paine led her towards a mode of reasoned belief. His way of showing how the Bible exposed itself as myth seemed ominous, yet brilliant. His clarity and commonsense approach gave his ideas a simplicity unrivalled by the theologians of his time. But in a world where religion reigned supreme and Rationalism was still in its infancy, his words had fallen only on the ears of a few freethinkers. His attack on the religious establishment had made him so unpopular that only six people attended his funeral.

No longer could Jennifer live in denial; she simply had to know more. It was one thing reading about the insights of great thinkers, another to experience them yourself. But she internalized Paine's ideas in a moment of illumination and experienced the enlightenment of rational thought. John Cottingham's work on reason as the chief source and test of knowledge followed. Not that she agreed with everything, but she was on a new course. Rabin introducing her to these works broadened her mind—and she quit pursuing her PhD. She gave up on her dissertation: *The Authenticity of the Holy Bible.* Through people like Paine, Cottingham and Professor Rabin, she learned that neither faith nor reason could authenticate the Bible; even if it were authentic, it was not *authentifiable*.

It only dawned on Jennifer months later that Professor Rabin's fishing story had been an allegorical answer to her question: rather than check the charter company's bona fide, he had taken its operators' integrity for granted, and therein lay the lesson on faith—a person could not entrust his or her spiritual fate to blind belief. The irony, though, was that neither man nor institution could guarantee spiritual salvation.

*****

Simon passed Rabin the silver casket. 'We're not coming with you, Uri.'

'Is there a problem, Shi'mon?'

'I'm taking Jennifer to Tel Aviv. She'll be safer there.'

Rabin nodded. 'She can also take a direct flight.'

'We should get going, then.'

Simon shook Rabin's hand. He turned to leave but stopped, for not far off he saw Giorgio approaching from customs. From the deep frown creasing his friend's forehead, it was obvious that something was wrong.

Giorgio and Rabin needed no introduction. They had met a few days before when Giorgio fetched Simon. He greeted the professor briefly, then led Simon to a less crowded corner of the terminus.

'The gendarmes have just left Rome,' Giorgio said. 'I'm told they know we've landed here and are on their way.'

'How long still to refuel?'

Giorgio shrugged. 'I'm not sure. An hour, maybe. The guys here are very slow.'

Simon looked at the flight schedules across the hall. The only flight out of Turkey left around eight, which meant Jennifer's departure would coincide with the gendarmes' arrival. He checked his watch. It was nearly half past four, Turkish time. He was still searching for an alternative when something caught his eye. The airport bookshop stood right below the flight-schedule board. Predictably, a woman was paying for a book at the register, and a man was riffling through magazines on one of the racks, but this was normal.

What was disturbing, though, was the clerk he had just seen disappear into a back office.

Simon had not considered any alternative plans, but his instincts told him to get the hell out of there. Their best bet was Adana, a two-hour drive north, where international flights departed all night. He and Rabin had flown internationally from there before, and it was a safe bet they would have an evening departure to Tel Aviv.

'We're driving,' Simon said. 'Giorgio, you and your staff are coming with us.'

'Nono, Simon,' Giorgio objected. 'You have enough to worry about. I'm going to see if I can refuel in time. If not, I'll take my people to Harbiye south of the city. I have distant family living there. Or I'll find us a bed and breakfast to stay overnight.'

Reluctantly, Simon shook Giorgio's hand. He would have liked to convince Giorgio otherwise, but he knew his friend's autonomy enabled him to look after himself and his staff. 'Thank you for bringing us this far, *mio amico*. If we're still here tomorrow, I'll go back with you. If not, see you in Rome.'

Simon did not wait for Giorgio to respond, but taking Jennifer's hand, proceeded towards the pickup zone outside.

'*Ciao*,' Giorgio greeted, waving. 'Take good care of her.'

Seeing Giorgio watching them leave, saddened Jennifer. Without him she and Simon would have probably been caught by the gendarmes by now. It was uncanny how quickly they had connected. Her decision not to run from Simon had been a direct result of the information he had shared with her.

Rabin took the lead and crossed the street to the parking lot in the far corner of the airport. With early summer temperatures hovering around eighty, he had parked his Range Rover under the only tree he could find. He disarmed the central locking system as the three of them crossed the tarmac.

'You drive,' he said, throwing Simon the keys.

Simon held open the front passenger-side door for Jennifer. This time, she got in.

Chapter 31

Simon set off keeping one eye on the rear-view mirror. He could have sworn he had recognized the person who ducked out of sight in the airport bookstore. It was the Capuchin monk named Brian Malone. Discalced and heavily bearded, Malone belonged to the Order of Friars Minor Capuchin. The order originated in 1520 when Observant Franciscan friar Matteo da Bascio sought to return to a simple life of solitude and penance as practiced by Saint Francis of Assisi.

Simon was sure he had seen Malone scurry into the back office of the bookstore. The monk's brown tunic and pointed hood was so distinctive Simon would have recognized it anywhere. Since becoming Antakya's resident priest the year before, Malone had shown great interest in the Antioch dig. Simon recalled meeting the friar soon after excavation started at the site. Simon had just left the council building when the fifty-five-year-old monk, lingering outside, had stepped up and introduced himself. Malone's persistent questioning had struck Simon as intrusive, but he assumed the clergyman would be naturally curious about excavations so close to the Cave Church of Saint Peter. He had presumed Malone's interest was genuine, but the monk's presence at the airport now made Simon think the Vatican had used him all along to monitor their progress.

Of course, perhaps Simon was being paranoid, but considering the circumstances, he could not afford ignoring Malone's presence. He had to accept the monk would compromise their escape to Adana. Anyhow, his being there at the airport—if it was him—was suspiciously well-timed. Malone tailing them meant he was feeding information to the Vatican. As Simon checked his rear-view again, he hoped, perversely perhaps, to see the friar's old beat-up Caravelle behind them. Knowing where he was seemed preferable to wondering.

Jennifer stared out of her window, blinking at the glare. Driving along the two-lane highway reminded her of Florida's interstates, except it lacked the lush, green vegetation of her home state; indeed, the harsh, desiccated landscape had an unnatural rawness to it. By the side of the road, a dust devil whirled over a vineyard. In the shade, hives of bees bustled, their legs laden with sacs of pollen. Up the valley, industrial sprinklers shot short bursts of water over the rolling citrus plantations at regular intervals, and in the distance, she could see workers tending cotton fields.

When they neared the outskirts of Antakya, the rush-hour had picked up. Simon turned left at a sign saying Türkmen Bashi Cd and accelerated towards the Hacilar exit half a kilometer up the road. He crossed the Orontes River at the second of seven bridges. With the Starius and Habib Neccar mountains now serving as a backdrop the view from Jennifer's window seemed dreamlike. Minarets rose above randomly spaced, two- and three-story Ottoman-era buildings, and she could hear the recorded voice of a *muezzin* ululating the *ezan* over loudspeakers miles away.

By the time Simon turned left onto the Reyhanli Yolu, she had momentarily lost her sense of direction. Only when he turned towards the mountain again and she read *Senpiyer* on the street corner post did she realize where they were going. The roar of the Range Rover's engine deepened as it accelerated up the curved road beneath Mount Starius. At the summit, a hundred-meter sandstone cliff loomed like a sentry. Scattered along its rocky face, eerie nooks marked the entrances to hundreds of ancient hermitages. The sandstone facade atop the plateau's jutting terrace made Jennifer sit up.

'*Senpiyer Kilisesi*,' she whispered. Then, as if awaking from a deep sleep: 'This is the Cave Church of Saint Peter! I'm right, aren't I.'

Simon's eyes scanned the parking area for somewhere to make a U-turn. 'Now if only it had a two-hundred-meter carpark in front of it like that tacky thing in Rome.'

She found his sarcasm amusing, but rather than laugh, she noticed the quickening of her heartbeat. Vatican tradition taught the Cave Church of Saint Peter marked the place where the Apostle Peter had first ministered to the gentiles. As someone who had studied religion most of her life, she had long had the church on her must-see list.

'You work here?'

'That I do.'

'That's not what I meant.'

The casket tucked firmly under his arm, Rabin got out of the Range Rover. He stopped as he passed Jennifer's window.

'Our site is *on* the plateau higher up,' he said.

'On?' She leaned her head out the open window for a better view of the mountain. 'What's up there?'

'We're excavating skeletal remains buried in ossuaries, which were found in a hidden catacomb. We wouldn't even have known they were here if a janitor at Mustafa Kemal University hadn't got it into his head to borrow a ground-penetrating radar to look for artefacts up top. Just like in Israel, it's usually the amateurs who make the biggest finds, but in this case, someone noticed their lab equipment was missing, and here we are.'

'No offence, Professor, but why are *you* here?'

Rabin understood her question perfectly. He was a Jew exhuming bodies in a Muslim country, while just across the Syrian border, an hour's drive away, radical Muslims were persecuting people for nothing more than not being Muslim. 'Initially the government thought the catacombs were Muslim and wouldn't let anyone in, but when a Star of David was found etched into one of the ossuaries, they contacted the IAA. As for the rest of it, I'm an Israeli. They've been trying to kill us since I can remember. You get used to it.'

'How old are the graves?'

'Anywhere from two thousand to about fifteen hundred years.'

His casualness was nauseating. The existence of two-thousand-year-old Jewish graves in biblical Antioch was extraordinary; the entire world needed to know about it. 'That makes them the original Jews who fled Saul's persecution, right?'

'Maybe, but probably not. If you remember correctly, Jews also lived throughout the Eastern Roman Empire after Titus sacked Jerusalem.'

'Sorry to interrupt, Uri, but we've got to get moving.' Simon leaned across Jennifer's lap to greet his colleague. 'Best of luck, and call if you find anything.'

But Jennifer could not leave yet. She was a few hundred yards from where important work was underway, work nobody knew about, and considering the gendarmes were still after them, this could very well be her one and only chance to see the site. She was sure if the Vatican did catch her and Simon it would mean death, and whether they were caught in Turkey or Israel, would not matter much at that point. At least if she saw the dig, she could die feeling she had not been totally robbed.

She opened her door as Simon was already pulling out. 'Wait,' she called out. 'I'm coming with you, Professor.'

Simon reached out to stop her, but she had already fled the Range Rover. 'We have to go, Jennifer,' he shouted.

'I'm not leaving. There's too much at stake. …'

Simon jumped out of the idling vehicle. Standing in the middle of the road, he shouted after her: '"Too much at stake?" Damn it, listen to yourself. You sound like some trite character from American television. What's at stake, Jennifer. Really, what's at stake?! You sound like a goddamned child! You, me, Uri—we can all come back here once our current situation's sorted, but until then you're just going to get us all killed with this idiot, nonsense urgency of yours!'

Jennifer stopped. Turning back, she stared at him. 'Seriously, Simon? I wouldn't even be in this mess if you hadn't "rescued" me. What did you rescue me from, jail? Great. So, I'd call the embassy and get an attorney. Now, however, I've got people shooting at me for something I had nothing to do with. I mean, seriously, Simon, go fuck yourself. If I'm going to get shot—which I probably am because of you—I at least want to check one thing off my bucket list, and since we're nowhere near the fucking pyramids, this is going to have to do.'

Simon had switched the Range Rover off and was getting out to chase after her. If she was going to see the archaeology site, she was going to have to run.

Jennifer darted towards the narrow path snaking up the side of the cliff face. The importance of the Cave Church could not be understated; Christianity had probably originated on the very spot where she was standing. Again, the Literalist ideas of her youth began overwhelming the skepticism that had driven her from school. There was, after all, no better place to prove that maybe the Bible's teachings matched the evidence on the ground. With the Vatican coming up short in so many ways, she had had her doubts, but perhaps she was seeking her facts in the wrong place. Perhaps she—not Simon or Rabin—would find something that undeniably proved the truth of the Gospels. Even if it did not, she had to try, and this thought propelled her forward, straining her calves and thighs as she raced for the top of the plateau.

Suddenly, though, the path split, and she realized she did not know where she was going. She searched for Rabin up ahead, but he had vanished. Embarrassed and still feeling insolent, she hated what she was about to do. But, if she was going to get to the dig site, she had no choice.

'Are you coming?' she shouted at Simon, who was still standing beside the Range Rover in the parking lot below.

'You don't even know where you're going, do you?'

Rabin stepped onto the path halfway down, from an area she only vaguely remembered passing. 'You've gone too far,' he said. 'It's this way.'

Jennifer jogged down to meet him and realized her mistake: a boulder jutted into the path and, immediately past it, a small trail led to the top of the plateau at an even steeper angle than the main path. It was not exactly hidden, but neither was it obvious. To her, hidden pathways indicated the people who had lived there had wanted to hide—and considering the site's dating and symbolism, first-century Christians would fit the mold perfectly.

'Uri, you're supposed to be on my side,' Simon called from a few yards behind them.

Jennifer instinctively turned. Then, thinking better of it, she continued following Rabin up the hill.

For his part, Simon was furious. What was wrong with this woman? It was already way past four o'clock, and with the gendarmes arriving around six and getting through customs by, say, six-thirty, they were cutting it close. Part of him wanted to grab her and drag her back to the Range Rover, but another part of him could not stand the thought of hurting her. He also admired her for her strong will; it was that same character trait, he knew, that had motivated her to take on the Vatican spontaneously and alone. Not that she had any chance of succeeding, and perhaps she knew that too, but—well, call it *courageous* or *stupid*, it was a rare quality, and he hoped her rashness would not get them killed.

Up ahead, the trail cut right, and Rabin disappeared behind a small promontory that, from a distance, blended so well with the rock face that the trail seemed to dead-end. The mystery of the place deepened, and Jennifer realized this was the first time since childhood that anything had seemed so magical. From the moment, she had asked God for wisdom, incessant mishaps had dogged her path. She had to have done something terribly wrong to land in so much trouble. Not that she was given to superstition, but there had to be a reason all this was happening, right? If God *was* granting her wisdom, then, He was certainly making her sweat for it. Would the letter's authenticity and something about the remains provide answers to her questions about faith? If so, would it make everything she was going through worthwhile? As she caught sight of the professor, again she rued her smart outfit, but at least she had worn low-heeled shoes.

Rabin turned, keeping an eye out for her. 'I should have warned you,' he said. 'Just tell me if you need me to slow down or give you a hand.' With so many loose rocks to negotiate, she could easily twist an ankle.

His chivalry was charming, but Jennifer would have gone up barefoot if necessary. In any case, she had always exercised.

As they continued climbing, she appreciated the hours she had devoted to these activities. The trail was even steeper, and the sweltering Mediterranean heat had her dripping. She wiped her forehead with the back of her hand and was relieved when they stopped at an embankment just below the crest of the plateau. A steel ladder was attached diagonally to a rock face. Beside it, a platform with a pulley system served as a primitive but effective means of hoisting equipment to the top.

After placing the casket on the lift, Rabin climbed up. 'Be careful,' he called down. 'The steps are slippery.'

Their altitude only became apparent once she reached the top. From her vantage point at the edge of the plateau she could see all of Antakya, from the sea on the far-left side of the valley to Havaalani Airport on the right. In between, the Orontes River separated the old and new cities, and in the distance, the Nur and Keldağ mountains rose like a pair of drowsing giants. When her eyes fell on the old city, she imagined being there in biblical times. Antioch would have been much smaller then, but she imagined it would still have been much like the older part of the city directly below them.

Only after Simon had hoisted the casket up and joined them, did she turn towards the site. Four prefabricated buildings with interlinking passageways stood on stilts in its center. To the left, a bunker housed two generators with elaborately designed air ducts for sound and pollution reduction. On the roof, rows of solar panels faced skywards. The kitchen, off to the right, had timber walls with canvas window flaps and an adjacent dining hall opened out onto a timber deck. Towards the back of the site, tucked snugly against the cliff, trees provided shade for an outdoor conference space. Next to it was what appeared to be the dig site, where, covered by a canvas roof, workers—mostly young, suntanned and casually dressed—unearthed the find. Some waved from afar, others greeted as they passed.

At a glance, the site reminded Jennifer of a movie set, but on closer inspection, she realized it must have cost a fortune.

Rabin waved her towards his office and she followed.

Simon excused himself; he needed to shed the gendarme uniform. 'I'll catch up in a few minutes,' he said, heading for the adjacent building.

Jennifer found his disinterest unbelievable. ‘Aren’t you even a little curious about what’s in the casket?’

‘Jennifer, I work here,’ he said, unbuttoning his shirt. ‘I see this stuff all the time. And, as for that artefact, I never wanted to find it in the first place. Hell, I lost my brother over it when I’ve got hundreds of things here I can look at that people *won’t* kill me over. Anyhow, you can tell me what it says when I get back, which by the way will be in a few minutes from now. Only this time, be ready to leave. We can’t waste any more time.’

Chapter 32

Rabin's office brought welcome relief from the afternoon heat. Jennifer cooled herself in front of the air-conditioner while taking in the ambience of the new surroundings. The warmth of the professor's well-worn décor of rugs, wood and leather, reminded her of her dad's studio back home.

An impressive collection of at least a thousand books sat tightly stacked on the bookcase. Tilting her head sideways, she read out some of the titles. With mostly unfamiliar names staring back at her, she soon gave up. The 1920s Partners Desk was the epitome of ordered chaos. Sitting on the edge of a cracked-leather chair, she smiled at his dusty laptop. She would bet he hardly used it. An empty coffee cup on a wood coaster kept company with a mouse that seemed to linger impatiently for someone to fire up its laser belly. A silver-framed photo behind the laptop caught her eye. She picked it up.

'Is this your wife?' she asked. 'I remember you telling me about the two of you being in Key West. Is she here with you? I'd love to meet her.'

'She's at our home in Mevaseret Zion, on the outskirts of Jerusalem.' Rabin placed the casket on the desk and pulled open the blinds behind it. 'I visit her once or twice a month, depending on what's happening here.'

'You must miss her.'

'As you get older you get used to it.'

Rabin retrieved the casket and invited her to follow him.

'Simon's good company, though,' he said, making his way to the laboratory in the back of the office. 'Like a son really. We first met in Jerusalem when he was studying there. He was one of my top students. I tried to entice him into pursuing archaeology, but he had his heart set on genetics. At least this find provided the opportunity for us to work together again. It's good to have someone from the hard sciences backing up our findings in archaeology. He's making quite a name for himself.'

Jennifer was only partially listening; her eyes were now scanning the shelves lining the lab's walls. Skeletal remains lay in plastic bins, some covered in decaying fabric. The sight of them made her queasy. Death still haunted her. She did not think she would ever get used to it. Turning away, she tried to shake off dreary memories of her mother's burial, and joined Rabin at the table in the center of the room.

'Have you worked with Turks before?' she asked, taking up position beside him.

The professor placed the casket on the table and washed his hands in a nearby washbasin. 'There is something I think you should know,' he said, shaking his hands so water droplets beat against the sides of the basin.

'About?'

'Simon.'

Blood rose to her cheeks. Was she so transparent? She had not even mentioned, Simon. She was wondering about him, though. But she hardly knew the man.

'Simon is Jewish,' Rabin said, drying his hands.

'Oh,' she said, wondering if his statement had some greater import than it seemed. 'I mean, not that it matters, but isn't Yilmaz a Turkish name?'

'John kept his ancestry a secret,' he said, joining her at the table. 'He felt getting into the priesthood was tough enough, but being perceived as a religious interloper would make it impossible. So, he changed to Yilmaz. Their real surname is Kepa. You do know what that means, don't you?'

'"*Rock*" in Aramaic, I believe.'

'Yes, and the name Jesus of Nazareth gave Apostle Peter.'

Rabin's statement was odd. She could not imagine a Jewish family deliberately associating itself with one of Christ's disciples—not, of course, unless they were Christians themselves, but then, how could they remain Jewish? Jesus might very well have been a Judean and, in the eyes of his Nazarene followers, the Messiah, but the fact remained that the *kohanim* and the rabbis of the Talmud had rejected Him. Despite this apparent contradiction, she was somewhat ashamed of her mistrust of Simon. He had done nothing but try to help her. That had made him *her* rock. Perhaps she owed him an apology for her reaction in the parking lot, but anyone would have done the same thing in her position.

Sitting on a stool by the table, Rabin absentmindedly began studying the artefact. Caskets like those served as safes for jewelry and coins, but they were usually iron. The gilded rivets reinforced the plate in the center, but he was sure it was merely cosmetic.

'What elaborate decorations,' he said, tipping the casket over. 'The lid is definitely Gothic—mid twelfth unto late thirteenth century. …'

Jennifer pulled up a chair and sat beside him. 'We don't have a key. Can you open it?'

He had already studied the mechanism on the way from the airport and knew how it worked. But did it still work? He rested the casket on its lower-back corners. When nothing happened, he tried the sides. Still nothing happened. He held the casket up. 'The clasp should release if I push one of these buttons,' he said pointing to the four small, barely visible pegs protruding from the casket's underside.

'That's if it still works.'

'It had better. We can't spray it with lubricant. That might destroy the contents.'

Tilting the casket forward, Rabin tapped lightly on the front of the artefact. Jennifer heard what sounded like metal bars grinding against each other, and suddenly, the locking spring released. The lock clicked, and she sat up, tense with excitement as the professor lifted the lid from the casket. Then, she sighed.

'That's it?'

Her heart, which had only moments before fluttered with anticipation, now seemed to fall through the floor. On the ruby-velvet lining lay a folded slip of paper. It was not a complete document, just a fragment. Not that she had no interest, but she had expected far more.

Rabin pulled on a set of cotton archivist's gloves. Having worked with ancient papers for nearly five decades, he knew what to expect. Hardly ever had he found an artefact this intact. Something this well-preserved was a blessing. Thank God it had been written on vellum and not papyrus, otherwise it would not have survived the trip.

Jennifer had also worked with vellum before. The fine calfskin ensured longevity, making it the paper of choice for the wealthy in ancient times. She watched anxiously as Rabin used a palette knife to lift the letter from the casket.

'What a find,' he said softly. 'Classical Latin. It wouldn't surprise me if this were an official document.'

Placing the letter on a cotton cloth, his eyes scanned the text for clues to its origins. The script was small and the blurred ink which made it difficult to read, forced him to position the magnifier lamp over it. In some parts, characters were illegible and the way the text ended abruptly at the bottom of the page did not bode well for a complete record.

'What is it?'

'Definitely a letter,' he said, pressing his nose against the magnifier's loupe.

'Can you tell who wrote it?'

'I don't see any signature, but it's obvious the writer is addressing someone directly.'

Nothing in his first reading of the letter seemed to indicate a context, but something in the opening lines made him wonder. Weathering had caused irreparable damage to the first two words, but based on what followed, he was certain they had once spelt a name.

'*...tius ....tus*,' he read the intact letters aloud.

'Is that it?'

He sat back. 'I think that's what it says. You try. I'm sure your eyes are better than mine.'

Reluctantly, Jennifer traded seats with the professor. Translating classical Latin in front of an expert of his renown was unnerving. She, of course remembered her diction, declensions, conjugations and cases by rote, but it had been some time since she had used it. She hoped she would not make a fool of herself in front of him.

Hunching over the loupe, she tried reading the letters in her head, then spelt them out aloud: '… *t-i-u-s* …. *t-u-s*.'

'I thought so,' Rabin said.

Disappointed with the result, she also sat back. 'Yes, I get the same.'

They traded seats again, and hoping the rest of the document would yield more information, Rabin centered the loupe over the entire sentence.

'"*...tius ....tus*,"' he read finally, '"a servant of Caesar's by his Highness's most gracious Imperial appointment."'

Jennifer felt certain she had read a similar phrase somewhere before. She thought about it for some time, then abruptly asked Rabin for a Bible. He nodded and she fetched a ragged copy of the New Revised Standard translation from the office bookshelf. Paging rapidly to *Romans*, she set the open Bible on the table. She continued flipping, one by one, to the salutation of each Epistle. In nearly all, Paul had opened with phrases like the one the professor had just read. The salutations in *Corinthians*, *Timothy*, *Ephesians* and *Colossians*, were almost identical in translation.

'"Paul, an apostle of Jesus Christ by the will of God,"' she read aloud. 'It sounds like something Paul could have written.'

'Maybe, but no more or less than any two letters today might sound similar because they both begin with "Dear So-

and-So." What we're looking at is a standard form of epistolary salutation throughout the Roman Empire in the first and second centuries. If anything, it only shows that Paul was merely playing on an existing trope by replacing mention of the emperor with a mention of his Messiah. It would be as seditious as, "I pledge allegiance to the flag of the Union of Soviet Socialist Republics," during the McCarthy Era in the US. Sure, it shows Paul was a political subversive, but that's nothing we didn't already know. For anyone who'd ever read a letter during this period, the intent of such a statement was unmistakable, but the fact that Christians thumbed their noses at the imperial cult—and were often tortured for doing so—is well-established and documented.'

Although the professor spoke in a kindly, fatherly tone, Jennifer felt humiliated. Thankfully, she was not his student; he probably would have flunked her on the spot.

'Well, at least we know it dates from the right period,' she said. 'Whoever this "servant of Caesar" was, he had to be someone working for Caesar, and "by his Highness's most gracious Imperial Appointment" must mean he carried the Emperor's blessing.'

Rabin held his breath. Constraint required patience. As a doctoral student, she should know better than to jump to premature conclusions—especially those based on her own personal bias. Refusing to let her conjecture cloud his judgement, he moved the magnifier to the next line.

'The author extends his gratitude to the recipient for his loyalty to Rome,' he said.

Jennifer slumped. They needed a name. That the sender was loyal to Caesar meant nothing. 'Does it at least mention the recipient?'

The professor did not have to answer. His ignoring her was enough to tell her it had not.

'Well, I don't get why the Vatican is bent out of shape about this,' she whined. 'An unsigned letter to an unknown recipient is about as dangerous as a declawed rabbit. Unless we're missing something, I don't see why they're after us. The rest of the text had better offer something more tangible, or we might as well give it back.'

Just then, Rabin's face lit up. Moving the loupe again, he read the following line aloud: '"Years have passed since stopping the uprising."'

Jennifer sat up. Rebellions were regular occurrences in the Roman Empire, especially in Judea. Judging by the Vatican's reaction, the text must refer to the Jewish-Roman wars. The problem was there being nothing, yet, from the letter to indicate this.

Turning to Rabin, she said, 'It could be referring to Jesus? He was a rebel. Could the letter have come from one of his enemies, someone like Herod Antipas?'

Rabin shook his head. 'Again, you're jumping to conclusions. At face value, we don't know if the letter's referring to the Boudicca or bar Kokhba, and Antipas wouldn't have used Latin.'

'What about Pontius Pilate then? He governed Judea. 'Pon-*tius* Pila-*tus* fits perfectly.'

Rabin could not imagine arriving at that name from two incomplete words. It was like recognizing a twenty-megapixel image from a handful of dots. The letters in the smudged name did match 'Pontius Pilatus', but they could just as easily match some unknown person named 'Brutius Domitus' or 'Austius Ignatus'. The Vatican's reaction—which it would naturally deny—was no proof of anything.

Still, he bit his tongue. Even if she was right, they did not have sufficient proof; hell, they were not even close. And, anxious to validate her beliefs, she was just spouting off anything that might even obliquely support her preconceived notions.

'Oh, come on, Professor. The missing characters—they match ...'

'No, Jennifer, not any more than they might match, "Hor-*tius* Quin-*tus*."'

'Who?'

'No one. Those are just random Roman names strung together to prove that the writer could be anyone and that, no, none of this necessarily relates to Jesus.'

'An uprising under Pilate relates to Jesus.'

'And?'

He did not need to explain any further. She knew exactly what he meant. On the other hand, maybe the letter implicated Pilate in Jesus's death. The canonical gospels, after all, did not, and it had been standard dogma for fifteen centuries that the Jews of Jerusalem, not Pilate, had convicted Christ. So, maybe the letter explained who really killed Jesus. As an Israeli, Rabin would see that as a contentious issue. Would the Vatican?

Suddenly, Rabin turned to face her. 'Listen, Jennifer. I know what you're thinking, but you need to stop expecting something that isn't there. You get your proof first, then, draw your conclusions. You don't start with a conclusion and look for proof. That's the difference between real scholarship and pseudoscience. People who look for evidence of aliens already think there are aliens, and unsurprisingly, what little proof they come up with is never conclusive. You should know this. You are a graduate student.'

The professor's reprimand was hurtful, but she refused to be intimidated by it. What the letter said and who the participants were far outweighed her ego getting in the way.

While Jennifer remained deep in thought, Rabin deciphered the next line: '"Another uprising, stronger in numbers and loyalty, has flared up and must be quelled."'

Jennifer's immediate intuition was that it referred to the siege of Jerusalem, but Pontius Pilate had been recalled to Rome long before that. 'It could be Jesus's followers—the Nazarenes.'

'Even if this were Pilate, as you suggest, he is not known to have persecuted Jesus's followers.'

'But Paul did when he was Saul. And since Pilate did not execute his own orders, one could ask who did. What if Saul was the recipient?'

Rabin had to admit that was a plausible explanation for the Vatican's behavior, depending on the rest of the letter. But it was not borne out by what they had read.

Jennifer sat still. Without names or real evidence, they had very little, if anything, to go by. Yet, she was not giving up. Even if her ideas were speculative, she had to carry on. Too much was at stake.

'Saul's persecution of the Nazarenes is an article of faith.' she said. 'Nobody questions it. The idea of a Jew from Turkey persecuting other Jews in Judea is odd though, don't you think? And yet, that's exactly what Paul in the Epistles says he was doing, so it's illogical to assume a man from Tarsus was acting on behalf of Judea's disenfranchised Jewish population. As with the Jerusalem Sanhedrin, he too would have had to bring those he accused before Pilate. Or if Saul openly killed Jews, he must have been acting under Pilate's personal direction. What's more, by Paul's own admission, Christ said to him, "Saul, Saul, why are you persecuting *me*?" We have always assumed the transcendent Christ was referring to his followers. If the letter is addressed to Saul, it would be logical to suggest that Jesus personally confronted Saul *before* His crucifixion. …'

'Jesus didn't militarize,' Rabin stated in defense. Despite her enthusiasm, he was not allowing Jennifer to draw him into her speculation. 'Calling the incidents leading up to the Passion a "revolt" would be an overstatement. Pilate would not have broken a sweat over the Jesus movement, so the Gospel story about his acceding to Jewish demands could be nonsense. The Church could maintain whatever it wants, but this anti-Semitic notion from the Gospels has been rejected by the clear majority of serious academics, making a letter that implicates a Roman Prefect nothing at all; it certainly would not make the Vatican want to hunt you down over it.

'Most scholars today agree that it was the unrest Jesus was stirring up over taxation that got him killed. You of all should know this. First, he ridiculed Levi of Capernaum, convincing him to quit his post, and later, he influenced a Jericho tax collector, Zacchaeus, to resign. That would have been enough for Pilate to have Jesus killed, but to top it all, there is the incident with the moneychangers in the temple. As governor, Pilate's primary responsibility was to ensure taxes were collected and sent to Rome, and under no circumstance was he to allow anyone preventing such taxes from being obtained. Just encouraging someone not to contribute was a capital offence. So, to stop Jesus's activities and to prevent similar incidents from occurring,

Pilate was compelled to make an example of a man he would otherwise have considered a harmless preacher.

'That's the general academic consensus, and it's borne out by everything we know from Josephus and the archaeology. In the end, exactly what you'd expect to happen is probably what *did* happen: Pilate had Jesus crucified on Mount Golgotha near Jerusalem for interfering with the collection of taxes. Even the sign on the cross, "King of the Jews," indicates nothing more than that Jesus was killed for political sedition. Perhaps—and I suppose this is a stretch—it implies that Pilate yielded to a Jewish demand, but it just as likely indicates he was deflecting blame for an execution he was compelled to carry out during the week of Passover. His reply to the protesting high priest regarding the plaque, "King of the Jews", says as much: "What I have written stays written." The priests had no power to execute in first-century Judea, and Pilate had no mandate to concede to anyone's demands but the emperor's.'

The professor's knowledge of scripture was impressive; not that Jennifer expected any less. She liked how meticulously he made the point. The clarity of his argument demonstrated his grasp of the subject. Neither was he alone in his thinking. Considering how Pilatus had shifted blame by implicating the Jewish priests, his campaign to crucify Jesus had been successful. Perhaps the letter indicated a third motive for Jesus's death, though, something eluding, and something that no one has ever thought of. Even if they abandoned all assumptions, there had to be a reason the Church wanted to recover the letter so badly.

'Assuming you're right, Professor, how does it affect the Church?'

Rabin had already refocused his attention on the letter and was not listening. Then something caught his eye. Having gone over the last sentence again, he translated it aloud: 'To avert creating another martyr, they must "corrupt", or "defile"—it can read either way—the faith.'

A chill rippled down Jennifer's spine. 'Professor, you're not serious.'

Rabin sat back, his brow twisted into deep folds. Even he could not believe what he had just read. His gaze shifted to Jennifer. 'The letter instructs the recipient to appropriate the *Nazarene* faith.'

She shot forward to see if the text said that; she needed to be sure the professor was not toying with her. It did indeed.

Finally, Jennifer understood the Vatican's desperation to get the letter back. The Nazarene link was the *smoking gun*, for not only did it connect the letter with the Apostles' persecutions, but it incriminated the Vatican's esteemed Saint Paul as well. Her mind raced. She had to make sense of it.

'Another martyr must refer to Apostle Peter, surely,' she said, her eyes glistening. 'There is no way he could have reached Rome safely with a contract on his head in Judea already. Given the letter is true and it refers to Peter, Paul's ministry to the gentiles was a complete apostasy—an abandonment of the faith if you will—perpetrated to corrupt a church the Romans had already unsuccessfully attempted to destroy by force. In other words, if the letter describes Peter's demise, and Paul is required to pose as Peter—to establish a Roman Church—and in so doing undermine the true Church, the entire Apostolic succession is nonsense.'

Rabin stared at her, a hint of a smile creeping across his lips. Mention of the Nazarenes made all the difference. Even he had to admit her hypothesis, though not without its limits, made sense. Yet, as much as he agreed in principle, without hard evidence to back it up, the letter meant little, if anything.

Jennifer gloomily turned her attention to the letter. The idea of Pilate and Saul persecuting the Jews and corrupting their faith was out of sync with Catholic doctrine. The credo of the Apostolic succession hinged on a Jewish rejection of the Messiah. The popes assumed the mantle of God's viceroys on Earth based on a scorned Christ and a Roman Peter. Only if the high priests had spurned God's Son and, in so doing, forfeited God's terrestrial seat in Jerusalem, would the Vatican's claim hold.

Jennifer's umbilical connection with Christianity aligned her with the gentile clique, which might have illicitly appropriated God's power and authority from the Jews. The consequences were far-reaching. She felt as if she should justify herself to the professor. She was about to apologize on behalf of Christendom when she saw Simon approaching. His clean-shaven jaw and wavy, wet, slicked-back hair indicated that he had just showered. His white-cotton shirt flapped like a flag as he walked, revealing his muscular frame beneath, and his tight-fitting jeans revealed his glutes and hamstrings, which rippled like a pacing lion's. He stopped in front of her, and she felt a little light-headed.

'I'm sorry to break this up,' Simon said, 'but we have to go.'

Jennifer felt sick in her soul. Her attachment to Christianity had caused her to believe strange things over the years. She saw that now. 'I can't, Simon,' she said, suppressing tears. 'We've only translated a few lines.'

'Goddammit, Jennifer! The gendarmes are an hour from landing.'

'They still have to get through customs, right? That could take another hour.'

Simon glanced down at Rabin. 'You have to help me here, Uri.'

Rabin got up. 'You two can discuss this in the car, Jennifer,' he said, replacing the letter in the casket.

The idea of leaving devastated her. When Simon pulled impatiently on her chair, she refused to budge. 'I'm not leaving.'

Rabin closed the lid carefully, then removed his gloves. 'Simon is right, Jennifer,' he said, taking the casket and making his way to his office. 'In any case, without evidence the letter means very little, if anything. To be honest, I can't see any falling like manna from Heaven any time soon either. So, come, I'll walk you back to the car. And, in the meantime, I'm locking this in my safe.'

*****

Jennifer descended Mount Starius like a peevish child. These setbacks had to end. She had had enough bad luck to last her a lifetime. Her interview with Cardinal Librarian Cardoni that morning had been fruitless, and now, she had stumbled on something revolutionary. If Rome had sanctioned Paul's persecutions and later his Church, it changed everything. It meant that Rome had engineered the founding of their brand of Christianity, and if so, the long-standing impression that the Jerusalem Sanhedrin was responsible for Jesus's death made sense. It had to, for on this charge rested the veracity of the Christian faith. If the Jewish priests had not purged Jesus, papal authority was a lie and the Jews remained the chosen people.

And yet this was all speculation. What they needed was evidence. She recalled Cardinal Cardoni saying *Q* originating in Antioch. Then she reminded herself of *Acts of the Apostles* recording the Antiochene gentiles were the first converts to be labelled Christians. When she looked up at the retaining wall beside her, adrenaline surged through her veins. Thirty feet above her lay the Cave Church of Saint Peter, traditionally the place where Peter had first preached to the gentiles. That made it, for non-Jews anyway, *the* root of Christianity. And what if it was all linked: the letter, *Q* and the Cave Church?

Simon unlocked the Range Rover and opened her door, but she ignored him and continued up the road. He stared after her, door in hand.

'Where are you going now?'

'The Cave Church.'

'Jennifer!' he shouted. 'For fuck's sake, Jennifer, get back here!'

'I'll be quick,' she called out.

'It's closed for renovations! The cave is falling apart—it's locked!'

'I'll climb over the gate.'

'What gate? There's a whole building blocking the way—and a pile of rubble is jamming the entrance!'

Chapter 33

Schreider sat hunched at his desk, his elbows pressed into the arms of his chair, his chin slumped on a pair of clenched fists. His dressing down at the Penitentiary had angered him, but it had not compared with the fury he had felt when Verretti had pulled a gun on him. The incident was entirely his fault, of course. He should not have lost his cool. His misjudgment would certainly cost him. Verretti getting the better of him spelt the end of his career. His perfect record was ruined.

The colonel's eyes shifted to the wind-up alarm clock on his desk. It was already half past four. In little more than a half an hour, most of the staff would be leaving for the day. Not being able to take statements from those who had heard or seen something irked him. It made no sense. Every aspect of the crime should be receiving equal consideration. His blood boiled again at the thought that Verretti would fail to take care of the important details. What kind of an investigation did that meatball think this was? All the man cared about was his damned ego. Mounting an internationally unsanctioned pursuit obviously appeared far more impressive than properly investigating the minutiae.

After reviewing the morning's events, Schreider's thoughts focused on the murder in the Penitentiary vault. Something about the priest's wounds still bothered him. His mind clouded over, and he forced himself upright. He should not be carrying on like this. He had to get it together. He activated the intercom and called for Weber.

Weber entered minutes later, beret in hand. 'Where are we going?'

'The morgue,' Schreider said, holstering his pistol.

'Did they call?'

Schreider could not say why he needed to go there. He just felt the urge to inspect Father Yilmaz's corpse. With the pursuit coming so quickly after the murder and the Maggiore removing the Father's remains from the vault before anyone had had a chance to examine it closely, made it likely they had missed something.

Marching down the Via del Belvedere, Schreider hoped the coroner had not left already, but he would break in if necessary. The cardinals had behaved strangely in the vault, and someone needed to find out why. In less than an hour Verretti would be in Antakya. He dreaded what would happen once the inspector apprehended the suspects. If the gendarmerie's treatment of the bomber was any indication, the two fugitives would be turned to bratwurst. 'Not again and not while I'm Oberst,' Schreider decided. He would do whatever it took to stop Verretti from getting creative with the law again.

Weber appeared stressed. He had never seen his commander act so out-of-character. 'You have to let me on board, Oberst,' he said, matching his commander's stride. 'I can't help you if you don't tell me what's going on.'

Schreider longed to tell the captain about the secret letter, but he had pledged absolute secrecy. On the other hand, with the Church withholding important information, he now felt relieved of his sworn responsibilities. As he turned left at the Belvedere fire station, he saw the coroner locking up, and he began to run.

'Doctor!' he called out from the arch entrance by the fire station.

The coroner, a rickety man nearing retirement, did not hear Schreider and carried on walking to the center of the courtyard where he had parked. He was removing his white jacket and placing it in the boot of his Alfa Romeo as the two Swiss guards approached him.

'Ah, Colonel Schreider,' the old man said. 'Actually, I wanted to talk to you about something.'

'I really need to see that body, doctor.'

Anticipating Schreider's purpose, the coroner had already retrieved his jacket from the boot of his car and was putting it back on. 'Yes, that's what I wanted to talk to you about. I was going to call you in the morning, but I suppose now's as good a time as any—besides, my wife's making *trippa* tonight and I could use an excuse to work late. Anyhow, there's something I wanted to show you.'

The old man moved more quickly than Schreider expected. In a moment, the three were inside the morgue, making their way past the stainless-steel dissection tables. Several tables from the door, the coroner stopped at a three-tiered cold chamber. He drew out the middle tray to reveal the body bag.

'I need to see the wounds,' Schreider said.

'I'm glad you said that, Colonel,' the coroner responded, unzipping the bag down to Yilmaz's torso.

When Weber spotted the gaping wound in Father Yilmaz's throat, his diaphragm contracted. Unlike Schreider, he had not had experience of death on the battlefield.

'I find deep breaths help, Captain,' the coroner said as he slid on a pair of latex gloves. 'There's a reason so many coroners are mouth breathers.'

Weber could not believe the coroner could joke at a time like this. The thought of gulping death was sending him into convulsion. Luckily, he had not eaten since lunch, or his food would already be puddles on the floor.

The coroner found Weber's weak stomach irritating. After all, the captain was a grown man, young and a member of the Swiss Guard. 'What a *bucaiolo*,' the old man thought, but gave Weber time to compose himself. Once the captain had his gag reflex under control, he continued. As he slipped a finger into the slit below Yilmaz's right nipple, the captain grew queasy again, but this time the old man did not stop.

'As you see, there is a puncture wound on the right side of the chest. There is also bruising to the chest here and the neck here. Last but not the least, we have the *coup de grace*, as the French say, the six-inch laceration across the throat.'

Schreider himself was now becoming a little unnerved—especially as the coroner was nonchalantly poking his finger into every wound—and he did not have time for a lengthy analysis. 'You said you wanted to see me about something?'

'Yes, Colonel, the location of the wounds speaks volumes. Based on the lacerations, bruising and blood drainage, there's a pretty clear sequence to them.'

The coroner picked a stainless-steel probe from his workstation. Careful not to damage muscle tissue further, he inserted the probe into Yilmaz's puncture wound and slipped the probe deep into the dead priest's chest until it thumped against a rib. Leaving the probe projecting from Yilmaz's chest, the old man again turned towards Schreider and began gesticulating as he explained.

To demonstrate how the killer had inflicted the wounds, the coroner asked the two officers to stand toe to toe. Schreider was to play the killer, and Weber, the victim. The coroner handed the colonel a surgical knife, directing him to hold it in his right hand. The old man then made sure the pair were the right distance apart before asking Schreider to mimic inflicting the wounds he had seen on the priest.

Weber cringed. 'Can we reverse roles?'

'No, no, captain. You are the right height, so I need the two of you as you are.'

'I'll be careful,' Schreider chuckled.

Frowning, Weber dropped his hands to his side.

Schreider flicked the knife around in his hand. With the blade now protruding from the back of his fist and in line with his forearm, he thrust foreword as if to slice Weber's throat. His second thrust swung towards the captain's chest, stopping just short of his ribs.

'Exactly as I thought,' the coroner mused. 'Good. You stabbed him just where the killer stabbed our priest.'

'Obviously,' Schreider responded. 'That's what you told me to do.'

The coroner was not amused: 'Yes, Colonel. Because *how* you did it isn't how it happened. You just demonstrated *how* someone with military training would inflict the same wounds in the same areas. The average person wouldn't hold a knife with the blade protruding from the back of his fist. Change that and you have an entirely different result. Try it again, this time holding the knife like a lay person.'

As an expert in hand-to-hand combat, Schreider knew exactly what would happen. His moves would be the same, but slower. Letting the blade protrude from the top of his fist, he repeated the moves.

'Stop!' With the knife tip inches from Weber's chest, the coroner held Schreider's hand. 'Now compare this with the probe sticking out of our priest over there.'

'I sliced in the opposite direction and finished to his left,' Schreider said, not needing a second glance.

'So now, Colonel, this can't be what happened either.'

The coroner had the two officers repeat the demonstration, but this time he let Schreider hold the knife in his left hand and like an amateur. As a final analysis, he had the colonel hold Weber's throat with his right hand. He then had him stab at the captain as an amateur would, with the blade protruding from the front of the fist. Inflicting the neck wound in the same way was impossible because of his right arm which was in the way. That meant there was only one possible explanation: the killer was an amateur who first stabbed with his left hand, while clutching his victim's throat with his right hand. He then let go of the neck and with the right hand slammed the priest on the chest.

'As a last act of savagery,' the coroner said, 'our killer slit the Father's throat.'

Schreider handed the coroner the knife and returned to Yilmaz's corpse. The coroner was spot-on. The thumbprint and bruising was clearly visible to the right of the neck and the chest.

The coroner looked grave. 'The killer made sure Yilmaz died instantly,' he said. 'You don't slice a man's throat after you've stabbed him in the lung. By then he is already drowning in his own blood.'

Chapter 34

Jennifer stood with her feet planted on the cobbled path, her arms at her sides. Her heart pounded in her chest, forcing bursts of blood richly charged with oxygen to her limbs—the result of her dash to the Cave Church. Before her was a twelve-foot-high, sandstone building with a gated entrance; beyond that, one of Christianity's oldest landmarks. With the Apostolic succession now in question, what better place to start looking for the truth than at Apostle Peter's first church?

She tried to see a way past the building which possibly consisted of an ablution and box-office, but to its left it had a three-hundred-foot rock face, and to the right a hundred-foot drop fell to the road and parking lot below. She thought of shimmying up the wall-mounted lamp at the entrance, but she could not even do that on her own. She felt like screaming in frustration, and the energy drained from her.

'What a paradox,' she thought. 'Here is a site dedicated to Apostle Peter's church, yet there's no proof he ever ministered in Antioch.'

The only person known to have ministered there was Saint Paul. Perhaps the time had come to place these biblical characters under the microscope. Interestingly, the only reference to Peter's presence in Antioch came from Paul himself. His Epistle to the Galatians stated that he had asked Peter to visit the area so they could clarify their differences. Their famous meeting was known as the 'Incident of Antioch.'

Saul, not Paul yet, first appeared in the Bible when Stephen Martyr was killed in Jerusalem. Of course, it was true that scripture depicted Saul as merely a bystander, but maybe he did have a hand in the stoning. At the very least though he must have incited the crowd, because soon after this, the Bible said, he set out to massacre other Nazarenes. The rest of the story was familiar to most people: his persecutions caused many to flee—some as far as Antioch. On his way to Damascus, Saul was reputedly visited by the resurrected Christ. He then disappeared and only resurfaced years later in Antioch where he attempted to convert the local Jews to his teachings, but they rejected him, saying he was preaching blasphemy because some of them had known Jesus.

Saul, on the other hand, had not met Jesus. He angered the Antioch Jews so much they expelled him from their midst. No matter where Saul preached, the Jews would try to stone him. Hellbent on establishing a ministry, Saul turned to the gentiles. Ignoring the Apostles' teachings, the Turk from Tarsus converted Antiochenes to his newly founded faith. His ministry led to a protest from Peter, whose practice was to accept gentiles *only* if they were baptized in the name of the Lord, kept the Law of Moses and were circumcised.

Peter's requirements were non-negotiable.

Saul later wrote: 'If ye be circumcised, Christ shall profit you nothing.'

It appears that conflicting ideologies had yielded different denominations early on, and there was no evidence that these two opposing factions were ever reconciled. Clearly, Peter's Jewish denomination, the Nazarenes, and Saul's gentile church, the Christians, were two distinct groups. But Peter had not ended up the founder of *gentile* Christianity because, if he had, all those who believed Jesus was the Messiah, Jews and gentiles alike, would still be keeping the Law of Moses.

There was no actual record of Peter ever preaching to the gentiles.

Saul on the other hand, immediately changed from being Saul to the Romanized version of his name, Paul, and started ministering *only* to the gentiles.

When a voice behind Jennifer spoke, she felt a jolt in her chest, and her heart contracted violently. She had heard this voice all morning, but now it sounded different. It no longer asserted authority but was soulful. Simon approached her, and she glanced up at him.

'Nothing makes sense anymore,' she said. 'I've spent more of my time exploring spirituality than anything else, and for what?'

'It's really important to you. That's obvious.'

'Well, yeah. our spiritual destiny is the most important thing anyone can focus on. It is the core of our existence. For a long time, I believed blindly like a child, and then it was all shattered. How do you walk away from that?' She began to sob and turned aside. Rarely had she been so emotional. 'I don't know what spirituality is anymore,' she whispered.

'I'll help you.'

'With what?'

'Find answers.'

'I can't get you into trouble over this,' she said sniffing. 'You have already done enough.'

'I got you into this, remember?'

Now, Rabin was lumbering towards them with a gait so lethargic it seemed to belong to a man twice his age. It was already past six, and between work and rushing off to the airport earlier, it was to be expected for him to be exhausted. Stopping beside Jennifer, he said, 'You know, no matter how many times I've been up and down this mountain, it's always a new experience.'

Although an earthquake had made entering the site unsafe for the public, the Turkish government had given him a set of keys in case access was needed for his research.

Jennifer beamed as he unlocked the gate. She rushed past the professor. For her, visiting a place where the Apostles had preached felt more intimidating than visiting the Vatican Library. She crossed the empty terrace. Despite having studied photographs of the site, she had no idea what to expect. Squares of hundreds of smooth cobblestones were set at regular intervals about two feet apart, and between them were tufts of grass and yellow wildflowers. Within the wrought-iron fencing cypresses climbed up the rock face, shading a handful of empty park benches. A steel balustrade atop a wall served as protection from the hundred-feet drop to the front, and opposite her was another sandstone wall. Then, she saw it: set into the cliff face on the far-left side of the terrace was the Cave Church of Saint Peter.

Simple yet beautiful, the sandstone-block facade measured around thirty feet across and twenty-three feet high—hardly a third of the size of the main entrance to Saint Peter's Basilica. As with the Basilica in Rome this church stood on its own portico. The structure itself simulated two Roman-arched aisles flanking a central nave, a design feature Jennifer had seen replicated in numerous other basilicas. Outside, each of the three arches was bricked up, had its own simple entrance with a stone lintel to support the weight of the masonry above, and included its own decorative window directly above its doorway. The main entrance, slightly larger than the adjacent two, had its own barrel vaulted motif giving it prominence over the side entrances.

Studying the facade reminded Jennifer of her father. After her mother, had died and she had accompanied him onto countless jobsites, he had taught her to review the buildings with him. It had taken her some time to learn the field jargon, but as the daughter of an architect, she had a natural eye for the differences in features and forms and had even worked as a part-time architecture tour guide.

Now, she called on those memories to understand what she was looking at; whether anything looked odd or out-of-place. The customary crucifix found at Christian landmarks was missing, but the central window featured a cruciform symbol with short, equilateral arms radiating diagonally. Oddly, it represented a circle- or sun-cross. She stared at this and was about to mention it to Simon and Rabin, when she noticed something even more fascinating.

'Is it just me, or is the central window an optical illusion,' she said, gazing upwards.

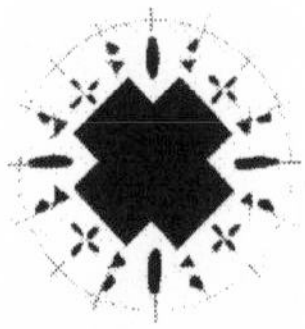

Simon turned away from the front-perimeter railing to join her. Other than the circle-cross, he could not see anything unusual.

Likewise, Rabin squinted upwards, and to him it was merely a circle-cross as well. 'I think it's just you,' he said.

She was not letting up: 'No, I mean, seriously. It's in the negative. The circle has eight segments, four with clover motifs resembling primitive fleur-de-lis. Each of these points up, down, left and right, representing north, south, east and west. Following the line around the upper fleur-de-lis and down to the first diagonal, you'll see it extend to and curl around its symmetrical counterpart on the bottom, crisscross the center of the circle and extend back up again, to form a vertical beam. And, if you do the same thing with the left and right fleurs-de-lis, the whole form is a perfect Maltese cross.'

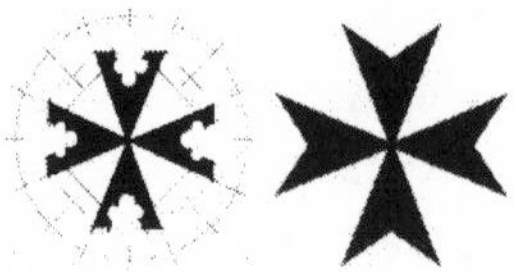

'Ha!' Rabin exclaimed. 'That's genius.'

'The side windows are the same,' she said. 'Their eight-pointed stars are also stylized Maltese crosses—and together, with the ovals above them, they represent Knights with lances.'

Rabin was astounded that he had not noticed this before or made the connection, and to his knowledge, neither had anyone else. 'It could also be Knights Templar. Both orders served here during the crusades.'

Jennifer could not agree about the Templar connection. She had already spotted the most convincing evidence yet, and though she was not sure if she was right, it would not hurt to point it out. 'Did you bring a pen and paper with you, Professor?' she asked.

He drew a pen from his shirt pocket and searched his pants for a slip of paper. In his wallet, he found a folded leaflet. Passing it to her, he said, 'It's an outreach letter from a local mosque. You might as well make use of it.'

Crouching and using her thigh as support, Jennifer sketched the facade's outlines, including the doors, arches and windows. She placed twelve dots at key points in the drawing, and using only two continuous zigzag lines, connected the dots. When she had finished, she stood up. She held the sketch up before the facade.

Rabin clapped his hands. 'A Maltese cross to the centimeter. To-the-centimeter.'

'How the hell did we miss that?' Simon asked, puzzled.

Stumped that no one had previously picked up on the design, he checked over Jennifer's sketch. He needed to make sure her proportions were not just a fluke and that the points she had chosen were not arbitrary because, really, a person could draw dots on anything and connect them with lines. It did not take long to confirm what Jennifer was seeing.

'My guess is also for the Hospitallers,' Rabin agreed. 'They sprang up in Jerusalem during the crusades and cared for destitute pilgrims to the Holy Land but soon, like the Knights Templar, they became powerful, enriching themselves with territory and revenue. When Islamic forces drove them from the region, they operated from Rhodes and later Malta—hence the name *Maltese Cross*. Their strength as a Catholic order became somewhat diminished by the time of the Protestant Reformation, and only during the early nineteenth century did the order resurface, performing humanitarian and religious work. Presently, they are headquartered in Rome and Malta. Like the Vatican, their enclave is extraterritorial from Italy, which means a significant amount of political pull. In fact, to this day they maintain their own military in Rome.'

Jennifer shuddered. The peculiar blend of pagan symbolism made it impossible to equate this site with Christianity or with Apostle Peter's ministry.

'This must be some kind of temple,' she said. 'Maybe to serve as a small hospice. The Templars used their eleemosynary mission to accumulate wealth covertly, but—and correct me if I'm wrong—didn't the Hospitallers' wealth come from land and banking, while the Templar made their fortune by trading in relics?'

Rabin nodded slowly. 'There are stories to that effect, but it's hard to say what secret organizations do and don't do, especially when they're a millennium old. At any rate, some scholars believe the Templar might have dug up something under the Temple Mount during the crusades;

medieval legend would have it that they found the Holy Grail, the Arc of the Covenant and John the Baptist's reanimated head, but then, the great thing about secret organizations is that you can make up all kinds of nonsense about them.'

Jennifer listened with rapt attention as Rabin made his point, and waited for him to finish, before asking her next question: 'Didn't the Cave Church once have graves in front of it.'

'As recently as the last century,' Simon cut in. 'It even had graves inside it.'

She looked up at the entrances in the cliff wall overhead. 'And the site sits right in the middle of the catacombs you're excavating. …'

Rabin was about to complement her on her observation when Simon put his hand up to stop him. 'I hate to say it again, Jennifer, and I realize you're likely to stay till we've got bullets in our heads, but seriously, we have to go now. The gendarmes must be landing as we speak.'

'But, Simon, …'

'What?'

'Well, I just can't *leave*.'

'Because you want to get us caught?'

'No, I. ... I just feel like I'm missing something.'

Chapter 35

The temperature had reached twenty-eight degrees Celsius on the landing strip when Verretti approached the terminal building at Antakya's Havaalani Airport. He had tried to nap during the flight, but with his men shouting above thrusting turbines and his mind racing every time he closed his eyes, he had settled on reading a magazine instead. Before disembarking, he had had his men synchronize their watches to Turkish time. He checked his watch again to make sure he had rewound the chronograph button. His chest tightened. It was nearing seven o'clock.

Driven by his desire to see Schreider completely shamed, he hurried into the arrival terminal. The inspector's eyes scanned the hall for Friar Brian Malone, but there was no sign of the monk. Then, stepping from a coffee shop, arms outstretched in welcome, Malone approached. Verretti wanted to give the man a dressing down right there. Their mission required discretion. Advertising the gendarmes' arrival could jeopardize the entire operation.

Malone was the only Capuchin in Turkey, personally assigned to his post by the pope; it would not be a stretch of the imagination, then, for anyone watching to suppose the friar's greeting a group of men at the airport might indicate an unsanctioned envoy. Originally from London, the friar belonged to the evangelical brotherhood of Capuchins, an order that lived in austere, simple conditions. Malone had joined the Capuchin order in Detroit, Michigan, and had since spent his days in prayer and contemplation, while also taking part in missionary activities and engaging in pastoral work.

The footsteps of Adjutant Lioni and the rest of the men clattered behind Verretti, and he quickened his stride towards the terminal exit.

Sensing he had perhaps done something to offend his guests, Malone sped after the inspector.

Verretti also knew Malone from his numerous visits to the Vatican. His meteoric rise in the order, combined with a four-year stint as chaplain in the British Marine Corps, had made the friar an obvious choice for the Vatican's special 'outreach' in Turkey. Verretti had often run into him at the Governatorato, where Malone was attending meetings with high-ranking members of the Holy See. For some time now, word had it that he played a clandestine role in Antioch. To maintain its position at the head of a world religion, the Holy See had commissioned him to keep an eye on the new discoveries made at an archaeology site above the Cave Church of Saint Peter. Managing a parish fulltime, in addition to constantly monitoring the archaeology site, claimed most of Malone's time. His parish now comprised around ninety souls, and with the Holy See ever anxious for news from the site, he worked tirelessly to perform all his duties with equal fervor.

Verretti paused briefly to let Malone catch up. As the monk reached him, the inspector began walking again.

'How far to your parish, Friar?'

'It's a thirty-minute drive, Inspector.'

'You can stop calling me by rank, Malone. We have to be taken for civilians.'

Engaging with Vatican officials on a first-name basis made Malone uncomfortable, and though he knew the inspector's first name, he would not call him by it. As a monk, his esteem for the Holy See and the Holy Father would not permit it—not even to ensure security.

Verretti crossed the road to the parking area taking the lead. 'I believe you know why we're here, yes?'

Malone nodded. 'The site is a five-minute drive from my presbytery,' he said, huffing. 'I hope they're still there. I had to come back down the mountain to fetch you and your men, so I don't know.' He slid open the door of his Caravelle. 'You'll have to squeeze in. I didn't expect so many guests.'

Verretti instructed Lioni to load their backpacks on the roof rack and get in. Once the last man had taken a seat the inspector signaled for Lioni to take the wheel. 'My man will drive, Friar.'

Malone handed his keys to the adjutant and wedged himself in the back, between two of the men.

Verretti then slammed the door closed and took his place in the passenger seat.

Lioni adjusted the rear-view mirror. 'Where to, Friar?' he asked.

*****

Lioni stopped in the courtyard of Malone's church just as the sun was about to set behind Habib Neccar.

Stepping from the Caravelle and onto the sandstone paving, Verretti waited for his men to offload their luggage. During the flight, he had pored over the operation's intelligence file. Apart from details on transport and arms, it had described the church. Built in the eighteenth century, but rebuilt after a major earthquake in 1872, the building featured a Roman-vaulted entrance flanked by four pointed rib vaults. It was reminiscent of Islamic architecture, such that, combined, these ribs spanned the entire width of the church's facade. Windows on the enclosed second floor overlooked the quiet church court where Verretti stood. To the far right, a staircase led to a four-story bell tower. The interior conformed to late sixth-century principles with its aisles flanking a central nave. The small Catholic cross that stood atop its slanting, terracotta roof, was the only other indication that it was a Christian building.

'I have prepared the guest quarters for you,' Malone said, smoothing the creases in his robe and adjusting the knotted rope around his waist.

Verretti approached the side entrance beside the church, Malone straining to keep up. On reaching the presbytery, the monk had managed to pass Verretti and lead the group across a tree-filled courtyard at the far end of which he unlocked the guesthouse. After showing the men around, he offered them drinks.

Before Verretti could decline, his phone rang, and after a brief conversation, he ordered Lioni to return to the van.

'My captain will need your help, Friar,' he ordered. 'Please go with him.'

Malone protested, but Verretti closed the door on him. He did not have the time to explain himself. He sat down at the head of the dining table. With their transport and arms about to arrive, he needed to go over his plan. His mission was complicated, and success would bring him great prestige. His quest to become the sole commander of the entire Vatican's security would be realized if he pulled it off, but if he did not, it would spell the end of his career.

Chapter 36

Simon stood at the edge of the terrace. Cautiously, to avoid detection, he peered through the balustrade into the streets below. His eyes scanned the road leading to the site. Fearing it would distress Rabin, he had said nothing about Friar Malone's presence at the airport.

The professor joined Simon. Having sensed his colleague's uneasiness, he had followed him. 'Are you expecting someone?' he asked, concerned.

The old saw of 'keeping one's enemies close' sprang into Simon's mind. Being apprised of Malone's whereabouts would have been preferable to guessing. He had no doubt the monk was an informant, and their escape would have been challenging enough without Jennifer's tantrums. 'I saw Malone at the airport, in the bookstore,' Simon said after a moment. 'When I glanced in his direction, he ducked into the shop's back office.'

Rabin had met Malone before. 'It could be a coincidence, Simon. Maybe your eyes were playing tricks on you.'

Simon shook his head. 'Not this time,' he said, standing back. Then, turning to rejoin Jennifer, he stopped short. 'Now where the hell is she?'

'I …' Rabin turned. 'She was just here.'

Simon ran back to the cave where he had left Jennifer two minutes before. Standing on the portico, he scanned the Cave Church's courtyard. 'Now where the Hell did she go?'

'I'm in here,' she called from behind him.

Simon spun around. Her voice had echoed from within the building. As he entered, he saw her standing behind the altar at the back of the cave. Apart from the stone structure and a chair on a two-tiered pulpit, the cave was devoid of furnishings. 'Don't do this,' he demanded, pausing between the two supporting stone columns just inside the entrance.

The amber of a setting sun shining light from the doors and windows overhead cast a halo around Simon's frame, making him look celestial. 'You were busy, so I thought I'd have a quick look inside.'

Rabin stopped beside Simon. 'You need to get going if you're going to catch a flight from Adana.'

Jennifer knew she ought to go, but her heart bid her to stay. She had so much still to learn. She was trying to find closure somehow—closure for the death of her faith but also for the deaths of her mother and her career. Christianity had been with her from birth. Her entire religious life hinged on the precepts that had been preached on this very spot; where the Apostle Peter had purportedly accepted Paul's ministry to the gentiles. She sighed. Neither the fifth-century fresco above her head nor the twentieth-century marble statue in the niche behind her were proof of this, however, she knew that.

'We'll be here for months at this rate,' Rabin said. 'It's a complicated site. If it were easy, we wouldn't still be digging up top. Why don't you come back later?'

That was the problem—she could not. Even if they evaded the gendarmes, her finances would never allow her to globe trot again.

'In all likelihood,' Rabin said, 'there's nothing more here.'

She hated to admit it, but perhaps the professor was right. She had to let go. Peter had not preached in Antioch. If he had, scripture would have said so. Despondent, she hunched forward, resting her hands on the altar and staring aimlessly at its dusty surface. That was when, she had another revelation.

'Don't altars sit atop relics?' she asked.

The words had hardly left her mouth when the altar shifted slightly beneath her hands.

Her head shot up. 'Did you feel that?'

Simon had been an Antiochene all his life and knew exactly what it meant. Turkey lay over two Anatolian fault lines. In the last decade, there had been four massive earthquakes. Tens of thousands of lives had been lost, and hundreds of thousands of homes, destroyed. In fact, the closure of the Cave Church had resulted from tremors like these. As he felt a second tremble buckle the ground beneath his feet, he finally lost patience with Jennifer.

'Now we've really got to get out of here!' he yelled.

The ground under Jennifer shook, moving the altar. As if on ice, it slid sideways and back. Her feet parted. She looked down. The stone blocks between her feet had separated from each other and the opening snaked beneath the altar. A roar filled the cave, and she looked up. To her horror, the floor between Simon and Rabin first shot upwards, then back down, crumbling as the earth sucked away. Her heart seemed ready to explode from the sudden surge of adrenaline.

Simon plunged to his side of the cave, landing against the wall.

Rabin also sprang away, landing on his belly in front of the archway at his side.

Simon's eyes locked on Jennifer, who stood spread-eagle over the chasm, her arms raised as she tried to maintain her balance.

'Don't move!' he shouted.

Jumping to his feet, it took only three strides to land on the podium. Using the weight of the stone altar to propel himself, he leapt forward, catching Jennifer around the waist as he dove past. He landed on his back with her on top of him, just as slate peeled from the ceiling. He rolled over her, in time to take the falling debris striking his shoulder blades. The altar disappeared behind them and he sprang to his feet. He hauled Jennifer to hers as the altar toppled into the opening.

Simon pulled her back. 'We've got to get out of here!'

The professor had waited in the vestibule to make sure Simon and Jennifer were safe, but as he turned to lead them, the mortar in the columns' stone blocks started crushing. He stuck out his arm to stop them. The imminent collapse of the triple-barrel vaulted roof and facade left them with no choice. They would have to turn back.

'The catacombs!' he yelled, turning.

Jennifer's heart felt it would explode in her throat. 'Is it safe?' she whined.

'Safer than being here, yes!'

Simon spun around and drew Jennifer towards the tunnel in the back corner of the cave. He had only managed a few steps when her weight pulled him back. He lunged towards the tunnel, but she nearly ripped his arm out of joint. Glancing back, he saw she had slipped down the chasm.

'Oh, my God!' she called out.

'Uri!' Simon cried. 'I need your help.'

Rabin saw Simon struggling to maintain his hold on the paving stone and moved in to grab hold of his legs.

Jennifer reached out with her other hand, but instead of getting hold of the paving stones, she slipped further down.

'Hold on!' Simon screamed. He braced his free arm around a floor stone and tried to pull her up, but both their palms were sweating, and he started losing traction.

Jennifer tried to pull herself up, but it was like being stuck in quicksand—the more she fought, the more she inched down the chasm. Realizing that further struggling was futile, she stopped. It was no use trying, she decided. As with her mother, her time had now come. Soon they would be together again. Dangling by her fingertips, she stared up at Simon. Their eyes met, and she felt calm.

'I'm ready,' she said softly. 'Don't worry, Simon, I'll be safe.'

When his grip slackened, her last thought turned into a wish. She wished she had had time to know him better. Then, their fingers parted.

'No!' Simon cried. He felt sick. Losing her was unthinkable; not after they had come so far together.

Suddenly the ground beneath Simon gave in, and he also tumbled into the chasm, head first.

The professor threw himself on his stomach, peering over the precipice, but he was too late—Jennifer and Simon were both gone, submerged in a haze of whirling dust.

The rumble was dissipating and the ground beneath Rabin stabilized. As the tremors ceased, the stillness echoed the silence inside him. He could not imagine losing two young people; not like this. He loved Simon and in the short time he had known Jennifer, had had the utmost respect for her. The world could not lose people like them. Not with so much to offer. People like them were a rarity. He could not imagine meeting more than a handful in his lifetime. He refused to give them up for dead. He must know for certain.

Light filtered through the church's broken façade, illuminating the space below. That was when he saw Jennifer; five meters or more beneath him, dusting herself, she looked as shocked as he felt. Simon stood by her side, checking if she was hurt.

'Jennifer, are you all right?' Rabin called out.

'I think I'm okay,' she said, examining herself in disbelief.

'And you Simon?'

'Apart from a few scrapes, I'm fine.'

Rabin was still lying on his stomach. Indeed, Jennifer was just fine and was now adjusting her skirt. Looking up at him, she smiled broadly. For a moment, the professor was struck dumb. Even caked with earth and dust, she looked angelic.

'Yup,' Jennifer said, 'totally all right, every part of me.'

'Don't move. I'm coming down!'

Rabin examined the chasm's wall for a secure surface. Inching closer to the edge, he searched for a foothold.

'No, stay there', Simon warned. 'We're going to need help getting back up.'

Rabin rose. 'Stay where you are. There's a ladder at the box office.' Picking his way over fallen rubble he set off towards the exit. 'Don't do anything stupid. I'll be back in a minute ...'

As Simon checked the chasm wall for stability, Jennifer called him. Ignoring her, he searched for a flat surface to place the ladder.

'Simon …'

When he turned, she was standing with her back to him.

'Are you hurt?' he asked.

'I think I saw something.'

He moved in behind her. Just past her was a man-sized recess. It must be a long-buried sepulcher torn open by the earthquake. He edged past her. Inside the chamber lay a sandstone ossuary, the front of which had been crushed by the impact of falling debris.

Jennifer's curiosity overtook her squeamishness. Joining Simon, she watched as he brushed the sand from a pearly, convex object.

'What is it?'

'A skull.'

Her hair stood on end. 'Don't joke.'

'I do this for a living, Jennifer. It's definitely a skull.'

Rabin returned from the ablution block carrying an aluminum ladder. He extended the parts and locked them into place. As he lowered it into the chasm, he urged Simon and Jennifer to climb up.

'We have to hurry, Simon,' he said, stomping the ladder down for a secure footing.

'Uri, you should come down here,' said Simon.

'No Simon. You know there will be aftershocks.'

'Come down first. We can leave as soon as you've seen this.'

Rabin hesitated. The last thing he needed was for the walls to cave in on them, burying them alive. But realizing his colleague would not insist if it were not important he gave in, and avoiding the displacement of loose rocks, he made his way down. After carefully looking Jennifer up and down, he approached the chamber. It was certainly a grave, and considering its location, it was undoubtedly important. He saw the broken ossuary and his heart nearly failed him. Without an intact inscription, identifying the bones would be a major challenge.

When a metallic object in the rubble caught Jennifer's eye, she reached out for it, but Rabin stopped her.

'It looks like a set of keys,' she said.

'And a sword,' said Simon.

'Is that common?'

'Not at all.'

Rabin pulled his phone from his pants pocket to call the workers at the dig site. They would need help recovering the remains. On finding there was no reception, he lifted the keys from the sand, dusted them and put them in his shirt pocket.

Simon could not believe his eyes. They never moved artefacts without meticulously recording and photographing their exact locations; never mind professional ethics, the Turkish authorities were fanatical about protocol.

'I know what you're thinking,' Rabin said, 'and I hate doing it this way too, but we really have no choice. The earthquake changes everything. If another tremor strikes, it will destroy everything anyhow.'

Jennifer could not have cared less about protocol. She just needed to know who they had found.

'The symbols of the Apostle Peter are a set of keys and a sword,' she said. 'The keys unlock Heaven's gates, and he used his sword to cut off a Roman soldier's ear during Christ's arrest.'

Rabin had expected something illogical from her, but now she was just being dumb. 'It proves nothing,' he said. 'Crusader knights also had keys and swords.'

'They didn't bury their dead in ossuaries though.'

'She has a point, Uri,' Simon broke in.

Rabin was astonished by their naivety. 'Both of you should know better,' he said irritably. 'Peter's keys were symbolic. These keys are real.'

Jennifer frowned. 'Are you saying that if these were Peter's remains there'd be no keys?'

'Who knows, but don't *you* think it's a bit convenient that there's a set of keys and a sword in a grave beneath this particular church? For one thing, unless there's a literal gate to Heaven, the whole idea that Peter carried actual keys is absurd. I could perhaps accept Apostle Peter having a sword, but that doesn't mean thousands of other people with swords weren't in this cave. So, we should get a specialist in ancient weaponry to examine this and confirm it's of the correct period first. Moreover, even if the keys and sword are both genuine, or the bones have all the right genetic markers for a first-century Judean, carbon dated to the right period too—say we can establish all of this—that in no way rules out the possibility that crusaders found the grave a thousand years ago. Everything has to check out—the sword, ossuary and keys.'

The professor's corrections were annoying, but he was right. As a Christian, she had learned to accept the Bible on faith, but in archaeology, every theory had to stand up to rigorous scrutiny that left no room for doubt. Evidence, evidence and more *evidence*; that was what science depended on. Sheer coincidence would never be sufficient proof.

'Then we should find out where the keys fit,' she said after a moment. 'If the keys weren't meant to open Heaven's gates, they must fit real locks somewhere, and whatever's behind those locks, is worth investigating.'

'Jennifer,' Rabin said, frustrated by her persistence. 'We can determine the age of the bones with carbon dating and have the keys and sword dated by their design and metal compositions. That will show us whether they date from antiquity and indicate the general area where they were made. We can also genetically test the bones to see if they have the same markers as the remains found in first-century graves in Israel; in fact, we can even test them to see if they match remains found in Galilee. But to unequivocally prove they're Apostle Peter's bones, we'd need something distinctive, like an ID or a passport with a photo of his face or something, and good luck finding that.'

Jennifer had no time or patience for lengthy processes. She wanted her faith proved empirically without all the rigmarole. An inscription would certainly help, but the front of the ossuary lay cropped off and shattered, and even if it were not, it would also have to be dated to prove its age. Perhaps it could be reassembled if all the pieces were collected, but that would take time, and she knew the likelihood of finding a name was nil.

Simon again checked his watch. It was seven o'clock. The gendarmes would be nearly up the mountain. 'We've really got to get the hell out of here. They'll be here any time now.'

Jennifer sulked. At the very least, she needed something to take with her.

Sensing her reluctance Simon started for the ladder.

'All right,' he said. 'I'm truly sick of this now. If you want to deal with the gendarmes, go for it. Play here in the dirt all damn night. I've humored your bullshit far too long, Jennifer. I've saved your life twice, and both times it would have been unnecessary if you had simply accepted that some things can't be proved. You are N-E-V-E-R going to find irrefutable proof of God's existence, but go ahead and get yourself killed looking. I'm not saving you again.'

Jennifer stared blankly at Simon as he climbed the ladder and disappeared over the top of the crevasse. But she turned back to the remains in the sepulcher. She was desperate. There was no way she would normally dig around in someone's remains, but this was her last chance to find something—anything—that would give back her faith.

'Please, God,' she whispered, leaning into the sepulcher.

There was nothing, as expected, but at least she had tried. Then her eyes adjusted to the almost darkened chamber and she spotted a bone. She lifted it from the soil.

'What's this?' Rabin shot forward. 'Give me that!'

She set a bone in his outstretched palm.

He flipped it over so that its most important detail was visible to both.

'Now, this might just prove something,' he gasped. 'You might just have made the most important find of the century, perhaps the millennium …'

The small fragment was singular in its simplicity, just a portion of a human heel bone. What made it special was what also made it painful to look at—a heavily rusted iron spike driven through its center. Only one other example like this existed in the entire world, and that had not been dedicated to Apostle Peter. Rabin pulled out his phone and, activating the flash, held the relic under the light.

'What a specimen,' Rabin said, studying the relic. 'It's almost identical to the two-thousand-year old remains we had unearthed in Jerusalem around fifty years ago. It belonged to a young man named Yehohanan. He was still in his twenties when he had died.'

Jennifer clenched her jaw and winced as she imagined the pain of having a spike driven through such a tender spot. And yet, she was elated by their find.

Rabin pivoted the fractured bone from side to side. 'The victim was crucified upside down,' he added.

'No Professor. How can you tell that?'

'The shearing on the bone where the spike penetrated. The direction is towards the bottom of the heel. In normal crucifixions, the sheering is towards the ankle. The way this is, could only have occurred if the weight had pulled down. Hung by the feet, the thin part of the heel would be under immense strain to support the rest of the person's bodyweight.'

Jennifer's lips twisted. His graphic account was disturbing. 'Well,' she said, 'we have a sword, some keys, and a heel-bone with a spike in it that indicates inverted crucifixion, in a church dedicated to Apostle Peter. Is there anything else we need to find to prove who this is?'

'No, Jennifer,' Rabin agreed, 'there really is not much else. We still need to test everything to confirm the dating is correct, but believe it or not, I'm also leaning towards this being Apostle Peter now. The odds of having so many relevant artefacts in one grave are simply too remote for this to be anyone else. All we need to do now is confirm the dating of these pieces and the Apostolic succession is a memory in my book.'

If Jennifer had learnt anything about Rabin, it was that he was not a man to make unqualified assertions. And, of course, he was right that if any piece they had found did not check out in every way, it would not matter what the three of them believed because no one else would be convinced. This, she realized, was the crux of his doggedness. She had not thought about Peter's upside-down crucifixion before. Now, the way in which he was crucified, where he was crucified, who killed him and even whether he was crucified were all crucial. The description of Apostle Peter's crucifixion was mentioned in the Apocrypha, but to establish the story's veracity meant proving that the pieces of evidence they had just unearthed were unimpeachably genuine.

What Jennifer found most unsettling about the grave was not that it could topple Catholicism; rather, she was wondering if Saint Paul had invited Apostle Peter to the area so the two could meet on common ground or had he lured the Nazarene there to eliminate him? Getting rid of Peter in Antioch would have been far less conspicuous than Judea. If Paul as Saul had incited the stoning of Stephen Martyr, he would have certainly had the stomach to effect

Peter's demise. That Paul had, at one time, persecuted other Nazarenes surely indicated that he was a psychopath. Maybe he had had a visitation on his way to Damascus, or maybe he lied to infiltrate early Nazarene's gatherings and destroy Jesus's followers from within. Considering that the man had behaved as sadistically, her assumption made sense.

'You really have to go now,' Rabin said, interrupting Jennifer's daze. 'What's left to do will take days, if not months, and if you don't go now, Simon might leave you. If that happens, all this will have been in vain because the gendarmes will confiscate everything we've found if they catch you here. At least if you two leave there's a chance they will chase you to Adana and not search the dig site.'

Rabin was right; any further delay would endanger her and Simon as well as the artefacts. The truth they had uncovered would be empty if suppressed and Father John's death would have been in vain. She had helped find what might well be evidence of an alternate Christian history—one that challenged Catholicism and Pauline theology, but corroborating a broader Christian tradition.

She helped Rabin pack as many of the artefacts as they could fit into his pockets, then climbed to the shattered sanctuary above and quickly negotiated the rubble. Though the front of the church had partially collapsed, the far-right exit was still passable, and they soon found themselves crossing the courtyard.

In the parking lot, Simon was sitting in the Range Rover, fractiously strumming his fingers on the steering wheel and scanning the mouth of the path up to the Cave Church. He started the engine and pulled towards them. He braked abruptly and swung the passenger door open.

When Jennifer handed Rabin the relics, he kissed her on the cheeks and escorted her to the Range Rover.

Watching him as they drove from the parking lot, the professor looked both avuncular and a little odd with bits of ossuary and bones bulging from his pockets. She leaned out of her window to wave him goodbye. As the professor disappeared, she heard his call the last time.

'Drive safely,' Rabin's voice echoed over the roar of the Range Rover. 'And call me when you get to Adana. Shalom!'

Chapter 37

The window in Friar Malone's guest quarters had no view of the Cave Church of Saint Peter, but Verretti paced in front of it anyway. Waiting for an important call, he had tried sitting at the dining-room table, but he was jittery and could not bear to be still. He and his men must not be discovered operating outside their jurisdiction. The clandestine nature of the operation prevented them from entering a foreign country armed to the teeth; they would not have made it past customs. The problem was, of course, that they could not accomplish their mission without weaponry and specialized transport. His stomach turned, as he realized how ill-advised their hasty departure had been. That was where Their Eminences Santori and Cardoni entered the playing field. The two cardinals had somehow managed to orchestrate a delivery.

Indeed, Verretti was so nervous as he paced that, though he had been waiting for a call, the shrill ring of his phone startled him. He answered and, after a brief exchange, ordered his men into the court in front of the church. As they waited, a second call came through, this time from Lioni. The adjutant and monk had been reconnoitering the Cave Church for the past half hour. Verretti needed to make sure the suspects were still at the site and had not left while Malone was fetching them at the airport. That would spell disaster. If there was any movement at all, Lioni was to pursue from a safe distance. Under no circumstance was he to engage without the rest of the team in place to facilitate the arrest. There was no room for error, and failing to act discreetly would jeopardize the entire mission; if not, cost them their lives.

To Verretti's dismay, the suspects had left and were heading north. As ordered, Lioni and Malone had followed them at a safe distance and, thus far, had managed to remain undetected. Verretti had Lioni's Smartphone linked to his, and the inspector now logged into the tracking application to view their position.

Darkness, meanwhile, was descending on Antakya, and the street outside the church was quiet. Across the court an ambulance and response vehicle waited under a tree to avoid streetlights. As Verretti approached, he noticed The Order of Saint John's logos on the vehicles and it puzzled him. It was the third time he had been the recipient of Hospitaller support that day. The first had been on the Puma helicopter that had transported them from the Vatican to Ciampino Airport. The second had been on the jet, which brought them to Antakya. A thought nagged at him, but he had no time to consider it. His only concern was that things went smoothly until his return to Rome.

Soon, a man dressed in a bomber jacket with a Saint John's insignia strolled from the shadows behind the ambulances. He was a sinewy man with epaulettes extending beyond his shoulders. Verretti stretched out his hand in greeting, but the man declined to introduce himself.

Verretti, decided to call the man Max. He had a sense that Max was not actually a Saint John's officer. Max's overdeveloped chest, bony face and slit eyes reminded him of a snake that had just swallowed a rat.

Max's eyes scanned the street. Seeing nobody, he waved and a second man in a similar uniform stepped from the shadows.

The second man opened the back of the ambulance. Beside the stretcher sat two crates. When the man opened the first, Verretti saw six MP5 MOD sub-machine guns, each with pre-attached ACOG scopes and S3 silencers. Extremely accurate and controllable in short bursts of fire, the MP5s would be of great use in midrange combat.

Verretti turned his attention to the second crate. This contained two-way communication sets, Glock pistols, extra magazines, ammunition and slings with ammunition pouches. The inspector pulled a Glock from its holster. Satisfied, he turned his attention to the medical kit. He had requested drips, syringes, needles and vials of local anesthetic. Max did not disappoint. Finally, Verretti asked about the hi-vis jackets he had ordered—some of the men would wear Saint John's clothing as disguise. This would come in handy in case of a roadblock.

'I take it someone's picking you up?' Verretti asked.

Max nodded, and Verretti divvied the keys between two of his men. Snapping up two magazines for his Glock, he ordered his men to arm themselves and, hopping into the passenger seat of the rescue vehicle, he told the driver to start the engine. He also attached his Smartphone to the windshield. Determining Lioni's position was crucial. He had an idea where their suspects were heading, but he could not base his mission on belief. Something could happen to Lioni and Malone, making tracking them impossible. That would be a disaster. When Lioni's phone flashed on the Google map, he sighed in relief. Now he had their location.

The rescue vehicle and ambulance circled the block and headed out of Antakya. At a crossroads about three kilometers outside town, Verretti checked Lioni's position. He was wary of ending up in Syria, and if they were forced to engage with any Muslim extremists, a diplomatic disaster would ensue. Family pride and personal ambition aside, the Vatican's existence depended on the success of the present mission, although Verretti certainly intended to avoid danger to himself.

As he directed the driver to turn right, the small, red dot representing Lioni and Malone disappeared momentarily.

This was going to be a long night.

Chapter 38

Surpassing even the glamour of the Rue du Faubourg-Saint-Honoré in Paris and London's Bond Street, Rome's Via dei Condotti was the epicenter of Italy's fashion industry. Lined with three- and four-story buildings, it boasted no fewer than seven palaces. On the street level, gaudy clothes clashed with the dignity of age-old architecture as the jet set clustered to experience the latest creations of Dior, Gucci, Valentino, Hermes, Armani, Cartier, La Perla and Prada—all household names to the sophisticates who frequented the quarter's shops.

Further up the street, a Late-Renaissance church, the Santissima Trinità dei Monti, served as a focal point from its position above the early eighteenth-century Spanish steps. In the Piazza di Spagna below, cameras flashed as tourists attempted to memorialize their vacations. Others stood agape, pointing to whichever landmark had caught their attention. At the famous corner eatery Caffé Greco, waiters scurried between tables, anxiously serving mirthful patrons as if they were royalty. Everywhere, as people gathered in the labyrinth of plazas, streets and steps, the electric atmosphere of the Via dei Condotti was palpable.

The Palazzo Malta—containing the headquarters of the Sovereign Military Order of Malta and the governmental and administrative residences of the order's Grand Master, Grand Priors and Deputy Grand Priors—was in the center of the Via dei Condotti. Built in the seventeenth century, the three-story, ashlar-block palace with its corbelled cornices boasted extraterritorial status, courtesy of the Italian Government. Two red flags were draped diagonally from the first-floor balcony above the main entrance, one with a white Latin cross—the state flag of the Sovereign Military Order of Malta—the other with a white Maltese cross—the flag of the Grand Master of the Order. Access from the Via dei Condotti was through a narrow archway opening onto a central courtyard. In the cobblestones of the courtyard, which was large enough to receive six vehicles abreast, was set an outsize Maltese cross. Curious passers-by would peer through the archway when it was open. At the far wall, another Maltese cross loomed over a fountain shaped like a lion's head.

His Most Eminent Highness, Grand Master Fra' Pierre Dubois, stood by his office window overlooking the Via dei Condotti.

'Lord Jesus, Thou hast seen fit to enlist me for Thy service amongst the Knights and Dames of Saint John of Jerusalem. I humbly beseech Thee, through the intercession of the most holy Virgin of Philerme, of Saint John the Baptist and the Blessed Gerard and of all the Saints, to keep me faithful to the traditions of our order. Be it mine to practice and defend the Catholic, the Apostolic, the Roman faith against the enemies of religion; be it mine to practice charity towards my neighbors, especially the poor and sick. Give me the strength I need to carry out my resolve, negligent of myself, learning ever from Thy Holy Gospel a spirit of deep and generous Christian devotion, striving ever to promote God's glory, the world's peace and all that might benefit the Order of Saint John of Jerusalem. Amen.'

Fra' Dubois could not remember when he had last recited the mystical vows of his knighthood. The vows—designed to act as a reminder of one's pledge to serve humanity—were a centuries-old tradition. His Maltese cross, which he rolled between his fingers when in meditative moods, was a symbol of the spiritual nature of his vows. In honour of God and the Holy Cross, brothers of the order wore it at all times. The four arms symbolized the four cardinal virtues: prudence, justice, temperance and fortitude; the eight points of the cross symbolized the eight beatitudes that Christ had bestowed upon his followers.

It had taken Dubois over thirty years to become Grand Master. His uncle, a former master himself, had introduced his nephew into the order as a promising aspirant. Like all grand masters before him, Dubois was the offspring of nobility. Born a Frenchman, his family was descended from Sir Adrian Fortescue, a knight of Malta martyred in 1539. The Council Complete of State of the Order of Malta had ordained Dubois eightieth Prince and Grand Master in 2010, allowing him to achieve the apex of the celebrated order's rankings. He recalled receiving his seal with pride. It had been a memorable occasion; in his early sixties at the time, he had been young for a grand master.

At an intersection in the Via del Corso, a limousine turned into the Via dei Condotti. Making its way towards the Palazzo Malta, the black-diamond Mercedes crawled through the throngs of sightseers. Dubois placed his Maltese cross in his pocket and buttoned up his double-breasted jacket. As the limousine stopped before the palace entrance, he crossed the room to his desk. He watched on a monitor as his guards opened the building's large, wooden doors. After it had advanced to the steel portcullis, an Order of Malta guard used a mirror on an extension pole to inspect the vehicle's undercarriage for explosives. Another guard spoke with the driver; after a moment, the guard leaned through the driver's window to identify the passengers in the backseat. Satisfied, he straightened, saluted and ordered the control gate open.

As the limousine entered the courtyard, Dubois studied a second monitor. A guard marched out from reception to open a door. As the first figure stepped out, the guard knelt to kiss the dignitary's ring. Dubois recognized the cardinal from his upright bearing and forthright demeanor. The second dignitary emerged, and the guard repeated the ritual. Dubois had known this cardinal since Pope John Paul II had appointed him Cardinalis Patronus to the Order more than fifteen years earlier. His duties of promoting the order's spiritual interests and acting as a liaison to the Holy See ensured they had met regularly over the past thirty years.

Above Dubois' desk hung a framed picture of himself standing beside His Supreme Holiness, Pope Gregory XVIII. As now, Dubois wore a red military jacket embroidered in gold and decorated with tassels, medals and other evidence of the great deal he had accomplished during, at that point, his brief time as Grand Master. Only one citation still eluded him, and it was the most prestigious of all—The Supreme Order of Christ. The papal order of chivalry owes its origins to the Portuguese Order of Christ of the Knights Templar. Traditionally awarded to senior Catholic heads of state, his elevated position amongst God's elite and his assistance in the current debacle certainly set him on a course to becoming the next recipient, but his position was also something of a double-edged sword. As prince and grand master of the autonomous order, Dubois governed both as sovereign and religious head. And yet, in addition to his title, 'Most Eminent Highness', the Holy Roman Catholic Church had also conferred on him the rank of Cardinal, thus binding him to the Holy See.

Dubois did not take his connection to the Vatican lightly. It only took a moment's reflection to remind him that a pope had once yielded to a king, allowing the elite of the Knights Templar to be burned at the stake. In 1307, King Philip of France had ordered the arrest of all French Templar, falsely charging them with heresy to appropriate their immense riches. Many of the accused 'confessed' under torture, obligating Pope Clement to issue a papal bull instructing the Christian monarchs of Europe to arrest all Templar and to seize their assets. After petitioning for papal hearings to determine their innocence or guilt, many Templar recanted their earlier confessions, but King Philip reacted by threatening military action unless Clement complied with his wishes. Based on their original confessions, Philip sent numerous Templar to the stake. This scandal resulted in Clement dissolving the order. In the years that followed, many surviving Templar Knights and their assets became absorbed into the Order of Malta.

The knights and dames of the Order of Saint John had, for nearly a thousand years, devoted their lives to caring for the needy and disadvantaged. Operating with complete impartiality and, at times, putting their own lives at risk, they cared for all, regardless of race or religion. Their mission included providing medical and social assistance, disaster relief and emergency services, as well as supporting the elderly, handicapped, destitute and orphaned.

Although the order had, through the ages, suffered considerable setbacks at the hands of enemy sovereigns, it had remained a formidable organization. The order now included more than thirteen thousand members, eighty thousand permanent volunteers and twenty thousand medical personnel in one hundred and twenty countries. Indeed, lending credence to its position as one of the planet's most powerful religious charities, its membership included CIA directors, Young Americans for Freedom leaders, high-profile military and intelligence personnel, NATO generals and even a former US Secretary of State.

Dubois acknowledged the knock on his door from the antique cherry wood table, which stood on the elegant Persian rug in the center of the room.

On entering, the guard bowed low. 'Your Most Eminent Highness, your visitors have arrived.'

'Show them in.'

Cardinal Santori entered before the guard had a chance to announce him. He moved swiftly to the chair farthest from the entrance, which position gave him a view of the whole room. Approaching Dubois cap in hand had embarrassed him, and his profusely sweating brow reflected this.

After Santori's entrance, Cardoni slumped in, seeming drained. In addition to the dramatic events of the morning, he had had to endure Santori's jabbering about the Order's excessive use of insignias on their paraphernalia and palace. In criticizing the Order, his dear colleague seemed to have conveniently forgotten the Vatican's own profusion of ceremonial gear and regalia. He grimaced as the parable of the mote and the beam crossed his mind.

'We must thank you for your help, Pierre,' Cardoni said, seating himself on the couch against the wall.

Dubois offered them drinks, but both declined. He then sat down opposite Cardoni. 'I've arranged for someone to assist your men in Turkey,' he said.

Cardoni needed a moment to catch his breath. The two flights of steps to the third floor, on top of such a hectic day and the two packs of cigarettes he had already chain smoked, made him truly wish someone else could have come in his stead.

'We hope to return the favor one day, Pierre,' he said finally.

'This can't go public. You know that, don't you?'

'That's not why we're here,' Santori said, adjusting the cushions behind his back.

Dubois' gaze settled on him. The man looked grim. 'Did anyone ask for a ransom yet?'

Santori swallowed hard but held his gaze. 'I doubt it will come to that.'

The cardinal sounded anything but confident. Dubois sat silently for a moment, before continuing, 'Is there anything else I can do?'

'Our men are very capable,' Santori said. 'They'll bring it back.'

'What about the suspects?'

'That's why we are here, Pierre,' Cardoni interjected. 'We need a place to finalize this matter.'

Dubois looked at Cardoni. As an affiliate of the Holy Roman Catholic Church, his order could not afford a calamity like this. That was why he had given in to their request for assistance. 'I'm not saying yes necessarily, but what did you have in mind?' Unlike the Vatican, which was a skilled, high-profile player, his order was involved in clandestine operations.

Cardoni hesitated; seeking favors never sat well with the Holy See. Such arrangements inevitably had unforeseeable consequences. But right now, they had no choice. 'We need somewhere else to operate once they're back,' he said at last.

'For God's sake! You can't bring them here. Have you seen all the people in the street? The moment you attempt to transport them they'll be in foreign jurisdiction.'

'We can't return them to the Vatican, Pierre. There's too much scrutiny on us now.'

'That's *if* your inspector gets them. My men didn't think much of him—said he was carrying on like a clown, brandishing guns like he was Sylvester Stallone. Has he actually ever been involved in anything serious like this before?'

'No, but that's beside the point. We really can't have those people in the city.'

'Why not get straight to the point, Giovanni?' Santori snapped. 'Can we use your villa, Pierre, on Aventine Hill?'

Santori disregarded Dubois' raised eyebrow. Feeling an anxiety attack coming on again, he stood up. He walked to the cherry wood table and toyed with the order's brass seal, which lay on a silver tray. 'You are equally responsible for all this, Pierre,' he said, stamping the seal down onto a bar of red wax. 'You forget it was your order that found that letter in the first place.'

Dubois turned to face Santori. Was that a threat? 'That was a thousand years ago, Leonardo. Just because members of our order handed the Church a musty piece of paper doesn't make us all co-conspirators in the deceit perpetrated before or since.'

'You know as much as us, Pierre!' Santori shot back. 'I don't see you rushing to expose the truth.'

Dubois rued the day the order had formed a pact with the Holy See. Santori was right though. Their suppression of critical information made them equally responsible. They might have avoided centuries of scrutiny, but as co-conspirators, every member of the order bore as much responsibility as the Holy See. The letter struck at the heart of both their creeds. He hated the mess they were in. He would try once more: 'Can't you take them somewhere else?'

Santori did not respond but, instead, headed for the door. 'We'll let you know as soon as we have more information, and thank you for the use of your facilities.'

'Yes, we must go now, Pierre,' Cardoni said, following his colleague. 'But we'll keep you informed.'

It took a few minutes before Dubois managed to walk to the window. He pulled the curtain back as the limousine drove off in the Via dei Condotti below. Soon the taillights of the Mercedes merged with the street and shop lights. The sound of laughter could be heard drifting up from the streets. The grand master scanned the sea of faces.

'No doubt they're Catholic, most of them,' he thought. 'God help us if they no longer think God exists.'

Chapter 39

Simon thought of jumping stop signs and passing slow traffic on solid lines, but prudence prevailed. It was better not to get caught for reckless driving; they were in enough trouble as it was.

Jennifer sat quietly staring out of the window. She did not feel like talking. After a day of nonstop action, the drive to Adana provided a much-needed break. It also gave her time to reflect on her new role as an investigative journalist. Every incident that day had potential for a major story: her failed interview at the Vatican, the murder at the Penitentiary, her flight from Rome with a suspected murderer, the letter and discovery of the apparent remains of Apostle Peter in Turkey—reporting on any one of these could win her a Pulitzer.

Of all these events, the letter was the most problematic. Rabin had not finished translating it, and even if he had and it supported her conjectures, any serious reader would struggle to accept that Pontius Pilate and Saint Paul had conspired to kill Jesus and His Apostle Peter. It implied that the Roman Church's original leadership had appropriated the Nazarene faith by eliminating its leaders. It also implied that Paul's claim of Christ's divinity had become doctrine over Peter's dead body. Peter's insistence on Jewish principles had made it impossible for the gentiles to claim the religion as their own without radically changing their lives and habits; of course, they would not have wanted to be circumcised or abstain from eating pork or ritually cleanse themselves every time they had sex. By silencing the Nazarene leadership, Paul would have had carte blanche to preach his version of Jesus as the gentiles' savior in and around Rome. The apparent ease with which he had preached a new religion was surely indicative that the Roman government was sanctioning his activities. A multi-decade ministry would not have passed unnoticed. To this day, verification of Paul's persecution and execution had eluded scholars. Some even believed the self-appointed apostle died of natural causes in France. Jennifer would have to wait for more information from Rabin to strengthen her argument, but she was certain of what she believed herself. Assuming the evidence was compelling enough, the sea of change that would ensue once she had published her story was too immense to even imagine.

Luckily the evidence was now safe with Rabin, and already, without verification or completing the translation, they partially demonstrated a truth, which contradicted canonical Church doctrine. Yet, until Rabin completed his analyses, she would be unable to corroborate her story. Readers would dismiss her claims as fantasy. She should have tried to keep that heel bone for herself at least. She could have slipped it into her pocket without showing it to

Rabin and simply presented it to *Geographic America* on her return home.

Simon checked the time on the dashboard clock. The two-hour drive would probably prevent his attempt to get Jennifer on a flight from Adana. Her damned thirst for answers to a failed faith had made that near impossible. They would probably have to find a place to stay for the night, leaving them more vulnerable to capture.

Leaving Turkey just hours after arriving might also be problematic for Jennifer. As a smartly dressed westerner, she was already conspicuous, and arriving at the airport covered in dirt as she was would arouse suspicion. She looked a mess. In his imagination, he could see a customs official accosting her for smuggling contraband. Seeing her staring out of the window made him realize just how impossible it would be for her to board a plane. Fortunately, Turkey no longer conformed to strict sharia dress code, so at least she did not need to wear a hijab and full-length abaya.

Maybe they should escape to Israel. But that meant driving through Syria. He had done countless road trips in the past, but it was no longer a good idea driving a pale-skinned westerner through the area, especially not at night. And not with an armed conflict in process. After the Syrian Civil War began in March 2011, ISI fighters had sent delegates into Syria and established a large presence in Sunni-majority areas such as Ar-Raqqah, Idlib, Deir ez-Zor and Alepp, some of which cities lay directly between them and Israel. With reports of westerners being the target of Islamist extremists, they could not risk falling hostage.

Simon's sudden turning off the E93 and onto a dirt road caught Jennifer off guard. He headed for the valley between two mountain ranges, and she felt her heart beating faster. Realizing it could not be the road to Adana, she asked, 'Where are you going?'

'My place,' he said. 'You need to freshen up.'

'It can't be that bad, surely.'

'Have you see yourself.' He flipped down the sun visor above her head and switched on the light. 'You're covered in dirt.'

She positioned the mirror to reveal her face. She did look a mess.

'Even if we made it on time, you can't fly like that,' he said irritably.

She wiped her cheeks, but the caked sweat and dirt stuck to her skin. Even her hair was standing on end and covered in sand. He was right, arriving at customs looking like that she would attract too much attention, but it was hard to accept defeat. She wanted to know what the rest of the letter said. Now she would never know.

Realizing her selfishness, she glanced over at him. 'What are you going to do?'

'I'm going back with Giorgio in the morning. We're leaving at ten. Well, we were; but I don't know anymore. It depends on how quickly I can get you out of here.'

The idea of him going back to Rome made her uneasy. Not that it was any of her business, of course. Once she was on a flight to Israel, she would be on her own again. She had had one of the most incredible experiences of her life, both at the Vatican and in Turkey, but she had to look to her own future. Her way forward had nothing to do with Simon's fate. She felt for him, but she could not involve herself with his destiny. How could she? She hardly knew the man—not to mention how only a few hours had passed since she had believed he was a murderer. She felt the pain in her chest return, and resolved to stop thinking about him and just relax. It would be an understatement to say she had had a full day. She needed something to take her mind off Simon, but there was nothing in the car, no magazines or books, and she again found herself contemplating her attitude towards him. She felt guilty. It was not like her to be so cold. Perhaps she did care. … Yes, she cared a lot.

'It's too dangerous, Simon. What if they discover he's your brother?'

'They don't know that yet.'

'But what if they do? They'll be waiting.'

'I'll use the letter.'

'To bargain with …?'

Jennifer was still wondering how she could convince him not to go when he turned off the dirt road and onto a driveway. Persian oaks lined the path, bringing back memories of a wine estate she had visited in South Africa. Beyond the trees and open fields, mountains framed the landscape like a theatre backdrop. Although the new moon prevented her from appreciating the landscape fully, the sky was clear enough for starlight to reveal some of its secrets. Her eyes were riveted to the drawn bow of the Milky Way reflecting in the ripples of a pond beside the driveway. She had never seen the stars shining so brightly. She opened her window, reveling in the cool lick of wind on her hair and face. She listened. In the distance, she heard crickets and frogs calling to their mates. The drone of the engine and sound of pebbles chipping away at the Range Rover's undercarriage reminded her of a discordant orchestra. She inhaled the scent of damp soil and wild scrub. The aroma filled her mouth with a zesty savor. It was like smelling a good burgundy before tasting it. That was something she had not had for some time either. The land had rawness to it, as if it had experienced hardship. Yet it seemed a strong, rugged and determined land. It made her feel more alive.

Flickering lights penetrated the vegetation, harnessing her thoughts. Simon was approaching a ten-foot wall. With a remote control, he opened a steel gate and drove into a large courtyard. On both sides, garages and stables lay between trees and shrubs. Two horses peered curiously over their stable doors. Simon rounded a fountain and stopped in front of a stuccoed veranda. He hopped out and ducked around the back of the Range Rover to open her door, but she got out and closed the door herself.

Jennifer was, however, in awe of what, based on Simon's brief description, she had assumed was no more than a humble farmhouse. Before her stood a work of art, a play of geometrical forms and angles entirely foreign to her. Unlocking the door and stepping into the foyer, Simon deactivated the alarm. She could sense from the powerful smell of fabric, leather and wood that the house was still new. As he lit up the spaces from a computerized pad on the wall, the interior transformed into a panorama of light and shadow. A circular table with a vase of wild flowers adorned the center of the foyer. Beyond, the living room flowed into a spacious garden. To the right, at the back of the house, was the kitchen. To the left was Simon's study. Behind that, a hallway linked a TV room and bedroom. Together with the table lamps, sculptures and rugs, these features spoke of hermetic refinement, an apt expression of Simon himself. With a contemporary, open plan and combination of single- and double-volume spaces—with subtly placed stone and brick walls counterbalanced with floor-to-ceiling windows and water features—the ground-floor area was breathtaking. Considering her father had been an architect, her reaction was quite a compliment. She knew of no other man who would appreciate standing there more than her dad. She wished he was there with her.

Her desire for a tour fell on blind eyes.

Without hesitation, Simon set off for his bedroom to the left. He opened the top drawers of his teak bureau and selected a light ash-grey lamb's wool jersey. He draped the garment in front of her to see if it would fit before passing it to her. Satisfied with the result, he set off again.

Jennifer followed as he strode into the *en-suite* bathroom, which walls he had painted desert red contrasting with a floor tiled in cream-grey marble. The décor was complemented by dark wood furnishings.

Simon started the shower for her and admonished her to be quick. He was praying they would not arrive at the airport too late, but felt it to be a vain prayer. They certainly would not make it in time even for the last flight. Retrieving a fresh towel from the linen closet and handing it to her, he turned to leave. As he passed through the bedroom, though, he stopped, suddenly feeling anxious. It was as if a cold fog had fallen over him, and the skin on the back of his neck felt clammy. Something was about to go wrong; he was sure of it.

Simon had had intuitions before; some form of sixth sense. His ability to predict things had started early. As a child, he had anticipated events weeks in advance. It was an unusual skill, which some considered a blessing. Others thought it represented occult powers and was therefore a curse. In the past, such individuals were burned at the stake. For Simon, it was normal, just the way he was born. He did not know how it worked, and recognized science had no explanation for it. Though his premonitions were as dependable as death itself, he had no control over them; they occurred on their own schedule, seemingly at their own will, making any sort of scientific validation through replicable testing impossible.

Even so, his foresight was real enough and he trusted it, in some measure, more than his other senses, it had proved reliable so often. It was this that drove him into his study. He crossed the room to a full-length painting hanging on the wall behind his desk. Tucking his index finger behind its Baroque frame, he pressed a switch. The painting clicked loose and tilted forwards. He swung it open to reveal a safe. He typed a code on the keypad, waited impatiently for it to unlock, and swung open the eight-inch steel door.

All his personal documents lay neatly stacked on the middle shelf. Items of jewelry and bundles of cash lay directly below that. None of these were a concern. He took his Browning pistol from the top shelf, pushed down the safety pin, then pulled the slide back and checked for a round in its chamber. Contrary to habit of returning the hammer and flicking the safety catch to its locked position, he half-cocked the weapon instead. He then took out his harness and felt the weight of the two magazines to make sure they were loaded. They were. Finally, he took a pack of notes and slid it into his back pocket.

After locking the safe and returning the painting back to its original position, he checked his watch. It was nearly eight. Jennifer had better get moving; they had already missed the chance to catch last flight, he was sure, and now they were at risk of being apprehended. They would still try for the airport, but failing to make a flight, they would have to head on for the Greek border. Yes, the birthplace of Western civilization was presently an economic mess, but Syria and Iraq were both out of the question, and Greece was at least devoid of the organized crime and corruption of Bulgaria. Along the way, they could stay at a guesthouse; that would be safer than staying at the farm. His heart throbbed faster. Somehow, he knew these were futile thoughts and there was something unforeseen about to happen.

He decided to check the flight times, but as he clicked the mouse to call up the internet on the desktop monitor, he heard a ticking sound come from the passage outside his study. At first, he told himself it was Jennifer closing the shower door, but given the distance between his bedroom and the study—plus the fact that he remembered closing the bedroom door—her presence seemed unlikely. There it was again! Remaining still, he turned the noise over in his head. What was it? It had almost sounded like the ticking of a window blind. This happened when the wind picked up, causing the pull-button to hit against the glass if the window was slightly open, as his housekeeper sometimes left it. This drove him crazy, especially at night when he was trying to sleep. To reassure himself he leaned over the desk and drew the blind back. He looked across the lawn at the trees in the garden. To his surprise, they were motionless. Not a leaf stirred.

His head swung towards the hallway. It could have been Jennifer, but he was doubtful. Then, he heard the noise again. Flinging the harness over his shoulders, he charged through the doorway. The adrenalin surge tricked his brain into believing he was moving slowly. His pistol was cocked and ready to fire at the slightest sign of movement. Years of

Israeli military service had kicked in. First response was attack, then follow-up. You did not stop unless your enemy was either dead or disarmed. Wars began with patriotism and ideals, but they soon became a matter of simple survival; turning living itself into killing to live, and for the soldier's own safety, mercy could only come to those lying on their faces.

Simon sprinted down the passage. Passing an open window, he saw two intruders in the courtyard, both armed. He halted on the other side of the window and peeked out. One man was already climbing through his bedroom window. He fired twice, hitting the man in the jugular and cheekbone. The intruder slammed against the bedroom window, spun completely around and dropped, blood spurting from his neck and head. Simon's next two rounds hit the second intruder in the chest, one near the heart and the other in the right lung. The force of the shots sent the man's body crashing through the bedroom window.

Pistol clutched in both hands, Simon continued to the bedroom. He knew more were on their way and desperately needed to know where they were, but there was no time. He had to get to Jennifer. Keeping his back to the wall, he approached his bedroom. Just before reaching the door, another assailant sprang from the TV room shooting.

Simon ducked just in time, and the first round clipped him in the shoulder; the second missed, striking the wall inches above his head. Adrenalin must have numbed him because he could not feel anything. He fired over the top of the desk, both rounds hitting his opponent in the sternum. The hollow-point rounds exploded the man's chest, leaving gaping wounds as they left his body. The intruder collapsed backwards, smashing into the grandfather clock and landing on the gore-splattered floor.

'Simon!' Jennifer screamed from the bedroom.

Simon did not wait to see if the wounded assailants stayed down. He reached for the bedroom door. There was no time to check whether Jennifer had locked it. Like a wounded bull, he bashed in the door. The timbers ripped from the hinges and crashed inwards. He tumbled forward, landing on one knee. A man was pushing the barrel of an MP5 to Jennifer's temple. A second man stood behind her, holding her arms behind her back. He posed the lesser threat. He would die second.

Simon's finger was poised on the trigger of his Browning, but his heart failed him. He would not risk getting Jennifer killed. He relaxed his trigger finger, but held his aim steady on the intruder with the MP5.

'Drop it!' he snapped.

'Drop yours,' the intruder with the MP5 said, 'or she dies!'

Jennifer's face was red and swollen. She was still wet from the shower and had not even had the time to cover herself, revealing her nakedness. They had also hit her and tears and spit pooled around her lips. Simon wanted to shift his gaze to her—wanted to make eye contact like they had when she had fallen into the chasm to let her know everything would turn out fine—but he dared not lose focus. Any wrong move and they would both die. He remained kneeling. Realizing he would have to move, his focus remained on the gunman. 'If you do anything stupid,' he said, 'you die first.'

Suddenly, Jennifer began struggling to free herself. The man holding her clapped his hand over her mouth. He squeezed down hard, but she shook loose.

'Behind you!' she cried.

Simon knew what she meant, but he had no time to react. He heard the telltale click of a pistol's hammer being cocked. The firearm was inches behind his head. When a voice ordered him to lower his weapon, he remained still.

'Do it now!'

Simon held his aim.

'I'll say this one more time!'

Simon shifted his gaze to Jennifer and their eyes met. She was determined not to return to Rome. She would rather die than surrender.

'Shoot me, Simon,' she cried. 'Just kill me.'

He did not waver. He needed time to make the right decision.

'Simon, shoot me!'

'No Jennifer, be calm. We'll get through this.'

Simon lowered his pistol. 'Just do as they say.' He could not see her die.

'Slowly ...' said the voice behind Simon.

Simon placed his pistol on the floor.

'Now slide it back towards me.'

Simon flipped the pistol back towards the man behind him. 'You are trespassing,' he said, his voice now composed.

'So were you.'

The voice behind Simon had a distinct Italian accent. It could only be one man. 'You're the head of the gendarmerie?'

'Let me introduce myself. I'm Inspector General Arnaldo Verretti.'

The synapses in Simon's brain flashed. If Verretti had wanted them dead, he would have given the order already. It meant he was after the letter. That bought them time. To get the letter, Verretti would need to keep them alive. They would use Jennifer as leverage. How many times had he foreseen this? He might as well have written the script himself. He needed time.

'What do you want?'

'You know what I want,' Verretti snarled. 'You took something that doesn't belong to you.'

'First, let her go. She has nothing to do with this.'

'Right, and I'm the Second Coming,' Verretti laughed. 'You know I can't do that.'

'I forced her to come with me. She knows nothing.'

'Then she has nothing to fear, does she?' Verretti was now in front of Simon, the muzzle of his Glock touching the Turk's forehead. 'The letter, where is it?'

Simon had to find a way to get Jennifer away from them. He could worry about himself later. Uri might also still be at the site. He often worked late, and he was likely to be awake tonight. He dreaded what would happen if the inspector decided to go to the site and found the professor still there.

The butt of Verretti's pistol struck Simon behind his ear. The skin split, and he fell sideways.

Simon struggled to right himself. The blow had caused a ringing in both his ears, but as if from a distance, he could still hear Jennifer pleading for him. He held his head, blood oozing through his fingers. He struggled back onto one knee. Verretti was not there to negotiate, that was evident.

But he did not know where the letter was. Their only hope lay with the professor. He somehow had to get word to him. He noticed Jennifer fighting to free herself and motioned for her to calm down, saying he was all right.

Verretti kicked Simon in the back, forcing the Turk to the ground. As Lioni ran through the door, he ordered the adjutant to handcuff Simon. He waited as Lioni—knee pushed into Simon's shoulder blades—drew their captive's arms behind his back. When Lioni was done handcuffing Simon, he helped pull him to his feet.

'Take him out and wait in the living room,' Verretti ordered. 'I'll be there in a few minutes.' Then, in a cruel, mocking tone, he added, 'We can't let our new friend go out in the nude now, can we. That would be unseemly.'

Simon heard Jennifer scream frantically as they dragged him from the room.

Chapter 40

Two thousand kilometers to the west, Colonel Schreider made sure Father Franco had retired for the day before he slipped into the Penitentiary. His Eminence Santori's summons that morning had sparked a sequence of events that seemed to be spiraling out of control. It was clear from the events that the cardinal was withholding crucial information regarding the Church, and if so, was Schreider still obligated to honour his pledge? Was it his duty to protect the Church's leadership even when they broke their own vows? It was only his faith in God that had brought him to the coveted position of commander in the first place. How could he protect a man whose actions were contrary to both God and man? He felt sick.

These thoughts appalled Schreider. Even thinking them was a betrayal of his pledge. How could he maintain his integrity? He turned to Weber, who was waiting for him to lock the office door. On the way, he had told his captain about the vault and the secret letter taken from it. He did not want his most trusted soldier to break his vows as well, but the man had the right to know the truth. Schreider would not have involved his second-in-command otherwise.

For his part, though, Weber would take a bullet for his commander. Not that he ever expected it to come to that—Schreider, he knew, would rather take the bullet himself. Defending Schreider was one thing, defying the Holy See, something else entirely; essentially, the colonel was asking him to commit treason against both God *and* country.

Weber was not insensible to the strangeness of Santori's behavior or the injustice if Schreider's suspicions proved true. Thus, he had joined his commander in what could yet prove the most quixotic mission either of them had ever undertaken. He stood beside the colonel, scanning the entrance to Father Franco's office. Satisfied no one had seen them enter, he closed the office door behind him.

'I'm not happy about this, Oberst,' he protested.

Schreider gave him a hard look. 'Suppose one of the cardinals is a murderer; I can't imagine their infallibility allows them to break one of the Ten Commandments and, then, blaming it on someone else, break another.'

Weber felt as if he were confronting the Devil. 'Damn it, Oberst! You can't say that.'

'We're the ones giving them their power,' Schreider said. 'Do they really deserve it? I need an honest answer, Franz—would you desert them?'

Weber looked down. His commander was questioning his loyalty to the Holy Father. 'I've taken a solemn vow.'

'So, you would defend them, even though they are breaking God's laws? What does it take then? Who do you worship, Christ or a bunch of old men in red cassocks making out as if they represent Him?'

'Are you testing me, Oberst?'

'Stay with me Franz. … Just tell me how you feel.'

Confronted with his senior's persistence, Weber contemplated the question. At last he said, 'They are the custodians of God's power and authority. We need them. Our salvation depends on them.'

'Yes, yes. I know that's what they tell us, but ask yourself, is that really the truth?'

Weber thought deeply. The idea of being disloyal to God's elite was frightening.

The more Schreider thought about it himself, the more he needed to know if his oath deserved his loyalty. Proof lay right there in the Penitentiary; of that he was certain.

Ignoring his captain's panic, Schreider moved over to the hearth. 'Look. The fact is that Santori probably killed Yilmaz this morning and blamed it on this Simon person, who stole a letter that the cardinals have admitted is evidence that the Church is lying to the faithful. In the light of that, I have no problem breaking an oath that was founded on a deception. I want to uphold God's law, not pledge vows that protect evil, and to do that we have to get into the vault.'

He pulled the pike from its holster and held it out to his captain. Like the Swiss Guard's halberd, the weapon consisted of a shaft and a spearhead, but instead of the customary steel axe, this spearhead was made from brass and in the shape of a fleur-de-lis.

Holding the pike out before him, Schreider demonstrated how, from the side, the spearhead looked like a two-dimensional three-petal fleur-de-lis. He also showed Weber how, viewed straight on, it resembled a Maltese cross with four leaves and eight points.

Schreider noted the confusion on the captain's face and lifted the pike to the circle motif cut into the side of the hearth, which also contained a Maltese cross. He inserted the spearhead into the center of the cross, aligning the fleur-de-lis petals with the arms of the Maltese.

The petals pressed against the fleurs-de-lis, driving them outwards. Suddenly the brass head disappeared into a hole. He continued sliding the pike deep into the hearth until it stopped against an object on the opposite side. He tapped the butt of the shaft to see if it would go any farther in, but nothing happened. When he tried to move the hearth forward but with the same result, he crossed to the other side of the hearth. Removing the symmetrically placed pike from the opposite wall, he inserted it into the matching cross. He slid it in as far as it would go and had Weber mirror each move. Standing on the library side, they pushed against the pikes to see if the hearth would shift towards Santori's office. Frustrated when nothing happened, Schreider rotated the pike.

A thud followed as the brass head slotted into place.

When Weber followed suit, the locking mechanism disengaged. Suddenly the hearth moved, revealing the secret entrance. 'There's no way the Maggiore would have brought a junior priest in here with him,' he said staring into the abyss. 'Not if the letter is blasphemous.'

Schreider stopped by his captain's side. 'Exactly, and did you notice anything about how we just opened the vault?'

Weber thought for a moment. He was dumbstruck to realize what his commander meant: 'It takes two to get in here!'

Schreider turned on his pocket torch. Taking the lead to familiarize his captain with the space, the colonel stopped at the first landing halfway down. After shining the light into the storage area beneath Santori's office, he descended to the chapel below the library. On reaching the altar, Schreider shone his light where Father Yilmaz had fallen. The blood had dried, but the stench of death lingered.

'Father Yilmaz and our suspect must've worked as a team,' he explained. 'I can't see why he'd enter the vault with his killer. It wouldn't make sense.'

'Unless our suspect used Father Yilmaz to get in and, once he'd found the letter, killed him.'

'That's possible, sure, but since it takes two to get in here, Father Yilmaz would've had time to flee his attacker before entering. Also, the killer left the murder weapon—a knife. Everyone knows about fingerprint evidence, so the only time that happens is *when*?'

Trained in forensics as a cadet, Weber knew the answer by rote: 'When a suspect's interrupted or trying to frame …'

'Precisely,' Schreider said. 'There must've been three people in here: two who opened the vault for sure, and a third who either interrupted a murder, or on committing the murder, tried to frame it on someone else. Now we must wonder who had a motive to kill Yilmaz—a person he opened the vault with or another person who wasn't with them to begin with. Or did Yilmaz and the third person such as Eminence Santori enter the vault, and when the suspect entered to steal the letter, he killed Yilmaz without harming the cardinal. Maybe it's just me, but it's hard to imagine the suspect taking on two, killing one but fleeing from the other. Moreover, consider that His Eminence was covered in blood when we were first called to his office. Adjutant Lioni was the first here and he and Father Franco can attest to seeing it. Hell, there are still splotches of blood and bloody footprints in the Maggiore's office and library, so the fact that His Eminence had contact with a bleeding Yilmaz is beyond any doubt. Now think about us chasing the suspect today. Did you notice anything out of the ordinary?'

'The clothes we recovered were clean. …'

'Absolutely.'

Weber mulled over Schreider's hypothesis. It made perfect sense. He had seen the clothes the suspect had shed in donning the gendarme's uniform. The cassock had not had a speck of blood on it. It could be the suspect had stabbed Yilmaz and sliced his throat without getting blood on him, and the Maggiore got soaked from trying to help the priest after he had been wounded, but since the Maggiore had the strongest motive to kill Yilmaz, that now seems unlikely. The Cardinal was after all, and by his own admission, trying to keep the stolen artefact secret. If the evidence and basic reasoning showed the suspect had not murdered Yilmaz, the blame could only fall on the Maggiore. Indeed, the fact that no one had suspected the cardinal sooner seemed absurd; it was only the priests', gendarmes' and Swiss guards' blind faith in the Church's infallibility that had kept them in ignorance.

'Come,' said Schreider.

He headed for the staircase, stopping briefly at the top to point out the bloody handprint on the side of the hearth where someone had braced himself; it was typical of an older man resting after struggling up the steps. They continued into Santori's office, where, standing with their backs against the door to the reception area, the two officers had a full view of the office suite. The Maggiore must have found the vault standing open after Father Yilmaz and the suspect had entered it. There was no way to open or close it from inside.

Schreider lifted a gold scabbard with a Hospitallers emblem from Santori's desk. He assumed the Maggiore had disposed of the dagger by now, but the implication of its emptiness was clear. Obviously, in his rage the cardinal had grabbed the dagger from his desk; he knew it was there and he had had a reason to take it. The Maggiore likely came upon Father Yilmaz at the altar. The suspect had returned during or after the murder, but finding he was too late to intervene, fled back up the steps, the Maggiore in pursuit.

Weber was convinced and joined Schreider at the desk. The front had bloody fingerprints across it, as if someone with bloody hands had turned to lean against it. From that position, the person would have a perfect view of the library behind the hearth. If it were the Maggiore, he would have been looking to see where the suspect had gone. Because

Father Franco covered the reception exit, the suspect had had nowhere to go but the library behind the hearth.

With Weber, hard on his heels, Schreider crossed to the spiral staircase at the back of the library. As he expected, the rear exit had blood on the door handle where the Maggiore must have grabbed it while in pursuit. Schreider returned to the office. He stopped in front of the hearth. Though faint, there was a bloody handprint in the center of the marble lintel. Why had he not spotted it before?

'Left-handed,' he said, holding his hand over the print.

Weber gazed at Schreider. 'Just like the coroner said.'

Schreider gave the captain time with his thoughts, and pulled out the first pike. There were bloodstains on one of the shafts, now barely visible. They were likely the last things the killer had touched. The colonel returned both pikes to their original positions against the wall, unintentionally revealing the last piece of evidence—it took two to open the passage but only one to close it.

He pushed the hearth over the vault's entrance and, once the doorway was closed, turned back towards Weber. 'There *is* one thing I've just remembered. When I arrived here this morning the dagger was still lying downstairs beside the body, and when I saw it, the Maggiore picked it up and wiped it with his handkerchief.'

'To remove his prints,' Weber said.

Schreider sighed deeply. If the Maggiore committed the murder, and it certainly looked that way, he and Weber were in one hell of a predicament. How do you charge a cardinal with murder? Not only did the Holy See abide by its own laws, but His Eminence Santori was one of their highest ranked leaders. Everyone knew of his aspiration to be the next Vicar of Christ, and no one until now doubted its inevitability.

Chapter 41

Verretti pulled out of the driveway, cursing. He fumbled in his pocket for his handkerchief, and adjusting the rear-view mirror to reflect his face, lightly pressed against his bottom lip. The pain became unbearable and he pulled away. A mixture of thickened blood and spit had soaked into the white cotton cloth. Lioni was a good gendarme, but he made a lousy paramedic.

The inspector attempted to focus on the task of recovering the letter, but his mind insistently replayed the scene that had unfolded a half an hour earlier as he stood in the bedroom with Miss Jaine. He had circled her, then stopped behind her and, curling one arm around her shoulder, had slid his hand across her breast and stomach. Attempting to stop his hand from gliding further down she had leaned forward, and he had pulled her back, pinning her naked body against his chest. He recalled painfully how the bitch had jerked her head back, smashing it onto his bottom lip, crushing it against his teeth and bursting the skin, leaving a deep wound. For a second he had nearly lost consciousness. In his stupor, he had relaxed his grip and she had swung around, smashing her elbow into his chest, making him gasp for air. As he landed on the bed, she had kicked, aiming for his groin. He had just managed to roll over, narrowly averting a disaster for future generations of gendarmes throughout Italy. He had not afforded her another chance. As she kicked again, he had shot up and slapped her, flinging her across the room.

He had ordered her to stand and get dressed. She had refused, and he warned her that she would either put her clothes on in front of him or in front of all his men. He had loathed himself for this, but had only been doing his job. He had certainly not been trying to win her affection. He had holstered his pistol and sat down, arms folded. At first, she had remained defiant, but then had turned her back to him. She had stared at herself in the mirror, tears running down her cheeks. Seeing she had no choice, she had submitted, sliding the top over her head and shoulders, dropping it down to her waist so it almost covered her crotch. A gentle shake of her head and her hair had fallen over her shoulders.

Verretti had waited until she had slipped into her skirt and shoes before standing up. Then, he had seized a handful of her hair and pulled her head back. He remembered the smell of her freshly washed hair. Any other time, and it might have been different.

To avoid more of her devilry, he had taken her into the bathroom with him. He had needed to rinse the salty mix of spit and blood out of his mouth. Facing himself in the mirror, he had watched the wound swell while a throbbing pain set in. Hoping she had not cracked a tooth, he had leaned closer to the mirror and flipped his bottom lip inside out. *Cazzo!* She had done a damn fine job on his lip for sure. He had realized he needed at least three stitches, maybe four. His gaze shifted to her reflection in the mirror. As much as he loathed her for getting the better of him, he had always liked a woman with fight in her.

It had taken some time to stop the bleeding. Afterwards, he had wiped his chin with a wet towel. Fortunately, his dark jacket and turtleneck shirt would not stain too badly.

He had then pulled Miss Jaine into the living room, where Lioni and his men were holding Simon. They had escorted their captives to the ambulances parked in a bush outside the main gate. With Verretti's lip stitched by a twitching Lioni, they had taken to the road again, half their mission accomplished. All they needed now was the damn letter.

To get his mind off his humiliation, Verretti decided he was driving. Some of the men sat in the cabin behind him. Cracking jokes, their laughter irked him. One could swear they were on their way to a football match. He turned from the dusty farm road onto the highway which led back to Antakya, spitting more blood-filled saliva out of the window. His men had strict orders not to speak out about what had happened there this night. He would hate to be the butt of Schreider's reaction if he heard his adversary had been injured by a woman. Apart from that detail, he would return to Rome victorious. He imagined himself arriving in a horse-drawn chariot like Julius Caesar, spear in hand, head held proudly high.

Verretti stopped at the road below the Cave Church where a cool breeze drifted across the Hatay valley. He got out, directing Lioni to park the ambulance. In the back, Simon sat handcuffed to a handrail, while Jennifer lay strapped to the stretcher. The inspector ordered his men to retrieve Simon. After they lifted him from the ambulance, he told Lioni to sedate Jennifer. Having anticipated a hostile response, Verretti already had his pistol drawn. When Simon hurled himself at Verretti, the inspector swung hard towards Simon's head, but the Turk ducked, narrowly avoiding the blow.

Simon surged back up, smashing his shoulder into Verretti's midriff. The impact of the blow winded the inspector, making him gasp for air. Simon hurled himself again, pinning Verretti against the steel door, but before he had a chance to strike, the gendarmes wrestled him to the ground.

Verretti hunched over, wheezing, and leaning against the ambulance door. After what seemed an eternity, his diaphragm spasms eased, and he could draw air into his lungs. That the captives should demean him like this was outrageous. It should never have happened, especially in front of his men. The Turk could be glad they were not alone somewhere remote; Verretti would have shot him on the spot.

Verretti signaled to Lioni in the ambulance and shouted, 'Now!'

As the rubber band around Jennifer's arm tightened, she turned her head towards Verretti. 'Please don't. Please ...' Lioni slapped the back of her hand, and she turned her head from side to side slowly. 'Please don't. I beg you, please don't do this.'

As the cold needle pierced her swollen vein, she turned her gaze to Simon on the ground. She drifted off, tears dripping from her face.

His men had hardly lifted Simon to his feet when Verretti sank his fist into the Turk's stomach. He did not allow Simon to catch his breath either, but hit him again as hard as he could. He then had two of his men escort their limp captive up the pathway to the archaeology site before slotting in behind them.

'Move!' he spat. 'We don't have all night.' He glanced over his shoulder at Lioni who was closing the ambulance doors. 'If we're not back in a half an hour, you know what to do.'

Chapter 42

It was half past five in the morning on Wednesday, 21 March 2012. Schreider knelt before the altar of the Cappella Paolina for the final time. Needing a moment of solace with God, he had slipped into the Holy Pontiff's private chapel. Together with the Sistine Chapel and the Regal Room—celebrated for their illustrious frescoes—the Pauline Chapel comprised an integral part of the Apostolic Palace. In the Vatican, where everything was immense, the Pauline Chapel seemed tiny.

No matter how hard Schreider had tried to rest, his thoughts had kept him awake. During the evening, he had considered taking a sleeping tablet but had not wanted to wake up sluggish. That he could ill afford.

After a night of anguish, he had finally made up his mind. As he bowed his head and closed his eyes in contemplation, he attempted to justify his plan to himself and to God. He remained there in stillness for some time. Then he rose to his feet.

Retrieving his metal morion with its trimmed heron feathers from the marble podium, he fitted it back on his head. To honour his final day at the Vatican, he had dressed in full military armor. The Oberst of the Guard only wore ceremonial gear during solemn occasions—on Good Friday and Christmas Eve, and during visits from major foreign dignitaries. And yet, Schreider did not care now. If his career or even life ended serving God over the papacy, he would do so with dignity.

With Christ on the cross gazing down at him, he prayed, 'Lord, I beseech Thee to bestow upon your humble servant your divine clarity and wisdom. Forgive me my sins and do not hold my numerous trespasses against me in this dark hour of my soul. Amen.'

He stepped up to the altar, bending with reverence to kiss the cloth. Straightening up, he raised his eyes to the white reliefs in the ceiling and read the inscription on the far panel: 'Vivere Christus est et mori lucrum.' It was *Philippians* 1:21. He knew the verse well. Roughly translated it meant, 'Christ is life and death is a boon.' Rather than crossing himself again, he saluted. He did not know why. Perhaps it signaled his struggle with his faith, or perhaps it underlined the recurring premonition that death was imminent. He shivered with exhaustion but not with fear. His conscience was clear. If he died defending righteousness against a corrupt Church, he would happily meet Christ.

He turned to go, but halfway down the aisle he stopped. Standing in the center of the nave, he turned, looking at the room around him. On every wall were colorful frescos, while in the corners, marble sculptures of scantily clad young boys held lanterns to light the way of the faithful. On the coffered ceiling, naked figures framed frescoes of biblical scenes. Facing the exit his gaze lowered to the wall on his right and fell on the most famous fresco, Michelangelo's *The Conversion of Saul*. It depicted Saul on the road to Damascus, after he had received authorization to slaughter Christ's disciples. Schreider turned to face Michelangelo's *The Crucifixion of Saint Peter* on the opposite wall. This painting depicted the several soldiers' crucifying an elderly man.

'The great Catholic paradox,' thought Schreider.

The details in these frescoes were incorrect. In the conversion fresco, Michelangelo had depicted Saul dressed as a Roman, fallen from his horse, and with Jesus appearing from Heaven surrounded by angels. In the other, he had portrayed the Apostle Peter hanging naked from an upside down cross. While the first event was recorded in Acts, historically speaking, Saul was a Jew, not a Roman patrician, and he would not therefore have worn—or even been allowed to wear—a toga; as for the crucifixion of Saint Peter, the story appeared nowhere in the canonical Bible, but had been lifted from the apocrypha. Now, studying the works anew, Schreider saw something else: Saul's spiritual rebirth occurred at the expense of his archrival, resulting in Peter's relegation to shame and death. This could hardly be a coincidence, surely.

Pope Paul III who had commissioned the chapel and frescoes had dedicated the building on the Feast of the Conversion of Saint Paul. Schreider recalled that Pope Paul III was a corrupt ruler. His birth name was Alessandro Farnese. During his long reign as pope, he had abused his authority to advance his own family's wealth and power using unabashed nepotism. The Farnese family had prospered for centuries before, but Alessandro used his ascendancy to further the family's interests. In his youth, he had fathered four illegitimate children. As pope, he had had the temerity to make all his grandchildren cardinals. At the time, they were still teenagers. The same pope had appointed Michelangelo to supervise the building of Saint Peter's Basilica. Strangely, he had designed it in the shape of an eight-pointed sun-cross.

How could any sane person condone Paul III's actions? Everything he touched should have been burnt to the ground. Schreider tried to imagine what would happen if current pontiffs were similarly corrupt.

This was a watershed moment for Schreider. For his whole life, he had thought of this chapel as the epitome of culture and art, but no longer. That which had aroused in him adoration and admiration now evoked disgust at the Church's lies and deceit. He did not like feeling this way. It was not how his parents had raised him. They had brought him up to be obedient, respectful and honorable—traits which now represented his antithesis. Not only was he violating his family's traditions, he was contradicting his own beliefs. He wished he had never come to the Vatican; he should not have made his religion his job. Like Martin Luther before him, he had arrived in Rome a naïve idealist and would leave it feeling bitter and betrayed. At this point, he was practically a Protestant. He wondered what kind he would be if he lived.

The colonel's footsteps echoed off the chapel's many reflective surfaces as he crossed its black- and white-checkered, marble floor. Marching into the Regal Room, he glanced at the pontiff's gilded throne, from which His Holiness presided as monarch of the Roman Catholic

Church. The permanent throne of the Bishop of Rome, the *Cathedra Romana*, stood in the apse of the Basilica of Saint John Lateran. A secondary throne, the *Cathedra Petri*, believed to have been that of Saint Peter himself, stood in the apse of Saint Peter's Basilica. However, this throne was purely decorative. Other movable thrones, each with its own movable dais, were scattered throughout the Vatican. The Regal Room throne and dais served as the pontiff's seat when entertaining heads of state and other dignitaries.

Schreider would honour his pledge to the Holy See one last time. He would have the pontiff decide his fate. Entering the command center minutes later, he strode straight to the surveillance room. He dismissed the stares of his men. This was not the time to explain his ceremonial gear. He halted by his communications officer.

'What's Verretti's status?' he asked.

The operator gazed up at his commander. 'He is nearing Rome as we speak, Oberst.'

'The suspects?'

'They have them, Oberst,' said a lieutenant, who had just hurried over from the surveillance desk. 'They should land any minute now.'

Schreider set off towards his office, beckoning the lieutenant to join him. At the reception desk, he ordered a corporal to get him a triple espresso. In his office, he laid his helmet on the desk and pressed the intercom button. 'Get me Captain Weber. If he's still in bed, fetch him. I need him in my office ASAP.' He turned to the lieutenant. 'Get the bomber in here. Five minutes. You have five minutes.'

'What about the gendarmerie, Oberst?'

'Did you hear what I just said?'

'Oberst.'

The lieutenant scurried from his office as the corporal reappeared with a stainless-steel mug. He placed the steaming coffee in front of Schreider before backing out obsequiously.

Schreider had barely taken a sip when Weber arrived clad in wrinkled trousers and an undershirt—his face still creased from sleep. The colonel waited for his captain to take a seat opposite him before asking, 'Franz, can I rely on you today?' When Weber nodded, he continued, 'We have to stop Verretti.'

Weber remained impassive. He was still half asleep. 'We're going to be in a lot of trouble for this, Oberst,' he yawned. 'But I won't forget all you've done for me as long as I live.'

Weber's statement, coming as it did from a partial dream state, did not bode well. Moreover, the captain was rarely pessimistic and never so straightforward. For him to say that, meant something. Meanwhile, Schreider seldom called the captain by his first name, and his doing so revealed how nervous he was.

The phone rang, and Schreider answered. It was his communications officer at the command desk. He listened, then said, 'His Eminence Santori, has he risen for breakfast yet?'

The officer had not finished speaking when Schreider threw the receiver down. Taking his pistol from the drawer, he leapt up. 'Let's go!' he commanded, holstering the pistol as he ran.

For the umpteenth time in the past twenty-four hours Weber had no idea where they were going or what they were about to do. 'Where are we going?' he asked, finding his feet despite his exhaustion.

Schreider was already out of the office before Weber could finish retrieving a sidearm from the gun cabinet. Having done so, the captain made sure to catch up with his commander.

Staff in the command center gawked. Running wildly, one half dressed, the other in full ceremonial gear, their officers made no sense. They were normally somber men; something serious must have happened.

'I want eight men in full combat gear,' Schreider barked across the room. 'Get them to the parade grounds in two minutes. I'll give further orders on the way.'

Weber seized Schreider's arm, forcing him to a stop. 'What exactly are we about to do, Oberst.'

Schreider did not shrug Weber off. He knew he owed his captain an explanation. The man had stood by him faithfully for the better part of a decade. 'The Maggiore and His Eminence Cardoni left for the Villa Malta half an hour ago. Based on what we saw last night and the fact that Verretti is on his way back from Turkey with the suspects as we speak, it's obvious what the cardinals are up to. Now, I need you to get to the parade ground to supervise the men I'm taking there. I have a plan, but there's no time to explain.'

Weber did not follow entirely but complied.

As the captain left, Schreider shouted across the room: 'Where is the lieutenant with the bomber?'

'Just arrived, Oberst,' the surveillance officer replied.

Schreider turned back towards the entrance, where four Helvetians now stood surrounding the bomber. On seeing the youngster, Schreider seethed. The boy's face was swollen and he looked half asleep. Schreider felt for him.

The poor kid had been acting insanely, but disarmed as he had been he had not deserved to be brutalized. He had not intended to hurt anyone; he just needed therapy and for someone to give him another chance.

Schreider could not give the kid most of that. He was not a therapist, nor was he a theologian. To make matters worse, the colonel also knew he might not survive the day, which meant he most likely would not be able to testify on the kid's behalf.

As the suspect approached, guards circling him, Schreider addressed him, 'I can't condone your actions, so I can't let you go. You need help. What you did was not right. That's why I'm sending you to Rome for psychiatric observation. It's for your own good.'

Schreider turned to the lieutenant.

'Make sure you take him to a clinic,' he ordered. 'They'll know what to do. Then, call Interpol. Explain what's happened. I might not be around tomorrow; let's just say I'm handing in my notice today. But I need to make sure the kid's safe. He's got mental issues, but he's no terrorist. I've got to go now, but do exactly as I say—if not for my sake, then for the sake of doing what's right.'

Schreider did not wait to see them leave but hurried on. Compared with what lay ahead, the bomb threat had been a sideshow.

On the parade ground, Weber had organized a section of their best men. They were in military uniforms and fully armed.

Schreider selected four men to join him in his Steyr Puch. The rest he ordered to follow in a second vehicle. When Weber headed for the driver seat of the second Puch,

Schreider ordered the captain out and told him to return to the command center.

Weber disregarded the order. The captain started the engine before Schreider could object and rammed the gas to the floor.

Schreider loathed what was happening. The last thing he wanted was for his captain to sacrifice his life as well. But there was no time to argue.

Seconds later, both vehicles roared towards the Porta Sant' Anna.

Chapter 43

The Villa del Priorato di Malta—renowned for the keyhole in its arched portone framing the dome of Saint Peter's Basilica in a distance—served as Grand Master Dubois's residence. Located at the edge of Rome's Aventine Hill, the tenth-century Benedictine monastery had passed first to the Knights Templar and then to the Hospitallers after the Templar purges. As with the Vatican and the Palazzo di Malta, the villa boasted extraterritoriality, giving it the freedom to operate per its own laws.

Standing beneath the Villa's allée of clipped cypresses, two of Catholicism's dedicated stalwarts scanned the Tiber River. Having received word of Inspector Verretti's impending return, the two holy men had slipped from the Apostolic Palace before breakfast. Their obligation to defend the Church was paramount in their minds. The Roman Church had seen numerous schisms, in 431, 462 and 1085 AD, as well as during the Protestant Reformation of the sixteenth through to the eighteenth century. Every threat had arisen from internal conflicts, but none had come as close as the present threat of destroying the Church completely. If the letter got out, it would eviscerate the core dogma, which distinguished Roman and its Catholicism from every other Christian denomination—the Apostolic succession and, by extension, papal supremacy.

Two people. That's all it took.

Two people and a letter could bring down the most powerful religious organization the world had ever seen. The cardinals' actions had not been about maintaining cohesion in the Christian world; cohesion had long ago been lost. No, their actions were about keeping Catholicism alive. Billions of the faithful entrusted their spiritual wellbeing to the Roman Catholic Church. Imagine if those faithful had discovered their faith had been misplaced. Then, imagine them turning against the Church. It would spell the end of the only unbroken tradition to survive from antiquity to the present day. It would also mean the two cardinals would be nothing more than a couple of old men in silly robes, stripped of their power and prestige. In such a context, it was clear that sacrifices must be made.

Leonardo Santori's gaze rested on the Vatican, where the rising sun now lit the copper green dome of the Basilica, the domicile of the Holy Roman Catholic Church for nearly two thousand years. The Church's doctrine was defined through ecumenical councils, and the faithful believed it to be guided by the Holy Spirit, thus making its moral pronouncements infallible. Salvation was also only possible through the Holy Roman Church. This was a divine law granted directly from God. Jesus Christ had founded the Roman Catholic Church when He appointed twelve Apostles to continue his work and teachings. The coming of the Holy Spirit upon the Apostles—an event known as

Pentecost—had signaled the Church's public inception. Independent of civil power and sovereign in all matters, the Church did not overtly claim political or temporal power, but she did assert indirect jurisdiction over moral behavior. She alone could interpret matters of spirituality, and she considered all humans to be bounded by her interpretation.

Santori stood motionless. Rome had been his home for nearly fifty years. He had spent more time in the Vatican than anywhere else, and yet he had despised every moment of it. How had this been? His ambition had propelled him upwards through the ranks of the clergy, and in a short time had found himself standing next to the throne of God, a champion for spiritual justice. And so, he had believed with all his heart, but acceptance from the inner elite, the guardians of the deepest secrets of the faith, had brought utter disillusionment. He had not created the illusion himself, but he had been tasked with keeping it alive. Persecutor, prosecutor, overseer of morality and eradicator of sins, he had rid the Church of its evils from within. What should have been a noble calling had turned into a dreadful nightmare. His experience in trials and excommunications had made him *the* champion defender of the faith. Seen against this backdrop, he had had an obligation to the Church. His fate and hers had become inextricable. He had often thought of burning the letter, as well as the other 'challenging' materials, which lay hidden in the secret archives, but like his predecessors, he had known that doing so would only delay the inevitable. None of it refuted God or Christ—in fact, some of it was better evidence of the Gospels' validity than any that was otherwise available—but every bit of it refuted the papacy's legitimacy and revealed the lies, which lay at the root of the Roman Church's true foundation.

The sun rose slowly in the east. Puffing on a half-smoked cigarette, Cardoni also watched as its rays lit the Basilica's dome. Blowing smoke through his nostrils, he felt drained. How he wished this day had never come. If only they could hand their problem over to the Italians. If only. He rejected the thought as soon as it occurred to him. The fugitives' knowledge of the letter made that impossible. Giving them over to the Carabinieri would be suicide. The Church would have to deal with the problem internally and without His Holiness's knowledge. He felt sickened by the prospect of what this day would bring. The shame of being found wanting was too daunting to contemplate. He could not imagine life without the Church. With no one to care for him now in his infirmity how would he survive? He was elderly. The Church was his home and provider. Her demise was not an option. He still had ten, perhaps twenty, years ahead of him. He was duty-bound to ensure the Church's long-term sustainability. Unfortunate as it was, there was no turning back. Admitting to what had transpired would seal the fate of the one true faith. It would be the end of everything they had lived for and their lives as well. If only he had known when he was younger what he knew now.

Though they were waiting for the call, the voice of a guard announcing the inspector's arrival still caught the cardinals napping. To Santori's disgust, Cardoni stubbed his cigarette against a tree and flicked it into a flowerbed, but there was no time to worry about it as they turned and walked back up the cypress allée and along the path leading to the Villa.

Falling a little behind, Cardoni lifted his cassock so he could move more freely and did his best to keep up.

Santori entered the villa via the garden entrance. He had to retrieve the letter, so it was imperative he be there when Verretti arrived. The captives he could see to later. Their status as non-Catholics set them outside the Vatican's jurisdiction, which would make dealing with them tougher. It was not simply a matter of excommunicating them. It would probably be necessary to have them taken out. It was regrettable, but there was no way around it. In centuries past, he could have had them burned at the stake. Not that he thought the Church should go back to its old ways, but the middle ages had certainly had its advantages.

Chapter 44

With outbound traffic at its peak, Schreider was anxious they would be too late arriving at the Order of Malta villa. If Verretti had already handed over the captives to the cardinals, he, Schreider, might as well forget about saving their lives. He had never expected to defend civilians against the Apostolate. But his vows to the Holy See had little meaning for him now. Had he promised to protect God's elite or His chosen? There was a difference. Now he sensed that the Church's elite were self-appointed and therefore not synonymous with the chosen. He prayed that he was right in this and that he was indeed defending those chosen by God against those who had veered away from His path.

Crossing the Tiber River at the Ponte Palatino, Schreider was pushing the engine of the Steyr Puch to its limits. From the iron bridge, he could see Palatine Hill, the most ancient part of the city, nestled amongst Rome's famous seven hills. But the Villa Malta, on the other side of Aventine Hill, was still some way off. As he cut through traffic, he checked his rear-view mirror to see if Weber was still behind him, and indeed, his captain was glued to his bumper like a bloodhound. He nearly radioed the captain to back off just a little in case of collision, but decided against it. He had worked with the captain long enough to accept that their relationship involved a certain clinginess on Weber's part. The captain was unmarried and, as far as Schreider knew, celibate. Schreider hated casting aspersions on his loyal captain, of course, but if he was honest, he had jumped to the same conclusion as others. Yet, he had never thought any less of Weber for it. Was not Michelangelo that way? The Church had certainly not disowned *him*.

By the time Schreider reached the remains of the Pons Aemilius, Rome's oldest stone bridge, he could see across the Tiber to where, behind a lane of giant sycamore trees, lay Aventine Hill. On the ridge, was the Basilica of Santa Sabina, and behind it, the Order of Malta's villa was lit by a ray of sunlight filtering through the storm-laden clouds surrounding it.

Upon leaving the Ponte Palatino, Schreider found the road ahead blocked-off, so their only option was to turn onto the Lungotevere Aventino to the left. This was in the opposite direction of where he needed to go. Frustrated, there being no time for detours, he kept going straight. Cutting across the center lane, his vehicle bounced as it negotiated the median, unbalancing the men in the back seat. With his hazard lights flashing and his hand thrust out of his window, he forced the oncoming vehicles to a halt. Many motorists gave him the *bras d'honneur*, but he ignored them, crossing the Lungotevere Aventino into the Via Ponte Rotto despite causing a major traffic jam. After circling the Temple of Hercules, he drove into the Piazza La

Bocca della Verità. Traffic at the intersection had slowed to a crawl, making crossing towards the Circus Maximus Valley a devilish prospect, and to top it all, the traffic lights at the Via della Greca intersection turned red.

Verretti's approach from Ciampino Airport on the far side of Aventine Hill meant the inspector would have less traffic to negotiate, but Schreider persisted. He had no choice, but to break the law, the Devil take what may. Yelling and gesturing for pedestrians to move, he drove onto the sidewalk in front of the Temple of Hercules and accelerated through the intersection at the Via della Greca and the Lungotevere Aventino. At the light, he slowed looking for oncoming traffic. Just as he thought he had found a gap on the opposite side of the Via della Greca, the light turned green, and a bus blocked his path.

The drive up the Via della Greca crawled at a snail's pace, and Schreider would have overtaken the bus, if oncoming traffic had not prevented him. He tried flicking his lights and swerving out of his lane to catch the other drivers' attention, but to no avail. After a while, though, the road separated into three lanes, and Schreider roared peevishly past the plodding bus. Turning into the Chivo dei Publicii, he checked his rear-view again. Somehow—and the Lord only knew how—Weber was still mere meters behind him.

The s-bend up the Chivo dei Publicii forced Schreider to downshift. The straight stretch of the Via di Santa Sabina allowed him to glimpse their destination, the Piazza dei Cavalieri di Malta. With only a few hundred meters left to go, he accelerated. Halfway up Santa Sabina the road became a one-way in the opposite direction. Dangerous as ignoring the sign was, there was no oncoming traffic, and he shot ahead. As he approached the Via di Sant' Alessio on the left anticipating oncoming traffic, he slowed briefly, then thought better of it and sped up again. Just as he did so, he saw a Saint John's ambulance race from the Via di Sant' Alessio towards the intersection. Judging by the speed of the ambulance, the driver had no intention of stopping; he was on a direct path with the Steyr Puch, and as anticipated, the driver skipped the stop sign, pushing in front of Schreider.

To avoid a crash, Schreider veered to the right, a move which set him on a collision course with the perimeter wall of the Basilica di Santi Alessio, so he wrenched the steering wheel left and floored the gas. His move straightened the vehicle and allowed him to edge in front of the ambulance.

Schreider glanced at the occupants in passing. It was Verretti and, in the driver seat next to him, his adjutant, Lioni. The inspector was screaming with his firearm pointing directly at Schreider. The colonel swung his vehicle left again, hitting the side of the ambulance. That did not deter Verretti from firing two rounds. The first smashed through Schreider's windscreen. The other hit the doorframe, inches above the colonel's head. When the Helvetian behind Schreider aimed his semi-automatic at the ambulance, the colonel ordered him not to shoot. He had to protect the captives inside.

The Puch and the ambulance entered the piazza in front of the Villa Malta side by side. Because Schreider had managed to keep Verretti to his left, the inspector would have to get around or past Schreider to reach the entrance to the villa in the far-right corner. Determined not to let Verretti slip past him, Schreider slammed into the ambulance.

Lioni attempted to use the ambulance's weight advantage to plough through the Puch and slam into Schreider, but to no avail—the Puch held its course. To pull around his adversary, the adjutant sped up, but this set him on a collision course with Sant' Anselmo University.

Using the lane between Sant' Anselmo and the Villa Malta to his advantage, Schreider sped up alongside Lioni. Then, with fifty meters before hitting the ten-foot wall, the adjutant slammed on the brakes. Schreider followed suit, locking the wheels.

Smoke blustered as rubber melted to the asphalt. With meters to spare before smashing into the wall, both vehicles stopped.

The Helvetians leapt out first. Rifles drawn, they surrounded the ambulance. Weber and his guards followed, but instead of aiming inwards at the ambulance, they formed a defensive cordon around Schreider's men, pointing their weapons outwards.

The back doors of the ambulance flung open and the gendarmes jumped out, but the Swiss Guard already had them in their sights.

Verretti climbed out of the ambulance, his face purplish and his veins bulging as he shouted profanities. He had lost three men in Antakya when they had captured Simon and Jennifer, which now gave Schreider the advantage of ten men to his five. But he believed his counterpart would not have the *coglioni* to open fire. He cocked the hammer of his pistol and advanced on Schreider. As at the Governatorato the day before, his gun was aimed at the adversary's face.

'Drop your weapon!' Schreider shouted at Verretti. 'Drop it!'

'Go fuck yourself,' Verretti spat. 'You drop yours.'

'You can't win this one, Inspector.'

'Neither can you, Colonel.'

With Verretti's hand now visibly shaking, Schreider decided to be the stronger of the two and lowered his gun.

Verretti did not move. 'Now, call your men back!' the inspector barked.

'I can't do that, Inspector.'

One wrong move and Schreider was a dead man. Keeping his eyes locked on Verretti, he called on two of his men to fall in beside the inspector. From the desperation in the Italian's eyes, Schreider knew the man was close to pulling the trigger.

'They need a fair trial, Inspector,' Schreider said, his voice more composed. 'You know that as well as I do.'

Verretti stopped meters from Schreider. 'Call off your dogs, or you are no longer part of this.'

Schreider took a moment to reflect. He reminded himself that he had made his peace with God. He lifted his hand for his guards to move in. 'Take his pistol!' he barked.

'Don't you dare, Helvetians,' Verretti spat. 'You try that, and I'll put a bullet in your commander's head.'

The Helvetians hesitated, but Schreider signaled for them to move in. 'I gave an order, Halberdiers!' The first Helvetian stepped in to disarm Verretti and the inspector swept his pistol towards him. That was when Schreider saw his chance. 'Now!' he shouted.

Verretti swung the firearm back towards Schreider but the inspector's momentary lapse gave the Helvetians the opportunity they needed. The first Helvetian went for the firearm, ripping Verretti's hand down as the inspector squeezed the trigger. The second dove into the inspector's midriff, knocking him down. Verretti fired in the fall. His first round hit the Puch behind Schreider. The second ricocheted off the tarmac, narrowly missing Schreider's leg. Together, the Helvetians wrestled the inspector to the ground, pinning him face down on the asphalt with his arms behind his back.

Verretti fought to free himself, but the Helvetian on top of him was too strong.

'Shoot these fuckers!' he screamed.

'No, hold your fire,' Schreider called out.

Verretti struggled to lift his head from the ground so he could face the colonel. 'I'll kill you,'' he cried. 'I swear on my fucking life!'

Schreider was not inclined to argue. He knelt on Verretti's shoulder blade. 'You're a prick, Verretti,' he said, holding his pistol to the inspector's cheek. 'A weasely, little, shriveled prick. But my guess is you already know that. You're a policeman for the love of God. You should be ashamed of being involved in this.'

Schreider stepped back. Knowing that in a moment the Order of Malta guards would fill the square, he entered the ambulance. Simon was handcuffed to a rail; Jennifer lay strapped to the stretcher. 'I'm here to help you,' he said. 'Move away so I can unlock the cuffs.'

Jennifer turned her head towards Simon, and 'help' was all she could manage to say.

Schreider could see from her cloudy eyes that Verretti had drugged her and ordered Simon to untie the seatbelts holding her down.

Jennifer wanted to walk on her own, but could not find her feet, so Simon lifted her and carried her from the ambulance.

Verretti thrashed violently. ‘Let go of me,’ he shrieked. ‘You can’t do this!’

Schreider opened the back door of the Steyr Puch for Simon and Jennifer to get in. He had just taken the wheel when armed guards charged from the Villa Malta gate. Close behind them followed the Maggiore and Cardinal Cardoni.

Schreider was uncomfortably aware that Verretti now had the advantage and ordered his men to retreat. He shifted into reverse as the first shots struck the Puch.

Weber returned fire with a burst of four rounds. His men followed suit. When two of the gendarmes fell, the villa guards dove for cover behind a parked car.

The two Helvetians holding Verretti also scampered for cover, and the inspector flung himself on his stomach beneath the ambulance. He aimed at Schreider’s Puch, firing several rounds in quick succession.

Schreider hit the gas, reversing towards the exit in the top corner of the piazza. Halfway back up the piazza, he twirled the steering wheel, spinning the vehicle one hundred and eighty degrees. Not losing momentum, he sped towards Via di Porta Lavernale.

Weber waited until his commander had disappeared behind the boundary wall before jumping into his Puch. He was about to call for his men to retreat, but he gave in to impulse. Instead of gearing up, he shifted into first. He stepped on the accelerator and his vehicle bucked forward, hitting the rear of the ambulance at forty miles per hour. Though he could not see the inspector, he heard the man crying out. He hoped he had hurt the bastard.

Gunfire exploded around Weber as he backed up. The windscreen of the Puch took several rounds and shattered.

He yelled for his men to take cover behind the vehicle. They ducked behind the Puch and fired across the bonnet and around the back. Reversing back up the piazza, Weber ordered them to take position on the running board and bumper. On nearing the perimeter wall on the far side, he shouted for them to hang onto the roof rack. Then, swinging around and changing gears in mid-turn, he sped down the Via di Porta Lavernale after Schreider.

Crawling from beneath the wrecked ambulance, Verretti ordered his remaining gendarmes to get back in. He leapt behind the wheel as an Order of Malta limousine and two urban assault vehicles with Malta guards raced through the gate of the villa. When the limousine stopped beside him and the Maggiore demanded the silver casket, Verretti was dumbfounded. How could the cardinal want the letter at such a time? He could not care less about the damn artefact. It was Schreider he wanted. He retrieved the artefact and threw the casket through Santori's window, but instead of returning to the ambulance, he wrestled the limousine driver from his seat. Ordering Lioni and the men to follow in the ambulance, he sped off.

Ensconced in the back of the limousine, Santori stared at Cardoni. He sighed, relief etched on his face. He had the letter back. Now their task was to deal with the fugitives. It would not be easy, but Mother Church came first.

Chapter 45

Schreider radioed command. 'Alarmbereitschaft Eins, now!' he shouted into the mic.

There, His Eminence Santori finally got his way. This call, though, was not to save the Holy See from harm, but rather to prevent carnage. He was now up against the gendarmerie, and if Verretti would get his way, the entire Italian Carabinieri. God forbid, the College of Cardinals would get caught in the crossfire.

Spewing orders as he sped across the Tiber, he called up the entire Vatican Swiss army. Wearing the mandatory ceremonial dress his men must secure the Apostolic Palace. If they were going down, they might as well do so proudly. The palace was also the only place where he could guarantee Simon and Jennifer's safety—at least until Interpol intervened. He could not believe he was securing the palace from its own occupants.

On his return, and with no idea where else to go, he sped into the forecourt of Saint Peter's Basilica. Veering sharply to avoid pedestrians lingering between the central obelisk and Maderno's granite fountain, the Puch roared up to the Bronze Door at the end of the colonnade. Behind the Bronze Door, a long, barrel-vaulted corridor led to Antonio da Sangallo's famed Royal Staircase, which in turn led to the Regal Room adjacent to the Sistine Chapel, where the Holy See was presently assembling. This was the colonel's destination.

As the Puch halted before the Bronze Door, a platoon of guards greeted him. He called Weber over and ordered him to assist with Simon and Jennifer. After helping them from the back of the vehicle, Schreider made sure Jennifer could walk on her own before accompanying them up the steps to the Bronze Door. In the corridor, several more guards were waiting. They had just formed an escort around Simon and Jennifer when the sound of screeching tires reverberated off the marble walls. Peering behind them, Schreider saw a black Order of Malta limousine and several urban assault vehicles race around the colonnade and towards the Bronze Door.

'Secure the entrance,' he shouted to his lieutenant at the base of the steps. Then, he turned to Weber. 'Take them to the Regal Room. I'll be there in a moment.'

When the lieutenant in the colonnade saw Inspector Verretti behind the wheel of the limousine with the two cardinals in the back he panicked. 'It's the inspector, Oberst,' he cried out. 'What should we do?!'

'Let the cardinals through, but no one else.' Schreider waited for the sergeant to organize his men into a tight formation in the street and on the steps in front of the Bronze Door. Before sprinting up the passage towards the Royal Staircase, he repeated his order: 'No one gets through but the cardinals. That's it.'

On reaching Bernini's statue of Emperor Constantine the Great, he found a platoon armed with semi-automatic rifles approaching from the Basilica Narthex where he had apprehended the bomber the day before. He stopped briefly to make sure two sections secured the passage, then continued, ordering the rest of the men to keep pace with him. Halfway up the staircase, he could hear Verretti spitting venom as the Helvetians restrained him at the Bronze Door. He did not look back.

As Schreider turned into the second flight of steps leading to the Regal Room, he thought of the Emperor Constantine. Why Bernini's five-story high, marble masterpiece mattered at that moment was impossible to say. Many times, he had admired it, but only now did it dawn on him that the statue begged a few questions. The work depicted the emperor gazing skywards while rushing into the Battle of Milvian Bridge. From the historian, Eusebius, we gather that Constantine had been startled by the appearance of a cross in the sky and after the emperor had his men paint crosses on their shields, his army indeed defeated his rival, Maxentius. The statue was inscribed with the legendary words of the emperor's vision: '*In hoc signo vinces*,' meaning 'In this sign you shall conquer,' and Schreider had read the words countless times, but he had never considered the kind of cross Constantine had seen. Next to the statue, the Vatican displayed a Roman cross. Is this what Constantine had purportedly seen? After all, the emperor had been a sun worshipper. Of course, some scholars would suggest that what he had seen was the Chi-Rho, representing the first two letters of Christ's name in Greek. As Schreider recalled, the early chi also represented the solar-ecliptic path across the celestial equator. Was it even possible to see a Chi-Rho cross in the sky? Did God impart signs like that? Schreider had begged for signs all damn day, yet he had received none. Then again, he was still alive, so maybe that was sign enough. He could not help appreciating the irony that the Vatican—the nerve center of Catholicism—had chosen the Royal Staircase as the formal reception area for foreign dignitaries, frequently royalty and presidents; to think that these worthies might be admiring the statue of a sun worshipper on their way to meet His Holiness.

At the Regal Room, Schreider stationed guards at each of the six entrances. Halting in the center of the hall, he saluted his captain. As Weber returned the salute, Schreider drew his sword. He swiveled into a right turn, lifting his knee waist high. In a final show of strength, and with all the grace of a Lipizzaner, he lowered his heel to the marble floor.

Schreider knew he might rue this day, but Weber's devotion gave him the courage to see it through, even if it cost him his life. Events were forcing him to stand up for his beliefs; for what he knew was right. The Church had done outstanding work in treating the sick and elderly, in feeding the poor and caring for orphans and housing destitute families. But the same Church had crucified those who opposed its views and convicted thousands to death for heresy, burning them at the stake and hanging them from the city's gates. Despite the Vatican's claiming to abide by divine laws as prescribed in the Holy Bible, it also had its own judiciary and a discrete legal system based on Italy's. The pope's judicial authority, which he exercised through the Prefect of the Supreme Tribunal of the Apostolic Signature, was a judicial system consisting of a judge, a tribunal, a Court of Appeal and a Supreme Court. All four courts had their seats at the Palazzo del Tribunale at the Piazza Santa Marta behind Saint Peter's Basilica. As head of the courts, the Most Holy Father presided over all matters as supreme ecclesiastical judge. His was the final say in any ecclesiastical judgment, and therein lay the problem. Although the Vatican's legal system prescribed sentences of up to thirty-five years, their courts were only mandated to prosecute minor crimes and give light sentences with limited penalties—a contradiction surely, but one rarely noted. Serious cases had to be passed to the Italian courts, and this should certainly be the case now. The Vatican had no authority as per to its agreements with Italy, to hand down death sentences, especially not for theft.

Nor was Schreider yet convinced that Simon and Jennifer would be fairly dealt with by the presiding pontiff, for whom he had a great deal of respect. Years of securing the Apostolic Palace had enabled him to build a close relationship with the Holy Father. In fact, Schreider had accompanied the pontiff on his morning walks many times. Setting out from the Fountain of the Eagle, the pope would choose a route around the back of the Vatican Radio Station. At the altar at the Madonna di Lourdes, he would stop to pray. On their return, he often asked Schreider to race him, then jokingly absolved the colonel when the younger man purposely lost. The pope frequently spoke of his life before becoming head of the Church. In his rise to the papal throne, he had spent much of his time campaigning for and establishing sexual ethics amongst the clergy. During this period, pedophilia scandals had shaken the Roman Catholic Church to its core; involving thousands of cases, his investigations had led to the defrocking of hundreds of priests and bishops. His no-nonsense approach in dealing with this plague had seen him elected to the papacy, although not by an overwhelming majority. His excommunication of senior clerics implicated in protecting the disgraced had silenced the Church's critics and had had enormous influence on world leaders and the faithful alike. His breakthrough in attracting young people back to the faith had also resulted in a steady growth in membership. Prior to his reign, it had appeared that the Church was on its way to extinction.

Yes, the Holy Father was an honorable man, Schreider decided. God willing, His Most Holiness would act wisely. Standing to attention, his eyes fixed on the Royal Staircase entrance, Schreider awaited the arrival of the cardinals.

Chapter 46

Jennifer raised her head from Simon's chest and wiped the tears from her cheeks with the palm of her hand. Disengaging herself from his protective embrace, she turned towards the empty hall. Her eyes scanned its four walls, which rose for fifty feet or more above them. The renowned Regal Room, situated at the heart of the Apostolic Palace, served as the antechamber of the Sistine Chapel during conclaves and as a reception hall when world leaders visited. Gleaming marble nudes framed frescoes of Church history beside stuccoed doorways. The hall was arguably the most lavishly decorated space in the entire city, and Jennifer had never seen such opulence.

A barrel-vaulted ceiling rested on a corbelled cornice, its open ends framing two massive arched windows. Through the window furthest from her, she recognized the southernmost building in the Belvedere Courtyard. Had it only been twenty-four hours since she had been out there, waiting for the library to open?

She turned towards the papal throne, which for many was the symbolic seat of God. She had dedicated her life to a religion she thought centered on humility and modesty, yet here she was gazing at the antitheses of these virtues. The richly gilded throne sat upon a three-tiered dais luxuriously cushioned in red velvet with carved cherubs perched upon its arms and the proud emblem of the Vatican poised above it.

Jennifer stood in defiance of immorality.

As sadness consumed her, her gaze alighted on Simon. The bell of Saint Peter's Basilica pealed in the background, and she closed her eyes. During their flight from Verretti and his men, she had wanted to let Simon know she was all right and that she did not blame him for anything. As she had lain half sedated on the stretcher unable to free her hands to touch him, she had wanted him to know that she accepted the blame for what had happened. None of it was his responsibility, except that he had not physically dragged her away from the Cave Church. She bitterly regretted ignoring his demands to leave the site. Her stubbornness had put his life in danger as well as her own. In any case, the letter was assuredly lost now, if not Apostle Peter's bones.

Was it naïve to believe that punishment for their 'sins' had long ago been relegated to the Dark Ages? Was it possible that the Church could execute them? Whatever the outcome, she longed for the nightmare they were trapped in to end. She wanted to be far away and free. Until now, she had taken her freedom for granted. She was a fool. She opened her eyes again and her surroundings confirmed that she was not dreaming. Their lives were still in danger, and their rescue by the Swiss Guard would surely result in a trial. If that were so, could they expect a fair one?

Chapter 47

Raging, Santori crossed the marble floor to the center of the Regal Room. He regretted not removing Schreider from his post when he had had the chance. Had he done so, none of this would have happened. Thank God, the letter was back where it belonged, and thank God for Inspector Verretti, whose swift action would enable the cardinal to defend the Holy See against this malignant attack. Santori was acutely aware that this was a chance to redeem himself, and he had faith in his vindication.

At the same time, Giovanni Cardoni emerged from the Royal Staircase feeling vile. His stomach churned as he took in the scene around the throne. There were the two suspects, hugging and encircled by a unit of Helvetians. He cursed under his breath as he recalled Miss Jaine's scathing accusations the previous day. He had underestimated her and so it was, to some extent, his fault all this had happened. He should have been more guarded in that meeting. She was a Protestant, and Protestants thrived on criticizing Catholics. But why? Had she forgotten how

Protestantism had its foundations in Catholicism? Both John Calvin and Martin Luther had been Catholic priests before spouting their heresies. Both had borrowed much of their theologies from Catholic ideals, the only major difference being that they had rejected papal supremacy. Really, all the rest was semantics and sophistry. In the end, as all other Christians, they abide by the teachings of Saint Paul.

Santori stopped just feet away from Schreider. 'I will have you court-martialed,' he snarled.

Schreider clicked his boots and saluted. 'Yes, Your Eminence, you've said that before. The fact remains that the suspects deserve a fair trial.'

At the thought of prosecution, Santori's heart crashed against his ribcage. Legal proceedings required evidence. 'We can't do that, Colonel,' he said. 'You know that.' There was no way he could disclose Pontius's letter in court.

Every muscle in Schreider's body stiffened. 'His Holiness must decide.'

'What if His Holiness tells you the same? What will you do then?'

'His Holiness is an honest man,' Schreider replied sternly. 'I trust in his judgement.'

'Are you insinuating that I'm not! What if I become the next Vicar of Christ?'

The Colonel stared the cardinal down through narrowed eyes. 'Then may God strike every one of us dead and level this cursed art gallery around us.'

Santori was opening his mouth to retaliate when the tramping of feet accompanied by the eerie swish of heavy robes silenced him. As he turned, wave upon wave of cardinals dressed in black, scarlet and gold were approaching. Heading the army of clergymen was Pope

Gregory XVIII; ferula in hand, fully dressed in the vestments of his office, white zucchetto, white simar and red amice, with a solid-gold cross resting on his chest, the Bishop of Rome entered.

Concerned by the apparent attack on the Church, Pope Gregory had risen early to meet with the College of Cardinals. Nearly one-hundred-and-forty strong, they had congregated in the Sistine Chapel next door. The theft of the letter demanded extreme caution on the part of the Holy See and level heads were essential. If revealed, its contents would prove devastating for the Vatican. The onus to clear the Church of this threat rested squarely on his shoulders. Even if it necessitated compromise, he hoped the Holy Spirit would help them arrive at an agreeable resolution. If not, the Church would collapse.

Schreider sank to his knees, bowing in reverence. He kissed the Holy Father's ring and remained there until commanded to rise. He slid his sword back into its scabbard and said, 'Your Holiness, I have delivered the suspects to you.'

'Oh, for goodness' sake!' Santori spat, cutting Schreider short. 'The colonel wants them to be tried in a court of law.'

Shifting his gaze to the cardinal, Pope Gregory took a moment to reflect. Trying the suspects in the Roman courts could put the Vatican at risk, but unethical behavior was not the solution. The Church might still command support in every Western nation, but these countries no longer swore absolute fealty to it, and its diminished military resources put limitations on their options. There had to be a way to resolve the issue peacefully and without involving anyone else. He ascended the throne and waited for his aides to arrange his simar before seating himself. Then, he ordered

Schreider to bring the captives to him. He stomped his ferula on the dais, compelling the attention of the College of Cardinals who immediately ceased their murmuring. The pope's intelligent eyes alighted with interest on the woman. Leaning into the male suspect's side, her face was pale and framed by tousled hair and her eyes seemed drawn and sunken.

Pope Gregory sat back. 'So, you are the inimitable Miss Jaine I've been hearing about,' he said, gazing down at her.

Jennifer was facing one of the most powerful men on the planet. Hearing her name come from his lips scared her. She wondered what he had been told.

As she remained quiet, Pope Gregory again took the initiative. 'I believe you have a doctorate in religious studies,' he said. 'Is this true?'

A million thoughts shot through her head, her fictitious persona being at the top of the list. Thinking about it made her sick. She had hated lying all her life, yet when it suited her, she was as guilty as anyone else, and look where it had landed her. She vowed never to lie again, but wondered if she was only lying to herself in doing so.

'Well, speak. I'm listening.'

When Pope Gregory signaled for Jennifer to move closer, she stayed put. After a moment, his benevolent stare drew her towards him.

As she stood before his throne, he studied her. Framed by a crowd of elderly, sagging faces, her beauty seemed seraphic.

'You represent *Geographic America*,' he said. 'Which is a fine publication, I have to admit. We have had a good deal of criticism from them. For the most part it's been fair.'

Jennifer thought of dismissing this, but changed her mind. She would speak her mind. His tone sounded respectful and considerate, and rather than lashing out at her, he seemed accommodating. Still, she should remain guarded till she understood his intentions.

'Your Holiness, I did not tell the truth,' she replied softly, surprising even herself. And she definitely did not feel comfortable addressing another human being as 'holy'. Moreover, she hated conforming to the dictates of a Church she now knew was fraudulent. Doing so made no sense. The pope was but another human being like herself. What was she honoring except the denomination's etiquette?

'Ah well, that is only part of it, of course,' the pope said. 'You've actually done many silly things of late, Miss Jaine. You visit our libraries under false pretenses, you accuse one of my cardinals of all sorts of despicable things, break into our bunker, then flee, only to crash a locomotive through one of our gates. This is not normal behavior, Miss Jaine. One does not expect this from a respectable person. Do you care to explain?'

Shame weighed heavily on her, but she straightened up. She had no idea how to respond. Perhaps a divine hand would guide her.

'Your Holiness,' she said, her eyes soft with humiliation. 'I promise; I did not intend to do any of it except meet with His Eminence the Cardinal.'

He pondered the verity of her words, before he said, 'Just tell me. Why did you really come to the Vatican?'

His inquiry struck at the core of her being. It felt as if it would rip her soul from her innermost self, exposing it for all to see. For a long time, she had wondered what had made her come to Rome. At first, she had thought it was to do the groundworks of her doctorate. When that had failed, her ambition shifted to succeeding as a journalist. But no, not even that was the true reason for her being there. Her impulse to visit the Vatican Library came from somewhere completely different—from a place of doubt.

Her shame fell from her as she said, 'I came to validate—or nullify—the foundations of my faith.'

The lines between Pope Gregory's eyebrows deepened. Her honesty was laudable, but despite her attempt at justify herself, she had not confessed to everything yet. 'Have you lost your faith, child?'

His shrewd honing in on her deepest wounds was starting to hurt her. Yes, she had lost her faith. Any faith—even the idea of faith. Faith no longer made any sense. That was because her faith—or lack of it—went hand in hand with the paradoxes she had discovered in the past. Now the evidence she had come across in the past twenty-four hours had substantiated her newfound agnosticism. She was reeling. The Church needed to be honest. For once, it should bring truth to the faithful.

Before Miss Jaine could answer Cardoni stepped forward. He knew her capabilities. Her method of exploiting their goodwill to launch attacks still lingered fresh in his mind. This time, though, he was ready. He stood in front of her, pugnacious. 'Faith is man's most precious possession!' he hollered. 'It is the root of supernatural life, the pledge of eternal salvation. Rejection of faith is the greatest of sins, abandonment the greatest heresy!'

Every time Cardoni spoke her hair stood on end. She loathed him completely and without reserve. She no longer felt like fighting with him though. Her truth was so far removed from his, they were never going to meet. 'I cannot have faith in a religion whose history and, therefore, precepts are based on falsehood,' she said plainly and honestly. 'Nor can I have faith in an institution that suppresses evidence of this falsehood by committing murder and bearing false witness.'

A rustle of mystification swept over the cardinals. Some moved forward to have a clearer view of her, straining to hear her speak.

Cardoni thrust out his chin. 'Disregard for the purity of faith has made you weak,' he said.

As a dedicated Christian, Jennifer had grown up abiding by biblical teachings. But the more she had studied, the more she had found discrepancies that challenged her beliefs. Now she had seen evidence to corroborate her earlier insights. Saddened, she said, 'My faith rested on the precepts of Saint Paul. In his *Epistle to the Romans* he teaches that all hope of salvation lies in faith and confession—if you "confess with your mouth that Jesus is Lord and believe in your heart that God raised him from the dead you will be saved."'

She paused briefly. She was not sure she should continue. Anything more would sound derogatory. And yet, something within compelled her. It was the same urge that had prompted her to enter the bunker and the same one that had made her stay at the Cave Church.

'I no longer trust Paul,' she said, her voice sincere. 'From what I have seen, he was an imposter.'

Cardoni could almost hear the desperate beating of his heart. Santori was right, she had read the letter, he was sure. It did not matter, because without evidence she had nothing. Now all he had to do was show her the error of her ways.

'Christ made Paul His chosen vessel to the gentiles,' he said. 'Our Holy Mother Church is living proof of that.'

Jennifer looked at him incredulously. 'Your Eminence, then why do you say it was the Apostle Peter who founded your Church?'

Jeers rose from the College of Cardinals. Her devilries had preceded her. Now they were experiencing her heresy first-hand.

'I think you should repent, child,' Cardoni said, raising his voice. 'For salvation of your soul, you must repent.'

The man scared her, not because she believed him, but for the many faithful out there who still did. Nevertheless, she refused to be intimidated. She had heard preacher's rhetoric like this all her life. Now she had had enough.

'Well, I won't,' she said.

Cardoni sensed a victory. Her defiance would turn everyone against her. 'Your obstinacy will see you damned to the eternal pits of Hell,' he said. 'Is that what you want?' Now all he had to do was feed her more rope—enough to hang herself.

She breathed in deeply, but the mustiness of the air prevented her from filling her lungs. If the danger she was in had not already sunk in, it certainly did now. 'There is no Hell,' she replied defiantly. 'Your Hell, a place of fire and brimstone where unrepentant souls burn forever, doesn't exist. There is no truth in this. Nobody knows if there is a Heaven or a Hell. No one. Why not just allow people to live good lives of their own accord? Let them make up their own minds. Let them choose their own destinies.'

As the mastermind behind numerous inquisitions, Leonardo Santori had had enough. He must intervene to defend the Church from this profanity. His colleague had done a masterful job in driving her into a corner, but it was time to bring this bickering to an end. Years of dealing with rebels like her had made him the Church's premier prosecutor. When he turned to address the College of Cardinals, his hands were clasped piously to his chest. 'If we are to perform Christ's work of salvation, we must rid the world of the deadly poison of heresy. Heresy proves that the Satan is alive and dwelling among us. As keepers of the faith, we must enforce and preserve the unity of the Church.'

Jennifer gazed up at Pope Gregory. When she spoke, her voice became serene: 'Faith is "things hoped for". I always thought it was that simple. I hope, Your Holiness, I hope for love, I hope for a good life, for peace, salvation, truth and above all, I hope for knowledge and wisdom. Can you provide that?'

Deploring her disrespect, the cardinals' groans bounced off the frescoes.

Santori pointed a shaking finger at Jennifer. 'Woman, you are in league with the Devil!'

*****

'Perhaps *you* are in league with the Devil.'

The room fell silent. Nobody moved.

The voice cutting in came from behind Jennifer. As if reluctant to come up for her, the man had kept quiet all this time.

Simon stood with his arms by his sides, his hands clenched into fists. 'Isn't Satan the Master of Deceit?' he asked. '"And you shall know them by their works" the Bible says. Is not one who practices deceit in league with the Master of Deceit?'

As if Lucifer, himself had spoken, Santori's lips curled upward. His trap has worked. Simon Kepa's interjection gave him, Santori, the upper hand. Contending with him was going to be far easier than the cardinal had anticipated.

Simon ignored the pain of the bruise throbbing in his temple. He stepped up to Jennifer's side and took her hand in his. She had made a brilliant stand, but these men would not let up. Anyone with her knowledge was a danger to their *raison d'être*.

'No, Simon,' she said, her vision blurred with tears. 'You do not have to do this.'

Heresy was no small charge. In the past, she would have been stoned on the spot or burnt at the stake. Seeking to combat entrenched arrogance with reason, Simon turned to Pope Gregory. 'Miss Jaine is right,' he said incisively. 'Anyone following Paul follows a false prophet. The very reason these men, as you know, Your Holiness, wish to impugn her is to suppress knowledge of Paul's falsehood.'

Shouts rose from the College of Cardinals. The heresy coming from their captives' lips knew no bounds. Something had to be done.

Pope Gregory stamped his ferula against the dais and raised his hand for silence. 'Let him speak,' he said. 'We must hear what he has to say. They have the right to defend themselves. No matter how painful we might find this, they have the right to speak their minds.'

When all was quiet, he looked at Simon. 'Please continue ...'

'I am Simon Kepa, a Jew from Antioch. My parents were from Antioch, as were their parents before them. As descendants of the Nazarenes who fled the persecutions of Saul, our tradition holds that he was an imposter. He did not speak for Yeshu; the man you call Jesus. We all know he had persecuted Him. Even the Gospel authors cautioned against him when they warned of false prophets. To them Saul was a false prophet. The Gospels date to decades after Saul's ministry and his Epistles. From that alone we can deduce they knew of his distorted views. Peter followed Jesus. He molded his ministry on the teachings of the Messiah. Why would that change? Why would Yahweh change His mind so soon? You say the Jews had rejected Jesus and for this God turned His back on them in favor of the gentiles. Yet, Peter never recognized Saul's ministry. He rejected it outright. Peter did not reject the gentiles for converting; he rejected Saul for perverting the teachings of Jesus. Two thousand years of hand-me-down hearsay will not suffice. When you tell your fold to have faith and believe with their hearts, you disempower them. When you say that you speak for God, you make them fear you.'

Simon paused to contemplate his final words. Then, he said, 'The power and authority you claim is neither God's power *nor* His authority. It is your own. Yeshu set people free. Paul enslaved them—as you do now.'

Santori stood amongst stunned colleagues. He was aghast at the words Simon had spoken. That it had come from a Jew made it even worse. What Simon had said could not be heard outside the Vatican's walls. Santori could not allow it. But, without the letter in his possession, Simon had nothing. Without the evidence to back up their claims, the Church would be victorious.

Jennifer was awestruck. As if from the lips of a Nazarene of old, Simon's words had profound meaning. She had misjudged him. All the time she had been with him, he had not made one comment on their find. It had made her doubt him. Yet, all along, he had shared her views. How had she not seen it? The Nazarenes continued to exist, which meant they had not accepted Paul's ministry. If they had, they would have been assimilated into the Roman Church. To this sect of Judaism, Paul was *the* false prophet.

'You used Paul to forge a link between yourself and Jesus,' Simon said finally. 'But that doesn't validate Paul. Paul is your god, not Jesus. Paul's opposition to Peter made him anti-Jesus, and strictly speaking, it made him anti-Christ.'

The College of Cardinals erupted. Their captive's heresy was deplorable. They could not stand by idly as these two desecrated their faith. Justice must be done.

Jennifer shivered. It was as if they were on trial during the time of the Spanish Inquisition.

With only a few Helvetians to stem an onslaught of Church dignitaries, Schreider marshalled more guards to surround and protect Simon and Jennifer. As he had previously sworn to protect the Holy See, he now vowed to protect the two accused with his life.

Santori was exhilarated. By goading his captives to reject Catholicism, he had turned the entire Holy See against them. Now all he needed was the His Holiness' assent. Intent on keeping the moment emotionally charged, he ripped his cassock from his shoulders. His eyes imbued with darkness, he cried, 'Simon Kepa, may the Lord have mercy on your soul!'

'My soul is not in your hands,' Simon called out above the shouts. 'But I'll tell you this—if you lie and kill and bear false witness, I pray for *your* soul.'

'We have heard their blasphemy!' Santori moaned. 'For their sins, they must suffer the worst the law prescribes.'

Stepping into Simon's embrace, Jennifer laid her head on his chest. What a horrifying experience! Did a cardinal hold their lives in his hands merely because they questioned Catholic dogma? Was execution at the hands of the Holy See a possibility?

Pope Gregory rose from his throne and stamped his ferula on the dais. Appalled by the cardinals' behavior, he cried, 'Stop this!'

Startled by the Holy Father's tone and enraged glare, the cardinals fell silent.

'We cannot do this,' Pope Gregory said sternly. 'We are bound to deliver them to the secular authorities.'

Santori shook his head in annoyance. He would have none of it. The Holy Father had gone mad. His weakness would lead to the Church's demise. Taking this matter beyond the Vatican's walls was not an option. The Church could not expose the truth to the world. They might as well commit mass suicide or burn down the Basilica.

Chapter 48

Suddenly, Schreider had a realization: ever since the bomber had accused the Vatican of being untruthful, the colonel had had doubts about his faith. This was what the female captive had felt—doubt. He had not shared the bomber's rage, but faith had ceased to be the anchor of his life. Now someone offered new insight, which for the colonel—until now a devout Catholic—had the ring of truth and reason.

The Church had not been entirely honest about its past. Rather than offering a true reflection of history, it had invented traditions to suit its doctrine. Through centuries of crafty manipulation, the Church's portrayal of events prevailed. Thus, erroneous doctrine was the basis of all Catholic belief. No wonder the cardinals were baying for blood. They were not combating heresy—they were hiding the truth. Chasing after a man and woman who had broken into the most secret parts of the Vatican and who were now propagating heresy had nothing to do with upholding the faith. It had to do with a bunch of frightened old men protecting their privileged lives from annihilation.

Schreider's gaze fell on the priests huddled together and contemplated his next move. The Maggiore was consulting with His Eminence Cardoni. Schreider cursed under his breath as he noticed their sardonic grins. Now he questioned his decision to bring the captives back to the Vatican. What else could he have done? There had seemed no other option. After all, he was still in the employ of the Holy See. Everything now hinged on the Holy Father. He prayed for wisdom. Could he take the law into his own hands again and make a run for it? No, it was too late for that. He would call for reinforcements. As he lifted his arm to activate the mic in his sleeve, he saw one of his lieutenants rushing in from the Royal Staircase.

Deathly pale and clearly panicking, the officer scanned the room. On seeing Schreider, the lieutenant raced towards his commander. His words came in short gasps: 'Oberst. We have trouble. Inspector Verretti ...'

Schreider did not have time for a fumbling officer. And he certainly could not cope with his adversary entering the fray. 'Not now, Lieutenant. Just keep the man at bay.'

'That's not the problem, Oberst. The *Corpo dei Carabinieri*. I think they're on their way.'

Verretti had obviously called on his family for support. With the carabinieri on their way, there was no escape. The colonel hoped Command had called Interpol as ordered, but that could be too late. Making a run for it was not possible. He had no choice but to stand his ground right there in the Apostolic Palace. Would he have to take the entire Holy See hostage? He shivered imagining the consequences.

'How long before they get here?' he asked.

'Twenty, maybe thirty minutes, Oberst.'

Schreider did not want the Italian authorities there. It would not surprise him if they charged him with treason. Well, if they did, so be it. He had no time for regrets and was listening to his conscience. There was nothing he could do but make this his final stand. 'Do what you need to do, lieutenant,' he ordered. 'Ensure no one gets in. Stand your ground no matter what.'

Schreider was about to turn to his captain to give him new orders when a corporal from the command center came running in.

'Yes, Corporal?' Schreider asked apprehensively. 'Can I help you?'

'Oberst, it's a civilian.' The corporal's bottom lip trembled. 'He insists on seeing you right away.'

'It must wait,' Schreider snapped.

The corporal stood at attention. 'He insists that he has proof that will free the captives, Oberst.'

Good God! This was madness. There was no way Schreider could listen to some maniac. Lives were at stake! But then it occurred to him that it could not be some nut, otherwise the man would not know what was going on in here. Perhaps it was a miracle; Schreider did not pretend to know the designs of Providence.

'Bring him here, Corporal.'

'He is already here, Oberst,' the corporal replied. 'I brought him around the back. He's waiting in a vehicle behind the Sistine Chapel.'

This was not a good time to leave the Regal Room. But his duty was to prevent bloodshed. What if the stranger could help achieve that? Realizing he could sprint there and back in a couple of minutes, he gazed at the corporal. 'If this backfires ...'

'Yes, Oberst. It's on my head.'

'No, it'll be too late. Now take me to him.'

Schreider passed the corporal as they ran. The two Helvetians sprinted down the staircase. Passing through the exit leading to the Sistine Chapel's courtyard, the younger man was panting; the colonel was not.

On exiting the building, Schreider saw a Steyr Puch parked twenty meters ahead of them. He headed towards the vehicle, but on reaching it, found the door standing open. To his dismay, the passenger seat was empty.

'Where is he?' he demanded.

'I don't know, Oberst. I left him here.'

Schreider cursed the day. 'No, God damn it!'

Chapter 49

'These people are innocent,' said a voice from the Sistine Chapel entrance. The voice was clear, calm and authoritative, a voice which commanded attention.

The words startled the College of Cardinals into silence. As one they turned towards the person who had just said that.

Surrounded by guards, their machine guns rammed into their shoulders, a stranger stood with his arms raised. Remaining still, the stranger asked if he could address the tribunal.

At that moment, Schreider marched into the hall, sweating heavily from his sprint back up the steps. Santori demanded he arrest the intruder, but the colonel waved him off, signaling his men to stand down. He had made his mind—the cardinal would no longer command them.

Santori was outraged by Schreider's disobedience and ordered his captain to make the arrest. When Weber also dismissed him, the cardinal stormed towards the Sistine's entrance.

'How dare you defy me?' he scolded Schreider. 'I gave you a direct order to arrest this man!'

Pope Gregory was thoughtful, observing Santori. The man exuded uneasiness. He was a good clergyman who had applied himself excellently as Major of the Penitentiary, but his aspiration to become the next Bishop of Rome seemed to be making him overly zealous. As a counsellor, he was brilliant, but he would never make it as *the* spiritual leader of the Church. A changing world required a people's person which was progressive, someone with warmth and amiability, not a dictator. The pope remembered how the fascists had behaved when he was a boy. Santori's pompous, domineering bearing was reminiscent of Mussolini's, whom the pope recalled hearing on the radio with his parents. The cardinal did not have the makings of an effective ambassador.

'By heaven, Leonardo, stop this nonsense,' Pope Gregory commanded. 'Let's first find out what's happening here.' Turning his attention to the stranger, he said, 'Could *you* explain to us who you are and what you are doing here?'

Cardoni stretched out to see across the hall. He had recognized the voice. Not only did it belong to a man of repute, but also someone who represented a threat to the Holy See. Cardoni recalled meeting with him at the Vatican Library's exhibition of the Dead Sea Scrolls. His research had made him an expert on religion in first-century Levant, but had also made him an incessant threat. The Vatican had frequently anticipated disclosures from his office with apprehension.

'Your Holiness, he is Professor Uri Rabin,' Cardoni said.

'From the Israeli Antiquities Authority.' The two had never met, but Pope Gregory knew exactly who Rabin was. 'Yes, the professor's reputation precedes him.'

Oddly thrilled to be meeting the professor, Pope Gregory ordered Schreider to escort the professor to his throne.

Jennifer's trepidation had given way to astonishment. Relieved, she leaned closer to Simon. Professor Rabin would fix this. Judging from his khakis and sun cracked loafers he had gone to work that morning and found the letter missing, then gone to the farm. She could not imagine how he must have felt finding the house broken into and blood spattered everywhere.

Simon did not share Jennifer's exuberance. Now he was concerned for the professor's safety as well. He regretted having helped John steal the letter. What had he been thinking? He had never imagined this would be the result.

Seeing the bloody lump on Simon's temple, Rabin was aware of the danger they were facing. It saddened him that Simon had not even had time to mourn John's death but was now a captive in the very city where that death had occurred. He feared for Jennifer as well. Her wit, liveliness and tenacity had impressed him a great deal. Seeing her and Simon in such a plight steeled his resolve to get them safely out.

Santori approached Pope Gregory. 'Your Holiness, this man has no business here.'

'I think we should at least let the professor explain himself,' Pope Gregory said firmly.

'But this is a matter for the Vatican State,' Santori said aghast.

Pope Gregory waved him off. His curiosity had been aroused and he wanted to hear the man out. 'Please Professor, continue. …'

Having been fortunate enough to run into Giorgio, Rabin had managed to get to Rome. The entire flight he had mulled over what he would say at the Vatican. He had not been sure he would be allowed into the city and had certainly not expected an audience with the pope; he had therefore no speech prepared. Now that he was there, he had no idea what to say. After all, Simon *had* stolen a letter, and Jennifer *had* been caught trespassing in a sensitive area. Of course, this was of little consequence compared with the mystery they had stumbled upon—a secret the Vatican had obviously guarded closely for centuries. But if the Holy See was intent on protecting itself from exposure, to what lengths would it go to prevent the exposure of past corruption? They were surely fighting a losing battle. No, you could no longer enforce hypocrisy with violence. It was no longer possible to burn a few books and reinvent history. The world had changed too much for that. Today's technology made truth less suppressible than ever. Simply tapping on a little black bit of glass and plastic that everyone kept in their pocket, they could send information whirling around the globe. Although the Holy Roman Church had, over two millennia, attracted billions of devout believers, making her the oldest, most powerful and wealthiest religious institution on Earth, every person in that room was aware she was sorely in need of renewal. The paradigm of obsolete sprang to mind. You could no longer demand obedience at sword point. If you did not like where you were living you could easily leave, and if you did not like what you were told to think, an incessant onslaught of media gave you innumerable choices. Though still quite barbaric, humanity was permanently, for better or worse, beyond the grasp of medieval superstition and suppression.

Remaining dignified, Rabin addressed the pope, 'Your Holiness, two people have violated your laws, and for that they should face the consequences. Of course, the penalty in question must fit their crimes—trespassing, theft, resisting arrest, fleeing a crime scene and assaulting officers of the law. No one in this room—not even the accused—will argue with that; nor would any sovereign nation on the planet. But before I go any further in this vein, let me say this—both people have come here to find closure.

'I could ask you to be lenient with them and leave it at that, but that is not the true problem facing us today. What is at stake is the Church's failure as a religious institution. For millennia, ordinary people have looked to Rome for salvation. When they sought spiritual guidance, the Church was eager to supply answers. The Catholic ideals of Christianity aimed to teach them what it takes to achieve salvation. But with all due respect, and without lodging any personal accusations, every one of us here knows that narration is not founded on truth.'

'Just say what's on your mind, Professor,' Santori snapped, thinking that if the professor mentioned the letter he would deny it and all this apostasy would end. 'I assume you have evidence to support these claims?'

Ignoring the cardinal, Rabin continued addressing Pope Gregory: 'Your Holiness, we have discovered the *true* remains of Apostle Peter. It was buried at the Cave Church site in Antioch.'

Santori's gaze fell on the Bishop of Rome, his face impassive. He had never heard anything like it. Reserved as

Rabin's words had been, the shocking news struck at the heart of the Church. It was beyond anything he had ever had to deal with in all his years as a priest, bishop or cardinal. 'Your claim is arrogant and erroneous, Professor,' he contested hotly. 'You know, of course, that we have Saint Peter's remains here in the Basilica.'

Pope Gregory leaned forward on his throne. 'The evidence you have is real, Professor? Are you sure?'

Rabin was about to do something he had never done before, but the extreme nature of the situation had left him with no other choice. Focusing on the pope, he said, 'I have confirmed the authenticity as first-century artefacts, and that, together with the location, means their authenticity is indisputable. It is not within the Church's power to suppress their existence as Turkish authorities are at the site, recording their existence, as we speak. This discovery means that the authority of the present Church, and indeed this tribunal, is founded on an erroneous premise. Now, to be sure, I'm not lodging any direct accusations against anyone present, but I must assert that, based on the evidence I have recovered, whatever authority exists in this room, is evidently secular.'

Rabin could not falter. The Vatican's ongoing discovery of relics had served as a source of funding for centuries. Pilgrimages to view relics of the saints had been a lucrative business since the fourteenth century. It was in 1968, though, that Pope Paul VI had announced the discovery of Saint Peter's relics, while Saint Paul's sarcophagus had only surfaced in 2006 in the Basilica of Saint Paul Outside the Walls. The way in which these relics suddenly appeared had given rise to speculation and doubt amongst scholars. No one had ever seen Paul's remains, while those of Peter turned out to be a few bone fragments that could have belonged to anyone. Professor Margherita Guarducci, who had led some of the excavations, discovered, by chance, the remains of Peter stored by her predecessor—the administrator of Saint Peter's Basilica. Perhaps unsurprisingly, Monsignor Ludwig Kaas had claimed these remains to be those of Saint Peter.

Any hint of his own misrepresentation now and the chance of saving Simon or Jennifer was over. 'Your Holiness,' the professor continued, 'I was unwilling to bring the remains here, as the Vatican would have every reason to confiscate and destroy them. However, if you wish to confirm their existence through an objective third party, you need only call the Turkish authorities, who are predominantly Muslim. That said, we have found a first-century ossuary with the inscription, "*Shi'mon Bar-Yonah*". As I assume you know, this is Aramaic for "Simon, son of Jonah", the given name of the Apostle Peter before, as the Gospels claim, Jesus of Nazareth renamed him. In the ossuary, moreover, we found a complete set of remains. Both the heel bones and wrists show evidence of having been pierced by iron spikes, with rust residue on the bones, as well as a spike remaining in one heel bone.

'Even more important, though, is the fact that all these bones have been forensically examined, and the examiner has concluded that they display trauma typical of an upside-down crucifixion, the manner of Apostle Peter's execution as related by the apocryphal *Acts of Saint Peter*, upon which your own Church bases its understanding of the Apostle's life. Finally, with these relics we found two keys and a sword. I need not explain the symbolism of this, but it does agree with the contents of the letter I read and can only assume the Church somehow recovered during the night without legal permission from Ankara to conduct policing activities within Turkey's borders.

'The letter itself is only secondary in this matter. Yes, its contents support the findings of our dig, but its existence is hardly necessary in the light of an imminent announcement on tonight's evening news.'

Extremis malis extrema remedia: desperate times called for desperate measures. Was it not only yesterday Rabin had chided Jennifer for jumping to conclusions prematurely? Now he was guilty of the same thing and bluffing one of the most powerful men on the planet. What else could he do? This was not the time for hesitation. 'At any rate,' he thought wryly, 'if the Church could make unsupported claims, why not he?' At least, if it came to it, he had something to show.

He breathed deeply and continued with assumed confidence: 'It is for this reason Miss Jaine is with us. She is a guest journalist from *Geographic America* as I'm sure you are aware, having vetted her yourselves. This world-renowned publication has secured exclusive rights to our discovery, and in Miss Jaine's absence, I have reported our findings directly to her editor.

'So, to settle this absurd situation amicably and extricate the Church from its unfortunate predicament, I suggest a truce. Before the Church makes matters worse for itself by harming those responsible for the relic's discovery—which, I assure you, will happen if the accused are harmed, as I have already apprised Miss Jaine's editor of the present situation—you can still prevent a complete collapse of your faith. We can only hold back for a brief time, and I know it won't be easy, but you can present yourselves as having been deceived and, with some minor modifications to your orthodoxy, inform the faithful while making yourselves out to be the unwitting victims of an ancient conspiracy. Our findings confirm every aspect of the Church's tradition about Peter except his presence in Rome and, therefore, the Apostolic succession. They do not repudiate Christianity per se. Consequently, the only ones amongst you who should be bothered by this plan are those who thrive on wielding absolute dictatorial power over the faithful. Those of you whose earnest desire it is to maintain this Church as an expression of monotheism and who wish to continue helping those in need and doing the will of God as you see it—those have nothing to fear.

'On the other hand, you can do as I'm sure the cardinal here wishes and eliminate me and the accused in secrecy, but the editor will call my office in Antakya this evening, and if I do not answer his call, he will run the story in their next issue and report our presence here to Interpol. I, meanwhile, will call Interpol myself if I leave here without the accused.'

The College of Cardinals were listening intently. They were puzzled and ill at ease. Rabin's report had stunned them.

Of all the cardinals, Santori was the most sickened. Whether the professor was telling the truth was beside the point, the Vatican could not afford a scandal. But this has now gone beyond humiliation. Saint Peter's true remains, meant they were doomed.

'You forget, Professor, crimes have been committed against our Holy State,' he said defensively. 'This *man* killed one of our priests.'

Rabin regretted it had come to this, but perhaps it was for the best. He had hoped for a settlement without bringing John into the equation. When the professor spoke, his voice was husky with sorrow: 'Your Eminence, your priest was not who you think he was. Father John Yilmaz was a Jew from Antioch. His real name was John Kepa. He was Simon's brother.'

A silence, the likes of which the Apostolic Palace had never known, fell on the Regal Room.

Rabin turned towards the College of Cardinals. 'Simon and John grew up as orphans,' he announced painfully. 'Their grandparents cared for them. For decades, they were the best of friends until the Church drove a wedge between them. John's longing to join the priesthood led to their estrangement. Believing that his older brother would not support his vocation, John found that your message of love and acceptance didn't apply to his only remaining family, and it wasn't long before the passion he felt for God's work turned into bitter regret. Knowing that John was alone in his disillusionment, Simon came here to support him. That is why they broke into your vault.'

Santori caught his breath and steadied himself. Satan himself and all the fallen angels might as well have been standing before them. John, a Jew and Simon's brother? Now how could he explain the Father's death? In a panicked attempt to save himself and the Church, he reached for Schreider's pistol. Ripping it from its holster, he swung the firearm towards Rabin's chest.

'You will not succeed, Professor!' he shrieked.

Santori snatched Schreider's pistol and viciously jabbed at Rabin with the gun's muzzle.

Simon leapt toward the two old men, but Schreider jumped in front of him. If anyone was sacrificing his life for the cause it was the colonel himself. He was not letting anyone take his place.

The Helvetians had their machine guns aimed at the Maggiore's chest, but Schreider signaled for them to stand down.

Santori had dedicated his life to protecting and promoting the Church. No one would destroy his life's work. The world depended on individuals like him. A world without faith—the faith of the Holy Roman Church—was not viable. 'We *are* the voice of God!' he cried. 'The mightiest tradition the world has ever seen; not even the Egyptians or Aztecs compare.'

Schreider had a feeling he was not going to live to see forty. He just hoped he would not die right that instant. 'I suppose there's no such thing as being prepared for death,' he thought, staring down the barrel of his own pistol. If it were the last thing he did, he would not let the cardinal kill an innocent man. Then, he recognized something the coroner had drawn his attention to the previous day.

His gaze remained on the cardinal, but he addressed the Bishop of Rome: 'Your Holiness, the person that killed Father Yilmaz is left handed.'

Shaking as he clutched the pistol with his left hand, Santori was trying to steady his aim. 'Good try, Colonel. How would you know? You weren't even there.'

Schreider's muscles clenched like a tiger preparing to spring. 'Your Eminence, but neither were you …'

The thought of not dying a traitor's death flashed through Schreider's mind. But would he die a coward. Silently praying that Santori would not squeeze the trigger, he stepped in to take the pistol from the elderly man, but the cardinal swung at him, narrowly missing the colonel's face.

Simon—a skilled student of Krav Maga—leapt towards Santori, seizing the cardinal's hand and forcing the pistol towards the roof. A slug burst from the barrel, missing Schreider's head by millimeters. The sound reverberated off the walls, deafening everyone in the hall. Before Santori could fire another round, Simon had pulled the cardinal's arm down, twisting it behind his back and flexing his wrist. The move softened the cardinal's hold, allowing Simon to tear the firearm from the old man's grip.

Santori struggled to free himself, but Simon proved too strong for his aging limbs. 'Get off me!' he moaned. 'You're hurting me!'

Cardoni placed his hand on Santori's shoulder. 'Leonardo, don't. Your madness will destroy us all.'

Santori's bloodshot eyes flickered momentarily towards his friend. 'They'll destroy the Church. We must stop them. We can't let them do this.'

Cardoni held his friend. 'Let go, Leonardo. We have nothing left to lose.'

Pope Gregory stood, looking somewhat sickened at the cardinals' embrace. He thanked God they were in the safe confines of their own Palace. Had this been anywhere else, they would have been doomed. He imagined what would happen if this had to go public. They would never recover again after this. He would have to act quickly and decisively. Turning towards Schreider, he ordered the Swiss officer to have his men place the rogue cardinals under house arrest. The Holy See would deal with them later.

On reaching the Regal Room's exit, Santori struggled with the Helvetians. 'I *am* the next Vicar of Christ!' he wailed. 'You all know this! The Church needs discipline. She needs to survive! I am the only one who can save you from the destruction you're bringing down on yourselves.'

Chapter 50

Pope Gregory now stood at the edge of the dais, ferula in hand, and gazing at the cardinals around him. The shocking revelation that one of their own had killed the Jewish priest seemed to have paralyzed them. With eyes centering on him, as if pleading for reassurance and guidance, waiting for him to provide leadership, it was his duty to unite them as one body and somehow find a solution to this dreadful situation. The old religion would now be obsolete. The Church of Rome had served them for thousands of years, but now needed to undergo profound change if it was going to survive. He knew not all the cardinals would agree with him; the traditionalists, who, like Santori, adhered rigidly to Church doctrine, would fight change. Reform was inevitable, and perhaps would end the schisms that had lasted for centuries. Nothing stayed the same, not even religion. Society had evolved to the point that dogma no longer sustained spirituality. Their followers would not expect their Church to be the same two thousand years from now, so why had they striven to maintain the status quo for the past two thousand years? Archaic dogma would stultify the Gospel of Christ, but creative change could initiate its growth.

Stepping from the dais the pope now symbolically made himself their equal. He handed his ferula to an aide, waving him away. As he passed Simon, Jennifer and Professor Rabin, they turned to follow him. The College of Cardinals filed into a horseshoe formation, allowing him to take up position in their midst.

Pope Gregory's demeanor was serene and his voice calm and deep as he spoke: 'The Church has survived difficult times, but never have we faced the possibility of her dissolution. For two millennia, we have remained the most powerful institution the world has ever seen, yet today we stand on the brink of collapse. We have achieved a great deal and preached the Word of God, but like a cancerous growth, the sins from which our prerogatives derive are suffocating us. It is clear from the events of the past two days that we have no choice but to change. Reform more radical than probably any of us can vision is required, or the Church will cease to be. Superficial change is not enough. We *must* penetrate to the heart of the matter, and for nearly all this time, those of us tasked with leading the faithful have known what that is.

Pausing, the pope waited until the echo of his voice slid off the marble walls around them.

Staring at Rabin, he said, 'What do *you* suggest we do, Professor?'

Pope Gregory's voice rang in Rabin's ears, but in the gravity of the moment, an answer eluded him.

Receiving only silence, Pope Gregory continued, 'Well, you have made your point and had your say. You have questioned the Church, our history, our doctrine and us. Now, it is my turn to say what I think of your ideas. Like us, Professor, you must get your house in order. The Church asks the same questions as science but in a different way. The questions we both ask are "Where do we come from?", "Where we are now?" and "Where are we going?". Science asks these questions from the vantage point of natural laws, while religion does so from a spiritual perspective. Rightly or wrongly, we arrive at different conclusions, but it is the Church that dares to go further and glimpse God.

'You have accused us of trying to speak for God, and perhaps you are right—we have assumed that right. You have wondered how anyone can speak *for* God, when arguably, just speaking *of* God limits Him. Mere human insight cannot define God you would say; it can at best *attempt* to know the unknowable. Yes, perhaps we and our predecessors have done wrong, but in altering DNA or speculating on the Big Bang, does not science also attempt this?

'We live in a world where life has become mundane,' the pope said, his eyes penetrating, his voice resolute. 'Everything has to be instant: gratification, communication, travel, results. We have all these at the touch of a button or a screen. In a world where increasingly sophisticated technologies allow us to observe the inner and outer fabric of the universe, telescopes, microscopes and particle oscillators have become an extension of our senses. X-rays, computerized axial tomography, magnetic-resonance imaging and position-emission tomography are used to peer deep into our bodies. Nothing is out of reach now. Our technology has made us powerful creatures; even our ancestors of only a century ago would have considered us superhuman. Sadly, though, it seems that technology has superseded the soul.

'Reductionism is the hallmark of science, and, because the soul eludes a scientific definition, science has reduced humans to mind and body. It is true that lack of evidence cannot support a belief, but it is also no argument against it. Contemporary thinking conceives of man only as a physical being. But isn't this a false perception? Might it not be that Paul, despite his treachery, was right when he suggested the trichotomy of body, soul and spirit? Or, as Our Lord suggests in the *Gospel of Matthew*—body, soul and mind? The inability of technology to identify the soul does not negate its existence. God is God. He cannot be commanded to reveal Himself. To some this proves His non-existence, but there are some in this room who have had personal encounters with divinity, which are as real as anything you perceive with your physical sight. Unfortunately, we cannot command the seraphim to dance to our tune, but we may hope that, as technology and science advance, we will discover the means to identify the soul. The arrogance of *assuming* the soul does not exist is like denying the existence of the sun because the clouds obscure our vision of it. Maybe science should set itself the challenge of discovering the soul. Billions the world over profess its existence. Can the atheist be so sure he is right? Truth is found through assiduous enquiry and not through conformity.'

The pope paused to ponder his next thought. What he was about to say he had never discussed with anyone. It was the result of years of solitary contemplation and prayer, but now elderly and infirm, the burden of carrying it alone was too great. He had long waited for the appropriate moment to share what to him seemed a divine revelation. If this day's events had not brought him to that moment, nothing ever would.

'Earth is not enough,' he said, slowly turning to regard all the cardinals. 'We live in a world that is running out of resources and real estate. Soon we will populate every inch of soil. The land will become barren, its resources drained. Look beyond Earth and our sun will one day perish. Look beyond that, and the universe will die as well. Without a soul, why do anything? Why religion and why science? Why the beauty around us? Poetry? Music? Love? Humanity has long known the Earth is not enough; we have intuited it, but still have continued to live in the same way. Hardwired into us is the realization that the soul, and spiritual immortality, do exist. Meanwhile, to ensure our long-term physical survival, we contemplate migration to neighboring planets in our solar system and even muse travelling to other solar systems in our galaxy, if not neighboring galaxies. Our refrain has become "Leave it to science!" But we do so at our peril, for in our own time, science has made Armageddon a possibility.

'The nature of humanity needs to change if we are to survive. Science will modify our DNA and create a new species of man that is better, stronger and more resilient for space travel, perhaps even immortal, in the hope our descendants will live on. Science will also create more durable, faster spacecraft, find wormholes and bend time. But perhaps even science has its boundaries. $E=MC^2$. Einstein's relativity has elevated us from earthly creatures to space travelers. Yet, it is this exact insight which shows us the impossibility of travelling beyond our own solar system. As impressive as the circulating theories and ideas sound, it is our mass that will prevent this. Even if it were affordable the time and energy taken to project *mass* to other solar systems or galaxies makes interstellar travel a theoretical dream. Unless we can rid ourselves of mass, there is no solar system within our reach. The only way forward is to let go of our physicality and attend to our immaterial, and God willing, immortal, soul.

'Should we discard this precious aspect of ourselves at the behest of a select few? Should a handful of scientists decide our destiny? Can we allow them to play God? If they deny the soul, should we allow them to continue this path of arrogant intervention? What if they are wrong? Scientists claim to create life, but I ask: can you create life with a soul? Clearly, if the scientists do not acknowledge a soul, they cannot. *Our* mistake has been to fossilize faith, but faith cannot be frozen in time. And while we cannot speak for God, neither can science be left to act in His place.'

Jennifer had been raptly listening to the pontiff's speech and was now agape with shock. For once the man had sounded holy. Not once had he spoken of Christ as the Savior or pontificated with the usual rhetoric. He had spoken of things that were relevant and current, and he had made a rational argument for why faith—at least a re-created faith—must survive.

In conclusion Pope Gregory proclaimed, 'To determine our way forward, I now invoke an ecumenical council. Let us search within ourselves, not just as Catholics but as scientists. Let us join hands and begin again. Together, humbly and with the Grace of God, let us pray that a new path be revealed. I do believe that solutions to the questions presented here today shall be found with patience, kindness and love.'

The pontiff's address was at an end and, after the united applause, he turned to Schreider and said, 'Take our young visitors to our doctor. Then, take them to my suite.'

He waited until Schreider had escorted Jennifer and Simon from the Regal Room. Then, motioning for Rabin to join him, Pope Gregory strode towards the exit leading to the Apostolic Palace's suites.

Passing through the stuccoed doorway, he said quietly, 'I hope you really did find Peter's remains, Professor. If not, you have just replaced Saint Paul.'

Chapter 51

A cool breeze picked up, drawing Jennifer indoors. Reclining into the soft cushions of the leather sofa, she gazed into the fire. She smiled as she recalled the events of the evening. Strolling into the kitchen earlier, Simon had pulled out a stool for her and suggested she join him by the stove. The kitchen consisted of three distinct areas: a central dining area with a bulky wooden table and twelve chairs under a wood and brass chandelier, the cooking area where Simon had started preparing supper for them, and a fireplace flanked by two armchairs and the sofa.

Upon their arrival, Simon had said he hoped she would like one of his favorite dishes, Alinazik. As he explained before he had begun cooking, the dish consisted of spiced lamb and eggplant served with vegetables over rice.

'So, it's a stir-fry,' she had joked dryly. 'You know we have that in the States, right?'

As she had seated herself at the table he had descended a spiral staircase to a cellar beneath the kitchen, returning with a bottle of burgundy. He had tasted the wine and then filled Jennifer's glass. Then, he had taken a knife from the wooden stand and sliced two onions.

Two hours later, and Simon was stacking more wood on the fire, the flames crackling and spitting sparks. Turning from the fireplace, his silhouette revealed his powerful frame. His calculated gaze rested on her for some time before he sat down on the far end of the sofa, propping her feet on his lap as if enjoying her presence. Though relaxed, his demeanor reminded her of their escape from the libraries when he had pulled her into the alley. He had held her then, only allowing her to move when it suited him. With one hand around her midriff and the other restraining her, his fingers had curled around her mouth. Her lips had parted slightly. She had wanted to bite him, but had not. He had smelled of adrenaline and testosterone. Presently, she became aware of the same scent, and it excited her.

She watched him over the book she was reading, and after a few moments, set the book on the floor. 'The professor used me as a scapegoat, didn't he.' she said.

Simon touched the cut behind his ear where Verretti pistol-whipped him two days ago. 'It worked, didn't it?'

Sitting up, she leaned towards him and began massaging the muscles in his neck. 'Does that hurt?'

He lifted his shirt, revealing his muscular torso. 'It's this one over here that bothers me,' he said, pointing to a bruise on the side of his ribcage. 'I think the inspector cracked my rib. I also have a bad one over here. Why don't you rub this instead?'

She punched him on the bruise. 'Oh come on, Simon. I'm not your personal masseuse.'

'You're not?' he asked, pulling his shirt back down.

She pressed the swollen area on his temple, this time just a bit harder. 'What about this one; does it still hurt?'

'Nope. Surprisingly, it's fine.'

Jennifer leaned back on the cushions, and his focus shifted to her silk top. Abruptly, he got up to get more wine.

'Professor Rabin's knowledge of Christianity is profound,' she said to his back.

'He has an amazing philosophy,' Simon said, pouring. 'The day he stops learning is the day he dies.'

Jennifer's eyes began to wander elsewhere. … 'I love that. I wish I were more that way.'

'Aren't you?'

Returning with the wine, he topped up her glass.

'Oh, I suppose.'

He placed the bottle on the floor next to the sofa and sat beside her. 'To life and discovery,' he said, lifting his glass.

'And to heroes who save damsels in distress two dozen times in three days.'

'And to the prettiest girl I've ever had the honour of dragging from a crime scene.'

Jennifer tittered. 'Ah, so if I'd been a dog you would have left me to my fate?'

Simon laughed. 'Maybe.'

'You know there are easier ways to pick up women.'

'Who said I was planning on picking up more than one?'

Now she laughed. 'I suppose you're right. Besides, you can really only topple the foundations of Western Civilization every so often.'

'Too true. But I could always go after the Dalai Lama next if I get bored.'

One of his hands lay along the back of the sofa, and she smacked it.

'Okay, okay. I guess what the Buddhists don't know won't hurt them.'

'Oh? You're not going soft on me, are you?'

'Well, I suppose if you insist. I mean, we are in a Muslim country. I could always build you and my second adventure girlfriend a harem in the backyard.'

Jennifer reached across him and pinched the tender spot on his ribcage.

'Ouch!' he exclaimed, pulling away. 'Hey! That hurts, damn it!'

'Take it back.'

'Okay, okay, there will never be a second adventure girlfriend. … Only multiple adventure wives.'

She tackled him in mock rage, and they tumbled to the floor, wrestling. Simon, of course, was not trying to win, and Jennifer soon found herself on his back, one elbow crooked around his neck. He reared up suddenly and she toppled to the floor like a rodeo rider tossed from a horse. He then leapt at her and pinned her arms.

'I give up,' he said.

'You? I'm the one pinned.'

'I still give up. I guess I will settle for one adventure wife if I must.'

Jennifer play struggled a moment more before what he had said sank in, and she became still. 'Wait. Are you asking me in a weird way that only you could ask what I think you're asking?'

'I don't know. Are you agreeing to it in a weird way only you could agree to something?'

'I'm not entirely sure, but perhaps I am.'

'Good.'

'Would I have to become a *giyoret* first …'

Before she could finish the sentence, he kissed her gently and long. She parted her lips, and he moved closer. He released her wrists, and cupped the back of her head with one hand. He slid his other hand under her top, touching her stomach. As his fingers grazed the sensitive nerve ends in her skin, she held her breath. Pulling her closer, his hand moved past her navel. Her low-cut jeans were just low enough. She gasped.

'You shouldn't do that,' she said, softly.

'I love the way you smell.'

Soft light from the candles in the candelabrum overhead cast a gentle glow on her face. She was smiling. His fingers loosened her belt.

She caught his hand. 'No,' she whispered.

'I want you,' he said.

The pulse of eons engulfed her with its eternal pattern of want, desire, defiance, surrender and joy. Time lost all meaning, but Jennifer did, for some reason, think of the date: Thursday, 22 March 2012. It was exactly nine months before the Mayan calendar predicted the end of the world. That zany prophesy. Why was everyone still talking about it? Why was she thinking about it? Why was she thinking anything at all?

Chapter 52

Professor Rabin's historic meeting with Pope Gregory had set a precedent for future cooperation, and the pontiff suggested sending a team of priests to the Antiochene site. If the Apostle Peter's remains at the Cave Church were authentic, it would point the way forward for Roman Catholicism. Rabin was open to the idea, but had warned that the final approval lay with the Turkish government. There was a lot to do before anything more than photographs could be made available.

Following his return to the site the next day, Rabin decided to revisit the Cave Church. Something about that find—momentous though it was—bothered him. Eager to return to work, he climbed down into the chasm and made his way to the sepulcher where they had found Peter's relics. Lighting the burial chamber with his flashlight, he pushed his fingertips through the sand. In their haste to get Jennifer to safety they could easily have missed something. Finding the sword and keys was an amazing bit of fortune. Peter was the disciple who had severed the ear of a servant of the high priest in the garden of Gethsemane, which accounted for the sword. But the keys still puzzled him, for they suggested the cave represented more than a grave. Was Peter's tomb the origin of something else? Could the cave have served as an entrance, an antechamber perhaps, which lead to something bigger? He pondered this. Rather than the gates of Heaven, it would make sense if Peter was in some way the gatekeeper to the catacombs. Anyone wanting to enter the area would have to get past him first.

No, Rabin decided, he was thinking like Jennifer now.

Simon descending the ladder could not have happened any sooner.

'Where's Jennifer?' Rabin asked.

'She'll be here in a minute.'

'Is she all right?'

Simon joined the professor. 'Don't worry, she's fine.'

Rabin wanted to inquire further but held his tongue. He was pleased to have his colleague with him again. 'The keys bother me,' he said, lighting the sepulcher. 'The sword I can understand, but the keys should be symbolic, not actual.'

'All we need is to find where they fit then,' a voice said from the shrine above.

Rabin looked up. Dressed in a cotton tunic, baggy pants and canvas shoes, Jennifer was staring down at them. 'How do you feel this morning?' he asked.

'Wonderful, thanks.'

'Did you sleep well?'

'I've never appreciated sleeping in a bed more in my life.'

To be sure, Jennifer appreciated the professor's concern, but she was naturally reticent about how she and Simon had spent their time on the farm. A lot of innuendos and puns came to mind, but suffice to say, there was not much farming going on.

'If the keys weren't meant to open the gates of Heaven,' she said, 'there should be a door with real locks somewhere around here.'

Rabin smiled. 'And where, dear Jennifer, do you suppose we might find said locks?'

'At a wild guess, I'd say follow the crosses.' The professor frowned, and she pointed to his feet, adding, 'I'm serious, you're standing on them.'

Rabin shone the flashlight on the ground. Sweeping the rubble and sand with his feet, he exposed a buried floor. In his preoccupation with the sword and keys, he had missed something significant: traces of an ancient mosaic. The pattern consisted of scarlet and yellow crosses typical of the Roman-occupation period. Amazingly, the design resembled Maltese crosses linked together. Samples exactly like those could be viewed at the Antakya museum. And yet, the pattern predated the Maltese cross on the outside façade by at least a thousand years.

Shifting sand away as he went, the professor followed it across the floor of the crevasse. The mosaic continued past the sepulcher to a far corner and disappeared beneath a pile of rubble.

After clearing the floor, Simon began wiping dirt from a rusty surface. He stopped suddenly. Before him at chest height was an opening the size of a keyhole.

Rabin became tense, and had to fight the urge to shove Simon aside. 'Don't let the sand get in the lock.'

'It's already inside. I'm trying to get it out.'

'We can't afford mistakes now.'

Simon did not appreciate the patronizing warning. He had been working the site for as long as the professor. Putting aside his irritation, he blew lightly around the keyhole, until the tiny vortices of air had cleared the chamber. Repeating the process, he cleaned a matching keyhole lower down.

Jennifer skittered down the ladder and joined the two scientists. 'Well, there's Heaven's gate. Now all we need are the keys.'

She had assumed Rabin had left them at the site, but the professor drew them from his pocket like a magician summoning a rabbit.

'I had a feeling we'd need them,' he said, smiling. He inserted the top key, wiggling it until it turned. The key rotated halfway and stopped. He swapped keys but got the same result. Standing back, he let Simon try, but he also failed.

Rabin asked Jennifer to try. After all, strange things had happened since she had arrived on the site.

Holding her breath, Jennifer turned the keys. Again, they stopped halfway. Disappointed but not defeated, she smacked the palm of her hand against the door and tried again. This time there was a click, and the door jolted open.

'Why am I not surprised,' Rabin said softly. 'Maybe God does exist and He's especially sweet on you, Jennifer.'

Simon slipped his fingers between the door and its frame. He pulled but only managed to open the door a few inches. Rabin then pulled on the top while he tried the bottom. After a final tug the hinges creaked and the door opened about a third of the way.

A musty stench wafted from the darkness and Jennifer nearly vomited. She was not sure if she could go in.

Rabin clicked on his hand torch and shone the light through the opening. He could not see much, but judging by the echo of their voices, or lack thereof, the space was small. By stretching his back and releasing the air from his lungs, he managed to squeeze through the gap.

Simon followed, his lean body sliding easily through.

Jennifer remained where she was for a moment and cursed silently. Even if she ended up dry-heaving by the end of it, she was going inside. Pulling her blouse over her nose and mouth, she slipped through.

Shining first left then right, Rabin quickly realized they were inside a catacomb. He decided, as the oldest and most experienced amongst them, he would scout ahead of his young friends. Considering the recent earthquake and the fact that many have occurred in the past, the tunnel's structural integrity might be compromised. Holding up his torch, he set off down a passage to the left.

The catacomb was circular, constructed around a central axis. Cut into a spinal area were four sepulchers, each with its own ossuary, but unlike Peter's ossuary outside, these were all intact. Completing the circle, Rabin returned to Simon and Jennifer.

'You are not going to believe what's in here,' he said.

Shining the light left to right he explained how the tunnel encircles a central pillar of rock, which has been carved in a Maltese-cross design like the rose window outside. Four niches were dug exactly at the four focal points of the cross in the shape of the primitive fleur-de-lis, and in each was an ossuary.

Approaching the tunnel clockwise, Rabin shone the flashlight onto the first ossuary.

Jennifer shivered. She was not sure she wanted to know what the boxes said. The last thing she needed now was being disappointed.

The professor stroked his finger lightly over the inscription. '"*Johanan Bar-Shi'mon.*"'

Jennifer did not hesitate: 'That's Aramaic for "John, son of Simon,"' she said hastily. 'Shi'mon is Simon-Peter, surely.' She felt silly for jumping to premature conclusions again, but this time she had good reason. 'Oh, come on guys. We already have Apostle Peter's remains. Do the sums. But who's John?'

'The answer to that, is around the corner.' Leading the way, Rabin stopped before the next sepulcher. Holding the light at an angle he read aloud: '"*Levi Bar-Shi'mon.*"'

Jennifer was about to mention 'son of Alphaeus', but this time kept her thoughts to herself. If her memory served her right, the *Gospel of Mark* cited Levi as being the son of Alphaeus. But, the reference pertained to an original Apostle of Jesus. Being a son of Shi'mon, this could not be the same Levi.

Jennifer had an idea, which, despite potential scorn from the professor, she felt compelled to share: '*First Peter* says a young man who went by both "John" *and* "Mark" accompanied the Apostle on his missionary work, and importantly, Peter refers to the young man as his "*son*". *Acts* and *Colossians* relate how Mark abandoned his cousin Barnabas and Paul, or Saul, at Perga, and returned to Jerusalem. Correct me if I'm wrong, but Perga isn't far from here, in modern-day Antalya, right. For two thousand years, no one knew *why* Mark ran. But considering what we know now about both Paul and Peter, it's pretty evident what happened.'

Jennifer's mind raced ahead. Aliases were not a new thing. Many of the Apostles who were under threat of persecution had two names. It was obvious why. 'Levi also went by the name, Matthew,' she said, casting her gaze up to Rabin. 'So, if Levi is Matthew and John is Mark, then the next one must be Luke, right?'

Rabin nodded and she laughed.

'Luke, son of …?' She expected another nod, but this time the professor's silence stunned her. 'The three Synoptic Gospel authors—and Peter's offspring.'

Jennifer had always wanted to explain why the Gospels post-dated the original Apostles. Now that she had found the answer, it was hard to believe. None of the Gospel writers were contemporaries of the original Apostles. Every pre-seminary student knew this. Their Gospels dated to at least a generation later. This was exactly what her fight with Cardinal Cardoni was about. If the remains were the offspring of Simon-Peter, there was the reason why the Gospels had been written later.

'Then the next must be, John.'

'We've already found a John,' Simon said.

'Not if he turns out to be Mark,' she shot back. She refocused on Rabin. 'Please don't tell me there's another, John.'

'Nope.'

She did not understand. Yes, John's work was different from the Synoptic Gospels and one could hardly consider him kin, yet it *had* to be, after all, his was the fourth Gospel.

Jennifer and Simon were following closely behind Rabin. On reaching the final grave, the professor lit up the fourth ossuary.

'"*Nathaniel Bar-Tlm*,"' he read aloud.

Jennifer felt faint. Matthew, Mark and Luke buried together made sense, but Nathaniel. Where did he fit? No one had ever offered a satisfactory explanation why some used his given name and others his surname, but tradition had identified "Nathaniel" and "Bartholomew" as the same man. In the synoptic texts, he was called "Bartholomew," or "son of Tlm," and in *John* he is called "Nathaniel." What was more, the Apostle Bartholomew's mission was not far from there either, in Armenia.

'*Mark* is the earliest canonical gospel,' Jennifer said, her mind ticking feverishly. '*That* every serious biblical scholar agrees on, and because of its language and references to the Jewish revolt, most date it to the reign of Nero, between 66 and 70 CE. Now, if Mark is Peter's son, that *does* make him a generation younger, and if he was a boy at the time of the crucifixion, he would have been in his forties at the writing of the Gospel that bears his name. Traditionally, he is believed to have died during Nero's persecutions in 68 CE, so it's not farfetched to think he could have written the Gospel or dictated it, before his martyrdom.'

She paused briefly to consider her next hypothesis.

'The *Gospel of Matthew* is dated between 80 and 90 CE, correct? Both the biblical texts and tradition are unclear on the date of his death. The Muslim tradition places him in Ethiopia, which is far enough away from Rome to escape the purges under Nero. And maybe he lived to a great age. If Matthew was born around the time of the crucifixion, he would have been in his fifties or sixties when he recorded his gospel. As for Luke, tradition has it he was from Antioch. Most scholars date his Gospel to around 80 to 100 CE. Tradition holds that he died in 84 CE, making him around seventy. That leaves Bartholomew …'

Simon stopped her mid-sentence: 'You're not going to resolve this now, Jennifer. These things take time.'

Her shoulders drooped. How could they be so patient?

Rabin also did not have time for further debate. They were unearthing what might prove to be a more momentous find than their initial discovery and he had to get his workers to come over to assist with the recovery of the remains. 'The faster we move the remains the sooner we'll have our answers,' he said, heading for the exit. 'For starters, Simon needs to do DNA tests to determine if Peter really was the patriarch. Then, we need to determine if damage to the bones forensically matches the traditions around each Apostle's death.'

Rabin was about to squeeze through the exit when the door abruptly slammed shut. He assumed it was the wind, but with the door requiring some effort to open, that was not possible. Then he heard the keys turn in the locks.

Simon pushed against the door, but it would not budge. Taking the flashlight from Rabin he shone on the locking mechanism, looking for a way to turn the keys from the inside, but the keys were no longer there. Through the keyhole, he saw a figure.

'Who are you?' he shouted. 'What are you doing?'

Jennifer's heart raced, and she felt suffocated.

Simon pressed his ear to the door. There was a splat, as if someone had slapped a piece of putty against the door. When there was another splat and two skidding noises, he backed up. He heard shuffling feet and the screech of a wheel growing fainter as it moved away from the door. Someone was climbing up the ladder, and then further shuffling. The sounds faded but the silence roared in his ears.

'What's happening?' Jennifer shrieked.

Simon was not saying anything, but he knew exactly what was going on. Years of military service in war-torn areas had given him a sense for distinguishing sounds. Often on night missions, they had had to rely on their senses to stay alive. Sound sequences could tell stories, and if interpreted correctly, they yielded all the information one needed. He was sure someone had stacked C4 against the door; the sliding was detonators being placed; and the squeaking was the laying of a detonator cord, which was hauled up the ladder to the shrine above. If it was a command-wire improvised-explosive device with an electrical firing cable, they were in serious trouble. The Cave Church was silent. The person must have gone outside to detonate the system. They awaited death.

Jennifer banged on the door frantically. She did not want to die—not like this.

Simon racked his brains. Depending how the charges went off, the C4 might free them if the tunnel did not collapse.

'Get back into the catacomb,' he said, pulling Jennifer and Rabin with him.

Jennifer did not comprehend the technicalities, but from their urgency she sensed the trouble they were in. As they scampered to the back of the pillar, she hugged Simon. She could not imagine being killed right then. Despite spending only days with him, she was already in love with him.

*****

A man rolled the detonator cord to one of the park benches outside the Cave Church. On the terrace, the temperature had soared to over eighty-eight degrees Fahrenheit. 'It's the hottest day this spring,' he thought as he sat down in the shade. He scratched his chin. The drops of sweat in his beard irritated him, but this was no time to fuss. He connected the detonator cord to the C4 clacker, a handheld device he had stolen from the British Military Corps many years before. He had felt ashamed at the time, but now that he needed it, he felt vindicated.

His life had not turned out as he had planned, and lately things had worsened. It had not always been this way; as a kid, he had had many friends and a large family, but as he aged he had found himself alone and isolated. He had joined the Church for the community of monastic life, but had found himself assigned to a monastery with no other monks. He had also joined the Church to escape the violent man he had been, but found himself called upon by the Holy See to perpetrate violence in God's name. The only reason he had not yet taken his own life was his faith. As a man of God, he felt suffering purified the soul. As his body succumbed to the aging process, he found himself less concerned with it. It was not that he was giving up, exactly. Life just did not matter much anymore.

And yet, death terrified him. He feared he would find himself even more isolated on the other side. When he prayed, he would ask God not to let him be alone, and to curry favor with Him, as a sort of apology for his suicide, he would execute the orders he had received from the Vatican—or, at least, from those cardinals still committed to Holy Mother Church in opposition to the Holy Father's new program. Not everyone appreciated Pope Gregory's point of view. The Church had flourished for two thousand years without liberals like him. Ridding the Church of the pope's new favorites would, it was hoped, make the Holy Father see the error of his ways.

Once he was finished here, he would head for the archaeology site and destroy Saint Peter's remains as well. He would make sure no evidence blemishing the Catholic faith remained, so he had to ensure that none of the discoveries made at the Cave Church that day were found a second time.

Standing, he wired the detonation cord to the C4 clacker. 'What a pity the Cave Church must go as well,' he thought. Admiring the façade—what was left of it—for the last time, he recollected proudly how the Capuchin Friars had restored the site in 1863. His predecessors had done a fine job then. A piece of church history would be lost forever, but so be it.

*****

'I'd put that down if I were you,' a voice said from across the courtyard.

Friar Malone turned towards the entrance. Engrossed in his thoughts, he had not heard anyone approach, but turning, he saw a man in a white t-shirt, faded jeans and a brown-leather jacket standing by a nearby tree. The man had a pistol aimed at the friar's chest.

'You're just in time, Colonel,' the monk said.

'Stop what you're about to do, Friar,' Schreider replied sternly.

Malone lifted the clacker to his chest. 'But we're on the same team, Colonel.'

'That's not true, Friar. You know that as well as I do. Now give me that handset. You're just making things worse than they already are.'

The monk did not trust the Swiss commander. He had heard how the colonel's betrayal had ensured that Their Eminences Santori and Cardoni were relegated to a Carthusian Order cloistered in the French Alps, where they would now live monastic lives of meditation, prayer and studying. Each cardinal—now stripped of his title and treated as a monk—had been forced to live in a small cell. Being a recluse himself, Malone had once almost found himself in the same monastery. He could imagine what the cardinals must be going through, severed from the opulent, powerful world of the Vatican.

For a clearer view of the church, Schreider moved to the center of the terrace. 'Where are they, Friar?' he asked, his eyes scanning the remaining entrance.

Witnessing his Church degenerating into mediaeval practices again was horrific to Schreider's principled mind. Fortunately, Pope Gregory had called on Schreider to ensure the safety of their captives as promised at the Vatican Palace days before. The colonel was also indebted to Simon for having saved his life. He did not think he would repay the debt so soon.

Malone hugged the clacker to his chest. 'They're doing the Devil's work, Colonel. We can't allow them to go on like this.'

'Put that down, Friar,' said a voice behind the monk.

Malone turned to see Weber standing behind him, the captain's pistol pointing at his chest. Schreider's distraction had allowed the captain to get in behind him.

'You wouldn't shoot an unarmed man, Captain,' Malone said.

Weber held his aim. 'You look armed to me, Friar.'

'Do as my captain says, Friar, and put down the clacker.'

Schreider waited for Malone to waver, then launched himself towards the monk, grabbing his hand. Malone resisted, but the colonel forced his index and middle fingers between the trigger and handset, preventing it from being triggered. Then, with all the force he could muster, he yanked the clacker from Malone's hand.

Weber plunged forward, dropping his pistol as he fought to retrieve the clacker, but Malone won. Lying on his back, clacker in hand, the friar stared up at Schreider.

Schreider aimed between Malone's eyes. His captain was perhaps not ready to shoot a monk, but by God, if the man dared activate that clacker, Schreider *would* kill him.

'I *will* blow them up, Colonel.'

'Yes, that does seem likely.'

'I am not afraid of death. In fact, I embrace it.'

The movement of a person's eyes could indicate a prelude to action. This was something Schreider had learned in basic training in Switzerland, and it had served well to keep him safe. Now, he watched Malone's eyes in a deadly staring contest. If he saw even the slightest flicker, he would shoot.

'What are you going to do now, Colonel? If you shoot me, you are eliminating a member of the opposing faction—which would make you no better than me.'

'Be rational, Malone,' Schreider said. 'Why do you let them dictate your faith? Think, Friar! Think about it. Don't let others decide your life for you. For once, think.'

Malone's pupils dilated and his hand contracted.

Schreider did not hesitate. He squeezed the trigger. As if in slow motion, the hammer hit the firing pin, and the powder ignited. The pressure of the combustion forced the hollow-point from its chamber, spinning the projectile along its way and spitting flames as it left the barrel. The slide kicked back, ejecting the cartridge, ramming the next round into the chamber and cocking the hammer into the firing position once more. Simultaneously, a tiny hole sank into Malone's forehead, and the back of the monk's skull bounced up as it burst open, then slammed back against the paving. The monk lay still, blood pooling around his head.

Adrenaline raced through Schreider's body, but he held his aim steady until Weber had pulled the clacker from the dead man's hand and disconnected the detonation cord. Then, Schreider holstered his pistol under his jacket and picked up the keys next to Malone's body. Following the detonator cord, he entered the Cave Church and descended the ladder. At the steel door, he removed the detonators from the C4. Finally, he inserted and turned the keys.

'Lazarus, come out!' he shouted into the opened burial chamber.

Moments later, Jennifer appeared. Behind her followed Simon and Rabin. They were shaken, but they were smiling.

Chapter 53

The frightening few days that had so nearly cost Jennifer, Simon and Rabin their lives lay behind them. Had it not been for Schreider and his captain, Malone would have sent the three to a stony grave. That Pope Gregory had assigned his own soldiers to protect the Church's apparent enemies was evidence of his commitment to change.

Making statements to the police and then disclosing their finds to the Turkish authorities had taken nearly all day. It was dawn before the professor had permission to relocate the precious remains to his laboratory.

Jennifer sighed with relief as she pondered the past week. With so much still left to uncover, she had decided to stay another day. She was determined to see how everything corresponded and had asked Simon if she could sit in on the DNA test.

Unearthing the relics of those so close to Jesus felt extraordinary. Not only did it cast light on the Apostle Peter's death, but if Matthew, Mark, Luke and Bartholomew were his offspring, the dates the Gospels were composed and the time of their authors' deaths would be empirically determined. Perhaps most significant was that each of the authors had warned his followers against *false prophets*. Given the context of the Cave Church find, the meaning of such admonishments had become clear. Not once in any of the Epistles had Paul warned of this. It would soon be an article of faith that the Synoptic Gospels were warning of the interloper apostle specifically.

Considering the Gospels were written after the Epistles, Matthew, Mark and Luke were intent on preserving the original faith. As per Pilate's letter, Paul had persecuted Jesus, then set his sights on Peter; the self-appointed apostle had then discarded the Jewish tradition in favor of his own Romanized doctrine, and it was this that made him a *false* prophet. Paul's ministry only flourished once he had silenced his Jewish critics. With Peter eliminated and no longer there to contradict him, he had annexed the Nazarene faith for Rome, and until now, Paul's doctrine had held sway.

It was eight o'clock on Saturday morning, and after a night of tossing and turning on Rabin's office couch, a quick shower in the communal bathrooms and breakfast at the onsite kitchen, Jennifer joined Simon in his laboratory, where he and his technicians were extracting DNA from the remains. Before entering the dry laboratory, he made her slip into a lab coat as well as a mask and hair net, and although he had her put on surgical gloves, she was to touch nothing without asking. The nature and sensitivity of their work called for extreme care, and if contaminated with extraneous material, the DNA results would prove worthless.

Simon introduced Jennifer to four technicians who had already spent hours preparing potential DNA by grinding the extracted bone and tooth material into a fine powder. No sooner had she sat down on a laboratory stool than she enquired about the time the testing would take. Apart from flying home the next day, she was not sure how much she could endure on an uncomfortable stool doing nothing. Simon reassured her that they could have the results that evening. However, with twenty-seven steps needed to yield DNA and the age and condition of the cells playing a major role, he added that he wouldn't place a bet on it.

Jennifer tried not to interfere with Simon's work, but she could not help herself. 'Why is everything done on site?' she asked from her uncomfortable perch.

Simon laughed. She might not *be* a journalist yet, but she certainly sounded like one. 'The Turkish government won't let us remove anything from the site until we are one hundred percent sure it belongs to persons of Jewish descent.'

'What are you hoping to find?'

'Connections.'

'Between?'

'The relics and people living today.'

With the dry material, ready for purification, Simon set off for the wet laboratory. As Jennifer followed, he explained the process: 'There are around twenty-five thousand Jews still living in Antakya. My objective is to link these historic figures with contemporary residents.'

'Do you expect to find relatives of the people whose remains we've just found?'

'It's possible.'

His nonchalance was sinful. How could he be so casual about it?

Jennifer had never considered the possibility that biblical figures might have living descendants. Their mythical status made it near impossible to imagine them being the ancestors of people she might pass in the street.

'Have you managed to connect any yet?'

'That's the next step.'

Conforming to the prescribed protocols, the wet laboratory, where purification took place, was separate from the dry area. Five more technicians and researchers were working at various stations when Jennifer entered. After relegating her to another laboratory stool, Simon joined his team. To facilitate DNA release, they transferred the dry material into tubes before adding agents to each sample. A high-speed centrifuge isolated the DNA by removing inhibitors that interfered with DNA amplification. With the purified material transferred onto strips in thermocycling tubes, an anthropomorphic robot used pipettes to dispense measured volumes of reagents and, once completed, the samples were ready for DNA isolation.

Simon's genotyping was captivating but also laborious and time-consuming. And with the weight of recent events on her mind, Jennifer drifted off. With a newfound aversion for jumping to conclusions—and irritating Professor Rabin—she was limiting herself to hoping the Cave Church's tombs were authentic. The remains of a victim who was crucified upside-down in a cave dedicated to Apostle Peter at least seemed like solid evidence. The adjacent ossuaries indicated that they held the remains of the Gospel authors. The inscriptions attributed Peter as the father, and though Matthew's and Luke's filiation did not agree with the canon and tradition, it made sense that he had fathered them. But, who was the mother, and where did Bartholomew fit in? Since they were buried together, there must be some connection. And how fascinating was the account of Paul's journey to Malta after his meeting with Peter and the fact that the Maltese cross featured in nearly every aspect of the Cave Church, including the tombs.

Jennifer smiled wryly to herself. She imagined how Professor Rabin would have reprimanded her if he had overheard her thoughts. She could not help herself; it was in her nature to question everything. At least she was learning to wait for evidence before she spoke.

Even so, she played now with the notion that Mary Magdalene had been Peter's spouse. The previous night she had been reading that Mark, while in Jerusalem, had stayed with a woman named Mary, and that his *mother*, Mary, had a large house in the city where Peter had also hidden. Mary Magdalene had been prominent amongst the women who followed Jesus. The Gospels held her in such esteem that she took second place only to the Virgin Mary. By calling her 'the Magdalene' or 'the woman from Magdala', she was differentiated from Christ's other female followers. Just as Apostle Peter had been Jesus's rock, so Mary appeared to have been His closest female friend. Mary Magdalene seemed to come to the fore during Jesus's last days. The Gospels record how Mary witnessed all three major events of the Passion of Christ: the crucifixion, the burial and the Resurrection. She vanished soon after the Ascension, and while legends abounded, her fate remained a mystery. Some traditions held that she had a child with Jesus and that she had gone to the South of France or Germany with Brother Lazarus. Others said that she had lived as a hermit in a desert cave for thirty years, fasting and communicating with angels. Various sources speculated that she was a leader in the early Church, and some churches even claimed possession of her remains. The first of these relics appeared in the eleventh century at the Abbey of la Madeleine in Vézelay, Burgundy. The second surfaced in the thirteenth century at Saint Maximin la Sainte Baume, Provence. A glass dome said to contain her skull still sat in that church's crypt. Mary's connection with that region extended into the nearby mountains where legend had it she had taken refuge in a cave. Perhaps she had fled there. Perhaps.

It also occurred to Jennifer that it was common practice in some cultures for a man to marry his friend's wife if the friend died, so perhaps Mark was Jesus's natural son and Peter's by adoption. If Mary was with Jesus first, but later married Peter as the story in the Gnostic *Gospel of Philip* portrayed, it would make sense for Peter to be aggravated when Jesus kissed her more often than seemed necessary. If Peter were in Antakya while Mary was in Jerusalem, would that indicate a separation between them? It would account for Peter's annoyance with Jesus's close connection with her. Or perhaps Mary had relationships with both Peter and Jesus, in which case, either man could have fathered Mark. That would explain the long tradition that had labelled her a prostitute, and would also explain why she had lived as a hermit after every man she loved had been killed. Considering all that had happened, Jennifer felt for her.

*****

By the time Simon had placed the purified DNA into a thermal cycler for isolation, Jennifer was exhausted. Apart from eating lunch at the canteen, she had been sitting on a stool for the entire day. 'Simon has a great team,' she thought, stretching her back. The way they had worked around the clock for twelve hours or more was extraordinary.

To determine the evolutionary relationship between the relics, Simon and his team had selectively amplified specific regions of the DNA, a process called fingerprinting. If they were related, the four evangelists would have inherited a substantial amount of Peter's fingerprint.

With the preparations completed, Simon asked a researcher to call Rabin on the intercom. He wanted his colleague present for the results. He saved the work onto a memory stick, and returned to his office to transfer the data onto his personal computer.

Rabin arrived as Simon placed several images side by side on his large screen monitor for comparison. The two scientists studied the results intently for some time, before sitting back.

Jennifer could hardly contain her curiosity. 'Well?'

Simon gazed at her with an amused gleam in his eyes and said, 'Mark was not Peter's son.'

'But the ossuary says he was.'

Simon shook his head.

Jennifer had just suspected as much, yet she could not get her head around the fact.

To highlight why Mark and Peter were not related, Simon compared their DNA. The differences were striking. He called up Matthew and Luke's fingerprints and placed them with Mark's. Though there were differences, there were, indeed, striking similarities to prove a blood relationship.

'It would appear all three had the same mother,' Simon said finally.

Jennifer was quick to pounce: 'But different fathers.'

'Two fathers,' Simon said, correcting her. There was a difference.

Rabin nodded approvingly. From the DNA fingerprints, it was clear that Matthew, Mark and Luke were half siblings. Mark, though related, had been fathered by another man.

Jennifer felt sick. She had anticipated that Mary Magdalene would be the mother, but the revelation of the celebrated biblical figure having been with two men still came as a shock. But who fathered Mark? There could be only one answer. …

'Jesus fathered Mark,' she whispered. 'And Peter was his stepdad. He brought Mark to Antioch and claimed him as his own, thus hiding him.'

For once, Rabin agreed with her. Of course, there was no way of knowing without DNA that had, per the Gospels, escaped into Heaven. As for Mary's DNA, they could have a sample of Mary's skull tested in France. That would shed light on the identity of the mother. But Rabin was already convinced. If the skull was indeed Mary's, the results would confirm their hypothesis. Jennifer's explanation was reasonable and it agreed with everything they knew about the Apostles and their culture.

Jennifer was deep in thought. Mary would have likely taken another husband. She would have been about Jennifer's age; young enough to start anew. *John* and *Mark* record how Mary was first to see Jesus's empty tomb, and it was to Peter she had then run to tell. They must have been close. The idea of Peter supporting Mary in raising Jesus's child and being separated so Peter could save Mark from Paul also made sense. Similarly, it explained why Mark had fled from Paul. Paul had not just been trying to rid the world of Nazarenes and pervert their faith; he had been out to kill Jesus's and Peter's successors as well.

Jennifer needed to be clear on the facts. 'Mark was the older of the siblings, which explains why his Gospel dates first and why his work differs from Matthew's and Luke's,' she said hurriedly, before adding: 'Put Bartholomew's DNA up.'

Simon complied, and he and Rabin were shocked. Unlike Matthew's and Luke's, Mark's DNA matched Bartholomew's. The two evangelist's fingerprints were nearly identical.

Jennifer could not be any happier. Not in her wildest dreams could she have anticipated discovering something as important. The find surpassed anything she could have imagined. 'You said, Professor, that there was a name problem with Bartholomew. Well, I looked it up last night, and "Bartholomew" has no translation. The "*tlm*" in "*Bar-tlm*" is never used in the Bible. It is a word much like "*y-w-h-w*", which itself has no meaning except for the name of God. I also read that some scholars believe it's related to the Aramaic "*telem*", making Bartholomew the "Son of the Furrow". We might then see this as "son of the ploughman", or it might be an early Nazarene code, a play on words. Many of Jesus's parables compare believers to seeds and God to a gardener. A furrow is a trench dug in the ground—by a gardener.

'If Bartholomew was Jesus's younger son, it would explain why he kept the connection to his brother even though they were physically separated, one being in

Antakya, the other in Armenia; and it would explain why a pseudonym was used by fellow Nazarene writers, while his given name, Nathaniel, was used by the Pauline John. The former was hiding him, but the latter intended to expose him. He was the son of the spiritual ploughman. And he is never spoken of except in passing in the synoptic texts. Only in *John* is there a story about him sitting under a fig tree, and his behavior when Philip brings him to Jesus is characteristic of a child. Even the *Gospel of Bartholomew* describes the interaction between Jesus and Bartholomew as that of a father and a son.'

Rabin expected nothing less. 'I don't suppose you'd got much sleep last night?'

Jennifer was about to put his mind to rest when she realized something. She could not believe she had not thought of it earlier. 'Bartholomew fits the two-source theory, which says that the *Gospel of Mark* and *Q*—the long-hypothesized *source*—served as inspiration for *Matthew* and *Luke*. Bartholomew as *Q* matches perfectly. He and Mark both recorded their memories of their father's death and Matthew and Luke later used *their* Gospels as *source*. Whether transmitted orally or in writing is beside the point. Mark, being the older brother would have influenced Bartholomew's work. We can test this hypothesis by asking Pope Gregory for access to the hidden Gospel I'd seen when I broke into their bunker.'

When Jennifer had finished, Simon smiled and Rabin clapped.

Never had the New Testament made more sense. Even the discrepancies between the Gospels, which had been an enigma for ages, suddenly made sense. And never in Jennifer's wildest dreams could she have imagined being a critical player in revolutionizing Christianity. But the evidence now clearly demonstrated that Paul had lured Peter to Antioch under false pretenses. Peter most likely arrived anticipating they would settle their differences or even start a ministry together, only to be persecuted anew. His crucifixion left Paul free to annex the Nazarene faith as he willed, and Mark, who had been old enough to accompany Peter, had fled back to Judea. With Jesus and Peter eliminated, Mary was left on her own to fend for herself and her boys. Hence, her sons recorded their gospels years later to undo the damage wreaked by Paul. What a tragic story! Mary Magdalene had seen both her husbands crucified by the same man. She had probably seen her sons killed too. Her date of death was never recorded. Tradition claims she was lifted to Heaven by angels. No martyrdom was ever mentioned. Had she lived out her elder years in a cave, having lost everyone she had ever loved?

Simon saved the work and closed the program. It was nearly six and the sun was setting.

'Supper,' he said, gazing over his shoulder at Rabin. 'My place. Seven o'clock. I'm also inviting Colonel Schreider and his captain. They're still down in the city. Pope Gregory has ordered them to stay until he can be sure the dissenting cardinals pose no further risk.'

Chapter 54

Jennifer stood on Simon's veranda. Dressed in a simple black dress, with a shawl around her shoulders and comfortable balmorals on her feet, she was sipping a cup of coffee. The glow from a distant peak backlit by the rising sun drew her attention. Wisps of vivid color reminiscent of peacock feathers fanned across the sky. As the glory of the morning sun lit the valley, she laughed silently as joy infused her being.

Jennifer remembered returning to the States the day after the DNA results. Flying first to Key West to see her father, she had related every detail of her epic journey. They sat at a beach cafe as she explained her abortive meeting with the high-ranking cardinal, the ensuing pursuit and her escape to Antioch where she unwittingly found Apostle Peter's remains. She told him about their capture and the shootout with Verretti, their trial and what she could remember of the pope's speech, then their second discovery and Friar Malone's attempt at destroying the evidence. Concluding her story, she said it had been an adventure like no other.

Her father restrained himself from reprimanding her for her break-in at the Library and not contacting him. He had been terrified. He was happy for her to be safe home again, but he had been just about to fly to Rome when she finally called him the week before. He had even bought tickets for himself and a return ticket for her.

Jennifer remembered apologizing for making him worry, but first escaping from, then being drugged and kidnapped by the gendarmes had made it impossible to call before she did. Anyhow, she was safe now, and since she was going to present her story to *Geographic America* for consideration, it seemed the trip would help her professionally. Her friend from the journal, who had helped her gain entry to the Vatican Library, had made her promise that *Geographic America* would have first claim on international serial rights. Strictly speaking, her trip had not involved the codex, but her friend said he would present the story to the managing editor anyway.

At her flat in New York a week later, Jennifer was acutely aware that although she had bid farewell to Simon in Antakya, he was still very much on her mind. It felt to her the time they had spent together had changed her. She pondered her attraction to him for hours. Was he in love with her? She had never had a 'one-night stand' before, and perhaps she was reading more into it than it warranted. Maybe their sleeping together was just stress release after the tension and the danger they had experienced. She wondered if she should visit him, and how would he respond if she did? The thought of finding out did not scare her half as much as being strapped to that stretcher in the ambulance, but it still frightened her all the same.

Meanwhile, she did have other problems—real problems. As she opened her apartment door, she saw a notice to pay the rent or quit, lying on the doormat. She needed the job at *Geographic America*, but it would mean going back to Antioch for sure. At least she would have an excuse. If Simon did not love her, well, she could be professional about it. Of course, it would hurt. It would *really* hurt. She could not help admitting to herself that she had fallen for him. If only she could take her mind off him long enough to deal with her life.

Attempting to bring herself back to Earth, she put the kettle on for a cup of noodle soup when gut-wrenching sobs took hold. Her despair was overwhelming. Her heart beat wildly, her gut twisted and she had to vomit. Did she make a mistake by sleeping with him? And would she make an even bigger mistake if she tried to go back? Tears poured as she sat on the living-room floor trying to make a rational decision. She had had boyfriends before, but she had never loved them. Not like this. It did not seem as if she could function without him. Listening to Anastasia's '*Heavy on my heart*' did not help either. By the time the artist belted out the final chorus, Jennifer was sobbing uncontrollably.

Over a week passed and Simon did not call. Her doubts increased daily, and with them came a fear of calling *Geographic America*. Although she now had the opportunity of a lifetime, how could she just turn up in Antioch without knowing if Simon wanted her there? It would be unbearable if it had just been casual for him. If that were the case, she would rather give the assignment to someone else.

She was a mess, sitting on the floor in a ratty hoody and a pair of gym shorts. A mug of cold soup stood on one side of her, a pile of Kleenexes on the other. She remembered glancing at her phone every few minutes, picking it up several times but put it back down, not wanting to bother someone who did not want to talk to her. She got up to stare across the Hudson at the New York skyline. Then, she noticed her reflection. She looked worse than after her beating by Verretti, and suddenly, she stopped caring what Simon thought. She called his laboratory and a researcher answered. They were extremely busy, but he would see if Simon could take the call. Minutes passed like centuries until Simon's voice came on the line. Their conversation started out cautiously with small-talk, but then he seemed to get his mind off his work and he relaxed. She found herself reassuring him that she did not have the job yet but that, if she got it, work would come first and he would hardly notice her. He chuckled and replied that he liked having her around and wanted to see her again. At that she had to restrain herself from singing. She was giddy and a little embarrassed by how much he affected her.

After the call, Jennifer felt more settled, though still was not certain where she stood. She could not tell whether he was just being friendly or if he wanted her there. After all, she would be in his space for some time. Would that scare him? It could. She told herself that being in a laboratory, surrounded by technicians and researchers, was not exactly conducive to romance.

She was still mulling over the conversation, when the phone rang.

Snatching it from the floor, she quickly repeated, 'Simon, you do understand I'm only coming because of the job, right? I mean, you will hardly know I'm ...'

The voice on the other end of the line cut her short: 'Shut up and listen, Jen.'

It was her friend, Ted, from *Geographic America.* He was offering her an assignment to investigate the latest discoveries at the Cave Church.

'Of course, yes,' she said. 'But how did you hear about the latest excavations?'

Professor Rabin had called to offer them an exclusive. He had also insisted on her. Actually, he had refused to work with anyone else.

'Yes, Ted. Email me the flight details. I'll leave on the earliest one you can get.'

Frantically, she ran to her room to repack her bags.

Simon insisted on picking her up, and ignoring the fact that she had booked a hotel took her straight to the farm. As he unloaded her suitcases from his Range Rover, he expressed his hope she would not mind staying over. Anywhere was better than a hotel.

She was not sure what he meant. Did he mean she was sleeping in the spare room? She only found out later that evening when they went to bed. Instead of turning into the spare bedroom, he hooked his arm around her waist and lead her to his.

Jennifer loved the firmness of his bed, the texture of his pure cotton sheets, the pure silk duvet, which felt lighter yet warmer than down, and the scent on his pillows. After showering, she slipped between the sheets still wearing a t-shirt, but he gently removed it before pulling her close. They laid awake for hours talking, his arm curved protectively around her neck. She never wanted to leave him again. She never would.

*****

The sun was rising now but the cool breeze from the mountains lingered, forcing Jennifer to draw her shawl tighter around her shoulders. It was April 6th, Good Friday. It occurred to her that she was unable to see herself celebrating Easter as she had before. Religious holidays had taken on a new meaning. Based on her new knowledge they seemed pagan. Luckily, she was spared the usual, gaudy consumerism she would have suffered in the States.

A hundred yards away, mourners were wending their way along an avenue of oaks to a small cemetery. By a nearby pond, children were skimming pebbles across the water, sending the ducks into a panic. Beside the empty grave was John's wooden coffin. In the brief space of time since his premature death, he had become a martyr for the Jewish community of Antakya. Were it not for John the relics might never have been recovered. Christians and Jews alike were reorienting themselves in the wake of the new information. Attitudes were changing and many were calling for a return to the original form of Nazarene-ism, at least insofar as anyone could tell what that was.

Professor Rabin stepped onto the veranda and straightened his black jacket. Out of respect for John and Simon, he had closed the laboratory and declared a day of mourning. He stood beside Jennifer as they watched the townspeople gather at the burial site. Some were conversing in groups, while others huddled around Simon.

Jennifer was studying all the new faces. 'Whose idea was it to call *Geographic America*?' she asked.

'What? To offer them the job, you mean?'

She glanced at Rabin but kept silent.

'Oh, I wish I could take the credit,' he chuckled, 'but really it was Simon's idea.'

She smiled warmly. She had made the right choice to come. She set the empty cup on the table and placed one hand on her stomach, just below her navel.

'Is something wrong?' Rabin asked.

'It must be something I ate,' she replied. 'Or nerves.'

'Can I get you something?'

'I'll be all right. I think I'm just anxious about meeting everyone.'

Rabin did not say anything, but he understood. Being raised Christian, she was nervous about how the Jewish community would view her.

Offering her his arm, he said, 'Let's go over. I'll protect you from the *bubbes*.'

Jennifer chuckled, and taking his arm they set off for the cemetery.

Schreider awaited Jennifer and Rabin at the gate. Now dressed in a dark-navy suit, he kissed Jennifer's hand. Every time he saw her, he sensed something about her. It was as if he were face to face with one of God's true chosen. Then he thanked Rabin for the hospitality and assured the professor he and his men had been well catered for by the Antiochene staff.

With Schreider was his captain and the six Swiss guards who had accompanied John's remains. They had taken it upon themselves to stand guard while the ceremony was in progress. Not that anyone had asked, but as soldiers sworn to serve and protect God's elite, they could not help themselves.

Schreider no longer served the Vatican, and although this had meant Verretti's promotion to temporary head of all security, the colonel had been glad to escape the Catholic establishment. His destiny was now his own. Having lost his belief that protecting the Holy See was serving God, he had resigned as Oberst of the Swiss Guard and was considering his own VIP security service for celebrities.

Simon pulled away from the quests and briskly walked over to join Jennifer. He kissed her warmly and asked if she would like to join him. When she assured him, she was fine by herself, he excused himself. Returning to the grave where he would lay his brother to rest, he struck up a conversation with the Rabbi.

Having never set foot in a Jewish cemetery before, Jennifer's eyes wandered. The graves were different from Christian burial sites, which invariably featured crosses and ornate angelic representations. Here, a tomb was a simple sandstone grave with a granite headstone, its only decoration, if any, an engraved Star of David. As she was staring at the symbol on one tomb, she noticed something unusual about it—the Star of David, which featured two equilateral triangles forming a hexagram at an angle, sat inside an eight-pointed star made of two squares forming an octagram. The age of the graves was immaterial; if they were adorned at all, they featured the emblem.

Jennifer studied the symbol. 'There is something familiar about it,' she thought. Then she remembered the design from the *Leningrad Codex* in the Russian National Library in Saint Petersburg. She had not personally seen the codex, but it had formed part of her curriculum. The *Codex Leningradensis*, as it was also known, was the oldest complete manuscript of the Hebrew Bible, and had been written by hand in Ancient Hebrew. For this reason, although scholars preferred an earlier manuscript written in the tenth century, the incomplete *Aleppo Codex*, the Leningrad served as an important source for reconstructing the Bible. Dating to around 1008 CE, written on parchment and bound in leather, sixteen of its pages contained decorative geometric patterns, one of which was the same as those on the graves around her.

Rabin noticed her intense stare, and curious, asked, 'I'm afraid of what might happen if I ask, but what have you found now?'

'I'm not quite sure yet,' she replied. 'You wouldn't have a pen and paper on you again, would you?'

Rabin patted his jacket and pulled a pen from his inside pocket. Disappointed that he could not find a piece of paper he passed her the pen.

'I'm afraid this is all I have.'

'That's okay. I'll use my hand.'

Jennifer drew the circle and eight-pointed star on the palm of her hand. She connected the eight points with four crisscross lines and filled in some of the segments. Then, she held up her hand for Rabin, showing the two perfectly intertwined Maltese crosses.

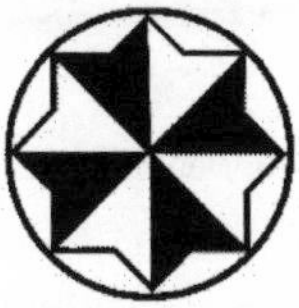

'You do your surname justice,' Rabin said proudly.

'Gift from God—me?' She smiled humbly. 'Hardly, Professor.'

'How many people do you think have stood before the Cave Church's façade and straightaway seen what you've seen? The same goes for these graves. No one has ever made the connection. It's ridiculous!'

'Well, thank you, Uri, but I think anyone could have done the same, given the right perspective.' She studied the symbol up close. 'What do you think this means?'

He contemplated her question. Symbols always stood for something; he of all should know. There was nothing random about them. Traditionally, the six-pointed star was Jewish and the eight-pointed star was Christian.

'Perhaps it is ...' he stopped himself. 'I shan't speculate.'

Jennifer could not leave it there. She had to try. 'Judaism meeting Christianity,' she said. 'Does Simon's family tree include gentiles?'

Rabin felt slightly embarrassed: 'No, you're the first.'

Jennifer blushed. 'I didn't mean it like that,' she chuckled.

What was he saying? People did not speak of gentiles anymore either; many Jews had intermarried with and invited into their faith the people in their vicinity. Why would Antioch be any different? 'I'm sorry,' he said, feeling his temperature rising slightly under his collar as blood rushed to his face. 'I didn't mean it that way either. In any case, you're not even married.'

Jennifer decided not to respond; it would only contribute to the already awkward conversation. Moving on to the next grave she noticed the tombstone was not as old as the others. She read the names: Mark and Mary Kepa.

'Those are Simon's parents,' Rabin said.

Her gaze took in the adjacent graves. 'These are all Simon's relatives?'

Rabin nodded. 'Going back hundreds of years.'

She read the inscriptions. A clear majority read: 'Simon', 'Peter', Andrew', 'Mark', 'John', 'Nathaniel' or 'Mary'. Then she saw a 'Yeshu'—Jesus's name in Aramaic—and her heart pounded. 'These are all Gospel names,' she said. 'Why didn't Simon say anything?'

Before Rabin had a chance to answer, a woman in her eighties accompanied by a girl struggled over to meet with them.

'*Shalom lach ladi,*' the old woman greeted Jennifer.

Jennifer realized the fragile woman had come over specifically to meet with her and was touched. 'Shalom,' she returned the greeting with a small curtsy.

Rabin interpreted the old woman's words as she spoke. She mentioned she felt Jennifer belonged with Simon and that Yahweh had brought them together.

The old woman's comforting words made Jennifer feel recognized and accepted, and after she had plodded away, Jennifer excused herself to Rabin; she felt boxed in and needed a short walk. Before she and the professor parted, though, another elderly woman approached, asking to speak with her.

'Shalom,' Jennifer returned the greeting.

To Jennifer's surprise, this woman not only expressed how she and Simon belonged together, she was more forthcoming and wanted to know when the two of them were getting married.

As the woman walked away, Jennifer turned to Rabin. Flattered by their kindness, yet perplexed by their zeal to see her and Simon together, she asked why the women had come to greet her in this way.

Rabin kissed her on both cheeks and stepped back, still holding her shoulders. 'Simon is very special to them,' he said. 'He is the elder Kepa. For people who believe in the old traditions, this is a big deal. Seeing you with him, they make their own conclusions.'

Chapter 55

When the professor excused himself to see if Simon needed his help, Jennifer stayed by the gravestones. Stunned by what she had just seen, she felt unable to join the ceremony yet. Instead of Old Testament names like Abraham, Isaac, Jacob, Solomon, David, Daniel or Ezekiel, Simon's ancestors carried the names of Gospel figures. Jennifer wanted to learn more, but with at least a hundred mourners filling the cemetery, she would have to wait until after the service. Wanting time alone, she looked around to tell Simon, but he had disappeared, so she headed away from the grave site.

Schreider noticed her leaving and ran up, asking what was wrong and where she was going.

She looked at him blankly. 'Anywhere,' she said.

Her ambivalence worried him. 'At least let one of my men join you,' he offered.

She declined, but set his mind at ease, promising to stay within sight of the cemetery.

To the accompaniment of women chanting sacred Hebrew songs, Jennifer set off up a narrow footpath. She did not understand the lyrics, but the gut-wrenching melodies, measured rhythms and poised harmonies pierced her heart. The haunting sounds evoked a vision of an unmitigated, ancient suffering.

The footpath led towards a nearby hill. A tree on its crest served as a focal point, and the scene was framed by the distant glowing mountain she had admired earlier. She set off for the tree, pushing overhanging shrubs and branches aside, while trying to protect her dress. As the sun rose higher in the sky, the air became hotter. Her breathing deepened as her muscles worked harder and drops of perspiration slid down her back.

The path was rough and seemingly unused, but Jennifer was determined to make it to the top of the hill. At least this time unsuitable shoes were not a handicap. Between rocks, rainwater had washed away sand, leaving stone-filled crevices. Halfway up the hill, she was still lost in thought. As she walked, she touched the leaves and flowers, wondering if the Nazarenes had done the same. Following in their footsteps made her feel like a Nazarene. She no longer considered herself a Christian; she was now a Nazarene. It was not possible to follow both Paul and Peter. It was like serving two masters. She chose Peter, Jesus's first disciple. He had cared for Jesus's children.

At least, that was what she now believed.

'There's dissonance though,' she thought. On the one hand, she had given up on blind faith, but on the other, she was convinced that Peter had raised Jesus's children. Was that belief? It was not purely speculation anymore, but they had no proof that Mark and Bartholomew were Jesus's offspring. They only knew the two siblings shared a mother—likely Mary Magdalene—with Peter's sons, Matthew and Luke.

What was faith anyway? Could she discard the faith of her childhood, which had been such a support in times of crisis? She had needed her faith to be grounded in truth, but even now there were no definitive answers. Peter had proved real, and his burial in Antioch demonstrated that God's power and authority had never advanced to the popes. The office given to Peter by Jesus would surely have passed to his offspring. That honour would have been bestowed on his firstborn. In ancient Israel, firstborn sons occupied a privileged position; receiving double the inheritance of their younger brothers, and during the period of exile in Egypt, belonging to God. Mark appeared in several other places in the Gospels, performing small tasks, and it was he who had travelled with Peter, so one could assume he was close to Peter. As *Q*, Bartholomew was also a contender, except that he too was not Peter's natural child. Between Matthew and Luke, though, it was easier to imagine. With Matthew's Gospel predating Luke's by decades, Matthew was likely the elder.

Jennifer wondered if the *Gospel of Matthew* appearing first in the New Testament had anything to do with his standing as *the* heir to God's power and authority. She discarded the idea. It was probably just coincidence. In any case, Apostolic succession was now relegated to the realm of fantasy—it no longer made any sense.

The distinctive fragrances, some sweet to attract bees, others spicy and fruity to draw beetles, moved Jennifer to pick a handful of flowers. Closing her eyes, she deeply inhaled their scents. Something tickled her hand. A ladybug was crawling up her finger on its way to the flowers. She smiled. It was a sign of good luck.

Heading for the shade beneath the tree, a further thought struck Jennifer. The Apostle Peter's birth name was Simon, but Jesus had called him *Kepa*—the Rock upon which He would build His church. *Shi'mon Kepa*—Simon the Rock.

After all this time and after repeatedly seeing and hearing the same name, it finally struck her: Apostle Peter's name was the same in Aramaic as the name of the man she loved. She looked for Simon at the cemetery. Was Apostle Peter his ancestor? If so, was it the same stalwart, dogged strength in that ancestor that had led Jesus to name Peter His successor? She thought of the grave she had just seen. Simon's dad was Mark—a family name, surely. She thought of the DNA fingerprinting. Simon did say they were fingerprinting various DNAs, hoping to establish connections between ancient and contemporary Jews. Had he thought of testing his own?

Drained, she sat down on a log. Surrounded by mountains, a few farmhouses, each with its own dam and lands, lay scattered throughout the valley. Sheep and goats grazed the fields. In the stable next to Simon's house, two of the horses were tossing their heads over the stable doors as if wanting to run free.

The chanting stopped and the Rabbi opened the ceremony with a prayer. Jennifer relaxed her shoulders. Her journey had started with a prayer. Before she had left for the Vatican, she had prayed that God would grant her knowledge and wisdom. Had she not got more than she had asked. None of her plans had come to fruition. Not a thing had worked out as expected. God surely had a mysterious way of doing things. He had turned her life upside-down. It was as if He had placed her on a collision course with destiny.

She smiled as she reflected that she should stop believing it was God who directed her life. If there was a God, He did not get involved. If He existed, as she wanted to believe, it was insane to think, as Lord of Creation, He would focus on her little planet, let alone her personal problems. Sitting on Cape Town's Table Mountain while hiking, she could hardly see someone walking in the streets below, and that was only a mile away. How could God see her from wherever He was. Yet somehow, she still suspected that He did—although that would be asking rather a lot.

From now on, she would follow her own intuition and make her own decisions. She no longer needed a creed to tell her what or how to think. Freewill most likely did not exist. Every thought she had ever had and every choice she had made had seemed like her own, yet there was no guarantee they had not been pre-destined. But she also knew that God could not be so cruel as to create a soul only to damn it. The alternative, of course, was that everyone went to Heaven, good or evil, Christian or not, but *Revelation* stated explicitly that there was a Hell, and believers had never dismissed the notion, for they lived in a world of suffering and needed to believe evil would be punished. Of course, all these thoughts were the stuff of speculation, and if two thousand years of debate had not settled the questions, she could hardly expect it of herself. Scientific empiricism and theoretical philosophies used to challenge her faith, but no more.

Sitting on the log under the tree and basking in the comforting relief of the shade, Jennifer felt a stirring inside her. She had always felt something like that and could not recall a time when it had not been. It was a sense of the life force, which impelled her on in life. But this was different, something else. The fluttering was slightly lower down, in her pelvis. She must be about to menstruate. She thought about it and frowned. That was not possible. She should have menstruated already. She always coincided with the new moon, but that had been … She was two weeks late! With so much happening, she had lost track. Could she be pregnant? She hoped she was not. Her gaze fell on Simon in the cemetery below. What would he say? She straightened up. She was being ridiculous. She could not be pregnant. She had just skipped a cycle. It must be the result of so much stress. Stress could easily cause a woman to miss a cycle. She sat motionless, still, without a breath. It could, though, couldn't it?

The old women's chanting rose from the valley below.

THE END

Acknowledgments

I owe my gratitude to the members of my family, friends and professionals, who over the years have helped making this project a success.
The first, of course, are my family and friends, who through their input and advice had given me direction when my compass veered from true north.

To the reviewers who through their critiques, sometimes harsh, sometimes complementary, but always fair, have made me more determined to achieve what seemed the impossible, I say thank you.

Particularly, I thank, *The Literary Consultancy* and their readers: Karen Godfrey, James Pusey and Dr. Stephen Carver.

I also would like to thank *Scribendi* and their team for the professional online editing service they provide. Particularly, I would like to thank: EM463, EM738, EM758, and the inimitable EM953, whom I would love to meet one day.

Last but not the least, for the special role each of my local editors and consultants have played in the initial creation of this work, I thank: Charl-Pierre Naude, Rachelle Greeff, Rinette Champanis and Rose Shearer.

Other titles by Izak Botha

Angelicals Reviewed

Do you have a soul? Is the soul a gift from God? Or is it something else? Does the soul guarantee life after death? Or is its purpose yet to be discovered? In *Angelicals Reviewed,* researcher of metaphysics, Izak Botha, challenges conventional thinking around the nature of soul and presents a startling new hypothesis.

In a groundbreaking study covering multiple disciplines, Izak shares his knowledge regarding the soul. In these pages you will discover:

- What individuals, groups, and societies believe regarding the soul
- How some accept, and others reject the notion of the soul
- How opposing doctrine differ or agree
- How views about the soul alter with time
- How the debate around the soul is ongoing
- And how the discoveries of cosmology and evolution influence the percepts of the soul.

As humanity dabbles with replacing God, the question surrounding the soul—existence, purpose, and destiny—becomes all important. If you have pondered these questions, this book is for you.

About Izak Botha

Izak Botha is a perpetual student of life, a former artist, athlete, performer with the Cape Town City Ballet, counselor, architect, entrepreneur, litigator versus multinational corporations, and now author of *Homo Angelicansis*, *Angelicals Reviewed*, and *Blood Symbols*, which made Semi Finalist in Publishers Weekly's Book Life Prize 2017.

Professor George Claassen of Sceptic South Africa evaluates Botha's writing as "a crucial analysis of evolutionary thinking that deserves to be read with care", while Todd Mercer of Foreword Clarion Reviews applauds for its "inquiry and line of logic that seem beyond the merely plausible—it is urgently imperative."

Settled on South Africa's Garden Route, Botha is presently working on his new novel.